OUT *of* CHARACTER

ANNABETH ALBERT

sourcebooks
casablanca

Published by Sourcebooks Casablanca, an imprint of Sourcebooks
P.O. Box 4410, Naperville, Illinois 60567-4410
(630) 961-3900
sourcebooks.com

Library of Congress Cataloging-in-Publication Data is on file with the publisher.

Printed and bound in Canada.
MBP 10 9 8 7 6 5 4 3 2 1

To my mom, who believed in Jasper perhaps even more than I did and who let me read her the epilogue at midnight. I hope I did Jasper and you justice!

CHAPTER ONE
JASPER

WE'VE GOT TO FIND A new prince.

April's latest text rattled around in my head as I shelved merchandise. My little sister was obsessed with our favorite game's most iconic character. And I, being me, had promised to deliver for our cosplay group. Letting April down wasn't an option. But where the heck was I going to find a dark-haired sea god on short notice?

"I need help. I'm in trouble, man." The voice startled me, almost causing a catastrophe of epic proportions because I had a dozen card-set boxes precariously balanced. No way could I turn around without toppling my last half hour of work, but I also wasn't in too much of a hurry. The voice was vaguely familiar, probably one of our regulars, and their definition of urgent issues differed greatly from the general population. Whoever it was could hold their dice.

"Give me a sec." Even as I shoved boxes in place, I kept my voice as cheerful as possible. A customer was a customer, and God knew that the little game store where I worked needed more of those.

"Here. Let me help." A large hand peeking out of a black

winter coat landed next to mine, steadying the stack, and we made fast work of stabilizing the display.

"Thanks. Though I think I'm the one who's supposed to be assisting..." My voice trailed off as I finally moved away from the display and turned to the customer. And it was trouble all right. Six feet and a couple hundred pounds of solid muscle of the worst kind of trouble. "*Milo?*"

Milo Lionetti did not belong in any game shop ever. I couldn't even picture him reading a comic book or shuffling trading cards. And I didn't care what the problem was—no way would he let himself be seen at the "Nerd Superstore" as he and his jock crowd had dubbed the place in high school. Nothing good could come of him being here.

"Yeah. I need—"

"To involve me in your latest stunt. Or are you here to gawk at the gamers?" I stared him down, all chipperness erased from my tone. Luckily, the shop was pretty slow for a Sunday in winter. There were a few random games going on at the tables in back, but no one was milling about the front part of the store to witness whatever the heck Milo had planned.

"I'm not here as a joke." Milo stepped close enough to the counter that I could smell his sporty aftershave. Even his body products were strictly jocks-only, and damn whatever part of me that found the scent appealing.

"Oh? Our restrooms are customers only. Need a gag gift?" It was the only other reasons I could think of for why he'd even set foot in here.

"No. I need *you*."

"For what?" I demanded. Even as some rogue electrical pulse zoomed up my spine, the words bounced right off my rigid torso. He was about eight years too late—four of them a miserable high-school eternity—and college hadn't softened my stance toward all things Milo one bit.

His eyes narrowed. "You do work here, right?"

"I do." Folding my arms in front of my red work T-shirt, I stopped just short of waving my employee keys in his face. He might have been less smug than usual, but I was no happier to see him than I had been back in school. Then as now, the sight of him heading my way was enough to get all my muscles tensing. *Red alert. Trouble incoming.*

"Good. Then you can help me." He shifted his weight from foot to foot. His tongue darted out to lick at his lower lip in the same nervous gesture he'd had since forever. And in that moment, he wasn't a bad high-school memory but rather the little kid who'd spent hours building complicated Lego structures with me. I missed that kid, far more than I'd give him the satisfaction of seeing.

"Come on. Out with it. What do you need?"

He took a deep breath, shoulders rolling back. "I need a complete play set of Frog Court cards in foil."

I laughed. Like full-out, whole-body chuckles, a few tears short of being a human emoji. When I'd recovered enough to speak, I couldn't stop shaking my head. "Tell me another one. Who put you up to this? Luther? James?"

Both of Milo's sidekicks were too stupid to know much about rare cards from the hugely popular *Odyssey* game, but this was the type of stunt they'd relished back in school. Send a dupe in with a ridiculous ask, embarrassing the requester and wasting the time of everyone involved.

"No, I'm serious." Milo held up his broad hands. Even in bulky winter wear, he managed to look ready to star in an Italian car ad. His short, dark hair was neatly trimmed, and he'd recently shaved. He didn't *look* to be drunk, hungover, or otherwise impaired, but no way was this anything other than some frat-boy dare.

"Uh-huh. Well, unless you have a spare five to ten grand and a burning desire to go treasure hunting, it's not happening. Not here. Arthur's had this place for years now, and I know for a fact he's never seen a complete set of all four cards, especially not in foil."

"Ten grand?" Milo paled as he gulped. "I need those cards."

"The money and a hunt," I corrected him. "They're not simply out there on the open market for the taking. Those are a serious collector's item, and people spend *years* looking to find a matched set."

Milo's eyes squished shut. "Damn it."

"Hate to tell you, but if someone made you promise the cards, they're having you on." Despite everything that had passed between us over the years, I actually felt for the guy a little. It sucked to be on the losing end of a prank. As I well knew.

"I...lost them." Milo went from pale to greenish gray, and for a second, I worried I'd be cleaning up puke next, especially when he swallowed hard.

"You lost what?"

"Bruno's cards." Milo's voice was low and pained. "I had no idea they were *that* rare. I—"

"Hold up. Bruno, your brother who's some sort of special forces, plays *Odyssey?*" I had vague memories of Bruno, who was a good four or five years older than Milo and me. He'd joined the navy right out of high school, and last I'd heard from the mom gossip network, he was one of the people who worked on SEAL boats and other top-secret stuff. Not the sort of person I usually saw across the gaming table.

"Yeah. A girl got him into it in high school, then he fell back into card games living in the barracks. He's wicked good at it too." Some of the pain in Milo's tone was replaced with pride, which I would have found cute on anyone other than Milo.

"Uh-huh."

"Won stuff off his teammates, that sort of thing. Anyway, he left a bunch of things with Mom and me before this last deployment. We played a few rounds when he visited."

"You played?" I blinked, trying to picture the badass SEAL support guy and jock king playing cards at their mom's pretty, white dining table.

"Quit looking so surprised." Milo made a dismissive gesture, nearly taking out one of the boxes of holographic dice we had by the register. "I can read the cards, same as anyone else. It's not a hard game to learn."

Actually, it was rated among the world's most complex

games to master, but far be it from me to convince a guy who'd probably played less than ten games total. "I'm still not sure how you go from him showing you how to play to losing a set of the rarest cards in *Odyssey.*"

Milo might be an idiot, but Bruno had always been smart on top of being brawny. No way would he have had those cards in an intro deck he used to teach newbies like Milo.

Milo rubbed his temples. "Whiskey."

"No kidding." I'd been right. His jerk friends and alcohol were never a good combo.

"The guys I'm living with had a party a while back. And there was this dude big into *Odyssey* there. I said I could play some and told him about Bruno's kick-ass collection."

Sensing where this was going, I groaned. "Tell me you didn't show him the cards."

"Whiskey and Coke. Like I said. Anyway, he invited some of us over to play last night and tells me to bring my cards. There was food and drinking and some friendly betting going on." Milo nodded, like I was supposed to sympathize with this tale of woe.

"*Odyssey* is not a drinking game. Or even one to try buzzed."

"Yeah, yeah, I know that *now*, Mr. Serious Gamer, but cut me some slack here. It's just cardboard." Milo still had the ability to make a simple eye roll condescending as all get out.

"Says the guy who apparently lost *near-priceless* cardboard."

"*I know.* And anyway, I'm good at the game. Even Bruno said so. Last night, I won several rounds in a row. His decks are that good, I guess, and then George says—"

Despite my determination not to feel sorry for Milo, my stomach took the express elevator all the way to the tile floor. "Oh, hell no. George Bryant? Our age or a little older? Tall guy, dark hair but longer than yours?"

"Yeah, that's probably him. He goes to Gracehaven but lives off-campus in a nice condo."

Yup, that was George, and if there was one person I disliked more than Milo and his squad, it was probably George. He'd cost me several of my best transforming cards with a dirty play style that might win him games but also made enemies out of most of the game-store regulars.

"He's in my year, and he's total bad news. Arthur had to ban him from playing here. That's the last guy you should have been betting with."

"Now you tell me." Milo's shoulders slumped further and he leaned on the counter. His eyebrows drew together as if he'd seriously expected a warning when we hadn't exchanged more than ten words in years. "He seemed like an okay dude right up until he suckered me into betting the frog family cards—"

"The Royal Frog Court, ultra rare—"

"Yeah, yeah. I get it, okay? And I lost." The pain was back in Milo's voice, which legit cracked. Damn. The guy really was hurting, and if he were anyone else, I'd pat his shoulder or something. "He wouldn't even play me to try to win them back. So now I'm screwed."

"Yup." I couldn't argue with that assessment.

"You don't have to sound so happy about it." Milo

pushed away from the counter, making the dice rattle in their boxes.

"I'm not." Seeing anyone screwed over by George wasn't my idea of fun, even if I didn't exactly have warm and fuzzy feelings for Milo himself.

"I tried to think of who I knew who might be able to help me. And you're the biggest gamer I know." His eyes were soft and pleading, the same look that had always earned us extra cookies from his mom. "Are you sure you can't help?"

"I'm sure. It's not like we have those cards here, and I'm on duty right now. I can't drop everything for a hunt for you." The way I saw it, Milo was boned, with or without my help, and Google could convince him of that as well as I could.

"After work?" More of that pleading face, and snapshots from every sleepover, every birthday party, every playdate danced in my head. He'd been such a great kid right up until he wasn't. And no way was I going to go down the path of trying to convince myself he'd changed back into the boy I used to know. We weren't friends now, and I wasn't particularly interested in changing that fact, opening myself up to that kind of pain.

"No."

"Is it because of high school?"

I wasn't going to lie. "Part of it. You think I've forgotten?"

"We're older now. And I'm sorry. I guess we were kind of jerks to your crowd—"

"You think? *Kind of?*" I kept my voice down, but I couldn't stop the sarcasm from seeping into my tone. I wasn't going to start listing incidents like I kept an accounting of all the hurts he and his crowd had dished out to anyone who dared to be smart, nerdy, or anything other than a vapid clone in their popular jock clique, but I deserved more than some half apology.

"Okay, some shit went down. Like I said, I'm sorry. Are you sure you can't help me? For old times' sake?"

"F—" I was about to lay into Milo about how far "old times' sake" had gotten me back when I could have actually used someone to defend me and all my geeky interests, but then my boss, Arthur, called my name as he came from the back of the store, and all I could do was shake my head. I was older now and I was my own damn hero. Maybe others didn't always see me that way, but I'd grown way past "old times' sake" sentiments.

"Jasper! Who has the private room booked?"

"It's that dads-who-game club," I told Arthur, trying to ignore the way Milo seemed to collapse further, despair rolling off him. He glanced at me again, and, apparently not liking what he saw there, he headed to the door, a slight limp to his steps. I had to stiffen my back muscles and plant my feet, trying not to feel anything as he walked away. Not curiosity about what had caused the limp and definitely not regret. I didn't have time for either.

He paused to hold the door for some patrons, light catching his expression. His eyes had transformed from pleading to resigned, like a world-weary soldier returning from a battle he hadn't won. His head was high even as his shoulders slumped, and he was perhaps more regal in defeat than he had been when he'd been so sure I'd agree. In that instant, he looked exactly like Prince Neptune. April would have freaked at the resemblance and would have begged him to cosplay with us. She always was a sucker for the story lines where Neptune faced losing odds and had to claw his way back from the edge of defeat. Maybe...

No. Not going to go there. Milo was no prince and certainly not anyone I needed in my life.

I was not going to be swayed by his worried eyes. Angry Milo and jerk Milo were easy to dismiss, but sad Milo had always managed to get under my skin. This time, though, I wasn't going to let him. He'd managed to get himself into a heck of a mess, but he'd have to get himself out again without me. I turned my back on him, same as he'd done with me all those years ago. But even as I turned, my stomach cramped, the battle between the urge to shut him out and the urge to swoop in with the rescue way more real than I would have liked.

CHAPTER TWO
MILO

THE COLD OF A NEW Jersey winter smacked me in the face as soon as I exited the game shop, but the chill in the air was nothing compared to Jasper's frosty expression when I'd asked him for help.

You think I've forgotten? Jasper clearly hadn't. Every mistake and transgression from high school had been there in his eyes. Every time I could have done things differently. All the moments I'd replayed in my head for years. Jasper wasn't the only one with a long memory. I remembered, too, remembered his cluttered basement playroom, the hours and hours we'd spent there. We'd been so in sync back then, him ready with the exact piece I'd needed at the perfect moment to complete our latest Lego build. Everything had been so much simpler, no need to ask...

Hell. I paused in front of the stationery store a few doors down to try to regroup. I hated needing help. Hated it. I'd needed far too much assistance in the last year, and every time I resolved to fix my own problems, some new situation would crop up to kick me where it hurt. And okay, some of that was my own doing. I could admit that. I'd been drinking the night before and was distracted in a way I didn't really want to examine too closely right then.

I'm so glad you came.

You're so good at this game. Like scary good.

Come on, don't you like a friendly bet, pretty boy?

I won fair and square. Unless there's something else you'd like to put on the table?

And there hadn't been. Even buzzed, I hadn't missed how George's voice had gone from warm and welcoming to cold and calculating. And in a single harsh look, I'd gone from distracted to heartsick, intuition kicking in a few hours too late. Not to mention literally sick, too, puking in the bushes, my notoriously weak stomach registering its opinion of what had gone down.

Such an idiot. I had to stop myself from beating my head into the exterior brick of the stationery store. The holidays were over, but the window featured a bunch of whimsical angels. My mom would love all the merchandise on display, and simply thinking about her gave me a sick, hollow feeling in the pit of my stomach. She too was going to be horribly disappointed in me. Again.

What is it this time, Milo? I could almost hear her too-weary voice, the one that said she'd been dreading this latest screwup. My fingers skated over the edge of the phone in my pocket. I could call her. Get it over with. Maybe she'd have better advice than Jasper after she finished being sad. Again. A-freaking-gain.

Chances were also high that she'd attempt to dip into money she didn't have to try to make this right. I withdrew my hand. I was going to have to solve this on my own.

In the window, a notebook cover featured a particularly

celestial-looking guardian angel, and the same sick stomach I'd been battling all day roiled again. Where had mine been last night? Mom was always saying that Dad was my guardian angel now, but I'd seldom felt as alone as I did right then. No Dad. No guardian angel. No common sense. *Ten thousand dollars.* Wasn't that what Jasper had said? For cardboard. Seriously?

I had only one thing worth that kind of money, and I sure as hell wasn't parting with it, no matter how much I'd screwed up. And he'd said something about a hunt too. Research. I had a stack of less-than-awesome grades showing how much I sucked at that skill. Jasper would know, though. He'd always been wicked smart, fingers flying over the keyboard, sharp mind organizing search results while my brain was still sputtering. I supposed there were other genius gamers I could try to recruit to help, but if the incident with George had taught me anything, it was that I couldn't trust my instincts about people.

And Jasper might die mad at me, but he was also honest to a fault. And nice. He'd never take advantage of even his worst enemy. Who was apparently me. *Damn it.* I wasn't giving up, though. I'd wait until his shift ended, try again.

It was cold, but I'd been in worse, and at least it wasn't actively snowing or sleeting. Luckily, I had gloves and a hat in my pockets, so I went around to the alley that ran behind the row of downtown shops. Sure enough, the old beater hunk of metal that Jasper called a car was parked in one of the spots behind the gaming store. Finding a convenient concrete planter to lean against, I settled in to wait, but I hadn't been there long when my phone buzzed.

Bruno's face flashed on the lock screen, and I almost dropped the phone. *Hell.* My pulse raced, my stomach rebelling all over again. I could let the call go to voicemail, but that was the way of a coward. Bruno got so little time to call home that Mom and I always made a point of answering if at all possible. He was out there saving everyone's asses and keeping us safe. The least I could do was pick up the phone.

"Hey, Bro." I tried to keep my voice steady, play it cool.

"Hey. I've only got a few minutes here, but I wanted to check in on my favorite baby brother." The phone crackled with every third word, but still the warmth in his voice came through loud and clear. His voice was deeper than mine, more naturally authoritative without trying. "How's it going?"

"Fine." Maybe the less I said, the better.

"Only fine?" Bruno's tone shifted, concern replacing the easy warmth. "You okay?"

"Yeah, of course. Nothing for you to worry about." I sped up, trying to convince both of us at the same time. "Job's going well. They said they might have more hours for me."

"Good. I knew when I told Juan about you needing work that you'd make me proud."

"Trying." God. Like I needed a reminder of all Bruno had done for me. He could have washed his hands of me a half dozen favors ago, but he was Bruno, full of patience and intrinsically *good*, a better person than I'd ever be. Jobs for a college dropout with an iffy record had been in short supply, but Bruno had leaned on his old buddy from high school to get me work in the online shipping warehouse. Decent hourly wage and health insurance, which had been the main incentive for me.

"Excellent. How's the leg holding up?"

"Fine. I mean, it doesn't really hurt these days," I lied. Rehab on my surgically repaired leg was a work in expensive progress, but the last thing I was going to do was complain to a guy who routinely dodged actual bullets.

"You're a fighter, that's for damn sure. When I first saw you after the accident... Well, never mind that. Proud of you."

And that right there was reason number one why I needed to get Bruno his cards back. He'd been my first call that terrible night, and never once had he complained about having to be the one to tell Mom or all the ways, big and small, that he'd had to help me in the months that followed.

"Thanks. And, uh...you hanging in there?" I never knew precisely how to ask about his work.

"Yup. You can tell Mom I'm keeping my head about me. Don't worry her, but shit's been real here." There was an edge to his voice that hadn't been there a second before, but then he exhaled hard. "Anyway, I'm hoping to get word that we'll be heading back to the States soon. Can't wait to see you both. Think you'll be up for an *Odyssey* game?"

"Maybe," I hedged, bile rising in my throat.

"It was fun, right? Nice to have something to do now that kicking the ball around is out..."

Soccer had been his sport first, then mine, and something we could always share. Except I'd gone and ruined that too.

"Yeah. It wasn't bad. Fun game."

"And you're a natural. Got those killer reflexes left over from the field."

Oh God. Panic joined the nausea party. *A natural.* George had said that too. And I'd been my usual cocky self and believed him. And look where that had gotten me.

"I'm not that great. Not like you."

"Hey, you'll get there. I'll show you more about deck building when I'm home. We'll go through all my cards, maybe have a beer now that you're actually legal."

"Sounds good." I had no idea how I managed to get the reply out without croaking.

"Soon." Bruno said the word like a prayer, and I knew he'd be in mine later. Real shit indeed. I wanted him home safe in the worst way.

"Soon," I echoed. This was it. I really was going to retch now. I was a crap brother and worse human. Bruno had asked for *one* thing after all he'd done for me, and I'd fucked it up.

A voice sounded from near Bruno. "Lionetti. Gotta go, man."

"Time's up." Bruno sounded weary, like Mom at the end of a long day. My chest ached as surely as if he'd landed a fist there. "Take care."

"Stay safe, Bruno." No way could I fess up, not right then, not with him heading out to God knew what danger.

"I try." And then he was gone, and I was left holding the phone, my entire body hurting like I'd been laid flat on the asphalt. In a way I had. I had to get those cards back. Whatever it took. Even if it meant—

"Milo?" Jasper emerged from the back of the game shop, wearing a bulky duffel coat and carrying a backpack that appeared to be more colorful patches than canvas. "What are you doing here?"

"Waiting for you." I was too wrung out from the call with Bruno to come up with anything other than the truth.

"Figured." Jasper's voice was marginally less hostile than earlier. As before, he looked...different than last time I'd seen him. Older. Good in a way that I hadn't been prepared for. Less scrawny for sure—more filled-out shoulders and defined arms that I'd tried like heck not to notice while he was stocking boxes. And failed miserably. His voice was more adult too. Firmer. "Was that Bruno on the phone?"

"Yeah. He's on some top-secret mission. Needs me to tell Mom not to worry." I gave a harsh laugh. "And needs me to be less of a dumbass, but what else is new?"

"You did screw up pretty spectacularly." Jasper shook his head like he was admiring the wreckage of my life.

"I did," I agreed mournfully. "And now I need help."

"So you said." Jasper paused, gaze dropping to my phone, almost as if he expected Bruno to emerge from it, special forces gear and all. "And I can't believe I'm going to say this—"

"*Please.*" My eyes squished shut as I did some major-league bargaining with the universe.

"My help is worth something. What you're asking for, it's not five minutes of work—"

"I know. I'm not asking you to do it for free." My head did a ridiculous bobble as I tried to will him toward a yes. And paying him would be hard, but I'd make it happen. Anything to avoid disappointing Bruno yet again.

"Good. Because I might have a proposition for you."

Relief coursed through me, so swift and overwhelming that my eyes stung from more than the cold. I had no idea what he was going to ask for, but I was going to do my damnedest to give it to him, even if it sucked.

CHAPTER THREE
JASPER

MILO LOOKED LIKE HE WAS in serious risk of passing out right there on the frozen asphalt behind the game store. I hadn't seen him that upset since freshman year of high school when we'd had our last real conversation—a fight that had left me in a billion pieces. I'd shattered exactly like a rocket we'd worked on once, a freak collapse destroying days and days of work, except that time it had been years of friendship crumbling.

"I don't get why you can't sit with us." My voice had done the wavering thing I hated on the walk home from school. I'd left school alone, Milo popping up two blocks into my trek, all cagey about why he hadn't been at the lockers like usual.

"Because the team sits together." The team. God. I was already sick of hearing about the soccer team and definitely sick of Milo's reverent tone when he talked about his teammates. "I may be JV now, but Coach says if I keep working, I'll be the first freshman to make varsity. I need to be one of the guys right now."

"But you were one of *us*." He'd sat with our crowd all through middle school and the first part of freshman year. Sure, the school was bigger, but we'd had the same core friend group for years now. We talked about our favorite games and complained about our least favorite classes, same as always, even though we didn't have many classes other than lunch together. But then he'd gone and made the soccer team, and everything had changed. I hated it.

He bit his lip, tongue darting out to soothe where his teeth had been, making my stomach do flippy things even as I knew I wasn't going to like what came next.

"I'm not a gamer. Not really. And I'm not gunning for honor society and math team like you guys. Coach says I'll probably get a scholarship somewhere even if my grades aren't all that. I'm just not a..."

"Nerd," I finished for him. "You don't want to be seen with the nerds."

"No!" Milo squawked, but something about his protest rang empty. "I can message you."

"Message? Like, why can't you talk to me at school? Or hang out at our houses like always. I don't get it." Coming to a stop at an intersection, I pivoted on my heel, staring him down, daring him to tell me I'd been imagining his weirdness lately.

"I don't think you should come over because... You know. You went to that meeting. The one for that club." He'd gone paler now and his voice was faint.

Heck. I never should have told him about that. I'd built it up to this huge deal in my brain the first part of the year, but then I'd finally gone on a day when Milo had had practice after school, and it had been totally fine. "The rainbow alliance? That one? There were like maybe fifteen people there—"

"But other people noticed." Milo's face had gone pale, lending a sickly cast to his skin. He looked like he had after we'd ridden that huge roller coaster last summer, right before he puked up his guts. But unlike then, I had zero sympathy.

"You mean your jock friends noticed. And now you can't be seen with me?"

"It's not about what my friends on the team might think," he said, even though it undoubtedly was. "My parents might find out too. My dad... Never mind. It's nothing. Maybe everyone will just get over it."

He didn't sound too sure, and the way his voice had wavered on the word *nothing* told me everything I needed to know. He was scared to be seen with me, and it wasn't simply about me being too nerdy for the jock crowd.

Now my own stomach lurched. Others might get over it, but somehow I knew deep inside that I wouldn't. Not ever.

He kept going. "And in the meantime, we can message and stuff."

Somehow I found the strength to straighten my shoulders, harden my stare, and toughen up my voice. "I'm not going to be your secret. That's not cool. Either we're friends or we're not."

I could still see his face as I'd walked away that day. His lips had been pale, but his cheeks were stained red, and his dark eyes had been hollow, an emptiness there that still haunted me.

"Anything. Whatever you need," Milo promised now even before I had a chance to lay out the bargain I was 100 percent sure he wouldn't take.

"Not so fast," I warned, holding up a hand. "You're not going to like this. But I need a Prince Neptune."

He blinked. "A prince who?"

"Prince Neptune. Only the most iconic character in *Odyssey*. The one on all the set boxes? The one starring in their novel series?"

"I'll take your word for it." He nodded rapidly. "So, you need his card? I can't part with more of Bruno's stuff—"

"No, I need *him*," I corrected. And to be fair, Milo wasn't the only one I expected to hate this plan. I had no freaking clue why I was even having this conversation other than that I'd had four more texts from April and one from my friend Kellan while I'd been at work. Everyone was counting on my ability to find a Neptune, and I really wanted to deliver on my promise. And okay, Milo wouldn't have been my first or hundredth choice, but then I'd heard him on the phone with Bruno, all sad. My better instincts had fled, leaving me here with this most ridiculous plan. "I'm part of a cosplay group. We go to different events as our favorite *Odyssey* characters—cons, tournaments, parties, that sort of thing. And we have a regular gig at the children's hospital. We go to see the older kids, play cards with the ones who feel up to it, take pictures with others. It's fun."

"Uh-huh." Eyes wide, Milo clearly didn't share my definition of fun. But that was fine. He didn't have to like this idea. In fact, it was probably better if he didn't, if he turned it down flat. We could both move on with our day that way, and at least I could say I'd tried.

"Whatever. We love it. The kids love it, too, and they're expecting us Wednesday, but our Neptune is doing a semester abroad and the backup my friend found fell through."

"It's for kids?" Milo sounded slightly less reluctant. I, however, refused to let myself soften toward him simply because he was still a big softie for little kids in need. He'd always been good with baby April back before everything went sideways.

"Yup. April's involved in the group too. She's counting on me." I wasn't going to beg, but I also wasn't above using his sympathies here. "I've got the costume for you. Our regular guy left it with me. The kids are expecting to see Prince Neptune on Wednesday."

"I, uh...I'm not scheduled to work that day." Milo sounded less than certain, but it wasn't a no.

"You have to wear the costume. Like, the whole time, no chickening out and no running from pics. That wouldn't be cool."

He gave a sharp nod. "If I do that, if I pretend to be this Neptune guy, you'll help me?"

His eyes were wide and pleading, and I hated the pull they had on me, the way they made me want to help without exacting my price. "After. After you cosplay with us, and if you're not a dick about it, then sure, we can do some hunting online, see what's out there."

"Any chance that we could bring that $10k price tag down?" His head tilted, same expression as if he were angling for extra fries at the burger joint.

"You're not making this easy."

"Sorry." Holding up his hands, he offered up a little smile, posture much easier now that he'd secured my help. "It's just…I'm not exactly swimming in cash right now."

"Somehow I'm not surprised. I mean, we can see what we find, but this isn't like ordering a new lamp. It's more like treasure hunting. People spend years tracking down rare cards."

"Whoa." Whistling low, his breath came in a frosty huff. "I don't have years. Bruno said he might be home soon."

"Well, then you might want to start praying for good luck." I resisted the urge to make a joke about the odds being in his favor because he wouldn't get the reference. Geeky pop culture was never his strong suit, even before his sidekick jock friends got their claws in him.

"I will." He was so earnest, even glancing skyward like he might actually be making a wish. I couldn't help my laugh. My chuckle warmed my chilled body, but I wasn't looking for any thaw in my opinion of Milo. I stamped my feet, trying to warm up further. It was cold, and Milo's earlobes were pink, peeking out from under his knit cap. How long had he been waiting? Was he freezing under that coat? I hated myself for caring, hated the rogue thoughts about all the fun ways two people could warm up. Because it didn't matter how good Milo looked and smelled—I was done crushing on straight, asshole jocks. And I needed to highlight, boldface, and underline that rule for Milo specifically. He'd trampled all over my feelings once. No way was I giving him any power over me now.

This was strictly a business transaction, a way to score a temporary prince and maybe have a little fun at Milo's expense. I couldn't wait to see his expression when he saw the costume. And yeah, I'd help him with what was sure to be a futile hunt because I'd given my word and that meant something to me. But no way in hell was I resurrecting a friendship better left buried. I'd get what I needed and get the hell away.

CHAPTER FOUR
MILO

"YOU'RE A LIFESAVER. I MEAN that." I pocketed my phone after collecting Jasper's number and the details for Wednesday. Wear a crown for some kids? That couldn't be too hard. In a way, I felt bad, like Jasper was letting me off too easily. "So…uh…why can't *you* dress up as the prince guy?"

"I'm another key character." Jasper's long-suffering expression said I couldn't possibly understand the intricacies of this cosplay stuff. Whatever. I was known for being a good sport. Like, I let myself get talked into a costume every Halloween. Some even had masks, which I wasn't a fan of. At least this wasn't likely to involve fake blood, which my notoriously weak stomach hated.

"Gotcha. So which one are you?"

"I'm the Frog Wizard. The kids love it." Jasper's little smile was far too appealing and far too short-lived. "And at the risk of feeding your already massive ego, no one would buy me as the prince. You'll be perfect."

"My ego is not that big!" I felt honor bound to protest. Also, I sure hadn't felt like all that in months and months. Being needed for something, even something silly like this, was…different. Maybe even nice.

"Yes, it is. Your opinion of yourself has always been more than healthy." Jasper had the audacity to roll his eyes at me. I didn't see what self-esteem had to do with being a prince unless…

"You saying the prince is a hot dude?" I mulled this over in my head. Yeah, maybe I wasn't bad looking, but I never knew what to do when people pointed that out. *Pretty boy.* I had to shove George's voice the hell out of my head, making myself focus only on Jasper. "Like, he works out?"

I wasn't that much taller than Jasper, but I was more built. And Jasper wasn't bad looking for a skinny guy. If you were into red hair and freckles and… *Yeah.* Not going there. I didn't see how muscles made the prince, but maybe the guy was simply that ripped. I resolved to do a few more arm curls before Wednesday.

"Yeah. The prince pumps iron." Another dismissive eye roll from Jasper as he picked up his backpack. "You can Google him. I'll have your toga Wednesday. See you then."

"Wait. Toga?" He hadn't mentioned a toga. I'd been picturing some sort of velvet robe, not a *sheet.*

"You backing out?" Jasper raised an eyebrow, all but calling me a chicken.

"No!" *Maybe.* God, I really hoped not. I still needed his help in the worst way. "How much skin are we talking about?"

"It's *kids*, Milo. Chill. All your essential bits are covered. You might be a little cold, but you're not risking an indecent-exposure citation."

"Good." Last thing I needed was another citation of any kind, but I sure as hell wasn't telling Jasper that. "I can deal. See you Wednesday."

"See you." Something about Jasper's tone told me he was expecting me to bail on him. But I wouldn't. Bring on the toga. Whatever it took to replace Bruno's cards.

Satisfied that I at least had help in my quest, I finally headed back home. Well, not *home*. Home was a two-story blue house not too far from where I knew Jasper's parents still lived. A new family lived there now. I'd seen them. Three kids. A mom and a dad. But not us. Bruno was halfway around the world, Mom had her small apartment, and Dad…

Well. Dad was somewhere. A better place, they said. I wasn't so sure. But I did know that him not being here had changed everything, taken that little blue house away for good. And after my accident, I'd had no choice but to stay with Mom for a while, but I hated feeling like I was crowding her already tight space, disrupting the new routines she'd worked so hard to find. So I'd moved in with some friends. Crappy apartment on the edge of town, a complex that had never seen a good decade, with thin walls and lax management, but I could afford my share of the rent. At least I hadn't had to worry about the whole application thing on my own.

And it was on a bus line, which was an advantage because I didn't take my car out unless I had no choice. It was a Sunday, so I had a wait for a bus, but that was fine. I had my phone and other distractions with me. No one was around at the downtown stop, so I pulled out my pocket sketchbook, did some doodles while I waited. I roughed out some crowns, trying to psych myself up for Wednesday, but somehow my pen strokes kept morphing into cartoon versions of Jasper. Messy hair. Easy smiles. I was being ridiculous, but it passed the time until the bus finally pulled up.

As I pocketed my sketchbook, my phone buzzed with a message. Jasper, almost like he'd sensed my obsession with getting the right lift to his expressive eyebrows.

Change your mind yet?

Gee. He had such faith in me. *No. You wanting me to back out? Got another prince on standby?*

The reply came as I found a seat at the back of the bus. *Nope. No such luck. Just making sure because Kellan says some hospital administrators are stopping by. It would suck not to have a Neptune for their visit.*

What the heck? He'd said *kids*. But a promise was a promise.

I'll be there, I texted even as the skin of my lower back prickled. I hated the idea of being embarrassed in front of anyone, but if this was the price of Jasper's help, so be it. He'd probably enjoy my discomfort, damn him. And the worst thing was that I couldn't say I blamed him. I'd been a shit to him in high school, and I'd been the one to trash the best friendship I'd ever had. No one's fault but mine.

Eventually I made it back to the apartment. As usual, Luther and James had taken over the living room, chip wrappers and beer bottles surrounding them as they battled in some first-person shooter game.

"Hey." Nodding in my direction, Luther stretched. The two of them had probably been at the game all day because the place reeked. Funny how they loved hating on nerds even as they were obsessed with wreaking fictional carnage. "You were late last night."

"What the hell? You his mom now?" Not even looking up from his controller, James made a pinched face, like even this amount of interaction was physically painful for him.

"Nah." Luther made a dismissive gesture. "I just want someone here to have gotten lucky last night. Damn sure wasn't me."

Lucky. My stomach gave a fresh roll. "It was all right."

"Eff those gamers, man. Serious lack of estrogen in their crowd if you know what I mean." Luther laughed at his own brilliance, but I didn't. "Was there even any booze?"

"Some." I shrugged. In my pocket, my phone buzzed. A weird thrill raced up my spine. Was it Jasper again? More warnings not to ghost him? I wanted to see, but no way in hell was I looking right then.

"Lame." Attention already drifting back to the game, Luther jostled James's shoulder. "Idiot. I wasn't ready yet."

"You never are. You guys gonna yak all night or what?"

"Or what. I need food." I headed to the kitchen and found that the jar of peanut butter I'd put in the fridge Friday along with a loaf of bread were both gone.

"Not cool, guys, not cool," I yelled, only to get curses back. Screw having roommates. I found a dusty can of soup instead and heated it up before retreating to my room so I could check my phone in peace. My room was the tiniest and the coldest, slightly bigger than a closet with space for a single bed, a small desk, and little else.

I flipped on my space heater and wrapped up in my comforter as soon as I finished the soup. And yup, my message was from Jasper.

Just remembered that you and search engines don't get along. This is Prince Neptune. If you see him on any cards, do NOT part with them, no matter how much you drink.

He'd attached a picture to the message and...uh. I had questions. *Wow. That's a toga*, I typed. At least, like Jasper had promised, the guy's junk and pecs were well covered. And he was indeed a good-looking guy—dark hair like me, Mediterranean complexion, and muscle. But that was most definitely a toga with all sorts of fancy gold accents. Wide gold belt with a seashell for a buckle. Tall gold sandals. This was going to be so embarrassing.

Jasper's reply came quickly, and considering the conversation was thus far centered on my coming humiliation, it was sad how fast my pulse raced, even before I saw the message. *It is. There's also a scepter. And his friend the Octopus Oracle is on a lot of cards too.*

My groan echoed off my narrow walls. *A talking octopus? Now you're just messing with me. Maybe I'd rather be one of the frog guys like you.*

Remember you said that, he replied. And I smiled. God only knew why, but I smiled, maybe for the first time since losing Bruno's cards. This was going to be so bad. Dorky costume. Public audience. But it was Jasper, and we were talking for the first time in almost eight years, and I was enjoying that far more than was smart. I needed to be careful, make sure that I didn't lose anything else that I couldn't afford to part with.

CHAPTER FIVE
JASPER

"IT'S GOT TO BE HERE somewhere." I pulled my coat tighter around myself as I dug through boxes. My parents' detached garage was freezing, but I had no choice but to keep looking. Wednesday was only two days away, and thanks to a heavy class schedule, this Monday night visit was my only chance to grab the garb before then.

"What exactly is it you're looking for?" My mom poked her head in the door. She'd put on a colorful knit hat and scarf for the trek to the garage, and I felt bad for making her come outside.

"A box of stuff Ronnie left before he and everyone else headed to London at winter break."

"We're holding stuff for Ronnie?" She gestured at the packed space that held remnants of five childhoods, various seasonal hobbies, holiday decor, and the usual assortment of bikes and yard-work tools.

"And Jaida," I admitted. Jaida and Ronnie had both needed to stash stuff before the big London trip, and I'd figured three more boxes wouldn't make that much difference. "But not much. Just cosplay stuff. And I need it for Wednesday."

"Oh? Did you finally find your prince?" Smiling, she waggled her eyebrows at me.

"Sort of." I wasn't quite ready to tell her about Milo. She was still friendly with Milo's mom, and I didn't need to take a ride on the Awkward Town express right then. Instead of meeting her eyes, I busied myself with moving a few boxes of Christmas decorations. At the bottom of the stack was a white box with Ronnie's blocky writing on it. "Found it!"

"Good for you!" She gave me a high five as I tucked the box in to my side and made my way back to the door.

"Yeah. I knew I would. Sorry if I made the mess worse."

"It's okay. Dinner is almost ready. You're staying, right?" Pulling her hat down over her ears, she led the way back to the house.

"What is it?" I was staying regardless because her cooking always beat dorm food or needing to buy dinner, but I didn't want to appear too desperate or I'd be headed back to my dorm loaded down with a week's worth of leftovers and snacks.

"Chicken enchiladas and bean soup."

"Yeah, I could eat that." I paused to stamp off my shoes in the mudroom. I stashed the box next to my shoes and backpack. If I was staying, I knew the rules, and I headed to the sink before she could remind me to wash up. April would be down soon, and she'd want a hug, so I scrubbed extra well under my nails and up my wrists, the process automatic from years of precautions.

"Jasper!" Right on schedule, April trooped down the stairs.

Her hair, same red as mine, was pulled up into a high ponytail, little wisps escaping to make her look far younger than fifteen. The baby of the family, she was also small for her age with delicate features and slim limbs, but she was surprisingly strong as she clung to me in a tight hug.

"Wash," Mom ordered.

"I'll set the table." Unlike most of my siblings, I never minded doing chores for my mom. I liked being useful, liked knowing that no matter how stressed and worried she got, there was something I could do for her.

The dishes were still hot from the sterilizing cycle in the dishwasher, and they felt good against my chilled hands. Already changed out of his uniform, Dad came in from the front of the house as I finished, and he went right to the sink too. We were all super well-trained. Anything to keep April safe.

"You're coming Wednesday, right?" I asked April as I took a seat opposite her. "Hospital administrators might stop by. We need our elf."

"I'm coming. Mom made me a new mask that matches the costume since it's still flu season, but it's hardly canon for the trickster elf to need a mask and gloves."

"You make your own canon. And you're one of our best players. The kids all love playing you."

"I am good." She gave me a toothy smile as Mom set the food on the table. I way preferred the times when April could tag along, one of our group, to when she was one of the patients we visited. She'd had another lengthy hospitalization that past summer, and like Mom, I worried constantly about rogue germs. But we also couldn't keep someone with her kind of energy home indefinitely. She'd most likely be dealing with the genetic blood disorder that affected her immune system the rest of her life, and it was always a balancing act between keeping her safe and letting her have the same freedoms as the rest of us.

"Did you find a Prince Neptune?" April asked as I took a portion of the piping-hot enchiladas. Her voice was even more eager than her texts, which was saying something. Neptune was unquestionably April's favorite character so finding a cosplayer for him, even if it were Milo, made me happy. Honestly, there wasn't much I wouldn't do to make April smile. Considering everything she had to put up with, procuring a prince was the least I could do.

"Yup."

"My hero." She said it jokingly, but that right there was a big part of why I liked doing things for her so much. In my friend group, I wasn't the resident genius or the best *Odyssey* player or the hottest person. I made an excellent sidekick. A bonus friend, there to make even numbers or crack a joke at the right moment. With April, though, every so often I got to play hero. I might be an afterthought for others, but with her I could be Super Big Brother.

"Thanks."

"Who is it? Someone from the college?" She leaned forward. April *lived* for college gossip, especially since she'd transitioned to online high school after catching several bad infections from bugs going around the school. She hated being the only Quigley kid who wouldn't graduate from our neighborhood school. She'd been down, and that was another reason why I was relieved to have found a Neptune, even if I was still less than thrilled with the who.

"No. It's…" *Oh hell.* She was going to recognize him right away, and Mom would as well, if she brought April. I took a bite of too-hot food, trying to buy time, and immediately regretted it as I scorched my tongue. And my stupid brain immediately leaped to a vision of Milo from the day before, his pink tongue worrying his full lips. *Damn it.* Why couldn't he be a little less hot?

Of course, if he weren't so appealing, he wouldn't be so perfect as Neptune. But that perfection was going to come at a cost to my sanity. For the hundredth time, I second-guessed what the heck I was doing. I'd texted with him for a good hour the night before, answering questions about Neptune lore that Milo could have discovered perfectly well on his own, only stopping when Kellan and Jasmine came to collect me for food. And really, I should have been grateful for the interruption. I wasn't supposed to find any part of this…arrangement fun.

"Who is it?" Mom prodded, concern evident in her eyes. She wasn't the biggest fan of some of the game-store crowd, and she was probably already visualizing someone entirely unsuitable to have around April.

Heck. No choice but to share the truth, or at least a version of it. "Milo. Funniest thing, but he came into the store, and we got to talking and he…volunteered."

"Milo Lionetti?" Mom frowned, which wasn't the reaction I'd expected.

"Heard he got himself into some trouble a while back." Dad's expression was even more grim.

"He sure is cute trouble," April added, which got her pointed looks from all three of us.

"I haven't seen him since the funeral." Shaking her head, Mom cut her food into neat pieces. "Poor Cathy. That boy has put her through the ringer on top of everything else she's had to endure. And she's not the only one. Jasper, do you really want to get involved with him again?"

"We're not *involved*." My fork clattered against my plate. Business. This was *business*. A transaction. A Neptune for Kellan and April and the kids at the hospital. Some help for Milo, but even that was more for Bruno, who hadn't deserved his dumbass brother losing his cards. *Involved* was not even remotely on the table.

Across from me, April smirked like she knew better. And then my phone buzzed in my pocket and I immediately wondered if it was Milo. *Damn it.* Even friendship would be beyond stupid. He'd proved enough times that he wasn't to be trusted.

"Good." Dad nodded firmly before returning his attention to his food. I got why they were both firmly anti-Milo. I'd moped for months when our friendship had ended, and they'd had to hear more than one tale of woe in the following years about Milo's new crowd and their idea of jokes involving the smart kids.

Involved. Back then, I hadn't allowed myself to hope for Milo being anything other than my best friend, especially once that friendship had been lost. I had been only starting to find other people cute back then, and while my heart might have had some private wishes, I tried hard to ignore any...*reactions* to his nearness. Unlike now, when my body most definitely had noted Milo was *all* grown up.

"You're months from graduation." My mom must have picked up my train of thought. Milo wasn't the only one who was an adult now. I too had the real world waiting.

"Yup. Don't need any distractions," I agreed. I had a possibility of a job in NYC after graduation, and maybe that was part of why I'd been so desperate to find a Prince Neptune. I still wasn't sure how I felt about leaving April and Kellan and everyone else here. Felt weird to be down to mere months. But at least I could make sure they were *good* months, and maybe eventually I'd sort myself out.

April's laugh cut through my tumbling thoughts. "I'd take a distraction about now. Especially if it looked like—"

"You're only fifteen. Maybe you spending time with Jasper's crowd isn't a good idea," Mom grumbled, which only made April groan.

"It'll be fine," I said before an argument could break out. "He'll probably only be Neptune the one time anyway."

Buzz. My pocket vibrated again. Heck. Maybe not even the one time if he was messaging to bail. Mom had a strict no-phones-at-the-table rule, so it wasn't until after I helped clear and wash the dishes that I got a chance to look at my messages. I leaned against the washer in the mudroom as I scrolled my phone.

Several from Kellan, of course. He wanted to show me his latest design for upgrades to his mage outfit. Unlike some of us, Kellan cosplayed as multiple characters depending on his mood and the event. And each costume needed approval from the rest of us. I added my thumbs-up and scrolled on. Arthur wanted to confirm my work schedule for the weekend, but none of those messages made my pulse thrum like seeing Milo's name.

Hey. Did you find the costume?

You're hoping I didn't. Don't lie. I laughed as I typed. *Yup. Checked the sandals. Size twelve. Think that will work?*

His reply came while I was still packing up. *Yeah. That's my size too. And uh...I've been wondering what goes under the toga?*

My answering chuckle was loud enough to make Mom glance my way from where she was putting away leftovers in the kitchen. *Oops. No distractions. No involvement. Seriousness only.* Except somehow my fingers didn't get the message.

You worried it's like a kilt? ROFL. And TBH, Ronnie and I weren't tight like that. Never looked.

That wasn't entirely true. I'd never hooked up with Ronnie, but I knew perfectly well that he wore something under the toga. I didn't want to examine too closely why I was having fun with Milo. And of course my pulse leaped with the next response. *Okay. I'm gonna bring some shorts or something, unless that's against cosplay rules?*

There's no rules. And sure, I'm not asking you to go bare-assed. Wear what you want under it.

But as soon as I typed that, my brain was filled with images of Milo in various stages of undress, a parade of all the possible underwear options. He probably wore boring mono-colored cotton boxers like all the jocks seemed to favor, but my brain enjoyed the mental fashion show waiting for his reply way too much.

Good. I have some white compression shorts. I'm probably overthinking this, right?

Yup. I'd been right. Jock gear. But there was something almost…vulnerable in his reply. Like he was worried about something more than ending up commando under a toga. I added a frazzled-looking emoji with steam coming out of its brain. *Quite possibly. You're nervous?*

I don't get nervous. Just don't like public humiliation.

Well, okay then. Nice to know how he saw cosplay. My fingers hammered out my retort even as my back tensed with a thousand unwanted memories. *Except when you're handing it out.*

I kind of expected that would end the exchange, and indeed there was a long pause, but the bubbles kept showing like he was typing. However, no message came, and I gave my mom a hug and headed out to my car. Still little bubbles, as if he was typing and erasing. And damn it, I was curious enough to wait a few more minutes while the car warmed up. Finally, the phone buzzed.

I'm sorry. You got a raw deal in school for sure. I was a shit. We all were. And I know it means dick now, but I'd do it differently if I could.

My chest did a weird flip as my hand tightened on my phone. He'd said sorry the day before, but I hadn't believed him. And honestly, I didn't entirely now either. He was likely only regretting that he needed my help and that I hadn't forgiven him easily. But at least he was owning that he was an ass back then—him and his lousy friends.

Even now, I could remember his jock buddies and their stupid jokes and the way Milo had always stood there, mouth a tight line, eyes grim, shoulders stiff like he was next on the chopping block. Except he never was. He'd been a golden boy for the popular crowd, and I refused to let my brain process the idea of him doing things differently. Because what if we'd never argued? What if we'd stayed friends? What if he'd stood up for me? Too many what-ifs for my head to hold, that was for sure. And I just wasn't ready for a world where Milo might have genuinely changed. Even if his apology felt good, believing in it—or *him*—would be beyond foolish.

CHAPTER SIX
MILO

"I'M NOT LATE," I ANNOUNCED, out of breath as I barreled through the hospital lobby to where Jasper stood. He was loaded down with a couple of bags, a large gold scepter, and a disturbingly accurate giant frog mask. My leg already ached from the fast walk from the bus stop, and I was pissed at it, missing the days when I could have easily jogged up to the hospital.

"Barely." Jasper was smiling, but my chest was still tight. I'd been worried he'd assume I was going to bail and call the whole thing off. I'd had another message from Bruno the night before, underscoring how badly I needed Jasper's help.

"Sorry. Bus took forever to come, but I made it." Inhaling slowly, I tried to resume my normal voice without sounding too defiant. Didn't need to start this thing off with my bad mood ruining our uncertain truce.

"That you did. And you actually beat some of the others. Come on, let's get changed." Jasper adjusted his bags, and I instinctively reached for two of them, leaving him with the props and his usual backpack. My hand grazed his shoulder, which was a miscalculation on my part. He was warm and solid and smelled like cedar, facts that my body took way too much notice of.

"Here. Let me help." My voice was huskier than it needed to be as I shouldered the bags.

"Okay. Okay. Careful. The red one has all the intro decks we use for playing the kids." Jasper strode across the lobby toward the restrooms, pausing near a soda machine to turn toward me. "And why don't you have a car?"

Oh, how I hated questions like that. I got enough shit from my friends over my reliance on the area's spotty transit. "I have a car. Just don't like taking it out, especially in winter."

That was true enough. My car was a classic Mustang that I'd spent hours restoring with my dad, and it was hardly a winter workhorse. But that wasn't the whole story, wasn't why my insides twisted up every time I had to drive, especially in bad weather. And I really hated caring what the hell Jasper thought, didn't know quite how to take his shrug as he entered the restroom.

Jasper glanced around the empty room as he pointed to the blue bag. "Your stuff is in here. I'll take the other bags in with me. Can't risk someone walking off with the cards."

"Yeah," I said weakly. Couldn't lose precious cards. For the billionth time since the weekend, I called myself all kinds of idiot. We exchanged bags and I headed into a cramped stall to change. It was weird, being back in a hospital with that distinctive medicinal cleaner smell, memories of my recovery and other less-than-pleasant associations making my injured leg tense further. My leg was already stiff from the too-fast walk from the bus stop, and the tight quarters didn't help. I took a minute to rub my leg as I took off my shoes before stripping down to my shorts. It was chilly in the restroom, and despite being behind the locked stall door, I felt weirdly exposed.

Unfortunately, the costume didn't help with that feeling as the thin fabric was all floaty as it draped over me, skimming my pecs and midsection before brushing my thighs and swishing around my knees. Bare arms. Bare legs. I'd worn a pair of compression shorts that I usually wore under baggier workout or soccer gear, but the toga was still rather...breezy. And strangely sensual. I'd never had silk sheets, but this fabric slid against my skin and made me aware of my nerve endings in a way I wasn't entirely comfortable with.

"Don't forget your accessories," Jasper called from the next stall.

Oh, yeah. Ornate crown. Gold arm gauntlets. Gaudy seashell belt. And...earrings?

"I don't have pierced ears." I tried to sound regretful, not relieved.

"They're magnets. And they're tiny. Not gonna steal your dude bro cred, promise. I've seen NFL players with earrings."

"Diamond studs are one thing. Seashells are..." My voice trailed off as I realized I wasn't going to win this one and in fact was probably decreasing my chances of help after we were done. "Whatever. Putting them on."

The magnets provided an odd pressure on my earlobes, like someone was tickling my neck and ears, but I tried to ignore them as I struggled to put on the lace-up sandals. No matter how I arranged the gold laces, my scars were still partly visible. Damn it. And of course Jasper noticed as soon as I emerged from the stall.

"Dude. Your leg—"

"*I know.*" My tone was harsh, but I didn't want to take questions right then. Or ever, really. Wasn't planning on baring any more than I had to for Jasper.

"Are you okay? The scepter is pretty sturdy if you need to lean on it." He handed it to me quickly, like I was in danger of falling right that moment.

"I'm fine. And uh...that's your costume?" Gripping the scepter tighter, I was actually grateful for the prop's support as I took in Jasper's outfit. He'd dropped a few hints in chat that I wasn't going to like the Frog Wizard's costume, but I'd figured on a hideous mask, not *this*.

"Yup. Warned you. Still want to switch?" Jasper's outfit was various shades of purple with teal and gold accents. Close-fitting velvet coat that was short in the front, long in the back. Lacy lavender neck scarf that probably had some fancy British name. Embroidered vest. Tassels in more than one location. Short, tight pants, sort of like the kind on the covers of the historical novels my mom loved, but with sheer teal stockings over the lower legs that tapered into gold high-heeled shoes. Oh and a floppy velvet hat.

"Um. No. No switching." I itched behind my ear, wondering if I was supposed to compliment him or what. He looked ridiculous. Also...surprisingly good. Like the outfit clung to his lean frame in a way that made him seem less skinny and more stylish. Elegant even. And if I were drawing a character, I wouldn't ever put red hair together with those colors, but somehow on him it worked, almost too well. "I thought wizards wear, like, stars and big robes."

"Not in *Odyssey*. There's all types of wizards. The Frog Wizard is almost more like a court jester. Some of his cards transform. Sometimes he's tricky, and other times downright devious. But he's known for his style."

"I can see. Those are some shoes. How do you even walk in them?"

"With practice." Jasper laughed, then sobered. "Wait. Speaking of walking, I didn't think... Is your leg going to be okay with the sandals?"

"It'll be fine." That was half-true. I would be fine, but I'd also be hurting later as my leg did rely on my shoe for a certain amount of stabilization. But I'd been putting in the time with the physical therapy exercises and figured I could spare an hour in sandals with no support.

"Whoops!" Two younger doctors in white coats and scrubs came in, door almost hitting Jasper. Both of their eyes went wide before they grinned slyly. Oh heck. This wasn't going to be good. I braced myself for some insult.

"Is it Halloween already?" The taller of the two doctors had a deep voice and was apparently in no hurry to take care of his business.

"Nope." Jasper shrugged, his smile as easy as ever, not in the least rattled despite his attire. "We're expected upstairs. Patient visits."

Somehow Jasper's confidence seemed to have defeated

the young doctors' urge to tease. It was something, the way their faces transformed from joking to respectful.

"I bet the kids will be happy to see you." The shorter doctor offered a warmer smile this time, but unlike Jasper, I didn't grin back.

"They usually are." Jasper still seemed perfectly at ease having the world's most bizarre conversation in a men's room. "We play the *Odyssey* card game with them."

"Wow. I used to play that in high school," the shorter doctor shared. I was a little afraid we were about to get into the specifics of the game right there, but then his companion added, "Good luck, guys."

Finally, the doctors went into the stalls, and we grabbed our stuff and headed out to the hall. Where more people would see us. I had to swallow hard.

"Come on. Let's introduce you to the rest of the gang." Jasper knew no such hesitation as he headed to the bank of elevators near the restrooms. He punched the button for floor three, sparing a grin for an elderly couple sharing the elevator with us. His comfort in costume was impressive, but he still carried the frog head under his arm.

"Why don't you put your mask on?" I asked, trying not to make eye contact with the others in the elevator.

"It's hot and dark in there. Hard to see where I'm going. And sometimes it scares the younger kids. Instead, I wait until they ask me to wear it for a picture or something like that."

"Makes sense." I wouldn't be in any hurry to put the giant mask on either. I followed him off the elevator to a waiting area where several costumed people were standing around. Most of the outfits I recognized from *Odyssey* cards—wizards and reapers and various anthropomorphic animals. A guy about our age in an impressive wizard's outfit strode over. His velvet robes dragged the floor and flowed down his arms. Why couldn't Jasper have needed another wizard? At least this guy was covered. And warm. I shivered again.

"You were right. He is the perfect Neptune." The wizard sized me up in a way that made me feel a bit like a bug under a magnifying glass, going as far as to circle me before reaching out to straighten my toga. It took all my restraint not to knock his hand away.

I settled for giving him a hard stare instead. "Uh. Hands off the costume."

"Sorry." Wizard guy shrugged. "Habit. I had fun altering this one."

"You make the costumes?" My head tilted as I considered him again. He was tall and wide, built like a linebacker, and he had a scruffy beard. He was the sort of guy who probably grew his first beard in junior high, and his hands were bigger than mine. I had a hard time picturing him threading a needle.

"Some of them." His grin had a lot of swagger to it.

"Kellan's a theater major. You'll be seeing his designs on Broadway someday." Jasper slapped Kellan on the shoulder, pride clear in his voice. I had no business caring about their easy friendship, but knowing that wasn't enough to stop an edge from creeping into my voice.

"Cool."

"You're shorter than our last Neptune. But I suppose you'll do." A petite red-haired elf gave me a regal nod. She had a mask embroidered with leaves covering her mouth and nose, and elbow-length gloves on as well.

"And this is April."

"Oh. Right. Your sister." The red hair should have tipped me off. But she'd been born when we were seven or eight, a surprise for the whole family, and had been little more than a preschooler when we'd stopped being friends. "You got big."

"You probably remember her as a tiny—"

"*Jasper.*" She elbowed him hard enough that he winced. And now both her mask and Jasper's interest in the hospital made more sense. She'd been born with some rare genetic blood disorder that impacted her immune system's ability to fight off infections and had been hospitalized a lot as a kid, especially before they found out what was wrong.

"Sorry. Meet my super ancient and wise sister."

"Dork." April rolled her eyes before giving me another critical look. "I told Jasper to find us a Neptune and you're not a bad look-alike, but you need to own it more. Like maybe don't look like we're asking you to chew glass."

"Damn. You're ice cold." Kellan sounded impressed, and honestly, so was I. April had a lot of personality packed into a small package, and I liked how she wasn't afraid to tell it like it was.

"Sorry." Straightening my shoulders, I tried to force myself to relax. Mine was hardly the most outrageous costume in the group.

And everyone else was laughing and joking and acting like this was the highlight of their week.

"Okay." Jasper clapped his hands, the clear leader of this motley group. Like his sister, he had a natural take-charge quality to him that I'd always admired. Jasper got stuff done. "Everyone ready?"

No. No, I was not ready to see yet more people. And privately, I was a little worried about seeing sick kids. Unlike Jasper's family, I didn't have a lot of experience with small children in the hospital. I didn't like the idea of kids being so close to something awful. I'd seen enough medical stuff myself the past few years to not want that for anyone, let alone a kid who should be out playing. My back tensed. I hoped I didn't freak out. But everyone else was nodding and murmuring, so all I could do was mutter, "Sure."

Jasper pursed his mouth and positioned himself next to me, almost like he expected me to make a run for freedom. But I wouldn't. I said I'd do this, so I would, no matter how chilly my bare legs were and no matter how embarrassing this became. I'd stick it out so that I could earn Jasper's help and maybe also so he'd stop expecting the worst where I was concerned. I didn't fool myself into thinking we could be friends again, but I wouldn't mind elevating myself in his opinion some. And if it took being Neptune to do that, then so be it.

CHAPTER SEVEN
JASPER

THIS WAS MY FAVORITE PART of the week, especially when I got to do it with April by my side. I liked walking the hospital corridors in costume, getting smiles from passersby. I knew firsthand how scary it could be visiting loved ones in the hospital, and if we made a sibling or grandparent grin for a minute, that meant a lot to me. And the doctors and nurses worked so hard that I liked bringing some lightness to their days too. Like the doctors earlier in the restroom. We'd made them laugh, and maybe Milo couldn't see the value in that, but I did.

Not that I expected Milo to see any of this my way. April was right. He looked like he was chewing glass as we made our way down the hall, jaw set, eyes straight ahead, shoulders back. He might as well be a prisoner we were escorting to an interrogation. He stiffened further as we reached the large and airy patient lounge favored by some of the older patients and their families—lots of art supplies and games and puzzles, and less of the toys and play equipment of the spaces intended for tiny kids.

"Smile," I ordered Milo as we paused at the door.

"Trying." His smile looked closer to that of a dog with a bellyache, and I wasn't sure whether to laugh or groan.

"Try harder."

"Hey, Jasper! How's it going?" Natalie, the room attendant greeted us, her Disney-print scrubs as cheerful as the rest of the colorful space.

"Great." I moved aside so everyone else could enter the room.

"You brought a new Neptune with you!" She smiled at Milo, who managed a nod.

"Yup. This is Milo." I gestured at him, almost accidentally hitting him in the chest. He was sticking close to me, and his nerves would be endearing if it were anyone else.

"Hey."

The kids had taken notice of our group, and moving slowly, they clustered around us. I loved feeling like an actual superhero for a moment, even if my superpowers couldn't extend as far as I'd like. Some kids were in pajamas and slippers, while others were in hospital gowns and robes. A few had IV poles with them, and as usual some were in wheelchairs while a couple of others had walkers. We got some smiles and waves from those who had seen us before, and as much as I didn't want any kid to have a long hospitalization, making our regulars happy made my insides all warm.

"So, who's up for a game of *Odyssey*?" I asked the group.

"Are you going to let me win this week?" Jenny, an imp

of a girl who reminded me a lot of a younger April, offered me a toothy grin as she leaned on her walker.

"No chance." I wasn't going to play one of my best decks, but I'd still give her a good game.

"I want to play Prince Neptune." Chase, another regular, spoke up from his wheelchair. His eyes were more tired this week, his skin pale, head slumping forward. His dad, who was an ever-present fixture on the ward, hovered nearby.

"I...uh..." Milo swallowed several times. His own skin was a worrisome shade of greenish-white. *Crap.* The guy couldn't even manage five minutes in costume. I should have known.

"Sure thing," I answered for Milo. He'd play Chase even if I had to personally shuffle for him and push him into a chair. "Let us get the decks out."

I steered Milo toward the table in the back of the room that I always used as a staging area for the decks and props.

"What's your problem?" I demanded as soon as we were out of earshot.

"I don't have one." His expression was more pained than sullen, but I still wasn't impressed.

"Yeah, you do. You think you're too good to play some kids?"

"No! That's not it." Milo was quick with the denial before pausing to lick his lips. Gaze darting away, he still radiated discomfort. He lowered his voice further. "I... Other than April when she was little, I haven't been around a lot of sick kids. Like that boy... He's really sick."

Oh. His reaction made a little more sense now. I'd been volunteering so long that I forgot that not everyone was used to sick kids and medical equipment. And Milo's unease stemming from a place of uncertainty and compassion was better than him continuing to freak out over being seen in costume.

"He is." I softened my tone and put a hand on his arm. His very bare, very warm arm. Oops. I shouldn't have touched him, and my voice sped up as a result. "Prince Neptune is his favorite character. He was in the hospital in the fall, and Ronnie always played with him. So how about you don't let him down?"

"I'll try." Milo's nod was firmer now, and he accepted the two introductory-level decks I handed him.

"Good. Let Chase play the purple deck. It's his favorite. And you'll need to shuffle for him."

"Got it." Milo headed over to the small table where Chase and his dad were already waiting. I took another two decks over to where Jenny was waiting to kick my ass. April and the others also found kids to visit with or play. Jenny was a good enough player that I needed to focus on the game, but my attention kept wandering over to Milo's table.

To my surprise, he was smiling. He laughed at something Chase said before plunking down a card, arm muscles flexing, crown catching the light. *Damn*. He really was the perfect Neptune. He'd never accept the compliment, but he did regal well, and the white of the toga contrasted nicely with his Italian looks. Something about the gold jewelry worked for him, too, and my brain kept buzzing with unwelcome thoughts about teasing his ears and neck.

"Jasper! How are the games going?" Ned, the

administrator of the hospital's charitable foundation, came into the room, followed by a young, dark-haired woman a little older than me. I paused my game with Jenny so that I could give them my attention.

"Great." I'd worked with Ned on some projects for the kids before, but my main contact with him had been through my parents when they'd needed to apply to the foundation for assistance with April's many hospital bills.

"And how nice to see April full of energy." Last time I'd seen Ned, April had been fighting off another bacterial infection, and he'd stopped by to see how my parents were holding up.

"Yup. We're lucky." And we were. Not all families got to bring their loved ones home, and I tried to never lose sight of that. We owed a ton to this place, to both the doctors and the administration. Thanks to Ned and the foundation, my parents hadn't had to lose their house when bills continued to mount.

"I wanted to come see your group today because Allison wants to tell you about our latest fundraising efforts for the foundation."

"Yes." Allison had a big smile and a bubbly voice. "Every year we do a big fancy dinner and silent auction, but this year we're doing something a little different."

"And fun," Ned added. He was like a proud grandpa, and I couldn't wait to hear Allison's idea.

"Yes! Fun. Costumes. It's going to be a costume ball."

"Oh my gosh. That sounds so cool." April appeared at our table, undoubtedly sensing the possibility of getting all fancy. But the annual fundraiser was the sort of thing with seats going for three digits and big law firms and accounting firms buying tables for their partners.

"Yeah, it does. But I bet tickets are going to be pricey." I tried not to sound regretful. We wanted the foundation to raise tons of money, and I didn't want them lowering prices just so some broke college students could attend. But then Allison smiled wider.

"Well, we're aiming for the corporate sponsors, true. But we're also asking a few of our regular visitor groups to join us. Mingle with the guests, do pictures, help make sure everyone's having fun."

"I want to do it." April bounced on her feet, practically quivering like a puppy. Homeschooling really was getting to her, and I wanted her to have this opportunity. And if it helped the foundation raise money, I'd be there.

"I'm in." I nodded, loving how April gave a happy laugh in response.

"And the rest of the group?" Allison pulled a small notebook from a pocket in her cardigan. "I'll need to know how many tickets to comp."

"We'll need Neptune," April said, predictably eager, while I was still counting in my head.

"I'm not sure…" Getting Milo to do this more than once probably wasn't going to happen, let alone something with bigwigs. Even now, I could see him eyeing Ned and Allison like they were seconds away from laughing at us, more of that unease he'd had with the doctors rolling off him.

"You know everyone's going to want a picture with him." April made the puppy-dog face she did so well that had gotten me into this mess with Milo to start with.

"He is rather...impressive." Allison smiled in his direction, but Milo busied himself with his game with Chase. Maybe his empathy for Chase could convince him to don the costume more than this once. Maybe.

"I'll ask him." Heck. Now I *needed* Milo to continue this gig, and that was not a comfortable thought at all. I much preferred being the guy swooping in with the big save, not the person needing a hand. My neck itched. He'd better agree. And now I had that much more pressure to help him find the replacement cards. I might need more than good luck to pull this off.

CHAPTER EIGHT
MILO

"SO, ON A SCALE OF terrifying to terrible, how bad was that?" Jasper's smug grin as we packed up our stuff said that he already knew my answer.

"I had fun." I wasn't lying. Once I'd gotten over the more... *breezy* aspects of the costume, I'd relaxed considerably even though it was still weirdly uncomfortable being in a hospital for no medical or personal reason. Seeing how the kids reacted to us had further unknotted my shoulders. They were so happy to see Jasper and his squad, and they acted like Neptune was a pop star, not merely an illustration on some cardboard. After a while, I'd become more into the whole thing, smiling for some pictures and playing a second round with Chase and another kid.

"Not too weirded out by the medical stuff?" Pausing from putting away the card decks, Jasper gave me a considering look.

"Nah." Actually, I had been at first, especially because of my own past. But I wanted to impress Jasper for reasons that were probably best not deeply considered. However, the longer he looked at me, the more truth slipped past my bravado. "Okay, it maybe took a little getting used to. I just...feel bad for them. I dunno."

"It's called compassion, Milo. Might be unfamiliar to you." Jasper laughed like he was making some big joke, but I didn't join in. Jasper didn't know shit about what I'd been through the past few years.

All of a sudden, I'd had enough of this stupid costume. I pulled off the crown and shoved it in the costume bag. "That's not fair."

Jasper simply gave me another long look. And okay, I got where his sarcasm was coming from. I didn't *like* it, but I got it. I'd been an asshole to him in high school, hadn't stuck by him, hadn't stood up for him when I knew good and well that I should have. It was easier to see what a jerk I'd been, especially now that I was trying to shake free of that world.

"I tried to apologize the other night. And I probably suck at apologies, but can we maybe not relitigate my past sins every five minutes?" Maybe text message wasn't the best medium for a grand apology. I didn't know because I hadn't tried to make that many before. But somehow Jasper made me want to try to be something more. "I'm not that person anymore."

Jasper gave a heavy sigh as he resumed putting the last of the decks away and zipping up the bags. "That remains to be seen. However, you did do a good job of making Chase smile."

"I tried."

"I believe you." Jasper's tone was less biting now.

And maybe he didn't believe my apology, but at least he believed that I'd been sincere with the kids, and that mattered. Some of the tightness in my chest loosened. "Thanks."

His smile also took on a warmer cast. "And now I can make good on my promise to help you."

"Here?" There were still some families in the lounge area, although Jasper's other friends had already headed out. His mom had come for his sister, and she'd had a hard stare of her own for me, which I supposed was understandable, all things considered. God only knew what she'd heard via the mom gossip network on top of the shit I'd actually done.

"No, not here. They have a movie night coming in next. Let's go to the cafeteria. The Wi-Fi is pretty strong there."

"Dressed like this?" I looked down at my toga. The administration people who had stopped by had been pretty chill, but I wasn't exactly dressed for the coffee bar. The idea of more speculative looks made my back sweat.

Jasper shrugged because of course *he* had no such issues. "I don't mind. I like making people smile."

"You're good at that."

"Why, thank you." Fully in character for a second, Jasper gave me a courtly bow and a wink. Then he straightened, regular Jasper again. "And if you want to change, we can do that."

"Yeah, I'm a little chilly." More like I was still slightly embarrassed, but I didn't want a lecture.

"Okay, okay. Back to civvies." Jasper led the way to the public restroom near the elevators.

"Ha. You sound like Bruno." I laughed, but inside, I tensed up at the reminder of why I was even here. Bruno had the military-speak down, along with that take-charge attitude. He was the better person for sure, and knowing how badly I'd let him down weighed on me, made my movements slower as I changed clothes.

Jasper was done first and was waiting on me when I emerged from the stall. He was back to a hooded sweatshirt and faded jeans, average college-student wear, but I could still see traces of the Frog Wizard in him. The regal posture. The knowing smile. The light, confident movements as he headed to the cafeteria. He always had a bounce to his step, that extra bit of energy that others lacked.

The cafeteria had a number of food stations including a coffee bar. And damn, I was tired. And thirsty.

"Do you want a drink?" I asked as Jasper pulled a sleek laptop out of his backpack. "I can get us something while you get booted up."

"Thanks. Yes, actually. Soda. M—"

"Mountain Dew. I remember." He'd always had such a sweet tooth and a thing for the junk food his mom seldom stocked.

He met my gaze, and years of history passed between us. Sodas and sleepovers and secrets. "Appreciate it."

I retrieved a bottle of soda for him because he always liked bottles more than fountain drinks and an espresso for myself. Taking the seat next to Jasper, I moved the chair so I could see the screen too. This put me close enough to smell him again, and our sleeves brushed. My body took way too much of an interest in his nearness, but I also couldn't move away without looking like a dick.

"You drink coffee?" Jasper raised an eyebrow as I slid him his soda.

"I got into bullet-proof coffee at college because some of the guys I trained with swore by it. And I had an early-morning PT appointment on the other side of town. I need some caffeine, but unlike you, I can't handle all that sugar anymore."

"If I didn't run on junk food, I'd starve." Jasper was already clicking around his laptop, opening browser tabs with impressive speed.

"Like your mom would let that happen." His mom wasn't a health nut, but with five kids, she did a lot more home-cooked meals than mine, especially when they were all younger.

"Truth." Laughing, Jasper took a swig of his soda, then gestured at his machine. "Okay. Let's start our hunt. I've bookmarked some of the most likely places. A simple search engine isn't going to turn up much."

"I know. I tried," I groaned. I had looked. Saturday night after the whole mess with George, I'd tried to see what I could find before I'd had the courage to ask Jasper for help. "And I suck at searching. Like, there's 2,000 results, and after five or so, they all start bleeding together in my brain."

Jasper nodded because this was hardly news to him. I'd talked him into doing most of the heavy lifting with group projects in middle school. His mouth pursed as his expression turned more thoughtful.

"How did you cope with papers at college? I heard you got a soccer scholarship somewhere out of state."

"It wasn't easy," I admitted. And with anyone else, I wouldn't share this much, but Jasper already knew me on a deeper level than some of the kids I'd shared a dorm with. "I practically lived at the writing center and still struggled. This one tutor there suggested that maybe I have some sort of learning disability. Like my processor doesn't run at the same speed as others."

"I can see that." Jasper didn't sound at all judgmental as he clicked away on his laptop. "There's help for all sorts of learning differences these days. But you're not at college now?"

"No." I sat back in my chair.

"Oh. Right. Your leg. Was it—"

"Can we talk about the cards now?"

"Got it. No more questions."

Predictably, as soon as his tone went cool, I missed his prying. God, I was a mess. "Sorry. That was rude of me."

"Nah. It's okay. I was being nosy." Jasper shrugged, but only some of his easiness returned. "Anyway, here's what I'm finding. Some partial sets for, like, $5K."

He tapped his screen, which had a bunch of pictures of cards with price tags with way too many zeroes.

"F—"

"Yeah, I know. It's a lot."

"There's no cheaper way to score these cards?" Squinting, I leaned forward, like that might help the screen show something different.

"Like armed robbery?" Jasper laughed, then sobered as he

clicked over to another browser tab. "Occasionally, you'll see one or two offered on a prize wall at a tournament. Like here's one this weekend in Philly. It's a decent competition. I won a bunch of transforming cards there last year."

"Hold up. You're good enough at the game to win prizes?" Turning in my chair, I studied him, almost like I was seeing him for the first time. He'd had a whole *life* in the years since we'd been friends. And he wasn't simply this computer wizard good at searches. He was...competent. Successful. A stranger.

"Why, yes, Milo. I've only been playing since I was sixteen. I'm on a popular vlog about the game. I've played at various regional tournaments. I'm not a pro, but I am good." His expression was closer to the Frog Wizard than the Jasper I knew. This guy was cocky. Radiating confidence.

"Better than George?" I tried like heck not to let on how freaking impressed I was.

"George cheats." Jasper made a pained face. "But yes, assuming he's not loading his deck with bombs, I'm the better player."

"Good on you." A stray thought wandered into my brain and wouldn't let go. "So you could maybe win that card?"

Jasper blinked. "You want me to enter that tournament, go to Philly on Saturday, and fetch you one of the missing cards? Is that all?"

"Well, when you put it like that..."

"It's a ton of work. It's not like some casual games with friends."

"I know." Pinching the bridge of my nose, I inhaled sharply. I should have known better than to share my big brainstorm. It wasn't like I could do it—playing with George had proved to me how very little I knew.

"But…maybe we could make a deal." Jasper voice had an edge to it I couldn't quite place. A slyness almost. Not like George-level sliminess but a little more calculating than I was used to from him.

"What sort of deal?" My head tilted as I considered him.

"You can stop looking like I'm about to ask for…personal favors."

I made an audible gulping noise. My brain hadn't gone there at first, but now he'd said it, vivid images danced in my mind, each more enticing than the last.

"Yeah. I know. The horror." He rolled his eyes as he laughed.

He couldn't be more wrong, but words failed me. And even if I'd managed to speak, volunteering for those kinds of *favors* probably wouldn't go well. He'd assume I was pranking him, and that would be the end of his help.

"Anyway…" He made a dismissive gesture right as the people at the table nearest to us stood. They glanced our way, and God, I hoped they hadn't heard his joke.

"Yeah?" I whispered, hoping he'd take the hint to lower his own voice.

"The hospital is doing a costume ball in a few weeks. I need you to be Neptune for that. And maybe a few other visits too."

"A costume ball? Like a bunch of rich old dudes in wigs and masks?" This wasn't the *worst* thing he could ask for, but it also wasn't the *best*.

"Probably." Jasper didn't sound too put out by the prospect. "And before you say no, I'm sure there will be other people in togas. Gods are always popular costume choices. Also, it would mean a ton to April."

Oh, that was low, making it about the kids. Of course I didn't want to let April or Chase or any of the other kids down.

"And you?" If he was going to go low, I was going to at least make him admit this wasn't only April wanting me to go.

"Fine. I'd like to have Neptune there too. And apparently I want it enough to drive to Philly in my death trap of a car." He finished with a groan.

"We can take mine if it's not snowing." My pulse sped up and sweat trickled down my back, but it was the least I could offer. If he were going to go try to win the card, I could give him a cheering section. Or whatever the heck observers did at these things. Maybe it was like golf clapping, but whatever, I'd figure it out.

"Deal. And if it is, I'll see if I can trade with Katie. She has an SUV now that she's all employed and stuff."

"She graduated?" Jasper's oldest sister had been in college last I'd heard. She'd always been nice. Super smart, like all the Quigley kids.

"Yup. She's a nurse now, over at the regional medical center." Pride laced Jasper's words as he smiled. "Her specialty is outpatient surgery."

"Wow. All I remember about her is her obsession with that one British band." It was hard to imagine that the gangly teen Katie had been was now in charge of people's lives.

"Well, like you said, people grow and change."

"That they do." I gave him a pointed look.

Expression more speculative as he narrowed his eyes, he turned toward me. "Tell me one thing different about you. And not the coffee-drinking thing. Something real."

I knew one thing. One big, giant thing, but no way in hell was I blurting it out right then. *Hi. I'd be down with whatever personal favors you wanted to request. Anything. Surprise.* And yeah, the news flash that he wasn't the only one into dudes wasn't going to go over well. I might not have his genius brain, but I knew that much. So I tried to think of other things.

"Unlike you, the junk food–tarian, I eat vegetables now. And I've got a tattoo..." I could tell by his face that he wasn't impressed by my answers in the slightest. And somehow, I hated disappointing him, wanted to prove something to both us. "Okay. Real talk. I got kicked off the soccer team. That's how I lost my scholarship and ended up back here instead of being able to rehab and stay in school."

I wasn't going to tell him the whole story, not right then, and maybe not ever. But considering that soccer had been the original wedge between us, it felt...significant somehow, sharing my greatest defeat with him.

Jasper whistled low. "Wow."

"You're not going to celebrate that I can't play anymore?"

"No. First of all, you got injured. I'm not going to cheer for anyone getting hurt. Second, I worked damn hard for my scholarships. I know how much losing them would suck. And no matter what you did, I can bet that getting kicked off wasn't your intention. You lived for soccer."

"I did." I had to swallow hard. "And yeah, it sucked. And you're right. It was my fault, but I didn't think... Hell, I didn't think, period."

"That does seem to be a persistent problem with you." Jasper sighed, but his tone wasn't unkind.

"Yeah."

"Hey." Surprising the heck out of me, he patted my upper arm. "For what it's worth, I'm sorry about the team."

"Thanks, man. That means a lot." And it did. Him voluntarily touching me, that meant something, too, made something fluttery break loose in my stomach. "And I do appreciate your help. I know my dumb ass got me into this mess, but I'm grateful you're bailing me out."

"I haven't bailed anything out yet." Jasper's laugh was warm and welcome.

"But you will," I insisted. Our faces were much too close now, but hell if I was going to be the one to move first. "I've got a good feeling about this tournament."

"Does your good feeling extend to the seventy-five-dollar entrance fee?"

"It could." The money wasn't nothing. My wallet felt every penny lately, but it also wasn't five-freaking-K, so I'd happily take it. More peanut butter and soup, maybe, but I'd also get a chance at some cards.

"Okay. We're on, then. You sure you want to spend yet another day slumming with the nerds?"

"Yeah. I am." And I was. Gamers might be an improvement over another weekend of listening to James and Luther bicker. And if there was one particular geek I was really looking forward to spending the day with, well, I wasn't going to tell Jasper that.

CHAPTER NINE
JASPER

"YOU DIDN'T WARN ME THAT gamers get up at the ass-crack of dawn." Milo was waiting where we'd arranged to meet, at the campus parking lot near my dorm. However, instead of me needing to search out his car, here he was standing in the cold on the sidewalk, stamping his feet and looking down at his phone. His knit cap, same one he'd had at the game store, was out of place on his usually stylish head. One of his many aunts undoubtedly knitted it. And maybe it was the cold or the early hour, but I was oddly touched that he'd left the car instead of waiting for me to find him. As a result, I kept my tone light as I followed him across the parking lot.

"Gamers do when they want to win prizes. Or stand in line for new releases. We're killer at standing in line."

"I'll keep that in mind for the next Marvel movie." He came to an abrupt stop between a beat-up Toyota and a classic Mustang.

"You still watch superhero movies?" I reached for the passenger-side door of the Toyota, but to my surprise, he unlocked the Mustang instead.

"You don't?" Smiling like he knew he had me, he gestured at the car. "You getting in?"

"Okay, now *this* is a car." I slid into the passenger seat as he went around to the driver's door, which also had a manual lock. The leather upholstery was butter-soft, and the car was super clean. Even the gear shift was dust-free and shiny. A car guy would probably call it pristine, and it seemed about as unlike the rest of Milo's life as one could get.

"It's all right." Milo shrugged like he didn't have the coolest car in the parking lot. Hell, simply the fact that he could drive a stick was impressive. His easy coordination as he backed out of the space and put it in gear made my body hum with awareness. But I didn't need to be finding anything about Milo sexy, so I tried to keep my attention on the car. I'd learned to drive on a minivan with a wonky starter, but Milo would have had his pick of cool cars.

"Is this the one your dad was always tinkering with?" His dad had been a mechanic at a garage in the next town over and had always had a restoration of some kind going. Growing up, I'd liked going over to Milo's, especially when his dad wasn't home and we could sneak into the garage to check out what he was working on.

"One of them. First one he finished that wasn't a job went to Bruno. Next one we fixed up together all through high school. All my cash went into parts. Got the keys graduation day."

"Wow." That was a lot of time and effort that I hadn't realized Milo had in him. And cash. I wasn't a car guy, at all, but I did know collectible items and this certainly had to qualify as one.

"You know...this car would probably fetch a whole lot of cards. Just saying."

"Nothing doing." Milo's voice hardened. "Dad wouldn't let me or Bruno sell our cars. The whole eighteen months he fought that liver disease, he kept saying they had the bills under control. But they didn't."

I groaned at the all-too-familiar tale. "Oh, how I know that dance. My parents have been there with April's medical bills more than once. Luckily, they've had resources like a fundraiser Dad's work did and the foundation from the hospital to keep from total bankruptcy."

"Yeah, well, not a lot of resources for my folks. Mom couldn't even keep the house. But they both insisted we keep the cars since we built them with him and the titles were in our names. It was like...the only thing he could leave us." Biting his lower lip, Milo didn't glance my direction as he made the turn that would take us to the highway. *Damn.* That was terrible. Simply thinking about one of my folks dying made my stomach twist.

"Bruno kept his car too?" I found myself strangely invested in this tale, wanting Bruno to have kept that last link to his dad, too, wanting him to value it as much as Milo clearly did.

Milo nodded sharply as he merged onto the highway. "Yeah. His is in special storage with a buddy of Dad's who collects classic cars and stores some for people. He almost... Never mind."

"What?" I hated when people did that. They'd get all

pensive and stare off into space and then try to act like they hadn't been on the cusp of some big revelation. Spill already.

"Nothing." Predictably, Milo didn't finish his thought, but his expression stayed distant and sad. "Just that I owe Bruno for a lot. That's all."

"I get it." I stretched to try to stay awake. This was weird, too, being on the road to an *Odyssey* event, especially without any of my usual crew along. The previous summer I'd had a trip cut short by April's illness, and that missed chance made me more determined to get a win here for Milo. Play hero, like I did at the hospital and with my family. "Katie and Brenda have both paid a couple of bills when my folks couldn't. It's what family does."

I probably should have let Milo stew in quiet, but I figured I could give him some conversation since he was the one doing the driving. Might be rude to fall asleep before we were even out of Gracehaven's city limits.

"Yeah. Family's good that way." Milo didn't sound all too upbeat about that. Probably still thinking about Bruno and his dad.

"I'm sorry about your dad. He..." I searched for a compliment that wouldn't sound false. "He was a good guy."

"You don't have to pretend. Everyone knows his liver went because of the drinking. And he yelled at you personally. More than once."

When we'd been kids, his dad had had a weird sleep schedule, especially on weekends. He'd never been violent, but he had been loud a few times. It hadn't taken long for most of our sleepovers to be at my house.

"Yeah. But he wasn't all bad. He'd take us for pizza." Weekdays, especially right after work, he'd been sober and sometimes he'd be the one to pick up Milo. He'd been funny then, joking around, a nice guy in that moment. And Milo had always alternated between being skittish around him and big-time hero worship. "You loved him, and that counts for something. And he built the car with you."

"And he went to a ton of my soccer games." Milo exhaled hard, and I wanted to pat him like I had at the hospital, but that had been a mistake. Touching him felt too good. Too familiar. Couldn't risk it.

"He did." His dad had been a sports nut, particularly for soccer, waking up in the middle of the night to watch the World Cup and cheering for Italian soccer teams with names I couldn't pronounce.

"It's weird. Missing some things but not others. Wanting the family back together, but also knowing it wasn't all that." Outside, there was a rogue flurry or two. I really hoped there wasn't snow while we were in Philly. Milo seemed weirdly antsy about driving despite being, as far as I could tell, really good at it. Like, he used his signals and changed lanes responsibly—that sort of basic stuff—but unlike the other times when I'd ridden with someone who drove a stick, the ride itself was smooth, not all jerky and bumpy, which was even more impressive given whatever was up with his leg.

"I get it. Parents are complicated."

Milo snorted at that. "Says the guy with the perfect sitcom family."

My hands fisted. I resented the hell out of that assumption. Milo didn't know squat.

"April almost died last summer. That…takes a toll. Jeff, he doesn't call home much anymore. Guess that's how he copes. And it's not the same as drinking, but I've found my mom, more than once, scrubbing the kitchen at 2:00 a.m. Dad, he's not perfect either. Works too many hours. Doesn't talk enough."

That toll was a big part of why I tried to help out so much. Seeing my parents so stressed made me feel helpless, and I hated that feeling. Any amount of chores or nice deeds was worth it if it made them smile a little more.

"I'm sorry about Jeff. That sucks." Milo had always gotten along with my older brother, who was in Bruno's year. Now he was out in Seattle working for a tech company, and we mainly had to use social media to keep up with him. "And you're right. I didn't know."

"No, you didn't." My mom's stress-induced cleaning fits and relentless insomnia could be particularly hard to cope with, but I didn't kid myself into thinking that I'd had it worse than Milo. "But it's not the suckitude Olympics either."

"True. I…uh…picked up some doughnuts on my way to you." He jerked his head in the direction of the back of the car, and I found a white bakery box right behind the console. As far as changes of subject went, that wasn't a bad one.

"Lee's?" Plenty of people in the area relied on chain places, but Lee's was a Gracehaven institution, and a love of their doughnuts was one of the few things our dads had in common. When I was a kid, my dad often retrieved a box on Saturday mornings when Milo stayed over, and we'd bickered over our favorite flavors.

"Of course. Picked out a couple. One's that chocolate-chocolate one you used to love."

He'd remembered that little tidbit, too, and I had to bite the inside of my cheek to keep from beaming. It was a doughnut, not an engagement ring, and going out of his way to get them probably only meant he'd been hungry. "Thanks. You didn't have to do that, but I'm not going to turn down chocolate-chocolate."

"Eh. I needed coffee and didn't want to wake Luther by rattling around the kitchen. He worked overnight."

Poof. A lot of my good feelings toward Milo evaporated at the mention of his bully of a friend. Maybe Milo's main sin was not speaking up, but Luther and James had been actively awful to me and my crowd in high school. Teasing. Pranks. Showboating. General assholery. Milo wanted me to believe he'd changed, but I wasn't sure how to trust that when he was still associating with jerks and bullies.

"Luther has gainful employment? And let me guess, James lives there too?"

"Yeah. They both work for a janitorial company. And before you give me a lecture, I didn't have a ton of housing options after my...accident. Their other roommate had recently moved out—"

"Probably wised up," I grumbled. Outside the weather

was equally bleak, with none of the sunny energy of my summer trip, and I again questioned the wisdom of trying to help Milo.

"Not gonna dispute that. They're kind of shit roommates. But it was that or keep hogging my mom's spare room. After Dad died, she found this little garden apartment over by the university. She can walk to work when the weather's nice. It's perfect. But small. She would have let me stay, but…"

"You felt bad. I get that. I'm glad my scholarship covers the dorm. But all my buddies were able to afford apartments for senior year, and I'm stuck in the oldest of the upper-class dorms. Still, though, I'd take my hole-in-the-wall over living with freaking Luther and James."

"Trust me, I would too." He gave me a little smile as we approached the outer limits of Philly. Somehow we'd killed an hour chatting. And that probably hadn't been the smartest because now he was even more of an enigma to me—a grieving son and a nice guy who brought me my favorite doughnuts, but also a pushover still relying on Luther and James way too freaking much. But that smile…that was the biggest problem, the way it made warmth start at my toes and snake its way north. It was going to be a long day, and I needed to focus on winning cards, not earning more smiles from a guy I was supposed to hate.

CHAPTER TEN
MILO

"WHOA." I STOPPED SHORT AS Jasper and I entered the hotel conference-center lobby. I'd been surprised enough when his directions led us downtown instead of to a strip mall in the burbs or something like that. And now we were surrounded by people. A lot of funny, nerdy T-shirts. Tons of deck bags like what Jasper was toting. More gender and age diversity than I'd been expecting—everything from little kids to clumps of teens to older adults. "This is a lot of gamers. I'd expected a game store like in our town."

"Bigger tournaments are usually in conference centers like this. They need more room than a single game store can provide. But the local game stores get billing as sponsors." Jasper joined a huge line waiting to get to the registration table.

"Cool. This is like nerd—"

Holding up a hand, Jasper hardened his tone. "You might want to consider your next words. Poking fun at gamers isn't going to make me want to win your cards back."

"I wasn't going to make fun!" God, was he always going to assume the worst of me?

"Oh?" His skeptical expression said yes. Yes, he was going to make those assumptions.

"I was going to say 'nerd heaven.' And it's a lot of people. That's all." Maybe calling it nerd heaven was bad because Jasper didn't crack a smile. I rambled ahead, trying to figure out how to redeem myself. "I didn't realize gaming was that popular. This is more than the turnout for some of my college's home games. It's impressive."

"It's massively popular all over the world. And this is actually a little smaller than some of the regional tournaments. I've played in bigger." Jasper's shoulders lifted, and his voice lightened the way it always did when he bragged. I wasn't supposed to find that appealing but it did something for me, his confidence infectious.

"Wow. And you have to beat all of them?" Suddenly, our prospects seemed much dimmer.

"No." Finally, I got a laugh out of Jasper. "I have to rack up points, then I get to pick things on the prize wall. I'm not looking to make the finals or even place. I'll let the people trying to qualify for the pro tour worry more about standings at the end of the day."

"There's a pro tour? Like, people making their living playing cards?" I'd never considered this before, and I probably should have. *Stupid.* I was so stupid to think that a couple of lessons from Bruno made me into some badass card-playing genius when there were people out there making real money doing this.

Jasper raised an eyebrow at me. "You name it and people have probably made money doing it. Gaming is huge, man. Vloggers and streamers make good money if they're big enough names. And the game companies pay too. I have a buddy who works for the Odyssey folks and he's in heaven, playing cards all day. But it's work too."

"And is that what you want to do? After graduation?" As far as I knew from the mom gossip network, Jasper was on some sort of math scholarship. I'd always figured he'd get a doctorate, be an important professor, but now I could also see him going the professional gamer route.

"Yeah. I'll probably join Conrad at Odyssey this summer, see what they have for me." Jasper didn't look all that certain as he shrugged, but then his voice brightened. "I've got a ticket to an exclusive launch party next month in New York for their new set. That'll be my chance to chat with the management people, see if they're still interested in me."

The line moved marginally closer to the front. My leg was already tight from driving and the line wasn't helping, but I tried to be subtle as I shifted my weight around. "I'm sure they will be if you're as good as you say you are."

"Oh, I'm good." He gave me a pointed look that made heat pool in my belly and made me forget all about my leg. "I've got other options too. Like, Ned from the hospital foundation has said I could do an internship there this summer, work in finance maybe. But I'll probably go with the game. Leaving Gracehaven's going to be so hard, though. Not sure I'm ready, honestly. But graduation awaits."

"Yeah." Undoubtedly, that was the right option for Jasper. And it wasn't his fault that the thought of him in NYC instead of Gracehaven sucked the energy right out of me. He'd be moving on to bigger and better things. As it should be. And I had no reason to let that make me sad. Pushing those thoughts away, I gestured at the crowd around us. "So how does this work?"

"I get registered and my decks get checked out, then I get a schedule of matches. From that point on, I'm pretty busy." Jasper bounced a little, like this was an excellent development. Him excited was simply too cute and I had to smile at him. "You're free to watch any of the matches, shop the vendors, or get some casual play in. I brought an easier deck like the ones we use with the kids if you want to try some of those games."

"That was nice of you." And it was, made my insides bubble to think about him packing up, thinking about me right as I'd been thinking about him with the doughnuts. Maybe—

"Eh. We can't have you bored." Well, okay then. Not a personal thing at all. I frowned as Jasper continued, "Most likely I'll barely get any breaks. Thank goodness for those doughnuts."

"I'll leave around lunch, get you a sandwich and some soda, and bring it back," I offered. Perhaps he hadn't meant anything by packing the deck for me, but I was still pleased enough to do him a favor. And he was trying to win the card for me after all.

"Thanks. That would be sweet." Not that *I* would be sweet, but the gesture. He undoubtedly didn't mean it as some sort of deep sentiment. However, my face still warmed at the compliment. I liked doing things for him, far more than was probably smart. It seemed to make me happy in a way I hadn't been in quite a while.

He fished a ten out of his pocket. "For my food. You got the doughnuts already. And my registration."

"Least I could do." After the parking fee we'd encountered, I wasn't too proud to take his cash. I pocketed the money as we shuffled forward again.

"Jasper! How the heck are you?" A tall Asian guy around our age who seemed to speak exclusively in exclamation points strode over to us.

"Eugene." Jasper gave him a high five and a big smile. "You playing or watching?"

"Playing! Always! This the new boyfriend? I heard about Rafe, man. Getting dumped sucks!" Even Eugene's style of commiseration was upbeat. And what was this? *Boyfriend?* I didn't have time to be rattled by the wrong assumption because I was too busy realizing yet again that Jasper had had this whole life at college that I knew nothing about. Hobbies. Majors. Future plans. And friends. *Boyfriends.* Undoubtedly, wanting to deck this Rafe on principle was not the right reaction, but I couldn't stop the sudden, swift surge of jealousy.

Next to me, Jasper sputtered. "Uh. No. Not boyfriend. This is Milo. We went to high school together. He's a newbie to the game."

"Hey." It didn't escape my notice that I was Milo-from-high-school and not a friend. Not that I'd expected more, but still. I'd figured after our talk in the car that maybe we were working back toward something again. Clearly, we still had a way to go.

"Newbie, huh?" Eugene sized me up, grin broadening further. "Hit me up in the casual area later! I always try to throw the noobs some tips between real matches. I'll be gentle."

My skin heated at the joke, and Jasper was also turning all sorts of shades of pink. I'd been around locker rooms enough not to be fazed by a mild crack or two, but my brain was still spinning around the whole *boyfriend* concept. My real worry was that Eugene was able to tell the direction of my thoughts, but right then two girls came up and stole Eugene away in a flurry of laughter and perfume. Dude had an entourage. I smiled as they walked away, but Jasper scowled.

"Sorry about that. Eugene's chatty, but he's harmless. Should have warned you that I brought Rafe last year."

Strangely, I wasn't anywhere near as horrified as Jasper apparently thought I was. If anything, I was still struggling with this weird attack of jealousy—mad at Eugene for knowing so much about Jasper's life and angry at this Rafe I'd never met because he'd had Jasper in a way I never would.

"It's okay." I kept my tone even, trying not to let on that my thoughts kept flitting over the fact that this Rafe undoubtedly knew what Jasper tasted like. Sounded like. *Felt* like. I shook my head, trying to get a grip. "You...uh...seeing anyone right now? That Conrad you mentioned? I just realized that I kinda hijacked your weekend."

"You did. I had to trade away shifts at the game store." Jasper's mouth twisted exactly like my gut at the reminder of what an imposition I was being. "But no. Not seeing anyone. Conrad is blissfully happy with another friend."

My surge of relief was almost comical. Yet something about Jasper's tone made me think maybe I wasn't the only one with jealousy issues.

"And that's bad?"

"It's—"

"Next!"

I didn't get a chance to find out Jasper's reply because we'd finally reached the front of the line, and Jasper had to show his ID, get a lanyard with a badge, and move down the line to a security-type woman in an event T-shirt and gloves who inspected Jasper's decks like they might be laced with actual explosives. I received a different-colored badge since I was simply watching. Finally, after all that, we entered the event space, which was full of rows of folding tables and chairs in the center of the big ballroom and a few vendor booths in the adjacent room.

The room buzzed with a flurry of activity and eager gamers ready to beat each other to a metaphorical pulp. Reminded me of game days for soccer tournaments, everyone all ready to get started. There were rows of tables, not playing fields, and way more colorful hair and nerd humor T-shirts, but the competitive spirit was similar. Later, they'd be dragging from a long day, but this early energy was contagious.

Two weeks ago, I would have laughed at the idea of finding card shuffling sexy, but watching Jasper get set for his first match made this weird mix of pride and awareness gather in my insides, mingling with that energy to bounce on my feet the way Jasper was always doing. He was simply so quietly competent at what he did, arranging his space and cards with practiced fingers. As kids, Jasper had always been the messiest kid in his family, far less ordered than I who had enjoyed sorting his Legos into little bins—but as a gamer, Jasper was methodical, everything evenly spaced and squared with the table. His play mat featured the same Frog Wizard he'd cosplayed as.

"It's possible your outfit is fancier than the actual one." I pointed at the picture. "But good job matching the colors and stuff."

"Thanks. I tried. He probably wears it better, but it's fun."

"Nah, you're cuter than his big warty head." The light words escaped before I could call them back. Jasper's eyes went wide and his head tilted. But then his opponent arrived, a younger girl with a serious expression.

Jasper shook his head like he'd misheard me and turned his full attention to the girl and the start of his match. I, however, couldn't move on that fast, couldn't stop from obsessing over my slip. I blamed how rattled I still was over the boyfriend revelation. It was yet more proof that Jasper was miles removed from the kid I'd once known. And worst of all was how desperate I was to get to know that person, to uncover his secrets. That sort of yearning was dangerous.

But I couldn't seem to stop.

CHAPTER ELEVEN
JASPER

"ARE WE SURE THE NEW guy is not your new boo?" Eugene found me in the lobby as I took a little break before my next round.

"Milo?" Mildly horrified, I looked up from my phone. I had it out because I'd been texting with Milo, who had gone to retrieve some food. This was a smaller convention/conference center and the meal options inside the complex were overpriced and limited, so I was especially grateful for Milo's offer to get lunch. But boyfriend? Absolutely not, and that little shiver that raced up my back could go the hell away.

"Yeah!" Eugene laughed, his voice as perpetually upbeat as ever. I liked him and considered him a gaming friend, but he did have an elevated opinion of his own sense of humor. "Tall, dark, and clueless. Just how you usually like them, right?"

"I don't have a type," I lied. If my crushes and sporadic dates had tended toward jocks, well, that was merely coincidence. And probably something I should work on changing. I knew better, even if my body didn't. Not a *type* and absolutely nothing to do with Milo.

"Yeah, you do." Eugene had been around enough not to buy my bluster.

"Well, so do you." I raised my eyebrows because the blond, bubbly friends he'd brought along were both totally his type, to the point that I wasn't entirely sure which was the current girlfriend. Both wasn't outside the realm of possibility either.

"Guilty." Shrugging, Eugene smiled slyly as he leaned against the wall. "And you're changing the subject."

"No, I'm not. And yeah, I'm very sure." Tired of standing, I took a seat on the floor, hoping that Eugene might take a hint and move along or at least drop this topic, but instead he flopped down next to me.

"He's watched all your matches."

No way was I explaining our arrangement, so I merely stretched, rolling my tight back muscles. "He's probably bored."

"Nah. He wants you." Eugene nodded like a guy who knew his way around attraction. Which he did, but he was dead wrong here. "He watches you like you're a slot machine about to come up cherries."

Well, that metaphor actually wasn't inaccurate as Milo was super invested in me paying out. And no way was there anything else in his gaze, his bizarre comment about me being cute notwithstanding. Distracted, I'd almost lost my first match until I'd decided that Milo meant cute in a dismissive way, like I was still a kid or maybe a pet dog, and not *cute*.

"You really need to stop going to Atlantic City." I knew that suggestion wouldn't go over well. In addition to playing *Odyssey* for fun, Eugene was something of a card shark with a poker obsession.

"Spending money. It comes in handy."

"I'm sure." I'd never had money I was willing to risk losing by gambling.

"And here comes your prince now. With food." Eugene gestured toward the front of the lobby where Milo was scanning the crowd.

I waved him over before answering Eugene. "Just because he cosplays as Neptune doesn't make him my prince."

"Wait a sec." Eugene's eyes went wide as his nose wrinkled. He wasn't a cosplay fan. "You're saying you got him to wear a toga and do that whole costume-brigade thing you do? And you don't think he's into you?"

If only. But I didn't get a chance to set him straight before Milo was right next to us with my sandwich and an endearingly eager expression. "It's still cold out so I got you cheese steak. Figured you'd need something warm. It's drafty in here."

Eugene's expression behind Milo's back was all-knowing. He needed to get a grip if he was seeing heart eyes while Milo was simply trying to keep me fed so I'd win his cards for him. And I needed to remember that too. Milo was only here because he needed something, not because he needed *me*. I should tattoo that difference on my arm because it was too easy to forget, especially when he plunked down next to me, our legs brushing as he squeezed in so others could pass.

"Oops. Sorry."

"No worries." I accepted the food from him and unwrapped my sandwich, which smelled as good as it looked.

"Food okay? You can trade with me if you want. I got meatball." Milo held out his own sandwich. Cute. He was cute in all senses of the word, and my stomach wobbled. *Danger. Danger.*

"I'm good."

"So you keep saying," he teased. Our gazes met, and his little grin made me want to pretend just for a second that he was here for me, that he was my guy, and that he actually cared about warming me up. He leaned forward. "Tell me about your morning?"

"Not bad. My transforming deck is getting a workout." I had a couple of competitive decks, but the transforming deck was my standby, and its tricky mechanic was working well against some pricier decks.

"Yeah, it is. You sure that you're not going for a top-eight finish?" Eugene asked right as his friends arrived with food of their own. He ended up with a girl on either side of him and some sort of fancy salad to eat.

"Nah. I mean, it would be nice, but I'm not all that."

"You're too humble," Milo insisted, bumping shoulders with me. "I saw you win a number of rounds. Lots of points?"

Points. Yeah. His cards. Why we were there. Sigh. "Some."

Truth was that I was a bit behind where I wanted to be, and I needed to rack up some more wins before someone else claimed the cards from the prize wall.

"You can do it." Milo's faith in me was both humbling and irritating because I wasn't sure what would happen if I failed. Would he want out of the bargain? Would I even see him again? I hated the uncertainty but hated myself more for caring so much.

We passed the rest of the meal break with more small talk with Eugene, who had all the latest gossip on our other gamer friends. Milo mainly let the conversation swirl around him, but he wasn't sullen about it. More like he was content to listen, and I liked his quiet presence far more than I should. If I could get past the whole jerk-from-high-school thing, I had to admit he'd probably make someone a good boyfriend. Not me, obviously. But someone.

"Hey. What about you? You have someone?" I asked as Milo walked me back into the main gaming space.

"Someone what?" Milo scrunched up his face, thinking far too hard for a guy who probably had a flock of girls following him, same as Eugene.

"You asked earlier if I had a boyfriend. And I realized that I'm not the only one giving up my weekend. You have a girlfriend who's going to care about your new toga-wearing hobby?"

"No." The tips of Milo's ears went pink. "No girlfriend."

"Back at college?" I pressed, way too interested in finding out who Milo had been the last few years.

Shrugging, he pursed his mouth. "Not really. I had friends, but nothing like that."

I read between the lines to see a string of hookups. "Ah. A player. Should have guessed."

"I wouldn't say that—"

"Jasper! I get to play you again." Naomi, a fellow

cosplayer who loved dressing as a reaper bride, greeted me. Her stuff was already set up, and I had to scramble to get my mat and cards out. No time to dwell on Milo's denial. And it wasn't my business what he had or had not been doing at college.

What mattered now was winning him the cards he needed. Not for the first time that day I wished I'd been able to finish that road trip last summer and play in the big national tournament. That would have honed my skills more for regional competitions like these. As it was, Naomi was a skilled player, one who had beaten me in both casual and competitive play before, and she demanded my full attention. Still, though, I was all too aware of Milo hovering nearby. At one point in the game I glanced over, and he gave me this encouraging smile that made my heart do a most unwelcome flip.

I messed up an attack step, and Naomi went in for the kill. I narrowly managed to block the lethal blow. I couldn't afford another loss. By my calculations, I needed this match and one more. No more looking in Milo's direction. Head in the game in more than one way. I had a mission and I couldn't afford any more mistakes.

CHAPTER TWELVE
MILO

I WANTED JASPER TO WIN, but not only for the reasons he thought. Rather, I wanted him to win because I liked the way he smiled when he won, liked the looseness in his step, liked the way he'd joke with me in between matches. Every win made me buoyant, riding high on his good mood. I hadn't forgotten about him needing points for the prize card, but I was having fun simply hanging out at the tournament, meeting his friends, watching him play. I liked seeing the hustle and bustle of the tournament, but also liked the way Jasper reigned over it, gamer royalty almost.

Everyone seemed to know him either from the vlog he was on or past tournaments and events. And they all liked him. He was... popular. Which shouldn't have been that surprising—he'd always been an easy-to-like guy, but high school was not kind to nice guys like Jasper. Yet he'd survived, no thanks to me. And now here he was, thriving. He'd found where he belonged, and I couldn't stop the ache in my chest as I wished I could say the same for me.

"Move to attack." Jasper narrowed his eyes. I'd watched and played enough *Odyssey* to know this was likely his Hail Mary move, a last-ditch effort to stay alive before Naomi did him in. And her smug smile said she knew it as she moved her cards into position to block.

"Any responses?" She sounded bored, probably already looking ahead to her next match.

"Yup." One by one, Jasper flipped his cards over, playing the scrolls to transform them into bigger attackers. Freaking brilliant. I'd seen him pull similar moves all morning, and I was still impressed. It was like watching a soccer star zip down the field, avoiding the defense and scoring the winning goal against all odds.

"Oh, f—flying monkey butts. Really?" Naomi thumped her own head. "How did I not see that coming?"

"Because I'm good." Jasper smiled, energy infectious, making Naomi smile back even as she groaned.

"Yeah, you are." After considering the board for a long minute, she stuck out her hand. "Good game."

I managed to wait until Jasper was packing up to hurry over. I smacked him on the shoulder. "You did it!"

"Yeah, I did. Ow." Jasper rubbed his shoulder.

"Oops. Too much?" Sometimes I didn't know my own strength. Or maybe he didn't want me touching him. "Sorry."

"It's okay. Your enthusiasm is appreciated even if your hands might need a warning label."

"Sorry." Feeling bad, I reached out and massaged his lean shoulder. And damn. I was woefully unprepared for how good touching him deliberately like this felt, heat rushing through me. He tensed before groaning and going more pliant. For a second that stretched into an eternity, the rest of the crowded ballroom fell away, and it was only us, him melting under my touch and me catching fire.

Then someone coughed and I remembered where the heck we were. My hand fell away right as someone jostled me from behind. "Pardon me."

"No problem." Heart still hammering, I moved out the way so a guy with a red deck bag could pass.

"Sorry," I said again to Jasper after the dude was gone.

"No problem. But you might want to warn a guy before you go handing out massages like that." Jasper's voice was light, but not particularly flirty. Still, though, something about his tone made my skin all toasty as I followed him to his next match.

"I…uh…might wander the vendor booths while you do this round."

"Sure." Jasper sounded distracted, but that probably had more to do with his next opponent, a middle-aged guy, than me. The weird energy thrumming between us was undoubtedly my own hallucination, and I tried to push it from my head as I made my way through the various stalls.

They featured cards galore and accessories like dice, but also T-shirts and things like magnets and buttons. I'd had no idea the level of merch gamers could collect. It reminded me of those dudes back at college who did their whole room as an ode to their favorite sports team. And posters. One booth had a long line of people waiting to buy art, and a woman with long, gray hair was signing each poster or small print.

"You in the market for a McMurtle?" Eugene appeared out of nowhere, entourage in tow.

"A McWhat?" My response got a big laugh from Eugene and his friends.

"She's Sylvia McMurtle. Famous *Odyssey* artist. Does a lot of the art for cards and other merch. Lives near here so she comes to the local events sometimes."

"And people pay for her signature?" I got that the cards could be super pretty, but it still made my head buzz that someone could get that popular simply from some drawings.

"And how." Eugene quoted a price for a print that made my jaw fall open.

"Wow."

"Yup. How's your boy doing? I think I've locked up a spot in the quarterfinals, but we'll see." Eugene all but blew on his knuckles as he humble-bragged.

"Jasper's kicking butt. He's probably one of the best players here." Aside from wanting to talk up Jasper out of loyalty, I wasn't kidding. I'd far rather watch Jasper than any other player, so that had to count for something.

"He's all right. Bet he at least adds to his transforming card collection with his points."

"Yeah," I said weakly. *Crap.* If all went well, Jasper wouldn't be adding to his own collection, and for the first time all day, my stomach rebelled. Funny how hanging out with Jasper calmed me down on more than one level. But now bitterness sloshed around in my gut and made my throat tighten. I didn't like keeping Jasper from getting something for himself.

Maybe there was something I could do. Something more than simply playing Neptune, which was more about his group. Something for *him*. It was strange the way he made me want to take care of him. But it wasn't really a nurturing sort of feeling. Like, I wasn't turning into my mom. More like I wanted him to ask—to *demand* something from me, something that only I could give him. Not for the first time, an erotic parade of images danced through my brain. There wasn't much I didn't want to give him. He wouldn't ever ask, of course, but that didn't stop me from wanting.

"There you are!" Almost like my fevered thoughts had conjured him, Jasper came striding toward us.

"That was fast." Heck. No way had he pulled out a win that quickly, but I didn't want to let my disappointment show.

"Yup." Then Jasper grinned, and I drank in his smile like I was chugging down electrolytes after a two-hour match. I might never get enough of seeing him beam.

"You won?"

"You doubted?"

"Nah." I went to clap him on the shoulder, but both the memory of earlier and Eugene's speculative look had me pulling back before I could touch him.

"Liar. And I missed a top-eight finish by five points!" Jasper bounced on his feet, all but dancing. He was so damn excited. And it was for *me*. It was humbling. I'd spent so much of my life being a selfish ass, while Jasper was the opposite. He did so much for others, and it seemed to genuinely make him happy. But unlike his sister and the kids at the hospital, I wasn't so sure I was worthy of that much goodness.

"Wow." I wanted to tell him thank you, but not with an audience. And even those words wouldn't be enough to describe everything happening in my brain.

"Come on. Let's go check out the prize wall." Jasper tugged on my arm before he seemed to realize that we were all but holding hands right there. He dropped his hand, but I didn't need any enticement to follow him anyway.

"Pick out something pretty." Eugene laughed as he waved us away.

I followed Jasper, but my head was still a churning cement mixer of weighty feels. I wanted to be bouncy like Jasper, but the not-worthy feeling kept rising to the top of the mix.

"Maybe you should..." I finally mumbled.

"Should what?" Slowing down, Jasper turned toward me.

"Should pick out something for yourself." Unable to meet his gaze, I studied the carpet, tried to catalog all the various shades of brown.

"Hey, a deal's a deal. What's with the sudden attack of guilt?" As always, Jasper wasn't afraid to call me on my bullshit. And yeah, that's what it was. Guilt. Obviously, I wanted the cards, but I also didn't want to keep being a crap human.

"I don't want to use you," I mumbled. "I mean, clearly I need your help. But..."

"But?" Jasper stepped closer, almost as if he were about to touch me.

With want gathering low in my belly, my hands clenched and unclenched. "You worked super hard today. Thank you."

Jasper exhaled hard, like I'd whacked him again. Emotions skittered across his face, but none I could label. Then, almost like he'd come to some unspoken conclusion, he nodded. "Well, I had appropriate motivation. And thank you."

"I mean it. I appreciate this."

"Good." Jasper resumed his journey to the big booth at the back of the room. "Remember that come the costume ball."

"I will." I wasn't supposed to look forward to wearing the costume with a room full of bigwigs, but the ball no longer seemed like such a punishment.

"Oh, heck." Jasper's face fell before I could finish sorting myself out. He pointed at the glass case at the front of the booth. "Only one of the two cards they advertised is left."

Crap. To have had him play so hard and come up short sucked. I gave him an awkward pat on the arm. "It's okay. One is better than none."

"Yeah. Here's what I'm going to do." Jasper rubbed his hands together. He was so damn good at not getting knocked down long. "I'll get the one Frog Court card, then I'll use the remaining points on another premium rare. We can hope to maybe turn it into another card for you via a swap or something down the road."

"We? You're going to keep helping me?" I'd been worried all day that this was as far as his assistance went. I couldn't ask him to keep giving up time to help me with my quest. But if he was offering...

"Guess this quest is growing on me." Jasper's crooked smile took all my anxiety and made it into something far warmer.

"Good." I couldn't help but hope that I was growing on him too, softening his dislike, redeeming myself in some way.

Jasper exchanged his points for the cards, but it wasn't until we were back in the car that he took the Frog Court card back out, holding the plexiglass case up to the light. It was a lot of case for a single card, but maybe if Bruno had displayed his cards like this, I would have better understood their rarity.

"Wow, it's so pretty." Jasper's awestruck expression was even more intoxicating than his usual smile. Something about his tone and the light in his eyes made my mind flit back to my earlier thoughts. He could have asked me for anything right then. *Anything.*

"Yeah, it is." My voice came out too husky, and I wasn't looking at the card. "Thank you."

"Didn't think I'd say this, but it was my pleasure." He turned toward me, and maybe he hadn't been expecting how tight the quarters in the Mustang were. Maybe I'd been leaning too close. Maybe our bodies knew more than we did. Regardless of the reason, our faces were suddenly centimeters apart. I could feel his breath, warm in the chilly air.

I inhaled sharply, but I didn't move away. Neither of us did. He opened his mouth slightly, pink tongue darting out to lick at his full lower lip. And all the want that had been simmering inside me all day finally bubbled over. I might die if I didn't get to know what he tasted like. I might die if I *did*, but it was a chance I had to take. Closing the distance between us in a graceful move despite my frantically beating heart, I brushed my lips across his. And waited.

CHAPTER THIRTEEN
JASPER

ONE MOMENT I WAS COLD and excited and ogling a rare *Odyssey* card, and the next I was kissing Milo. And still excited and not cold at all, and hell, was that a priceless card I was holding? Thank God for decorative display cases because I would have crushed unsleeved cardboard.

Because.

Kissing.

Milo.

Right that second, his lips glancing across mine in a sweet, almost hesitant kiss. Anyone less strung out on adrenaline would have had the good sense to pull away. But all I seemed capable of doing was sighing and leaning in closer, all that delicious energy from winning surging inside me. My little noise must have seemed like encouragement to Milo because he repeated the gesture, lips lingering, less sweetness and more hunger.

That hunger blocked all my usual bad-idea sensors and replaced my inner warning system with an elevated awareness of Milo's every atom. The softness of his lips. The faint brush of his stubble. His rapid breathing. His big hand connecting with my shoulder. But not to push me away. No, he hauled me even closer, my thigh getting up close and personal with the console. And not even the possibility of bruising was enough to slow me down.

I. Was. Kissing. Milo.

At fourteen, I'd dreamed of this nightly, a tightly held secret yearning, never uttered aloud to a single soul. And I'd had a million daring ideas for how to plant one on him, all of which faded come morning, stark reality keeping me quiet. He'd been my best friend, and that had been enough right up until he wasn't. Never once had I considered that *he* might kiss *me*.

Further, he wasn't anything like Dream Milo. Dream Milo was smooth. Practiced. In charge. Effortlessly talented at kissing. This Milo was...tentative. A little awkward, which was usually my forte. However, I'd kissed enough actual people since those dreams of Milo to know where noses went and how to manage the art of both kissing and breathing at the same time.

Mixing light, fluttery kisses with harder presses, Milo seemed to be still figuring out everything from the right amount of pressure to the position of his face. And his fumbling should have been a turnoff, should have made me laugh at the least. Because Milo Lionetti being bad at kissing? No one would believe me.

And yet there I was, still kissing him back, actively enjoying the process of stumbling our way from eager-but-bad to better to starving-for-more to brilliant bursts of pleasure radiating with each pass of our lips. And somewhere in the middle of my neurons having a fireworks show, Milo gasped again. Him forgetting to breathe was one the sexiest things I'd ever seen, and I couldn't resist taking advantage of his parted lips to deepen the kiss. Our tongues met, making a fresh round of sparks explode behind my eyes, and—

Honk. Somewhere deeper in the parking garage a car honked and we flew apart. I looked around, but our windows were all foggy and I couldn't see anything.

"What the heck?" Milo looked like a beautiful wreck, bright-eyed, lips swollen, cheeks flushed. But his hotness transformed into horror, pink cheeks going pale and tone shifting from husky to indignant.

"You. Kissed. Me." No way was I letting him pin this on me. Sure, I'd kissed back, rather enthusiastically, but he'd made that first move.

"I know. I shouldn't have done that." Groaning, Milo rested his head on the steering wheel. "God. We have to get out of here."

I could already tell it was going to be a long, cold drive back home. "You can't leave me on the side of the road."

"What?" Milo blinked at me as he started up the car. "Why would I do that?"

"Uh, maybe because you're freaking out?"

"Well, yeah. Obviously." His gaze kept shifting around, like he was afraid to look directly at me for more than a second.

"*Obviously*. Look, I'm sorry if your little experiment didn't go like you planned, but you don't get to blame me."

"It wasn't an experiment." Making a face, Milo gestured at the still foggy windshield. "Come. On. Stupid heater. The one thing that I don't like about this car."

"The hell it wasn't an experiment." Now I was mad. And I didn't get mad very often, but I'd had about an eight-year running start on this head of steam. "Look at you right now, desperate to get away from the fact that you kissed me. And I could tell it wasn't something you do on the regular. You haven't kissed a guy before, have you?"

"You could tell?" Milo made a horrified noise that would have been adorable under other circumstances. "It was bad?"

No, actually it was stupendous, gloriously *good*. But I wasn't admitting that. "The fact that you don't know whether it was good or bad is more proof that this was some sort of walk on the wild side—"

"Stop saying that." Milo punctuated his demand by finally putting the car in gear and heading to the exit.

"Oh. I'm sorry. You just happened to collide mouths with the guy you couldn't stand until a few days ago. Yep. Totally normal everyday occurrence. Dude bros do that all the time, right?"

"Would you *stop*?" Milo braked harder than necessary at the bottom of the parking-garage ramp.

"Watch it." I almost lost my grip on the card display case. Turning, I gently transferred it to the back before something could happen to it—like me losing all patience and launching it at Milo's head. Which would be ill-advised and totally unlike me, but I wasn't exactly feeling the most composed right then. Better not risk it.

Milo glared at me as soon as I settled back into my seat. "I never said I couldn't stand you. You're the one who hates me—with good reason."

"Oh? You did a really good impression of it for years." I still wasn't over high school. Earlier in the day, I'd thought some of my hurt was mellowing, but now the kiss had brought everything I'd tried to ignore right back to the surface.

"I *know*. I fucked up. Both back then and again right now. I gave you a bad kiss you didn't want in the middle of a parking garage where anyone could have seen us." Milo made the turn out of the parking garage to head for the interstate. His tone was as mournful as his eyes. "I get why you're so angry at me. I do. But you've also got it all wrong."

I was willing to admit that I was being a little bit of a jerk, jumping to conclusions based on a mutual past I'd rather forget. And almost all of my jerky behavior had to do with how damn good that kiss had actually been and how quick Milo had been to regret it. "Educate me."

"I probably deserve the dude-bro crack, but I'm not...experimenting. Or straight." Milo's voice was far softer now. "Trust me. I've spent years wishing..."

"Oh?" Planets shifted, realigned, fundamental truths of my universe rearranging themselves within that one syllable.

"I'm not brave like you, okay? I mean, that was probably clear in the whole terrible-at-kissing thing. But that doesn't mean I'm confused."

"It wasn't *that* terrible of a kiss," I allowed, some of my anger giving way to massive befuddlement. Hurt was there, too, but I was trying to ignore that ache behind my sternum for the moment. "But seriously? You've never kissed...anyone?"

"A couple of pecks with dates I got talked into. I have... something of a rep." Milo quirked his lips as we hit another red light, his braking more controlled now. "Like as the nicest guy among my friend group—"

"Not a high bar," I grumbled.

"Granted. But I ended up hanging out with several girls who didn't want to go there for a variety of reasons. And then I got the rep for being a great just-friends date for formals and stuff. My buddies would tease me about spending life in the friend zone with these unattainable crushes. But that was easier than admitting the truth."

"Which is?" I wasn't trying to be mean and make him say the words. I was genuinely curious as to how he might put it.

"I...like...guys." Each word seemed pried loose from Milo's soul. I had a strong feeling he hadn't said this aloud before. But he could have. He could have told me.

And that hurt I was trying not to feel bloomed fresh and raw in my chest, tinging my voice. "But...you knew about me. You were one of the first people I came out to. Did you know back then?"

"Sort of. I wasn't, like, positive." Milo was clearly hedging, and his gaze was firmly fixed on the on-ramp to the highway. "Everyone kept saying how some guys were late bloomers, and I kept thinking my attraction to girls simply hadn't arrived yet."

"Sexuality isn't something you order up on demand like the latest movie."

"I get that. Thanks." Milo accelerated and completed merging before he continued, voice somewhere between exasperated and apologetic. "Not all of us have it together as much as you did back then. Or even now. And anyway, yeah. I kinda knew...something."

"You could have told me! We could have gone to the school club together." A vision of an alternate past danced in my brain, one where I could have kept my best friend, had him right there with me.

"No, we couldn't have."

Poof. My daydream evaporated under the weight of what had actually happened, who Milo really was.

"Of course not. You had the soccer team and—"

"The team being all over anyone who was...different was part of it. Not gonna lie. I was scared shitless simply from their teasing about you, and most of that had to do with how smart you were. I couldn't stand the idea of them rejecting me next."

"So, your fear of being bullied turned you into a bully?"

"I didn't say I was proud of it, okay?" Milo's voice was strained, and his skin was mottled, a weird mix of too pale and flushed. If we were ten again, I'd swear he was on the verge of tears. "But it wasn't only the team and fear of being teased."

"Oh?"

"It was my dad. All right?" Milo's tone was defensive, but his words poked me like a spear nonetheless.

"I should have known." And maybe I had, the way he'd always been so nervous around his dad and the way he'd been so crushed that his parents had heard I was gay.

"That night...after you and I argued, and I was a dumbass and let you walk away, I kind of mentioned at dinner that we'd fought. Not about what. But that we weren't friends anymore. And Dad... He got this hard look. Like mean. And he said, 'Good.' And I knew right then that I couldn't be gay."

"But you were."

"Yeah. And you were my best friend. But he was my *dad*."

"I get it. I mean, you could have told me. But I see why you thought you couldn't." I didn't like it, but I did see how messed-up fourteen-year-old Milo could make that calculation. After all, we were riding in a monument to Milo's complicated relationship with his dad. He'd loved Milo. And he'd also been toxic as hell. Both things could be true, but I wasn't sure whether Milo had fully arrived at that conclusion yet. "And you never told? Anyone?"

"Not really. Kissing newbie, remember?"

I wasn't likely to ever forget being Milo Lionetti's first real kiss, but I nodded. "I'm not an expert, but I hear plenty of closeted guys get it on, especially with each other. But I'm guessing you don't make a habit of hookups."

"I don't. I mean...I guess I could have. There have been moments...chances here and there. But...it never felt right. Felt wrong."

"Because it's a sin in your mind?" I was so not up for a morality debate.

"No. Like, maybe at one time, but not now. But it's more because of what you said. I was a bully to avoid getting bullied myself. I never joined in with the cracks in the locker room, but silence is no excuse. I knew what I was doing, staying with that crowd, watching them hassle the honor-roll crowd. I was a coward, and I'd chosen what felt like the easiest path. Figured my dad was less likely to find out if I stuck to the jock crowd, but it seemed like I'd be the worst kind of hypocrite to be messing around on the down low."

Milo having a weird sort of conscience was somehow fitting. I still didn't like what he'd done, but knowing he'd been so hard on himself did somewhat soften my tone. "That doesn't stop a lot of people."

"Maybe not. But I was already a shitty enough human, you know?"

"Maybe you had reason to be shitty," I allowed. "I mean, sure, you didn't have to let your friends be assholes, but I kind of see why you couldn't come out. You couldn't risk being thrown out of the house. I'm not going to pretend that I know what I would have done in your shoes. I had it easy."

Unlike Milo, there really hadn't been any drama. Long before I got up the courage to tell Milo freshman year and to go to the high school club, my mom had guessed. My parents had a huge social circle and extended family. I'd known several same-sex couples growing up, and telling her the truth had been ridiculously easy compared to what some kids faced.

"Thanks." Milo nodded sharply. "And I wouldn't say you had it easy. You were so brave. You had all that teasing in school for being a nerd, and the people who could have stood up for you didn't."

"I had friends." Not him, but I'd had plenty of others, both in high school and college. I'd never been truly alone, and it was starting to feel like maybe despite having the crowd of Neanderthals, Milo had been more alone than me.

"I'm glad." Milo's tone was pained, and I wasn't sure whether it was from the conversation or the snow flurries hitting the highway with more regularity now. *Crap.* We were supposed to be on the cusp of spring, but Mother Nature hadn't received the message yet. "I'm not trying to excuse what I did. And I'm still here, taking the least complicated path. Still with the shitty friend choices."

"I can't argue with that. You could always try something radical. Get new friends."

"Working on it." The look he shot me was so vulnerable that a tremble raced through me that had nothing to do with the weather outside and everything to do with Milo and the way he was steadily working his way past my mountain of grievances against him.

"You know, Kellan and the rest of our group didn't hate your presence at our gig." I wasn't quite ready to offer up myself as a friend, but maybe if he saw that he had some options, he might further distance himself from his old crowd. "Just saying that you might not have to look far."

"Playing Neptune isn't the same as a cheap place to crash, but I get what you're saying. Thanks."

"And now your dad is gone." I didn't like pointing out the obvious, but it needed saying.

"Yeah, he is. And that's part of what I get all...tangled up in. Like, I didn't *want* him to die. At all. But...yeah. Anyway. He's gone, and I'm pretty sure Mom knows."

I made a startled noise. That, I hadn't been expecting. Milo's mom was a meek but nice woman who probably should have left his dad decades ago. My mom had said she seemed to be thriving now, on her own with a recent promotion at the college in the registrar's office. Still, though, I had no clue how she'd take this news from Milo. "She knows?"

"Uh... I had to stay with her after my accident. And remember how I'm bad at search engines—"

"*Wow.*" I choked on some spit. "Your mom found your porn browser history? *Rough.*"

"Pretty much. I thought I'd cleared it, but then one day there was a sticky note from her on the monitor with instructions on how to actually erase the history. And she added a little line about loving me no matter what and being there if I need to talk."

"That's cool. But you haven't taken her up on that?"

"I'm...not good at hard talk."

"No kidding." My own mom would have hounded me until I gave in and talked. But Milo's family had never been as big on conversations, particularly embarrassing ones. Outside, the flurries were picking up, creating a fine white powder—still not sticking, but worrisome.

"I'm working up to talking. It's not her I'm worried about as much as Bruno."

"Ah. You think he might react worse to that news than the fact that you lost his ultra-rare cards?"

"Maybe. He could be like Mom and surprise me. Or he could be another Dad. And, dude...I can't even tell you how much he's done for me. I fucked up. Big time. And he was there for me."

Milo could have maybe thought that through before he gambled Bruno's cards, but I also didn't want to kick him while he was already so down on himself.

"I get it. You're nervous. Coming out is a big deal no matter how old you are. And it's hard enough even when you have a good support system." The words tasted bland, like I was a one-person welcoming committee for our campus LGBTQ+ organization and reading off a pamphlet. But maybe it worked on Milo because he exhaled hard.

"You're right. And yours should have been better. Should have included your best friend. I'm sorry."

As far as apologies went, this was far better than the weak-ass one he'd tried to hand me via text. "I'm not going to say I forgive you because...it's still a lot. But I understand better now. Thanks for that."

"I don't expect you to forgive me. Which is why I shouldn't have kissed you. That was why I freaked. Mainly."

"So...to recap, you freaked because you thought I didn't want it?" I replayed his reaction again in my head, seeing it in a far better light now.

"You're the one who said it was bad!"

"I already said it wasn't terrible. It was...good." I tried to balance how much praise the guy needed to hear against my own losing efforts to protect my emotions.

"It was? Maybe—*whoa*." Milo sounded hopeful right up until the car wobbled. Not a full-out skid, but suddenly getting home in one piece needed to take priority over wondering whether Milo had been about to ask for a repeat. And if he had asked, what would I have said? Monitoring the road conditions seemed like a far better use of my time than trying to sort out the avalanche Milo's revelations had caused in my brain.

CHAPTER FOURTEEN
MILO

SO. I KISSED JASPER. THAT was a thing that happened. And then I told him...well, not *everything* but close enough. Close enough that when we almost skidded off the highway, that wasn't even the third most nerve-racking moment in the last hour or so. Traffic slowed down to deal with the increasingly dicey road conditions, and my grip on the steering wheel tightened. My leg ached from doing the clutch. I needed to deliver Jasper back to his dorm in one piece. That was all that mattered.

"Think we should take the next exit? Try to wait this out?" Jasper wrinkled his forehead, his expression, as always, a window into his emotions. I liked how he was so easy to read. There was no guessing with him. When he was happy, the whole world knew it. And right then, he was worried, same as me.

"It's probably only going to get worse. And we're close enough to home." I hoped that was true. I hated driving in weather, and I didn't want Jasper catching on to exactly how freaked out I was. But maybe there was a way out of the pounding in my head. "Unless... You drive in the snow a lot? I'd be willing to swap drivers."

"Ha. Much as I'd like the chance to drive a classic beauty like this, I can't drive a stick." Jasper laughed, which was good as it probably meant my efforts to hold it together were working, but it also meant I had no choice but to push forward.

Trying to keep my mind off all the possible doomsday scenarios, I made my voice light. "That's okay. I'll teach you sometime."

"I...uh...might take you up on that. You sure?" Jasper shifted in his seat. Maybe he was cold. Wishing I had a more fun way to warm him up, I adjusted the heater again.

"It's the least I can do. You're saving my bacon. One card down. Three to go." Optimism wasn't my strong suit, but I tried to channel my inner Jasper.

"Hmm. We'll see." Jasper sounded more like me for a change, pragmatic and guarded. "After this cold snap clears, maybe. I'd hate to ruin your clutch though."

"Let me worry about that." I wanted him excited about this prospect. And if it meant more time together, well, there wasn't really a downside I could see. It would be worth a repair if it meant doing something for him after all he'd done for me.

"Okay. Deal." Jasper nodded then stretched his neck. A rogue thought about what I'd like to do to that neck danced through my brain, but I forced my eyes back on the road. A couple of miles passed in silence before Jasper said, "Milo?"

"Yeah?"

"I'm sorry you had it so crappy. I wish I'd known." His voice was soft and a little uncertain and warmed me more than the unreliable heater.

"Thanks." Keeping my eyes on the road, I had to swallow before continuing. "I wish...lots of things."

"Yeah." Jasper's sigh held an entire library's worth of meaning. We drifted into another silence, this one less tense but still potent. Our conversation had left us in a strange place. He now knew more about me than almost anyone else, but I still had no idea if we were friends again, or if such a thing were even possible. And I'd lived with regret so long that my hope muscles were all atrophied to the point that I didn't know what exactly I wanted here. Learning to hope again only to fall flat on my face would suck.

And yet, as we neared Gracehaven, something kept fluttering inside me. Not hope maybe, but its restless, more anxious cousin. I wanted...*something*.

"Is your group doing the cosplay thing again this Wednesday?" I kept my voice casual, distant even.

"We are. It's not always all of us every week, but those of us who can, try to go at least weekly."

"Cool. I... Cool." I wasn't quite sure how to move the conversation to where I wanted to nudge it without seeming overeager.

"Are you asking because you want to join us?" Direct. And this time I appreciated that quality in him that much more because it saved me a lot of waffling.

"'Want' is a strong word." I tried to keep my eyes on the increasingly slushy road even as my brain felt equally difficult to navigate. "But we've got more cards to track down. And the weather's supposed to be bad most of next week, so teaching you to drive a stick might have to wait. If showing up as the toga guy gets me more of your Google-wizard searching skills, then I'll be there."

"Sure." Jasper sounded as carefully indifferent as me. "Prince Neptune is always popular with the kids. I was planning on only making you do the command appearance thing for the costume ball, but sure, you should come Wednesday. If the weather's bad, I'll drive you home so you don't freeze at the bus stop."

"Sounds good." Actually, it sounded terrifying, but I now had a guaranteed time this week to see Jasper, so win. Also, we finally reached the Gracehaven exit, which I took slowly. "No sudden moves" seemed like a good motto right then. The campus was relatively dead for a Saturday night, everyone probably huddling indoors, but the lights of the library and the dorms added a certain warmth to the winter scene.

"It's neat that you get to go here. I know how much you wanted it as a kid." Most of the students at the near-Ivy college were from out of state. Townies like Jasper getting big scholarships were relatively uncommon.

"Yeah. I got lucky. If I hadn't won the scholarship, I still would have stayed local. I couldn't see going too far from my family."

"You're a good guy," I said as I pulled even with the sidewalk near Jasper's dorm. The parking lot was deserted, most cars covered with a thin blanket of snow like they'd been there all day. "And you're the opposite of me. I couldn't wait to get out of this place. Thought college would be a fresh start."

"What happened?"

Part of me wanted to spill the entire tale right then, but the other part of me was still recovering from having my emotions scraped raw earlier. I already felt too exposed. No way could I air all my dirty laundry at once.

"Guess I couldn't outrun my issues." I shrugged. "Team wasn't that different from high school. A top-rated Division I program like that...it comes with certain expectations. Don't know why I was expecting anything different."

"It's okay to want to be someone different, Milo." Jasper's face was unusually tender, and I had to look away quickly.

"Yeah."

"Guess I better go." He shifted in the seat, gathering his stuff. "Don't forget about the card in the back."

"Like I could. Thanks again." I wasn't ready to say goodbye, wasn't ready to head back to Luther and James and that chilly apartment, but I wasn't sure how to make Jasper linger without looking desperate. Or like I was angling for another kiss. Which I wasn't. Okay, maybe I *wanted* that, but I also wasn't going to ask.

"Hey, what's this?" Jasper reached down to his feet and came up with one of my sketchbooks. "This must have come loose from under the seat when we stopped so fast."

"Sorry." I reached for the book.

"Don't be." Jasper didn't seem to be in any hurry to hand it back. "What is this anyway? Drawings?"

"Kind of," I admitted, but kept my hand out. "Give it here."

"You still draw? You always were the best at detailed

Lego plans. And I remember the teachers all loving your art projects in elementary." Jasper moved like he was going to open the book, and I plucked it from him.

"Yeah. Art time was cool and all, but you don't need to see my scribbles."

"You're twenty-two now. I doubt they're *scribbles*." Laughing, Jasper shook his head, then brightened. "Wait. Are they like naughty drawings? Nudes? Because now that you told me that you're—"

"Good night, Jasper." Forget lingering. I'd forgo my chance at another kiss if it meant avoiding this conversation topic.

"Okay, okay. I get it. You don't want to share. But I'm just saying that if you've got that whole Tom of Finland erotic art vibe going, I'd be interested in taking a peek."

"Great. Now I'm going to have to google who that is."

"I think search engines have gotten you in enough trouble. I'll send you some links as inspiration. For your scribbles."

"Thanks." My teeth dug into my lower lip because Jasper was being nice and cool, and I was back to being a dick all because I didn't want to show off my drawings. "Maybe sometime I can show you one of my better doodles."

Jasper's slow smile was worth the way that offer made my stomach revolt. "I'd like that. Night."

He opened the car door, letting in a gust of cold air. No kiss good night, and I couldn't help but wonder if letting him see my sketches would have made a difference there. We seemed to be in a weird space where we had definite plans to see each other again, weren't actively enemies, and yet weren't friends either.

"Night." I stopped biting my lip as Jasper got out of the car. *Maybe...*

Nope. He left the car without a second glance. But right when I was about to put the car back in gear, he stuck his head back in.

"Just so we're clear..."

"Yeah?" Heck. Maybe undefined limbo land was better than some warning I wasn't ready for.

"I'm not going to tell. Not anyone. That's your business. And I'm not out for payback."

"I appreciate that." My throat went tight like a water balloon, trying to contain emotions I had no idea what to do with. I didn't deserve his kindness, but I also wasn't stupid enough to turn it down.

"See you Wednesday." Slamming the car door, he then jogged up the path to the dorm, deck bag flapping behind him. I watched him the whole way to the door because I was worried he might go flying on the slick sidewalk. But when he swiped a key card to enter the dorm and slipped inside the heavy wooden doors, it wasn't relief that rushed through me.

It was weird, missing someone moments after we'd spent over twelve hours together, and yet there I was, driving away, feeling like I was leaving something precious behind. I parked carefully in the covered spot that was the one positive to this arrangement with Luther and James. My leg was so stiff from the hours of driving that I had to suppress a groan as I unfolded myself from the front seat. After some deliberation over whether to lock the card in the glove box, I ended up hiding the bulky case in my jacket along with my sketchbook. Considering that I'd left pieces of my soul all along the interstate, I so was not up for another tense encounter with my roommates.

And damn it. Luther and James weren't alone. The two sorority sisters who lived in the apartment beneath us were perched on the couch, holding beers. A recent comedy was on the TV.

"It's fu—*freaking* cold out," Luther said by way of greeting as he paused the movie. "The ladies had to cancel their plans to go out because of the weather, so we thought we'd kick back and see how much snow we actually get. Beer in the fridge if you want one."

I had zero desire to be a fifth wheel, and James's glare as he scooted closer to the brunette said that he didn't want me horning in on his conquest. As if. "Nah. I'm tired. Gonna go crash."

"Aww," the blond whose name might have been Brittany said. "Luther, turn the volume down."

"It's okay. I've got headphones."

"Where were you all day, anyway?" Luther fiddled with the remote.

"There you go, playing Mom again," James snarked, saving me from a reply as I retreated to the kitchen. My stash of soup cans was getting low, and someone had eaten my bread again, but I quickly made a packet of instant noodles while the movie started back up in the living room.

Not wanting more interrogation, I snuck the food back to my freezing room. I didn't want to lie to the guys, but there were certain conversations I wasn't ready to have. Jasper was right. I needed better friends. Stat.

Jasper. Setting the noodles aside, I pulled out my sketch- book and settled on my bed. A few quick lines and I had Jasper's expression when he'd won against that girl in his second-to-last match. I added a flashy vest in the Frog Wizard style. The more I sketched, the more my muscles loosened back up. I wasn't anywhere close to the person I wanted—*needed*—to be. However, looking at my drawing next to the rare card, I felt like maybe I'd at least found the path. And for better or worse, Jasper was key.

CHAPTER FIFTEEN
JASPER

"YOUR PRINCE IS HERE AGAIN." Kellan laughed as the elevator dinged. He lounged on a sofa in the waiting area near the bank of elevators as we waited for the others on Wednesday.

"He's not..." My voice trailed off because Milo was indeed striding toward us in his Prince Neptune costume, which I'd handed him in the downstairs lobby. His bus had been late, so he'd arrived after I'd changed, but he'd made fast work of getting ready. He looked fantastic, all the gold accessories glinting in the bright light, dark hair tamed under the crown, and muscles flexing under the toga as he moved. His limp was more noticeable than it had been on Saturday, and I had a feeling he'd raced too fast from the bus stop.

"Hey." He nodded at the group of us, coming to stand near Kellan and me.

I wasn't entirely sure how to greet him. Everything had changed on Saturday, and not simply because of the kiss. We'd been through something together, and that deep conversation had lingered in my head all week. Milo was gay. And maybe not as big a jerk as I'd assumed. But I also wasn't sure that we were friends, and I sure as heck wasn't asking him his thoughts, even though we'd been texting the past few days. I'd spammed him with various drawings I found of both fan art of Neptune and the Tom of Finland–style drawings that I'd teased him about. He still hadn't shown me his stuff, but we'd had several funny conversations about what I'd found. I wouldn't call our conversations flirty, but I also wouldn't call them not. Thus, I stood there, uncharacteristically short on words.

Kellan didn't share my internal dithering and stuck out a hand for Milo. "How's it going?"

"Not bad." A muscle worked in Milo's jaw, and he glanced around the waiting area. He'd never been the best at small talk, but right when I was about to save him, he turned to Kellan. "So…uh…is there a spring show at the college?"

I half groaned and half laughed. "Now you've done it. We'll be here all afternoon."

"Funny you should ask." Kellan grinned broadly and ignored my crack. "I've been busy all week on the costumes for our musical revue coming up."

"Cool." Milo's mouth quirked like he wasn't entirely sure what that was but didn't want to ask.

"It's a bunch of music numbers from various Broadway plays. Kind of like a mash-up or remix," I explained for him, having already heard all the details from Kellan multiple times.

"It's super fun," Kellan added, stroking his beard. "You should come."

My eyes went wide. *Hold up.* I wasn't so sure about my worlds colliding like that. And sure, I'd been the one to tell Milo that Kellan wouldn't make a bad friend, but that was a little different than my current bestie inviting my former friend to a non-cosplay event. It wasn't a *terrible* idea, but my neck prickled regardless.

"Maybe." Glancing at the elevators, Milo looked more ready to escape than to agree to see the show. "How bad are ticket prices?"

"Do you have a student ID?" Kellan asked.

Milo shook his head, face shuttering.

"No problem." Oblivious to the minefield he'd wandered into, Kellan continued on, cheerful as ever. "I get a certain number of comps, and this is the rare performance that my folks aren't coming up for."

"Um. Thanks," Milo said right as the elevator dinged again.

"I'm here." April rushed ahead of my mom, voice muffled by her mask. "Sorry we're late. Mom had a call."

"You're right on time." Kellan gave her a smile.

"Good. And Neptune made it again. Nice job." April nodded at Milo, who shrugged.

"I'm here. Still a little chilly though."

"You'll adapt." She was nothing if not pragmatic. She'd make a good leader someday, and there wasn't much I wouldn't give to see that she got the chance.

"Okay, are we ready?" Kellan asked, and the group murmured agreement. We all headed to the same lounge as the week before.

The same medical assistant was on duty, and there was a mix of new and old faces to greet us.

"That was nice of you," I said to Milo in a low voice as we entered the room. "About Kellan, I mean."

"You said to make friends. Was that okay?" Milo offered me a crooked smile, but his eyes were worried. Vulnerable even. "I mean, I don't have to take the tickets."

"Take them." Strangely his uncertainty made me surer.

"Okay. Maybe."

"I'll be going to at least one show. Maybe we can sit together," I offered before it hit me that I was being awfully chummy with a guy I was supposed to still have a grudge against. And being nice and making sure he didn't have to sit alone was a far cry from an actual date, but that didn't stop my pulse from revving.

"That might be cool." Milo shifted his weight from foot to foot, almost like he was doing fast internal math about how likely any of his buddies would be to see him at a show consisting of musical numbers from hit Broadway plays. "I'll check my work schedule."

"You do that." I put the odds of us actually going at subzero.

"Prince Neptune came!" Chase had a weak smile for Milo as his dad pushed him over.

"Hey, Chase! How's it going, buddy?" Milo crouched next to the wheelchair, and some soft place inside me pinged.

"Okay." Chase's voice was lethargic, and I exchanged

a worried look with my mom. "I had a new infusion today. Sleepy."

"Are you up for a game?" Milo asked, voice as gentle as I'd ever heard it.

"I can try."

"Good." Milo's smile was as tight as my chest felt. After rising from his crouch, he followed me as I set my deck bag on the rear table. He lowered his voice to a bare whisper. "Give me your two easiest decks. Don't want to exhaust the little guy further."

"I can do that." I picked the decks from the box and handed them over. "Pretty cool how you remembered his name."

"He's a hard kid to forget."

Maybe I'd accidentally skipped lunch. It had to be the only reason for why I was suddenly all fluttery. Milo getting into the whole reason behind our cosplay should not have been enough to have my heart going all soft and gushy.

"You're..." I swallowed, trying to get it together. "Give him a good game."

"I'll try." Milo took the decks and headed over to a table with Chase and his dad.

Before I could find a game of my own, my mom wandered over from talking to one of the other dads. "I'm going to go grab a coffee. Long day today for me. Do you want anything?"

"A soda?" I asked hopefully, knowing full well her opinion on junk food. She worked from home in the accounting department for the college, and on days with more activities for April or family stuff, she often got up way early. Maybe she'd be too bleary-eyed to protest the soda.

"How about a nice refreshing water?" Laughing, she shook her head at me before her expression turned more somber. "And what's up with you and Milo?"

I scratched behind my ear. *Crap*. Now I was picking up on Milo's nervous habits. Next thing I'd be having sympathetic stomach issues. "Not sure I know what you mean."

As usual, Mom saw right through me. Her whole face sagged. "Oh, Jasper…"

"He's changed." The assertion came quickly but so did the second-guessing. "I think."

Shoulders slumping further, she blew the bangs off her forehead. "I hope you're right. He used to be such a nice boy. I don't know what happened there."

I did, at least some of it, but I couldn't share any of it with her. I'd promised, and my word meant something to me.

"I—"

"Jasper, will you play with me?" A little girl I had seen once before came over, balancing on her crutches and saving me from more Mom questions I didn't have answers for.

"Sure thing."

"I'll be back." Mom sent me a warning look as I grabbed two decks. The conversation would be revisited, I was sure, but at least I had a reprieve while she headed for coffee. I didn't like her being all overprotective like this, but given my history with Milo, I could understand her not believing that he'd changed. Hell, I was struggling with it too. As much as I was enjoying spending time with him, a part of me was still cautious, putting up barricades around my heart and warning me against trusting too much too soon.

Grabbing a seat next to Milo and Chase, I smiled at Chase who was patiently explaining how to block a two-headed creature to Milo. I turned my attention to my own game, but every so often I spared a glance for them, my insides doing that weird flutter again as Milo fetched some water for Chase. Eventually, Chase declared himself too tired for a rematch.

"Okay, buddy. Another time?"

"Yeah." Chase's smile made all the work of talking Milo into cosplaying worth it.

"Come and play with Alexandra and me," I offered. "We can teach you some tricks for multiplayer style."

"Thanks." Milo pulled up a chair, and we were all deep into the game when my mom returned.

"Here you go." She slipped me a bottle of some organic soda I'd never heard of along with a cryptic look as her eyes darted back and forth between Milo and me. She settled in to talk with Alexandra's mom on one of the nearby couches. Backing up some of his bragging, Milo turned out to have some good instincts—he was brash, quick to attack, willing to take risks. However, he kept forgetting to plan multiple turns in advance.

"You can't go all in every time," I advised, and Alexandra nodded. "Try to visualize your optimal board state a few turns from now."

"But attacking is fun. I don't like being on the defensive."

"I know." And boy, did I. Less than one game and I could already see Milo hated being exposed and open to attack. In keeping with his personality and our long history, he preferred to make quick, ill-advised attacks to avoid being a sitting duck. "You're going to lose to Alex three turns from now, though, if you don't sit tight. Trust me."

Milo made a pained face like I was asking him to wax his eyebrows. "Nah. I better attack this turn, or I won't be around in three turns because you'll take me out."

"Actually, I won't. That would leave me open to Alex, and I'd prefer to win this round. Like I said, think ahead. But suit yourself."

"Fine," he huffed, then smiled for Alexandra. "You winning wouldn't be the worst thing in the world."

"I win a lot." Her eyes sparkled. "What happened to your leg? I'm here because I had surgery on mine. Again."

Milo was silent for a long moment. "A mistake. A mistake happened. And I had surgery too. More than one. Swear the second was worse than the first."

"Word." She gave him an awkward high five. "Anesthesia makes me puke."

"Me too."

"Somehow I'm not surprised," I added.

"Hey, I don't *always* hurl."

"But when you do, it's generally spectacularly awful." This sort of teasing felt good, almost too good, like no time at all had passed and we were back to joking about the amusement-park trip the summer before freshman year.

"You might have a point," Milo agreed before ending his turn. Alex, who was surprisingly bloodthirsty, took me out on her next turn despite my best plans to avoid defeat. That left her and Milo, who drew a card and frowned. "Heck."

"You can't bluff worth s—"

"Alex," her mother warned, looking up from her crocheting.

"Sorry." Alex's smile didn't dim one bit. "Come at me."

And Milo did, losing in short order. "Heck. Good game."

"Warned you," I reminded him a short time later as we cleaned up the cards.

"That you did."

"Jasper, are you coming for dinner? I've got chili in the slow cooker." My mom already had her purse and coat, and she barely spared a glance for Milo.

"Uh." I had been planning to do more card searching with Milo, but I didn't want to admit that to her and risk a lecture later. "I have plans. And a test to study for. Sorry."

"It's okay. Stop by tomorrow any time. I'll have some leftovers for you in the fridge."

"Thanks." I gave her a fast kiss before she and April headed out.

"So…" Milo shuffled his feet. "Guess I'll get changed. Good luck with your test."

"Dork," I teased, the light mood from earlier carrying over. "The plans are with *you*. Unless you've changed your mind?"

"Nah. We're on." Milo's smile in that moment was close to perfect, warm and open and dangerous. Dangerous because it made me want in a way I hadn't wanted in a very long time. With each interaction, Milo was wearing down my defenses, making me forget all the reasons why we couldn't be friends—or anything else.

CHAPTER SIXTEEN
MILO

"BACK TO REGULAR ME." JASPER'S smile seemed a little down as he met me in the bathroom after we finished changing. We stowed the costumes and headed to the hall.

"You sound sad about getting changed," I teased him. We'd been in a light, good place all afternoon, and I wanted to keep it going.

"The Frog Wizard is more fun than me." Jasper's tone was still a little mournful, and I couldn't tell how serious he was. I liked him in costume a lot more than I'd thought I would, but I also liked him like this, in his scruffy jeans and a sweatshirt with a twenty-sided die on it. I tried to decide how sincere a compliment to give him as we approached the cafeteria.

"I wouldn't say that. You're—"

Jasper cut me off as he pulled up short. "What's that smell?"

"Ugh." It was truly rank. Not at all the coffee and roasted-meat smell of the week prior. My stomach gave a precarious lurch. "Burned cabbage? Flaming kale? Whatever it is, my stomach is seriously rebelling."

"Hot-dog machine malfunction," the bored cashier standing near us supplied.

"We can't work here." Groaning, Jasper adjusted his bags. "Which sucks because I had ideas for you I wanted to go over."

I had plans, too, plans to enjoy his company. I had...thoughts on him not telling his mom that we were going to hang out, but I had no room to complain. Besides, she'd glared my way more than once that afternoon. I couldn't blame Jasper for not wanting to hear her opinion on us being...whatever this was. I didn't know what to call someone who sent me pics of sexy drawings and who teased me almost like flirting but who might still hate me with good reason. And even with all that uncertainty, I'd still been looking forward to this.

"Dang it. Maybe—" I was about to propose sucking it up and working here anyway, but then a fresh wave of the stench hit my nose. My stomach had definite opinions about this smell, and none of them were good. Sighing, I shuffled my feet. "Nah, I guess you're right."

Instead of heading for the exit like I'd expected, Jasper stood there, head tilted and mouth pursed. Damn, he was cute when he was thinking.

"Hey. You still like pizza?"

"Is the sun yellow?" When I was younger, I was pretty convinced the only food better than pizza was my grandmother's ravioli. And damn was I tired of various variations on canned soup.

"There's a new place near the university. Hipster vibe. Lots of California-type flavor combos. If I'm running you home anyway, maybe we could split a pie first?"

"Uh…" Was he asking me out? And if so, how did I feel about that? Also, what if we ran into some of his fancy college friends? The questions racing through my brain must have taken longer than a split second because Jasper frowned.

"Never mind. Forgot you need to keep our…association on the down low."

"I don't," I said quickly because somehow I knew this chance might never come again. I'd made that mistake once before, and no way was I doing it again. "We can go. The pause was me doing mental math. You know how it goes."

It was a little white lie, and not that far from the truth because there was always more week than cash lately.

"Oh, that I can relate to. I get paid Friday and it was my idea. I'll treat you."

Now that was even closer to a date. But I'd kind of backed myself into a corner. "Okay, but next time's on me."

"It's a plan." Jasper's smile was worth any nervousness on my part. And I'd pretty much sealed the deal on not one but two outings. He marched toward the exit with purposeful strides. "Come on. Let's find my car. You've seen it before, right? Don't go expecting too much."

"What? You think I'm some sort of car snob?" I faked offense, letting his answering laugh warm me even as the chilly air greeted us outside.

"Ha. Not only is mine tiny, old, and in dubious repair, but it's also messy." Jasper headed to the parking garage at a fast clip, then slowed, glancing down at my leg. "Oops. Sorry."

"It's okay." I hated slowing him down, but there was also no denying that my earlier trot from the bus stop already had the surgically repaired leg aching. "And no surprises there on you being messy."

"Yeah, much to my mom's frustration, I never did figure out the whole clean-as-you-go philosophy of hers." Jasper stopped by a little compact that had probably started life white but was now dingy and dusty with more dents than I could count and an assortment of bumper stickers.

I didn't miss the two with little rainbows on them, but I wasn't repeating my earlier mistake and making him think I was uncomfortable to be seen with someone who was proudly out. Forcing my eyes away from the bumper stickers, I slipped into the passenger seat as soon as he unlocked the door, moving aside an assortment of soda bottles, textbooks, and gaming supplies. I hefted my bag onto my lap while he stowed his collection of stuff in the back seat.

"You want to put your bag back here?"

"Nah. I'm okay. I'm used to more cramped spaces on the bus." My pulse sped up as I remembered what I'd finished up while waiting for the bus. I wasn't ready to have Jasper poring over my sketchbooks, but I'd done something specifically to show him. As he got in the driver's seat, I opened my bag. "You still want to see one of my drawings?"

Jasper's eyes went wide and bright. "Totally. Did any of my picture spam inspire you?"

"Sort of. I've been working on this one. I tried Neptune all sexy, but that was just weird—"

"I'd still like to see that." Jasper winked.

"Not now." It was hard enough getting up the courage to show him this one thing. I held out the page I'd already removed from the sketchbook. "So, this is kinda crap, but it's my version of Neptune as a Disney prince."

"Oh. My. God." Jasper did a fake swoon, which was pretty fucking gratifying, even as my heart still pounded. "This is incredible. I had no idea you'd kept working on your art and become this good. Have you been in shows? Were you an art major?"

"Slow down." I gave a shaky laugh. "Like this right here? This is the first I've shown something to someone since my dad had opinions on why I wanted to take art instead of shop in high school."

"Uh, because you're good at it? Seriously, you're way too good at this not to show it off."

"Feels weird," I admitted. "And I'm not *that* good. Watching some tutorial videos isn't the same as being art-major talented. It's just something I do when I've got restless energy."

"Well, I disagree. Keep doing it." Jasper nodded like he'd made a royal proclamation as he turned on the car. "And maybe some time you'll let me see more?"

"Maybe." After I purged all my doodles of him from my sketchbooks, perhaps then I could find the courage to show him more. He did seem to like it at least and wasn't actively laughing at me.

We headed back downtown toward the university and

the little shops that lined the streets closest to campus. Jasper drove like zombies were chasing us.

"I'm reconsidering teaching you to drive a stick." I chuckled as my teeth rattled. "Where did you learn to drive, anyway?"

"My mom."

"Explains a lot." For a nice lady who drove a minivan, Jasper's mother tended to drive like she was going for a personal best. "And I'm kidding. I'll teach you, but my baby doesn't like rough handling."

"Oh?" Jasper's voice dropped. *Fuck.* I hadn't meant to make a dirty joke, but now here I was with more thoughts about his hands and where I'd like them.

I made a choking sound right as he parked—an adventure in and of itself. "Careful."

"You forget I'm a math genius. Estimation and rapid calculations are strengths of mine."

"Maybe so, but I saw the dings on your bumper," I retorted, laughing again. I'd forgotten how fun he could be to joke with.

"Those were there when I got the car." His eyebrow wag made my face heat, and I wasn't entirely sure why. "Come on. Let's get some food."

The small pizza place was between a barbershop and a coffee shop packed with students.

"Almost forgot to ask. What's your test in?" I asked as we walked up the sidewalk from where we'd had to park.

"Stochastic processes. It looks at mathematical modeling including discrete and continuous-time Markov chains and Poisson processes."

"I don't understand a word you said," I admitted as we entered the pizza parlor. It had more of a hippie vibe than Italian, with light wood decor, beachy colors, and bold fonts on a giant wall menu.

"Oh, it's fun," he said and launched into a detailed explanation as we got in line to give our orders. I tried to follow along with his mini-math class as I surveyed the potential places for us to sit.

As in the coffee shop, clumps of students dominated the tables, many with books and laptops out. Most were in groups of three or four, but the smaller tables along the far wall were all occupied by twosomes. Some were clearly friends, but others were probably couples. Trying to guess which were which was a fun game. Two guys with ball caps at the back of the room were deep in conversation. Probably frat bros. Then one touched the other's hand, holding it as he smiled. Okay. Not bros.

And now I was back to wondering if people would assume Jasper and I were on a date. And if we were, how did I feel about that? Like, part of me definitely wanted this to be a date, preferably one that ended in another try to be not-terrible at kissing. The other part wanted it, too, but that part was a little seasick at the idea of all those eyeballs on me.

"See anything you want?" Jasper smiled at me, wide and unrestrained, hair still wild from his quick costume change, light reflecting in his summer-sky eyes. I'd suffer more than a little discomfort to earn more of those smiles.

"Yeah." My voice came out too husky.

"And? Which flavor?"

Oops. He'd meant pizza. "You know me. More meat the better. Anything from the carnivore section of the board would work. Or whatever you want. You're the one who's been here before."

"I am." He nodded solemnly, and I still wasn't entirely sure we were talking about pizza. "Trust me?"

"Absolutely." That much was never in doubt.

"Good. Go snag us that table over there. I need room for the laptop. I'm going to surprise you with something delicious."

"I can't wait." My steps were almost Jasper-level bouncy as I hurried to claim the table. I liked him giving me orders and didn't want to dwell on why that was. And it was true. I couldn't wait for whatever came next.

CHAPTER SEVENTEEN
JASPER

TELLING MYSELF THAT THIS WASN'T a date didn't make my pulse slow one bit as I made my way to the table Milo had claimed. To my surprise, he wasn't on his phone as he waited, but rather he had a mini sketchbook out, expression intent as his pencil moved across the page. I allowed myself the pleasure of watching him work for a few moments before I set the little plastic tent with our order number on the table.

"Oh, there you are." His smile made my toes curl inside my sneakers. "Gonna tell me what you got?"

"Nope." I grinned at him. "Gonna show me your sketch?"

"I don't usually draw around people I know, but I had this idea and you didn't laugh at my earlier one—"

"Of course not!" I glared at him. He was crazy-talented and couldn't seem to see it. His Neptune had looked exactly like a promo piece for a Disney movie. Preferably one where the prince got his guy.

"Okay, okay. This is a rough idea of something I might do bigger if you don't think it would be too stupid." He tore the sheet out of the book and passed it over.

My breath literally caught, as if my oxygen had snagged on all the too-sharp emotions assaulting me. It was Chase, but not Chase like he'd been that afternoon, tired and hurting. Rather, it was Chase as a superhero, cape flapping behind him, wearing a big smile like the one he'd had for Milo that first day.

"Wow. That's incredible. You have to give that to him and his dad. Please. I bet it would mean a lot to them."

"Okay. I'll try to do a bigger version. Better. Less smudgy." Milo's mouth pursed like he was seeing something different than the near-lifelike drawing in front of us. I'd always had mad respect for anyone who had art skills, and I had enough artsy friends to know when I was seeing true talent.

"Perfectionist."

"Maybe." His cheeks turned an adorable shade of pink, but the tilt of his chin said that he was secretly pleased at my compliments.

My phone buzzed, and I used him turning to put the sketchbook away to sneak a glance at my messages.

"Oh, cool. This is actually relevant to our card search."

"Yeah?" Milo leaned forward.

"I told my friend Conrad about our quest. Not the why, of course, but I wanted his opinion on locating the remaining Royal Frog Court cards on the cheap."

"What did he say?" Milo's mouth stayed flat, but his eyes glimmered, like he didn't want to get his hopes up.

"That Odyssey tends to pretend that the secondary market for cards doesn't exist. And that corporate doesn't have a secret vault of them where he can score them."

"Darn." The glimmer was gone now, and I slumped in my chair, hating that I didn't have better answers for him.

"But it wasn't all bad news. He and Alden are coming down this weekend to film a special episode of the *Gamer Grandpa* vlog we're both regulars on. He says he's going to do some hunting and we can talk about it Saturday night. Alden might have ideas too."

"So you'll keep me posted?" Milo's tone was cautious. And somewhere in between wanting to give him something worth getting excited about and my own complicated feelings about the gathering, inspiration struck.

"Actually, I can do one better. You free Saturday night?"

"You want me to meet your friends?" Frowning, Milo leaned back. He wasn't nearly as positive as I'd presumed.

"Well, you've already met some. Kellan will probably come too and bring Jasmine. They've both been on the program more this year. We're filming at Professor Tuttle's house, and his husband is making food."

"I wouldn't want to impose." That wasn't a no, but like earlier when I'd made the pizza invite, Milo's discomfort was hard to read. Like, was it a new-people thing or a not-wanting-to-be-perceived-as-a-couple thing?

"I already told Conrad that I needed the cards for a friend, not myself. And the professor loves a crowd. One more won't be a problem. In fact, it might even be good," I admitted.

"Ah. Good for the get-Milo-new-friends quest or good for not wanting to appear jealous of your friends coupling up?"

Damn. He was too perceptive. "I'm not jealous."

Milo merely raised an eyebrow.

"Okay, not jealous *much*. I'm used to being seen as just a friend, the goofy one in our crowd, not date material. It's not like I was in love with either of them. And I've had boyfriends." I sounded way too defensive, and Milo continued to study me carefully. "It's more that it's...mildly annoying to see them all lovey-dovey. Maybe I miss when they hated each other, but I'm also happy for them. Really."

"I'm in." Milo nodded like he knew something I didn't.

"Okay. But—" The arrival of our food cut me off from telling him that I didn't *need* a buffer. And I had a feeling he would have seen through the denial anyway. It was weird, being happy for my friends, but also wistful that I hadn't been able to finish the road trip with them. I didn't want to be with Conrad precisely, but I sure wouldn't have minded playing hero for him. The past weekend with Milo had shown me how good that felt but also made me more aware of what I'd missed.

"Now this is an amazing smell. Unlike earlier. Tell me what I'm about to eat?" He gestured at the steaming pizza that the waiter had set on a serving rack between us. Milo's intent expression was overtly hungry—eager eyes and open mouth—and heat rushed up my spine. I wanted to see that look more.

"This half is buffalo chicken. The other is barbecue brisket."

"Wing flavors on a pizza? I love it already." Milo smiled widely, like I'd known he would. He'd always been more than willing to try different pizza toppings growing up. Now I was, too, and even before he reappeared in my life I'd sometimes thought about him whenever I tried something outrageous.

"You're easy."

"Maybe." His shrug and half smile had a flirty edge that felt new. And dangerous. When he sampled the pizza, eyes fluttering closed and tongue catching stray drips of sauce, the heat inside me turned to an inferno.

Even forcing my attention onto the pizza didn't work. The flavors, which I usually loved, weren't anywhere near as captivating as Milo's face.

"So…boyfriends? Plural?" he asked as he helped himself to more pizza, voice way too deliberately casual.

"Not like a parade or anything. But, yeah, I've dated. I like dating more than random hookups for sure. But people have a way of not sticking around." That sounded a little too emo, so I tried to make my voice brighter. "Stuff happens, and maybe we weren't that serious to start with. They get back together with their high school person, or they go on a semester abroad and want to be free to sample the local everything, or they fall for someone at their internship. I'm still friends with everyone."

"Wow. I can't…" Milo shook his head.

"Can't imagine there's that many people willing to date me?" I narrowed my eyes.

"No, not *that*. More that I can't imagine it for *me*."

"But you want it?" My breath rushed out. I was far too invested in his answer. "Someday?"

His cheeks colored before he nodded quickly, not meeting my eyes. "Yeah. Someday."

I wasn't entirely sure where the conversation went from

there. It felt significant somehow, but also like handling a live snake. Then he laughed, and everything was okay again.

"Right now, I want a significant relationship with this pizza. Like bring it home to meet my mom and change my social-media status."

"Oh, my mom meets everyone in my social circle. Including this pizza. I got her hooked on another one they do with fig jam and prosciutto."

"I'm gonna mention this place to my mom too. Pretty sure my relatives back in Catanzaro would flip at some of these flavor combos, but I'm sold."

"I still remember that stuffed-pasta dish your grandma would do."

"Ravioli alla Calabrese? Me too." Milo helped himself to some pizza from the other side. "Someday I'm going to have my own place. And a fridge where my ingredients don't up and disappear overnight."

"Mood. I want more than a hot plate in the dorm."

"Yup. Then I'm gonna learn to cook like my *nona*. I've got a list of stuff to try. Dad always gave Mom a hard time about her cooking never living up to Nona's, so she doesn't have any patience for it now, but there's a recipe book some cousins put together. And I figure there are videos on how to do stuff."

"I can help you find some good ones." My chest constricted. I wanted that future for Milo. Better living situation for sure, but also somewhere he felt free to be himself, to draw and cook and chase away the memory of his dad and his stupid opinions on art and food. "Speaking of searching, let's see what we can find for our card hunt."

I set up my laptop, and we polished off the last of the pizza and split a giant brownie as we searched. But sky-high prices for even non-mint cards were super frustrating. The best brownie in town wasn't enough to stop Milo's frown.

"I wish this were easier."

"Me too. I bet Conrad will have ideas," I said as we packed up. "And I'm not giving up either. I work tomorrow. I'll talk to Arthur, see if he has any inside hookup on rare cards."

"Thanks. You've done a ton already. I appreciate it, man." Milo clapped me on the shoulder as we headed to the exit, and for a second it seemed like he was about to put an arm around me, but then he dropped his hand. Our eyes met as we reached the door, and the glimmer of the moment that had passed was still there. He might not have done it, but he'd thought about it, and he'd *wanted it*. And now I did too.

The cold air greeted us, a sharp reminder that no matter what cozy meal we'd managed together, reality was still lurking. I wanted to run to the car, but I matched my pace to Milo's, mindful of his leg. And despite the chill, I didn't mind going slower, not when Milo glanced up at the gorgeous full moon, then over at me.

"It's a nice night."

"Yeah." My breath hung in front of me, not unlike my heart which seemed perilously close to simply presenting itself to Milo on a platter. *Don't do it*, I reminded myself, moving more of those mental barricades into position. We could maybe be friends. Maybe even friends who kissed. But no way, no how could I fall for him.

"Thanks," he said softly. "For everything."

"I wish we would have found more leads, but at least the food was good." We reached the car, and I used the clicker that only sometimes worked to unlock both doors.

"It was amazing." He looked right at me as he said it, too, and I shivered.

"So where am I taking you?" I asked as we settled into our seats and got buckled up.

"How about 1435 Birchwood? That would be nicer than going to Luther and James for sure." He recited his old address with a wistful smile that made me remember memorizing our addresses and moms' phone numbers together in prep for being allowed to walk home from school.

"Sorry." Maybe I should invite him back to my room. Not for...*that*. But because he seemed so reluctant to go back to his place, and him sad was apparently my personal kryptonite.

However, right as I was about to offer, he sighed. "It's over by that big shopping complex off Wilson."

He gave me the rest of the directions, then started fiddling with my radio as I pulled out of the parking spot.

"It's dead," I informed him. "Gave up the ghost in the fall."

"I could replace it for you. Stereos are easy. I did mine."

Him offering made my chest all warm, but I had to laugh. "A new stereo in *this*?"

"Okay. Maybe not. You say I need new friends, and you're not wrong, but we gotta find you a better ride."

"Says the guy who currently swears by the bus."

I meant it as a tease, but his face shuttered. "I've got reasons."

"I know. Your car's a collector's dream. I didn't mean it in a bad way."

"I know." He exhaled hard. "Driving...sometimes makes me a little nervous. Since the accident."

"I didn't know. But you drove to Philly. Rather well."

"Well, yeah, I *can* drive. Not gonna lie, though, my nerves were real. It's hardest having someone in the car with me. Not personal to you. Just..."

"You were driving? In the accident?" It was the first time he'd seemed at all willing to discuss the accident, and I didn't want to lose a chance to know more about him.

"Yeah." His voice became distant and far off. "We were on the way back from a party we had no business being at. Right in the middle of the season, so it was against team rules to be out that late, and none of us were twenty-one yet. I was the most sober of us, which wasn't saying much."

"It wasn't your car, though?"

"It belonged to a buddy of mine from the team. Ended up with an insurance nightmare because it wasn't mine and theirs didn't want to cover. Anyway, it was a stupid thing. Thought I saw a deer in the road, and I swerved to miss it but overcompensated, and we ended up rolling into a ditch. It was bad."

"I'm sorry." It felt like all I could say and totally inadequate at the same time.

"Don't be. You're not the one who fucked up."

"Did anyone…" I let my voice trail off because my morbid curiosity wasn't helping Milo's audible pain at recounting the experience.

"No one died. But they could have. So easily. It ended up that I was the worst of the injuries. Small justice, I guess."

"You made a mistake. A huge one. But that doesn't mean that you deserved such a gruesome injury." Stopping at a red light, I sneaked a glance at his face, which was a mask of pain. Eyes shut, mouth fixed and hard.

"Yeah. I get that. And yet…I put my family through such shit. It wasn't that long after Dad passed."

"Which may have played a role, I'd bet."

"Quit trying to make excuses for me." He groaned and slumped further in his seat. "Sorry. You're being nice. But I don't deserve nice. Not about this. I know full well what I did was wrong on so many levels. And I didn't deserve Mom and Bruno's help either. He came. There was…police involvement. Charges. I didn't lose my license, but it was close. And there were fines. Bruno helped me handle all of it. Said I could repay him over time."

"He's a good brother," I said.

"Yeah. And how do I pay him back? I was a dumbass again. Got myself fleeced. Was drinking. Again. At least this time I walked my butt home. Progress?"

"In your defense, I've played George. He can be…persuasive."

"He flirted with me," Milo admitted softly as I passed the shopping center.

"I'm not surprised." I'd suspected as much ever since Milo told me he was into guys.

"You figured?"

"He'd flirt with a fire hydrant if he thought it would get him primo cards. He tried it with me and a number of my friends too. Flirts with the guys who are into that, but he's charming with everyone. And none of us lost cards worth as much as the Frog Court to him, but it wasn't for lack of trying on his part."

"Oh. So it wasn't just me." Milo's tone was hard to read as I turned into the apartment complex he'd indicated. "Second building on the left."

"Did you want it to be specific to you?" I asked gently as I parked a little way down from the building. Milo hadn't asked, but I figured that neither of us needed Luther or James ruining what was otherwise a pretty damn good day.

"No. I didn't want... Okay. That's a lie. Maybe I was flattered. At first. But then he made me feel... I dunno. Slimy? Used?"

"Yup. That's George. He's a charming bastard when he wants to be."

"I'm never drinking again." Milo gave a firm nod, meeting my gaze. "That was it. I'm not going to say I'll never be a dumbass again, because I'm still me, but I also don't want to be that guy who never learns his lesson. Not anymore. I want...something more. To *be* more."

"I believe in you." Patting his arm, I put all my conviction into my voice because I sensed he needed that, needed someone who believed he could change. And maybe no one had said that to him in a long time because his eyes went glassy and his lower lip trembled.

"Thanks," he whispered.

"I mean it."

He didn't reply, instead leaning into my touch. Moving slowly, he turned toward me and stopped when our faces were millimeters apart. It didn't take a genius to see what he wanted, and while I appreciated the hesitation, no way was I turning him down, not in that moment. I nodded slightly, and that was all it took for him to find my mouth.

Like the first time, it was sweet and slow at first, and his hesitance was even more of a turn-on now that I knew I was the only one to ever do this with him. And even though he'd been the one to initiate the kiss, his deliberate, soft movements made it easy for me to take the lead. He was a fast study, mimicking me as I nipped at his lips. I sucked on his lower lip, and he shuddered, groaning softly then immediately doing the same thing to me.

Pulling him closer, I did what I'd been dying to do for *days* and deepened the kiss, exploring his mouth. He tasted sweet, like chocolate, and vaguely spicy, and his inquisitive tongue was about to make me unravel. His little noises were even better—gasps and whimpers and soft groans like he was as utterly desperate for this as I was.

But I was also a little too aware of being in a public parking lot, engine still running, and the last thing I wanted was to out Milo to his jerk friends. Reluctantly, I pulled away, breathing hard.

"Not as terrible as the first one?" He gave me a soft, shy smile.

"Nowhere close to terrible." My voice was all husky, and even knowing we were way too exposed, I was still tempted to haul him back for another kiss. "You should probably get inside before one of us freezes."

"Or spontaneously combusts."

"That is a risk." We laughed together as he gathered his stuff.

"Drive safe. Text me?" he asked as he opened the door.

"I will." No point in playing it cool. I would text, exactly like how I'd give him more non-terrible kisses if I got the chance. And despite everything, I hoped I did.

CHAPTER EIGHTEEN
MILO

"READY TO GO?" AS HE'D done on Wednesday night, Jasper had parked a bit down from my building, but I'd been waiting outside for him and didn't have far to walk. "Tell me you didn't have to stand too long in the cold."

"It wasn't bad." I didn't want to keep him waiting because he'd been nice enough offering me a ride to Professor Tuttle's house. And okay, I also wasn't wanting the drama from Luther and James if Jasper came up to fetch me. I wasn't going to repeat the mistakes of high school, and I'd tell them where they could shove it if they hassled us, but I wasn't looking forward to that conversation.

I did a fast glance around the parking lot because I also couldn't resist the chance to lean in and give Jasper a quick kiss hello. It wasn't a long one—no tongues tangling like the other night—but Jasper's small, pleased smile said he appreciated the gesture. And that made me repeat it another time before settling into my seat and clicking the seat belt.

"Wow." Jasper rubbed his mouth, cheeks still pink. "You're definitely getting better."

"Yeah?" I liked knowing that, and I resisted the urge to wriggle in my seat like a puppy getting praised for a new trick.

"Your improvements have been noted, but you might need more practice later." Jasper's voice was light as he drove toward the exit.

"I could be down with that." I started racking my brain for ideas of where we could go park that might allow for more kissing. I'd never done the whole parking thing in high school, but I'd heard enough from the guys in the locker room to know such places existed.

"Good. But first, we've got to get to the professor's."

"Darn." Laughing, I stretched my legs. His car was suspiciously cleaner, and I had a feeling it might have been for my benefit. "Thanks for the ride. I could have done the bus—"

"No, you couldn't have. It's freezing." Jasper spoke exactly like someone who assumed it was his personal responsibility to take care of everyone around him. I'd been watching him these past few weeks, and the boy who'd liked to help his parents with chores had grown into the adult who never said no and was always there with an offer to help whether it was his family or Kellan or me. As much as I liked being in that circle, I also found myself wanting to take care of *him* too.

"Well, I appreciate it. Maybe there's something I can do for you?"

"We'll see." Jasper's tone was decidedly flirty, and

while I hadn't meant it as a sexy thing, I wasn't turning down those ideas either.

"You're right about freezing." I tried to adjust his heater, which was only marginally more functional than his stereo. "I'm ready for some sun."

"Me too. Of course, the sun and I have a love-hate relationship." Jasper laughed as he stopped for a red light. Saturday night traffic was predictably bad, but I didn't mind the extra time with him.

"I remember some of your terrible sunburns growing up."

"Yup. But I'm so ready for warmth."

"Oh, I can keep you warm." I was still testing this whole flirting-back thing, but I liked how it made my chest expand, like I needed extra room to contain these light feelings.

"Of that I have no doubt. Thanks to you, I had rather…heated dreams last night."

"Hey, you're the one searching out sexy drawings, not me." I lived for his texts lately, both the ones with and without images. They weren't quite sexting, but they weren't all G-rated either. I liked the flirting and also the little snippets of his life, like him mentioning being tired from classes and work.

"We need to keep you properly inspired." Jasper waggled his eyebrows at me right before turning into a neighborhood of stately older homes near the campus.

"You are. I'm totally inspired." I shifted in the seat, needing to move away from the flirting if we were almost to our destination. "And in other art news, I finished the drawing for Chase and his dad. Think they'll be there this week? Wait. Am I invited to cosplay? Didn't mean to presume."

"Neptune is always welcome. You too." Jasper's voice was far warmer than the air in his car. "And I'll call tomorrow and find out if he's been discharged yet. If he has, my mom has an address for them. We sent cookies and some *Odyssey* cards for Chase at Christmas."

"Your family is always so nice." I wanted to be more like that too. Thoughtful. The kind of person who thought before they acted.

"Well, it's mainly my mom, but thanks." Jasper frowned as we slowed in front of a house with a packed driveway. "Okay, now to find a parking spot nearby."

"I don't mind walking if it means sparing your car more of your stunt parking."

"Hey now. Remember that crack when I cash in my voucher for learning to drive a stick."

"We're going to an empty parking lot." I braced myself against the seat as Jasper did a parallel parking maneuver that was probably illegal in three states.

"Promises, promises." He winked at me as he straightened out the car and put it in Park. We were still at an alarming angle, but the heat in his eyes had me right back to thinking about all the things we could get up to at the end of the night. But first I had to be social and hope I didn't embarrass Jasper in front of his genius gamer friends.

"Do you need me to play this a certain way?" I asked as we got out of the car. "I am well acquainted with the 'let's make my ex jealous' move, thanks to more than one sorority sister needing a last-minute date to a function we both wanted to skip."

"Neither of them are my ex. Like I said, we're all friends. It's just…weirdish now. And is that you offering to be my date or you being scared I might claim that without clearing it with you?"

"Which gets me more practice kissing after this is over?" I gave him my best smile, even as my heart threatened to pound its way out of my chest.

"You surprise me more every day." Jasper shook his head, and I wasn't sure if that was a good thing. "And you look like you did right before that roller coaster. So, no, I'm not going to make you hold hands or anything like that, but if you can manage not to freak if someone makes the assumption, I'd count that as progress."

"And the kissing?" I didn't particularly like that his expectations were so low, even if he wasn't wrong about me being nervous.

Jasper glanced down the street, then gave me a lightning-fast peck on the mouth. He pulled back to study me closely. "Okay. You're not melting like a snowman. I think you might be cool for later."

"Good."

"Milo?" He stopped right before the house, which was a Victorian in immaculate repair. His face was serious enough to make my stomach flip.

"Yeah?"

"I meant what I said the other night. I believe you can change. Don't prove me wrong."

"I won't," I promised, hoping like heck I wasn't lying because the absolute last thing I wanted to do was hurt him. Especially right then when what I really wanted was to get better at kissing him senseless. And better at...*everything* when it came right down to it. I'd decided at some point in the last few weeks that I wasn't going to settle for spending the rest of my life as a loser. I wanted more, and that meant finally being willing to crack that closet door and let a little fresh air into that dank, windowless space that had been my home for far too long.

"Jasper! You made it. We're about to start filming." An older man wearing a *Gamer Grandpa* T-shirt under a thick cardigan opened the door after Jasper rang the bell. "Thanks for meeting here. My old bones haven't been getting around as well these days."

Leaning heavily on his cane, he moved aside for us to enter.

"I don't know about old. You look ready to kick some *Odyssey* butt, Professor Tuttle." Jasper had a big smile for the man, then gestured as me. "This is Milo. He's the friend who's been playing Prince Neptune with our group."

I almost preened at having graduated to friend. And I supposed "Milo the guy I've been sending racy fan-art drawings to and kissing good night" didn't especially roll off the tongue, even if it was maybe more accurate. But *friend* meant I was doing something right—and also meant there was more at stake if I screwed up.

"Welcome." Professor Tuttle nodded at me. "We've got plenty of food for after we film. I assume you play?"

"A little." I had at least learned something recently: not to brag about my skills playing a game that most of these people probably had played for a decade or more.

"Good, good. We won't put you in front of the camera. Yet." His sly wink made me smile. I followed him and Jasper to the rear of the house. We tossed our coats onto a pile on a bench in the hall before entering an impressively renovated kitchen that smelled like enchiladas and made me forget to be nervous about meeting new people.

Another older gentleman with a red apron and salt-and-pepper hair placed a steaming tray of rice on the counter. I guessed he was Professor Herrera, Professor Tuttle's husband, even before the introductions were made.

"Call me Julio," he said breezily. "And help yourself to a drink."

"What can I help you with?" I asked, ignoring the cooler of drinks on the floor at the end of the island. Jasper and the professor had started talking filming specifics for their vlog episode, drifting toward the dining room where I could hear Kellan's deeper voice amid some unfamiliar ones.

"Can you cook?" Julio asked, raising an elegant eyebrow. He was a drama professor, and I could totally see him onstage himself. I hadn't known many older same-sex couples, and he and Professor Tuttle fascinated me.

"Better than I can help with the vlog stuff," I admitted. "But not like expert level."

"Fair enough. In that case, you can stir this pot." In short order, Julio had me in an apron, stirring a giant pot of beans with a long wooden spoon while he carried on an entertaining monologue about the hazards of loving a gamer. I liked that he didn't require much conversation from me, which gave me ample time to peek into the dining room where the play mats had come out and much discussion was had as to who was playing whom.

And Jasper was right in the middle of things, talking animatedly, hands flying, smile never dipping. Others had louder opinions and might have been objectively better players, but to me, Jasper was the sun to which my eyes kept returning.

"How long have you been friends?" Julio asked, probably catching on to the direction of my gaze.

"Uh...this time around, like, two weeks? But we went to school together." I left out a giant chunk of our history while also trying not to outright lie.

"He's a great kid. One of my favorites of the Gamer Grandpa gang."

"He's the best." Of that I was sure, and watching him with his friends from a distance only made me more aware of how lucky I was that he was having anything to do with me, especially given our past. And I didn't ever want to be the one who dimmed that light inside him, that light that I couldn't get enough of. Even now, it wasn't only kisses I was counting down to, but simply getting a slice of that attention and energy. Forget spring. It was his warmth I wanted to bask in, even if meant risking getting burned.

CHAPTER NINETEEN
JASPER

MILO WASN'T THE ONLY ONE with kissing on his brain. As my friends and I took a break from filming so that Professor Tuttle could go find a missing deck in his office with Jasmine's help, my thoughts kept drifting back to Milo's unexpected but very welcome new interest. The kisses hello had been sweet, especially knowing he was risking James or Luther seeing. I had no clue what we were doing other than that I liked it and wasn't about to put a stop to it, not yet.

"So. Your friend. The one with a burning desire for the Royal Frog Court cards. He's...different." Conrad looked up from shuffling cards. He seemed older than the last time I'd seen him—nicer clothes, good haircut, all those real-world employment perks.

"Hey, we welcome jocks here too." In a good mood from a rare win against Conrad, Kellan laughed. He tinkered with the cameras for the next segment.

"He's not a jock." My emphatic denial surprised me, so I softened my tone a little. "Exactly."

"You like him." Conrad raised an eyebrow, apparently all- knowing about matters of the heart now.

"I don't *dislike* him." I glanced back at the kitchen, hoping he wasn't in earshot of this little exchange.

"Well, as long as he's got nothing in common with that jock guy from high school who was such a jerk."

Heck. Of course, Conrad would remember that story from one night when he'd needed a place to crash. We'd had one of those sleep-deprived oversharing conversations where I probably should have kept my mouth shut rather than sharing all my Milo angst.

"Um…"

"Oh, Jasper. Really?" Frowning, now Conrad was the one to glance at the kitchen. "I know you're big on seeing the good—"

"People change." I was back to being defensive about something I wasn't entirely sure about myself. I wanted to believe in Milo, but a mountain of past evidence told me to be wary. And there was a difference between believing and trusting, a distinction my overclocked brain kept obsessing about. "They do. I've seen people change."

"Not as often as we'd like." Conrad sighed like he was oh so ancient now. "And it's your life. But I feel like I should have words with this guy anyway."

"*You're* going to give a scary don't-mess-with-our-friend lecture?" Alden sounded both impressed and dubious.

"If he doesn't, maybe I should," Kellan mused. "I mean if you and Jock Neptune are—"

"No one is giving anyone else a lecture." I glared at Conrad, not really mad as much as frustrated. This was why I'd brought Milo in the first place. Being the single friend sucked. But my shoulders also sagged. I was setting myself up for a big disappointment if Milo wasn't as changed as I'd begun to hope.

"Okay, okay. Besides, he seems cool so far." As always, Kellan was quick to change directions. "The kids at the hospital love him. And look at him helping Professor Herrera, who usually doesn't let anyone help in the kitchen."

My gaze returned to the kitchen where Milo was grating a large block of cheese and laughing at something Professor Herrera said. Milo seemed totally at ease, perhaps even more so than I would be in there. I was always a little intimidated by Professor Herrera, who never had a hair out of place and who counted actual Broadway stars among his friends. My heart did this weird gallop watching Milo, remembering him talking about learning to cook and seeing him actually go for it, even if only to be helpful.

"And we found it!" Professor Tuttle came back in, followed by Jasmine and with two new decks for us to examine and talk about.

"Let's get the filming wrapped," Jasmine said as she moved to fiddle with the cameras, undoing Kellan's adjustments. The two of them had taken over a lot of the editing from me, and their little squabbles over minute differences were fun when they weren't making me feel even more conspicuously single. "I've smelled what they're doing in the kitchen. I want to enjoy it sometime before midnight."

"We will." Professor Tuttle settled into his spot in front of the

camera, but he was careful to finish up right as Professor
Herrera came to tell us that the food was going to get cold.
He helped Professor Tuttle up and already had a plate
waiting for him at the kitchen table. The two of them were
legit relationship goals, not unlike my parents. I wanted
someone to take care of like that, someone to—

"Snagged you the last Mountain Dew." Looking
adorable in one of Professor Herrera's aprons, Milo handed
me a can. "And here's a plate."

"Sorry if the filming took too long." I put my soda at
the table and joined the line for food.

"It didn't. And now I know a bunch of new tricks."
Milo's smile was so bashful and genuine that he was damn
lucky that I didn't kiss him right there, especially when
Kellan wrapped Jasmine up in a hug, lifting her off the
ground. And Conrad was having some sort of conversation
with his eyes with Alden, one that made Alden blush. Bah.
At least I got to soak in Milo's cuteness instead of drowning
in the sea of the happily coupled.

Eventually we all filled our plates for our late-night feast
and found places to sit. I ended up at the table next to Milo
and near Professor Herrera. None of us ever drank before
gaming, but now that filming was done, Conrad and Kellan
had beers with their food. Milo, however, stuck to soda,
whether in solidarity with me or as part of his newfound
resolution I wasn't sure, but I appreciated it.

"Thanks for loaning me your friend," Professor Herrera
said. "He's a fast study."

"Hey, I thought I was your favorite helper." Kellan faked being wounded, undoubtedly because Professor Herrera was one of his advisers.

"Was that you grating two pounds of cheese?" Professor Herrera laughed. "Now, everyone eat up. I don't want leftovers."

Milo pulled his chair closer to me, explaining which parts of the various dishes he'd helped with, and I again resisted the urge to touch him because his enthusiasm was so infectious. I liked how everyone tried to include Milo as we talked—Professor Tuttle getting him talking about classic cars while Kellan involved him in a discussion about the upcoming revue. I waited until Professor Herrera returned to the kitchen to ask Conrad what I'd been trying to get at all evening.

"So tell us, oh Great Odyssey Employee, do you have any inside scoop on getting the Royal Frog Court rares?"

"There seriously isn't a vault of rares or something we get to raid on our lunch hour. I know some of my coworkers who are collectors, too, and they still have to navigate the secondary market, same as everyone else. But I put out some feelers. I know some people now."

"We know," Kellan and I groaned simultaneously.

"I heard George, the jerk who Arthur banned, bragging that he got hold of a set," Jasmine shared. Next to me, Milo stiffened, and I tapped his foot with mine, trying to let him know that I hadn't told and wasn't going to break his trust like that.

"There's no way to guarantee George's cards are legit." Kellan stretched, eyes pinched together, a rare sign of irritation from him. "He'd probably part with them, though. For a price."

"And no one wants to pay his prices." Conrad sounded like he knew a thing or two about George's tactics.

"Is this George criminal or merely underhanded?" Professor Tuttle stroked his chin. I hadn't meant to include him in this conversation, and the last thing I needed was him thinking we needed law enforcement or something.

"A scuzzbucket, but he's careful to walk the line," Jasmine answered for me. "I definitely wouldn't do something stupid like try to play George for the cards."

I had been considering doing exactly that all week. I had something he might covet—my ticket for the Odyssey launch party next month, and I also knew I had the skill to at least have a chance of beating him. But Milo tapped my foot hard as he frowned. He wouldn't be down with that idea, but I wasn't completely discounting it yet either. I liked the idea of the big rescue, probably more than I should have, but Milo kept making me want to save his day.

"Why play George when you can hunt treasure?" Conrad leaned forward. "One of the people I know at the office told me about these secret treasure hunts. Like geocaching or letterboxing puzzle hunts where you can find rare items as the prize. She thinks there might be one around here with one of the Royal Frog Court cards as the lure. She gave me some top-secret links."

"An old-fashioned treasure hunt." Professor Tuttle rubbed his hands together. "I approve."

"Have you ever seen one of those cards?" I asked him.

"The queen, once. Had a chance to win her, but I was

outwitted. Later, I thought about acquiring a set for display here, but I ended up getting us some better cameras and microphones instead."

"And an air fryer," Professor Herrera added mildly as he handed out cookies. "I've heard about some secret treasure hunts around the campus too. There was one with Broadway tickets."

"Exactly. I've been doing some investigating with these links and I think it may be legit." Conrad leaned forward. "Of course, with all these things, the rule is that if you take something, you have to leave something of value behind."

"I've got that other rare I won at the tournament in Philly. We can use that as the trade."

"That would be awesome. When can we try?" Milo's eyes were big, and the hope there made me ready to agree to anything—even setting my alarm.

"I work tomorrow afternoon, but maybe we could try in the morning."

"I'll bring the doughnuts." Milo's big smile was worth any lack of sleep.

"As long as it's not the crack of dawn, you can call us if you're stumped about campus clues." Conrad leaned closer to Alden, who nodded.

"And me." Professor Tuttle yawned. "And I'll make some inquiries as well. I may not know as many people as Conrad these days, but I'll see what I can turn up."

"Thank you, sir." Milo nodded at him.

"And on that note, I think it's getting late." Professor Herrera started clearing plates from the table. "The professor needs his beauty rest."

"Oh, hush. Once upon a time, I could greet dawn after a night of cards." Professor Tuttle smiled fondly.

"We'll help clean." The six of us managed to get dishes done and camera equipment stored in short order. As soon as we were outside on the sidewalk, Milo pulled out his phone.

"Sorry. My phone was blowing up in there. Wouldn't stop vibrating. I better make sure it's not my mom." He clicked it on and then groaned, breath hanging in the chilly evening air. "Oh, F my life."

"What?" I touched his arm, finally getting the contact I'd been craving for hours, but his thundercloud expression had my back tightening.

"James and Luther are having a party. Again. Damn it. I don't want to go home and deal with that crap. And there goes any chance of sleep before our early start tomorrow."

Finally, an easy problem I could solve. "So don't."

"Don't what? Get an early start? I'll be fine. Extra coffee or whatever. Just wish my stupid door locked."

"You don't need to deal with all that. Come back with me." My heart battered against my rib cage, like hurricane-strength winds sweeping through me, equal parts terror and anticipation as I waited for his answer.

CHAPTER TWENTY
MILO

JASPER WANTED ME TO COME back with him, and I had to pause so that I didn't echo the solid "Hell yes" my body was giving to that idea. Too eager wouldn't be cool, so I took a breath.

But before I could speak, Jasper added, "Not for *that*. I wouldn't want you to feel pressured…"

"I don't," I said a little too quickly. If anything, I was now worried about being the one doing the pressuring. "And I don't want to put you out. I can deal with my stupid roommates."

"You're not putting me out. I have one of those chairs that unfolds into a spare bed. I slept there last time Kellan and Jasmine had a fight. It's not bad." Jasper's voice was as quick as his strides on the way back to the car.

"Okay." So much for my idea of going somewhere and parking. Screw James and Luther. There was now a very weird vibe between Jasper and me after such a nice, cozy evening where it had felt like we were dancing toward…*something*, and I had no idea how to fix things.

Jasper drove the short distance back to the university, parking in the same lot where I'd dropped him off last time. The campus was cold and quiet, Saturday night fun all probably happening off campus. Like at James and Luther's place. I barely avoided growling out loud at the thought.

"Am I going to get you in trouble with dorm rules?" I asked as he found a parking spot.

"No. This is the oldest of the upper-class dorms. I think sometimes the college forgets that they haven't demolished the building yet. And there's an RA, but he's cool. No sign-in sheets or anything like how the freshman dorms have."

"Cool." Needing to feel useful, I grabbed one of Jasper's deck bags once we were out of the car. "Lead the way."

"Heck. I forgot to tell you." Stopping short of the door, he glanced down at my leg. "No elevator. This building is *old*."

"I'll be fine." Four flights of stairs later, I was less sure, but no way was I going to complain about pain now.

Jasper's room was on the top floor, at the end of a narrow hallway that snaked its way around, vintage wall sconces and dark colors making me feel like we were in some old and musty castle. The lock, however, was the newer kind and Jasper used his key card to let us in to a little room. It wasn't that much bigger than mine, but size was the only similarity. Color was everywhere—bedding advertising a popular movie franchise, a mountain of pillows, an overflowing bookcase, and tons of posters for *Odyssey* and other games and movies.

"No comments on my superhero bedding." His laugh lacked some of his usual certainty.

"Nah. I dig it. I was going to say that your room is way neater than I expected." I toed my shoes off, leaving them next to his by the door. I liked how they looked lined up together.

"Tell that to my mom." A pink stain spread up his neck. "And...uh...I might have cleaned up some this morning."

"You were planning?" Maybe there was hope for more kissing after all.

"Not *planning*. But I figured I'd show you the place at some point." Jasper shrugged, his deliberately casual tone as hard to read as his flushed face. Giving up on trying to figure him out, I returned to studying the space, gaze landing on one of the many pieces of paper on the giant corkboard over his desk.

"You kept my Neptune drawing?"

"Well, duh. It's *good*. It might be a collector's item someday."

"Thanks." The amount of faith he had in my talent was almost enough to make me think something could actually come of my doodling. I pulled my mini sketchbook out of my coat pocket. "You...uh...want to see what I was working on while I waited for you?"

"Of course. And give me your coat." Jasper threw both our coats on his desk chair while I found the right page. Returning to my side, he peered over my shoulder. "It's the Frog Wizard! In a tux with tails?"

"I was thinking about the costume ball," I admitted. I'd drawn the wizard with the mask on and amphibian features. No way was I ready for Jasper to see how I drew *him*. "I figured he'd wear one of those old-fashioned tuxedos, like on the *Titanic* or something. Definitely the tails and a bow tie."

"Hmm. Maybe Kellan can rig me a tie for the occasion. Can I show him the drawing? Please?"

"Yeah." So far, Jasper's crowd seemed far cooler than mine. Kellan was kind of a big teddy bear of a guy, Jasmine was sweet, and Conrad and Alden were nice if a little protective of Jasper. And the two professors were like the sort of grandpas everyone would love to have—lots of food, funny stories, and genuine support. They made me miss my dad, or rather the dad I wished he'd been more often.

"You're so good at this." For a second, Jasper rested his hand on my back, head falling to my shoulder, but then he seemed to remember himself and straightened. "Sorry."

"Don't be," I said softly.

"Anyway, it's late." His voice was too bright and too fast. "And I'm going to take the chair bed thing because of your leg—"

"Which is fine. Not hurting," I lied.

"I'm also shorter than you and it's kind of narrow. Like a kindergarten nap mat, really."

"Then—"

"I insist." He steered me toward the bed, then dropped his hands all fast again.

"Jasper?" I turned to face him. This weirdness had to end.

"Yeah?"

"Do you *want* the chair bed?"

"Yeah, of course. I've slept there before." More of that fake cheer, and I wasn't ruling out the possibility of needing to shake him.

"Sure. But do you *want* that? Because I'd be cool with sharing." My gaze was stapled to his mouth and *cool* was a vast, vast understatement.

"Oh. Uh. I'm trying really hard here to be a good guy." Swallowing audibly, he glanced away.

"You are a good guy." I rested my hands lightly on his shoulders. "And I get that you're working overtime on the whole consent-is-sexy thing and to make sure I don't feel pressured just because I need a place to crash, but..." Licking my lips, I let my voice trail off as my courage started to ebb.

"But?" The hopeful curiosity in his voice functioned like a shot of bravery to my soul, made me pull him closer.

"But." Dipping my head, I brushed my lips over his. "You promised me more kissing practice. And I waited twenty-two years to kiss you the first time. I'd rather not miss another opportunity."

"You make it hard to do the right thing," he whispered, face still close enough for me to feel his breath.

"Maybe stop trying. Maybe do what you *want* instead of what you think you should."

"I'm more concerned about *you* and what you truly want. And need. But this..." He ghosted a kiss across my mouth. "This is what you want?"

Everything. I want everything. Unable to speak, I could only nod. And then he was leaning in again, mouth finding mine, and it was sweet and soft and perfect. His hesitance was still there, and in a way it contributed to the perfection. No one had ever treated me so carefully, so gently, and the pressure in my chest grew with every pass of his lips. I seriously didn't know how to process this level of tenderness, but all I knew was that I wanted more. All of it. I wanted everything.

This time when he pulled back, questions still in his eyes, I chased after him, claiming another kiss before I found my words. "You *are* a good guy, you know? The best guy. And even good guys get to have fun sometimes. If you want that, I mean..." I let my voice trail off, suddenly unsure again.

"I want *you*." He squeezed my upper arms. "No question there. But—"

"No but." I was practically levitating at his admission, mood soaring. He wanted me. Everything else could figure itself out. "I want you too. And you make me want to be a better person. More like you. And that has to count for something, right?"

"It does." He gave me another soft kiss, this one lingering, evolving into a deeper exploration as our tongues tangled. We shuffled closer to the bed, and my sketchbook hit the floor. I'd never wanted anything this badly in my whole life. Not making varsity soccer, not winning my athletic scholarship, nothing compared to how much I wanted him. He swept his hands up and down my back, and I stretched into the contact, preening like a cat and no longer caring about playing it cool.

"Milo?" Jasper's voice was all husky and low and made heat unfurl low in my gut. "I really don't want the chair bed."

"Good." I interrupted him with another pass of my mouth, putting all the warmth flowing through me into the kiss.

"Wow. You make me feel like I chugged a two-liter of soda."

My head tilted as I considered him. "Like you might puke or like you might never sleep again?"

"Definitely not puking." He laughed and tugged me the rest of the way to the bed. "More like my heart won't stop racing."

"Mine either," I admitted as I sat next to him on the edge of the bed. "But, like, I'm the one who *should* be worried. You've done this before."

"Not with you." His eyes were so serious that my nervous laugh died in my throat. Instead, all I could do was press another kiss to his mouth and hope he understood how much his words meant to me. How much *he* meant. And maybe he got the message because he kissed me back with an urgency that hadn't been there before. Eventually we tumbled backward. Between the sheer number of pillows and the narrow width of the bed, there wasn't a ton of room, and he ended up half on top of me.

"This okay?"

"Uh-huh." In fact, if it got any more okay, I might seriously expire of happiness, but I couldn't find all those words and simply kissed him instead. He used his tongue again, which let me do my new favorite thing on earth and mimic him. Every time his tongue brushed mine, my body surged like I'd scored on a penalty kick, crowd roaring, adrenaline spiking.

I'd waited for this. For him. Even if I hadn't quite known why, I'd waited. I'd denied myself this because deep down I didn't think I deserved it, but when Jasper kissed me like this, I felt...worthy. Like this whole trying-to-be-a-better-person thing mattered and like it might truly be possible. Because anything that felt this good had to mean that I was doing something right.

He kissed my jaw and my ears and my neck, and I did the same for him until we were both breathless and moving together, him pressed tightly against me now.

"I want to touch you." He rested his hand on my chest, right over my pounding heart. "Can I touch you?"

"Uh-huh. Whatever you want." And I meant it. I had no agenda of my own other than to be what he wanted, what he *needed*.

However, this was Jasper, and he didn't take, even though I offered. His generous nature probably had no clue about how to be selfish. Instead, he *gave*. More kisses, now accompanied by touches which were at first gentle and barely there grazes of his fingertips and then bolder. Pausing to meet my gaze, he waited for me to nod before snaking a hand under my sweatshirt and past my T-shirt to find bare skin.

I groaned. Or maybe he did. I was losing track.

"I want to do it too," I whispered.

"Oh, yeah." He sat up enough to pull his hoodie off, and I took the hint and did the same. *Game on.* My body hummed, that rush of adrenaline back a thousandfold when our bare torsos connected. We kissed and touched and explored, and not even the roar of a packed stadium could compete with how good he made me feel. His little groans and gasps were the best reward ever, making me feel both deeply connected, rooted to this place and time, and weirdly restless.

"Want…" I wasn't sure precisely what, only that I *needed* in a way that I'd never needed before.

"Yes." He didn't seem to be in the same hurry as me, giving me another leisurely kiss.

"Help me out here," I groaned when he let me up for air. "This is the part where I don't know what comes next."

"You, hopefully." His grin was downright wicked, and I loved that he could somehow still tease while we were both so wound up.

"You first." Now I knew exactly what I wanted. Sure, I wanted pleasure for myself, but more so for him. I wanted to see, to touch, to experience, and I wanted all of it for him.

"This?" He skated a hand across my waistband, then over my straining zipper.

"Uh-huh." I repeated the gesture to him, loving how it made him groan low and soft. Our slower pace evaporated in a cloud of *good* and *better* and *best* sensations piling on each other as we explored and touched. Faster kisses now. More urgent hands. We shimmied out of our jeans, some silent agreement driving us on. Suggestions, then requests, then demands were whispered between us. He touched me and I touched him, and somewhere in between endless kisses, I discovered that I did know what to do after all.

"Need…" he panted against my lips.

"Anything." Joy coursed through me because this I could give him, this I could do and apparently do well enough to have him groaning, eyes fluttering shut. Watching his face was like reading cue cards, learning what worked and getting instantly rewarded for my efforts.

"It's too good."

"No such thing." I managed a laugh that ended on a moan as he did something new with his thumb.

"Gonna…"

"Me too." My whole body shuddered as he claimed my mouth for another kiss, this one desperate and seeking.

"*Yes.*" Our groans mingled as our bodies tensed. The whole world burned bright, everything illuminated but also every detail reduced to simply this moment, this beautiful, bright second when together we were more than I'd ever been alone.

"Milo." Eyes blinking open but still breathing hard, Jasper touched my face almost as if he were seeing it for the first time.

"I'm here." My ability to make sense, however, was not. But what I wanted to say was that this was real, not imagination, and the fact that I was *here* seemed to be the single most startling thing in my whole life.

"We're kind of a mess." He gave a shaky laugh.

"Luckily, you like mess." My grin was probably rather dorky, but I was too happy to care. "And it's mainly on us, not your bedding or your nine hundred pillows."

"Hey, don't knock my pillows." Still laughing, Jasper stretched, managing to retrieve a towel from his dresser without leaving the bed. "I like studying in bed. They keep me comfy."

"Yeah, well, you have me to cuddle with tonight." I accepted the towel and followed his lead in cleaning up. "Maybe a few of your stuffed friends could hang out on the chair you're not going to be using."

"Okay, okay." Jasper tossed two at the chair in the corner, then I did the same, and then we both collapsed in a fit of laughter because it was like a very silly, very naked pillow fight. I took advantage of having a little more room in the bed to tickle him lightly until he was back on top of me, pinning my hands down.

"You're mean." He chuckled and his eyes danced, but my chest tightened.

"No, I'm not. Not anymore. I don't want to be mean ever again."

His expression sobered before he brushed a soft kiss over my mouth. "I believe you. Even though I probably shouldn't. But I want to believe that you've changed."

"I have. I am. Feels like one of those videos where they go from black and white to color to make a point. Like...the old me didn't even have a clue as to how much he was missing, not really. But now I've seen what could be possible, and there's no way I want to go back to a grayscale life."

"It's not going to be easy."

"Nothing worth having ever is." I echoed one of Bruno's favorite sayings as my pulse sped up again. Jasper was right. This wasn't going to be simple. Or easy. I could still end up screwed. And I still had to deal with all the dumb stuff the old me had done. Wanting to change didn't mean I was going to be able to leave any of that behind. All I could do was hope my past wouldn't steal my present before I had a chance to enjoy it. But there was also no way I wasn't going to take this chance. And if I gambled big enough, maybe my future would actually be worth having.

CHAPTER TWENTY-ONE
JASPER

"I COULD GET USED TO you being my alarm clock." I blinked over my shoulder at Milo. My actual alarm had gone off, too, but Milo's soft kisses were far more welcome than any chime. We'd fooled around again before sleep, and never had I been so grateful for my attached postage-stamp-sized ancient bathroom. Senior perks and all that. And judging by Milo's smirk, we'd be needing my pitiful supply of hot water again. Soon.

He dropped another kiss on my bare shoulder. "It's a hard job, but someone has to do it."

"Well, something's hard…" I snuggled into him. We really should have slept in clothes in case of something like a dorm-wide fire drill, but Milo was a freaking furnace and I'd barely needed a blanket. Bliss.

"Dork. Should we get up?" He didn't seem in any particular hurry, stroking his big palm down my torso, but his voice was also far too alert for the early hour. I hadn't been up this early on a Sunday in a couple of years.

"You totally grew up and became an annoying morning person, didn't you?"

"Eh. I'm a work-whatever-shift-they-give-me person and a hope-insomnia-finds-someone-else-to-bug-soon person. But I don't hate mornings." Milo got a little bolder with his explorations, hand dipping lower. "Especially like this."

"This is good." I made a noise that was somewhere between a squeak and a groan as he pulled me closer.

"We're not getting up right now, are we?" He was still chuckling as his mouth found mine for a lengthy kiss.

"Probably not." I rolled so that we were face-to-face, me mostly on top of him. I loved how easily he went to his back. He might be bigger, but he had no issues letting me take charge, which was sexy as hell. "Complaining?"

"Never." Stretching, he wiggled so he was more directly under me, our torsos aligned, and electricity sparking everywhere our skin touched. "After all, I'm the one who has a lot of lost time to make up for."

He laughed, but his words pricked against my otherwise happy bubble. I hated that I cared, hated that it bugged me that I was strung out on hoping he was changing while maybe he was just looking to get lucky for the first time.

"Is that what this is?" I meant to try for casual, but my voice came out too sharp. *Damn it.* "Trying things you missed out on?"

"No." Eyes solemn, he reached up to kiss the tip of my nose. "I didn't mean the still-a-virgin sex thing. I meant lost time with you, specifically. Missing out on that."

And just like that, my happiness bubble repaired itself. He was getting damn good at saying exactly what I needed to hear.

"You really missed me?"

"Yeah," he said softly, stretching for another kiss, and this time I met his questing lips. There was something magic in how a single kiss could make me all warm and light. "And maybe I didn't even realize how much until I saw you again. Like, really *saw* you."

"I am cute." I had to joke or else the rising tide of emotions was going to pull me under. Sweet Milo might be even harder to handle than Sad Milo.

"And smart. And a good guy. A really, really good guy." Milo punctuated each of his comments with another kiss.

"Even though I didn't sleep on the chair?"

"Especially since you didn't sleep on the chair."

And then as simple as that we were back to kissing, more purposeful now, until we were both breathless and definitely, positively not leaving bed anytime soon.

"*Jasper.*" Milo breathed my name like I truly was the answer he'd been seeking. And his eyes were glassy, but when his gaze met mine, I felt *seen* in a way I wasn't sure I'd ever been before. Maybe there was something to what he'd said about seeing me for the first time because I certainly felt like I was seeing him in a whole new light these days too.

Inspired by his comment on missing out on things, I slithered down his delicious body. He hadn't been lying about the tattoo—it was a tiny one, an Italian flag, right above his hip bone. *Lost a dare*, he'd said. *Sexy*, I'd said, right before I'd kissed it. I did it again.

"What are you..." He half chuckled and half groaned

as I painted his torso with kisses, inching lower. Finally reaching my destination, I took him in my mouth, teasing and showing off my collection of tricks.

"Oh...do that again. You're...incredible. *That*." I loved how damn responsive and appreciative he was. In fact, while I'd done this before, I'd never done it with someone so unabashedly grateful.

"Like that?" I asked before redoubling my efforts.

"Yes. Please... So good... That's...it. Please." A steady stream of wonder and praise escaped Milo's lips before he buried his face in one of my pillows to muffle his moans. Being able to coax that sort of response from him was my new favorite thing, and more than enough to have me tumbling over the edge with him a few moments later. I rested my head on his firm stomach for several long minutes, luxuriating in the way he idly stroked my hair as we both worked to reclaim our breaths.

"Okay. Wow. That was..." Milo gave me a dopey grin. "Are you gonna chuck a pillow at me if I say I'm not sure how I lived without experiencing that?"

"I am pretty good." I pretended to gloat as I finally left bed to search out another towel and some clothes. "Was it worth skipping coffee?"

"Oh, we're not skipping coffee. I owe you a doughnut. You pull up the GPS app and start deciphering clues, and I'll worry about food for us." Milo sat up in the bed, covers pooling in his lap. And damn, I could write an ode to his broad, sculpted chest that would make my English lit professor impressed.

"I'll walk with you. No sense in you doing the stairs twice." I sped up getting dressed as Milo climbed out of bed.

"Quit worrying about my leg."

"Can't help it. I inherited my mom's genes. It's what I do. I worry over all my friends." Now that I didn't have Milo warming me up, I shivered in the chilly air as I yanked on a shirt. I needed spring to hurry up.

"Well, if it means I'm a friend…" Milo paused as he pulled up his jeans.

"A friend who looks damn good naked." I couldn't help the leer because he really did.

Milo's laugh was deep and musical. "We better find that coffee before you tempt me into saying screw this hunt."

"There's another joke there…"

"Behave." He gently walloped me with his sweatshirt before putting it on. "Doughnuts. Now."

"Okay, okay." I grabbed my stuff and led the way back downstairs, slowing my pace for Milo. "And I'm freezing, so we'll take the car."

"All right." Milo grimaced and I couldn't tell whether it was leg pain or frustration with my thinly veiled attempt to spare him the long walk to the doughnut place.

But my plan didn't entirely work because I couldn't find parking near Lee's Bakery. Milo ended up hopping out to wait in line while I circled the block. When I returned, he had a white box and two steaming cups.

"Yours is hot chocolate. No soda before noon." Laughing, he settled back in the passenger seat. "And I got you your favorite again, so try not to die of chocolate overload."

"I'll try." I ended up driving us back to campus and parking in the lot near the library so we could enjoy the food.

"Now tell me how this works, anyway," Milo said as he grabbed a second doughnut.

"So, like the public geocaching sites, you're hunting hiding spots. These are even more secretive, with hidden lairs that you have to decipher clues to find, and themed caches. This site is all devoted to *Odyssey*, so if we can follow the clues, then there might, *might* be a card we can trade for inside. I've got the rare I won, plus two other ultra rares to try to equal the value."

Milo frowned at that. "I don't want you to have to use your personal stash of cards."

"Eh. I found these the old-fashioned way, cracking packs." Shrugging, I looked away. Honestly, I'd gone from resentful that Milo needed my help to being rather invested in his quest. I wanted him happy and wanted him to have a chance to redeem himself with Bruno. And helping him, having what he needed, made me feel twenty feet tall. "I got super lucky with finding the cards, but I haven't found the right deck for them yet. I don't mind using them to help you."

"Well, I appreciate it." Milo glanced around the parking lot before giving me a fast kiss on the cheek.

"Thanks." My skin heated as I pulled out my phone and navigated to the site I'd bookmarked. "Let's look at the first clue."

Milo quirked his lips as he looked down at my phone with me. "It's a lineup of *Odyssey* cards?"

"Yeah, but it's a puzzle. Why these cards? Why this order?" Thinking hard, I tapped my fingers against my thigh, mulling over possibilities.

"Is this where we call your friends?"

"Chill. Let me think." I could have called someone, of course, but I desperately wanted to solve the puzzle myself, wanted to be that kind of hero for Milo.

"Does it maybe have to do with the drawings?" Milo pulled out his sketchbook. "Like, they each have a human character in the foreground and a different building in the background."

"I love it when you talk art to me," I quipped as I helped him run through possibilities. Names of buildings in the pictures. What they represented. First letters. Our food was long finished, and the air in the car was frosty, but nothing was triggering a clue worth heading out into the cold for.

"Maybe we're overthinking it." Setting his pencil aside, Milo frowned. "I mean, they are all brick buildings. Not that we've got any shortage of those here—"

"*Brick*. Of course." Grinning broadly, I all but crowed as I opened the car door. "The Brick family donated an obscene amount of money for the Brick Science Hall, like, a century ago. Now, why four cards?"

"Are there four floors?" he asked as he followed me out of the car.

"Are we sure I'm the genius one in this operation?" I matched my strides to his as we made our way past the library to the old science hall. "Let's head to the fourth floor. And Boy Wonder, how about you figure out why it's those four characters."

We took a creaky elevator up to the fourth floor while debating what the characters represented on the card could mean.

"An archer, a gravedigger, some sort of chicken farmer, and a goth-looking chick walk into a bar..." Milo cracked.

"The farmer is raising a falcon army. And she's a reaper," I corrected automatically as I racked my brain, trying to make sense of the clues. "Which is sort of like an angel of death in the game."

"Well, there's enough dead creatures up here." Milo gestured at the glass cases of taxidermy creatures lining the wide hall.

Thinking of the gravedigger part of the clue, I crouched low to the floor, looking under the cases. "Perfect starting point. Look for a little hidden cache that will have our next clue."

"Like a falcon?" Coming to a stop in front of a case with a large black bird in it, Milo joined me in stooping low. The displays were creepy, and I wanted to find our clue fast.

"There." I ran my hand along a decorative arrow on the front of the case, and right below it, on the underside of the case, I found a tiny box that held a code to type into the app.

"Oh, hell, this clue is all math." Peering over my shoulder at my phone, Milo frowned.

"I have you." Finally, a chance to look smart. "It's a recursive function. Professor Tuttle teaches a whole honors seminar on them. And he's well known as an *Odyssey* player all over campus, thanks to the vlog. I bet the clue has something to do with him. Maybe we should walk toward the math building while I try to figure out the problem part."

"You do that." Milo's awed expression made me warm all over. I liked impressing him, probably more than I should have, both in bed and out, liked having skills he needed. Being the person to rescue him made me bound ahead toward the elevator until I remembered his leg and returned to his side.

"We make a good team." I switched my phone to my scientific calculator app as we exited the building.

"We really do. I can't believe we found that clue."

"We'll find the next one too," I promised as we huffed our way across the frigid campus. God, I hoped I wasn't about to let him down. I wanted Milo to have the cards, but more than that, I wanted Milo to have a reason to stay changed. Because I'd seen a glimmer of who he could be—the artist, the wannabe cook, the sensitive person who kissed me like his life depended on it—and I wanted that person to stick around. And somehow the cards seemed to be key. Now we both needed that clue. And fast.

CHAPTER TWENTY-TWO
MILO

JASPER MADE MATH SEXY. I liked how his tongue snaked out when he thought hard about something, liked how his long fingers flew over the screen of his phone, liked how he bounced on his feet as if his whole body were powering that beautiful brain of his. Heck, I even liked how he said big words like *recursive function* like they were nothing at all. The math building was like him—impressive and shiny with a wide, welcoming layout. It was a far cry from the ancient and stuffy science hall, and I enjoyed wandering around as Jasper wrestled with the math problem in the building's large atrium. After taking in various sculptures, I moved on to the line of bulletin boards near the hallway with faculty offices where Jasper stood.

"Maybe I could get down with math if it means scoring sweet deals like these." I gestured at the collection of homemade ads for everything from used laptops to bikes to rooms for rent. I stilled my fingers over a colorful piece of paper advertising a cheap room close to campus. "Join us!" it proclaimed, but it was the little rainbow in the corner that held my attention. It had a row of tags along the bottom with a name and phone number. The rent was slightly more than I paid James and Luther, but maybe...

Jasper glanced up from his phone. "Oh, that? It's not just a math major thing. There are flyers all over campus for people renting rooms to students."

"Students." I moved my hand away. Not for me, and I should have known better than to unleash my hopes, even a little. "Not like a college dropout working at the online packing facility."

"Wait." Stepping closer, Jasper put a hand on my arm. "You're thinking of moving?"

"Nah. It was just a thought. Probably not possible." I tried to keep my voice even, but somehow my resignation came out more. I couldn't seem to hide my deepest wishes and the worst of my truths from Jasper. "Most places want a credit check and have that have-you-ever-been-arrested question. Stupid of me to think—"

"No, no, it's a *good* thought." Jasper's tone was too bright, words coming too fast. However, his enthusiasm was cute, not fake. "And yeah, these sorts of deals tend to want students. But..." His tongue darted out again, as if he was back to doing hard math. "An aspiring art student with a steady part-time job at the packing place might work as well as a math major."

Oh. I exhaled hard because I'd never thought about being a student again. I'd assumed I'd lost my shot at college, hadn't dared let myself dream of anything else. Frankly, I hadn't thought I deserved it, but the light in Jasper's eyes and his voice made me want to dream again, made those hopes surge.

"I need to hire you to be my hype person." I laughed nervously. "You really think I could do something with art?"

"I know you could." Jasper squeezed my arm, his grip warm and steadying, even through my coat. "You've got a special talent. And even if it's classes at the community college or something like that, you should pursue it. And explore the housing situation."

"Maybe." It was almost too much to take, the sudden infusion of hope dizzying. And daunting. Jasper might be ready to dream big on my behalf, but I had reality tethering me in place. I might want, but could I truly outrun my past? I wasn't so sure. I looked away. "How's the math problem coming?"

"It's coming." Jasper apparently wasn't done helping, and he tore off one of the slips of paper and stuck it in my pocket before continuing. "There's not many places for something to hide here. I looked all around the doorframe for Professor Tuttle's office and his mailbox slot. I keep expecting one of the numbers here to line up with a room number, but so far no luck. Sorry."

"No worries." Now it was my turn to pat him. "You keep working. I'll go back to pacing—"

"Wait. Pacing." Jasper's eyes went big. "Milo, stand at Professor Tuttle's door and count out twenty-one paces to the south."

"Got it." That took me back into the atrium, but I stopped exactly on the twenty-first step and awaited further instructions from Jasper.

"Now fifteen paces east." Jasper clicked away on his phone.

I carefully pivoted and measured out the steps, landing in front of a sculpture that was probably supposed to represent some math process but it looked like endless spirals to me. "Now what?"

"We hope this thing isn't alarmed." Coming over to where I stood, Jasper laughed as he crouched down near the base, which had many legs like a spider. "And here's to hoping I don't topple it."

"You won't." If he could think I was capable of doing something with my art, the least I could do was believe he wouldn't bring this thing crashing down upon us.

"I love your faith in me." His smile was spring break in Florida warm.

"Always." I kept staring at him, willing him to believe, even after he went back to searching. His triumphant noise broke my concentration, though, and had me bending to join him.

"And here it is." He came up with another tiny box, which revealed a laminated scrap of paper. "Another clue to scan."

Pulling out his phone again, he came up with a new page, this one a picture that looked like an overhead shot of a play mat with all the *Odyssey* game pieces arranged on it.

"What's this one?" I asked. "A game board?"

"It's set up like it's midgame. That's the card library—"

"Library." I grinned at him and pointed out the windows across campus to the majestic library near where we'd parked.

"Okay, Boy Wonder, where are we headed when we

reach the library? It's huge, and I don't have much longer before I have to run you home and be at work." Frowning, Jasper tapped at the clock on his phone.

I studied the board more closely. "Apparently the depths of hell, if you go by the cards spread out."

Jasper pursed his mouth, eyes narrowing before they snapped open wide. "The lower levels. Basement it is."

Hurrying across campus, we didn't talk much, and I tried to ignore the cramping in my leg. The campus was pretty deserted as everyone was probably either huddled up studying or still sleeping off their Saturday night. I'd spent a lot of years around this place thanks to my mom's job, but unlike Jasper, I'd never imagined myself actually here as a student. However, as we passed the art building, I had a brief what-if moment as a pair of students exited the huge doors of the gleaming glass-and-steel building. Could I really go as far with my art as Jasper seemed to think? Maybe not here, but somewhere? It was like a peek at a future I wasn't sure I'd ever get.

Once in the library, we made our way through the stacks and study carrels down to the dusty lower levels, which got increasingly lonesome and musty-smelling with more cramped shelves and worse lighting.

"Damn. It's crowded down here." Jasper pulled his phone back out as we reached the lowest and darkest level. The shelves were tight enough that we had to walk single file until we reached a wider aisle. No other humans were in sight down here, which wasn't surprising as there weren't any study carrels or group rooms down here. "I don't even know where to start."

"Okay, so we're in the library, in the depths of hell, and if we follow *Odyssey* lore, what happens next?" Like him, I was a little overwhelmed at the sheer number of books because no way could we search even this one level before Jasper had to be at work.

"A reaper appears to guide us." Jasper laughed, then started pacing as he sobered. "More seriously, we use our scrolls to cast something and then move to attack."

"Did you say reaper? The angels of death, right? How about that?" I pointed at the farthest wall, which had a long, narrow painting above the shelves. It looked old, all muted colors, and a whole flock of angry-looking angels surrounding some sort of horned beast.

"Yes." Jasper made a happy noise that made my body remember exactly how much I'd loved everything we'd done the previous night and that morning. "You're brilliant."

He gave me a swift, hard kiss that had my skin heating even more. Maybe if we didn't find the cards, we could put our relative isolation down here to good use.

"Nah. You're the smart one." I followed him to the shelves directly below the painting. Remembering how he'd found the first two clues, I started by running my fingers under shelves. Jasper, however, hung back. His face wrinkled in that deep-thinking mode he had.

"Now, which of these books are about attacking?" Eyes narrowing, Jasper bounced on his heels before grinning. "Or scrolls. Look."

On the uppermost shelf, a series of particularly dated

books caught my eye, some sort of encyclopedia set about the Dead Sea scrolls.

"Scrolls!" I ran my fingers under the shelf that held the books, but I found only cold metal. Undaunted, Jasper examined each book. I caught on to the idea, and standing next to each other, we worked inward. I liked being a team together, liked figuring this stuff out with him, and even if we didn't find a card, this was still my favorite morning in a very long time. Leaning in, I brushed my lips over his temple.

Blushing, he turned toward me. "What was that for?"

"Nothing. Just...I'm happy. That's all."

"Good." Jasper snuck in another quick kiss. "You make me happy too."

My chest had maybe never been that full. I couldn't not kiss him in that moment, but when I went in for the kiss, he wasn't ready and I got a mouth full of hair. In trying to right himself, he bumped into the shelf and several books rained down on us.

I reached out to steady him, trying to shield him from the book tsunami. "Whoa."

Laughing, we kissed for real, then bent to retrieve the books and replace them on the shelves.

"Wait. Look behind." Jasper hopped up and down, but I was taller, allowing me to make the discovery that it wasn't a solid wall behind the books. My hands found a box that was lurking, tucked between the books and the wall. "Of course. Move the scrolls, reveal the bounty."

"This is too big to be another clue." I withdrew a flat wooden box with the *Odyssey* symbol etched on the front. My hands shook as I held it out to Jasper. We opened it together and peered in. Another card with a digital code on it was on top, then two random *Odyssey* cards that meant nothing to me but earned a whistle from Jasper. And then we gasped in unison.

"The queen." The card was encased in thick plastic, and Jasper trailed a finger down its front.

"*Yes.*" I pumped my fist before giving him a loud kiss on the cheek that resonated in the quiet. "We did it."

"We did." His smile could have powered the Empire State Building as he withdrew the card and handed it to me. He fished out the plastic-sleeved rares from his coat. "Now we update the digital log with what I'm leaving behind. I'll use a code name for us for our find."

"Dynamic duo?" I grinned at him because that was totally what we were. We were an excellent team.

"That works." Jasper clicked around on his phone for a few moments before we carefully replaced the hiding spot and headed out of the stacks. "Now let's get you and your prize back to your place."

"Our prize." No way was I taking all the credit when it had been both of us, working together.

"Okay." Jasper paused right by the elevators, turning back toward me. "Milo..."

"Yeah?" I wasn't sure I liked his cautious tone. Or his super-long pause, interrupted only by the ding of the elevator arriving.

"Nothing." He gave a weighty sigh that I liked even less than that pause. He hit the button, and we were on our way out of the library before he spoke again. "It's nothing. Really. Just that I hope you—we—find the other two cards. So that Bruno never has to know."

"Yeah," I agreed readily, trying to keep up with his fast pace toward the parking lot. And judging by Jasper's frown, that hadn't been the right answer. "Is that bad? I just don't want him to think I'm a screwup. Again."

"I know." Jasper voice was even, but his eyes were sad. "But... maybe all you can do is be you?"

Well, wasn't that the question of the week! And I had a flip answer ready, but the part of me that truly was trying to change, the part that felt safe and true around Jasper but no one else, that part let a whisper escape. "What if that's not enough?"

"It is. You are enough." Jasper's voice was firm as he squeezed both of my arms next to his car, looking deep into my eyes. For a second I thought he was going to kiss me, right there in the open, and shockingly, I was disappointed when he shook his head as he released me instead. "You don't believe me."

"I..." I couldn't lie. "I'm trying."

"Okay." Shoulders slumping, he nodded. "I'm going to be late if we don't hurry."

"I can do the bus—"

"On a Sunday? You'll be waiting an hour. No." Jasper gestured for me to get in the car. "We'll just hurry."

"My life is in your hands," I joked as we sped through town, but I meant it on multiple levels. What if I wasn't changing fast enough for him? What if he got tired of waiting for me to figure my shit out?

Before I could find anything resembling an answer, we arrived back at my place. And I'd had every intention of kissing him goodbye, but he was looking straight ahead, not at me. I glanced up at the apartment window and couldn't tell whether the curtain actually moved or not. *Crap*. My stomach cramped.

"You're going to be late," I said instead of kissing him, patting his leg like that might make up for my weak goodbye.

"Yeah." Jasper finally looked my direction, and when he did, his eyes were sad again. "Text me?"

"You know it." I smiled for him but wasn't surprised when he didn't return it. I slowly made my way up to the apartment where I discovered nine million beer bottles, a dozen empty pizza boxes, a weird stench, and Luther asleep on the couch, arm batting at the window. What the hell? I could have kissed Jasper after all. I was such an idiot.

"What happened here?" I put all my disgust at myself into my tone.

"Sorry." Luther blinked awake, shoving his dingy hair out of his face, and yanking his T-shirt down. "Must have fallen asleep out here."

"You reek, man." I was so not in the mood to sugarcoat it. "Good party?"

"I guess. James went home with someone." Luther managed to seem rather shocked that no one had chosen him and his three-day-old T-shirt to get lucky with.

"Good for him." The less we said about who went where last night the better, as far as I was concerned.

"Yeah. He better show back up by tomorrow, though. Job's sending our crew across town." Luther made a pained face. The two of them worked for a janitorial services company, managing to make more than me even as they complained bitterly about the work, which involved a lot of cleaning up after construction and renovation projects. "It's at the hospital. I better not get sick, all the viruses there."

"Dude. All the viruses *here*." I gestured at the filth before heading to the kitchen for some trash bags.

"Okay, point taken." Luther groaned and headed to the bathroom.

Even after I heard the shower click on, I couldn't shake my unease. I should have been happy. We'd scored one of the missing cards. But I could still see Jasper's sad eyes, the questions he hadn't asked, the kiss I hadn't given him. I tossed a few more beer cans before fingering the scrap of paper in my coat pocket with the information about that room for rent. I needed to get out of this place. And hell, what was that about James and Luther being assigned to a hospital? Was it the children's hospital?

Even if it was, no way could I bail on Jasper now, not after he'd done so much for me. I took some deep breaths. I could do this. I was a changed—*changing*—person. It would all work out. I had to believe that, had to ignore the wobble in my stomach. Jasper was counting on me, but maybe more important, *I* was counting on me.

CHAPTER TWENTY-THREE
JASPER

MY PHONE DINGED WITH A message as soon as I let myself into my room after work, and I didn't have to look to know who it was. *I miss your room.*

Because your roommates trashed your place? Jaw tight, I typed fast. I was still all kinds of mixed up where Milo was concerned, even more so after our awkward parting. I'd had that moment in the parking lot when I'd gazed deep into his eyes and I'd seen uncertainty. Like peering into a murky crystal ball and seeing the shadow of a guy who didn't quite believe he was worthy.

He might be trying to change, but he was also scared to death of the possible consequences of those changes. And that made it hard to trust that any changes he made would stick. Which Milo was he going to be long-term? My best friend or the guy who ghosted on me when I needed him? Frustrating as all of that was, however, he was also the guy who had held me all night long, the one who made treasure hunting fun, and the one I couldn't wait to see again. Not surprisingly, my heart still thumped when a reply came in.

Well, that and your room has *you*

So you miss me? I wasn't above making him say it, and I took way more satisfaction in the three dots that said he was replying than I should have.

So much. Is that cool to say? We left things kinda... He'd added an emoji of a guy with question marks over his head. *My fault?*

I exhaled hard and flopped onto my bed, coat and all. It was actually made, for once, Milo having somehow accomplished that even in the rush of getting dressed. It wasn't his fault that I'd had a minor freak-out at the realization that I might be heading for heartbreak with someone unable to give me what I needed. I'd been so happy to find the card, but resignation had come fast on the heels of the initial rush. If he couldn't tell Bruno that he'd messed up with the cards, was he ever going to come out to anyone else who mattered to him? It was one thing to sneak a few kisses in quiet spaces, and another to decide to live fully and openly. To be the sort of boyfriend I craved, the one I could trust with my heart.

We're cool. I lied because as much as I was twisted up over him, I also wasn't about to end this or to be the kind of guy who gave him an ultimatum simply because we'd shared some incredible hours together. My pillow still smelled like his shampoo, and my head danced with all the good moments of the last twenty-four hours. My gut might say we needed to have a serious talk, but my heart wanted to give him space to arrive at the same scary, wonderful place as me.

Good. His one-word reply would have further frustrated me, but he'd added an image. And my breath hung up on my rapidly expanding heart. It was *him*. Not a goofy selfie, but a cartoon-style drawing. Same sporty haircut, same winter coat, and a text bubble that said "I'm sorry."

Boom. Forget hoping I wasn't falling too hard for him. No, I was falling *soft*, landing in a vat of cotton candy, all sticky and sweet.

Thanks. Cute drawing. My heart wanted to say so much more, but my gut was still working itself out.

Milo's reply came fast. *I should have kissed you goodbye. Been thinking about that all afternoon. Another missed chance.*

Sad Milo was back, and he wormed his way past my pitiful attempts to protect myself. *There will be more chances.*

That earned me a happy-face emoji. *Soon?*

I laughed aloud to my empty room. It felt smaller and colder without him in it. *Wednesday after cosplay?*

I owe you pizza.

I replied with a smiley face of my own. *Wanna have it in my room?*

There was a longish pause, but the wait was worth it because cartoon Milo was back, this time with heart eyes. I touched my phone, like that might bring him here sooner.

It's a date. I started counting down the hours as soon as I sent the text, knew I'd be angling to see him even before that. I had it bad, and that was a huge problem. I should know better than to give Milo Lionetti extra chances, but here we were, and hell if I could pull back now.

―――――

"Looking good, Neptune." I gave Milo an exaggerated

once-over as I emerged from my stall in the men's room at the children's hospital Wednesday. He looked damn good in his toga, perhaps more so now that I knew exactly what he had under there. I could preach how superficial looks were all day long, but there was no denying Milo's attractiveness.

"That's Prince Neptune to you." He nodded, expression all haughty and regal. Last night, he'd drawn cartoon Milo in the toga, and his chin had exactly that same tilt.

"Oh, is that how you want to play this?" I gently poked him in the chest. We were alone in the restroom, and I'd missed him for three days now. I'd earned a little flirtation.

"Maybe." His mouth quirked like he knew exactly how my thoughts kept flitting to images of that toga on the floor.

"Remember that later." I made him silent promises with my eyes that I fully intended to make good on. Three days with a lot of texting and an hours-long phone conversation last night had done nothing to quash my desire for him. I needed a Milo fix and soon.

"Counting on it." His warm smile said that I wasn't the only one with a craving, and he stroked a broad finger down the side of my face before dropping his hand.

"Let's go find the others before I'm tempted to do something impulsive."

"Like this?" He stole my breath with a fast kiss. Sure, we were alone, but this was also a far cry from lost in the basement stacks in the library.

"Exactly like that." I beamed at him while contemplating the wisdom of yanking him back into a stall for a much more thorough kiss.

Undoubtedly reading my mind, Milo gave an exaggerated regretful sigh. "Better lead me to my kingdom."

"Dork." I bumped shoulders with him as we made our way out of the restroom and toward the waiting area where we were meeting everyone else as usual.

"You love it."

"Yeah." I did love this light and easy place we'd found ourselves, but the mere mention of the l-word had my muscles tensing. And I didn't have time to dwell on why that was, not with Kellan already coming over to greet us. He had a new costume, this one an elf druid. While I appreciated the artistry, he looked a bit like a hairy green beetle. I hid a smile by rearranging my bags.

"Hey, my dudes." Kellan had a big smile and hearty handshake for Milo, who had apparently earned his favor on Saturday night. "Tell me about the hunt."

"It was a success." Milo's unabashed happiness made my shoulders lift even before he added, "Jasper is brilliant."

"You weren't so bad yourself." My tone was way too fond, but I was too happy to keep it cool.

"You guys are ador—"

"Made it." April came rushing up, and all of a sudden, I cared way more about my tone. April and my mom didn't need to hear Milo and me being overly friendly or see Kellan teasing us about it.

"Okay, let's go." I hurried us along the corridor before any other banter could lead to uncomfortable questions and teasing. As it was, I felt my mom's eyes on the back of my head. I'd been avoiding her for days because I wasn't ready for a lecture but also didn't want to outright lie about how I was spending my time these days. I was an adult and I needed some space to sort out my own thoughts about Milo without her overprotiveness entering into an already complex equation.

"Hey, Jasper." Natalie, the attendant, welcomed us to the lounge as we got set up. I carried the deck bag to the back table, not terribly surprised when my mom followed me. I was asking her about her day while unzipping the bag when Milo came over, his mouth a thin white line.

"There's no Chase." His whisper was urgent and stricken. "Did he..."

"Let me find out." I patted his arm before I could think better of it, and I didn't miss my mom's raised eyebrow.

"Do you know what happened with Chase?" I asked Natalie, who was nearby, helping a little girl navigate with an IV on a pole. This wouldn't be the first time we'd lost a patient who was a regular. Loss was a part of this gig, and I remained profoundly grateful that April was still with us. I mentally crossed everything I had that Chase was okay.

"Discharged." Mercifully, Natalie had a wide smile for me. "He finished this latest course of treatment and was strong enough to send home."

"Thank goodness." I had to briefly shut my eyes against my sudden wave of emotions. I turned to return to Milo, but he was right behind me, eyes shining. *Damn.* He really did care.

"Do you have the drawing you did for them?" I asked him.

"Yeah." Glancing around, he withdrew a folder from his

backpack. His reluctance to hand it over to me was palpable, especially since we had more of an audience than I'd thought. Still, though, I couldn't resist opening the folder. The full drawing he'd done from his previous sketch was nothing short of stunning.

"Oh, let me see." Natalie peered over my arm, and my mom along with a few others had wandered over too. Milo was turning ten shades of pink with all the attention, but everyone was murmuring well-deserved praise for him. I wanted him to believe in his talent even half as much I did.

"That's so beautiful. Could you do one for us?" The mom of the girl with the IV had tears in her eyes. "I can pay."

"I don't need money," Milo said even though he probably did. He pulled out a bigger sketchbook than his usual pocket one and a case with some pencils. "I could work on it while she plays the game with someone, if that's okay?"

"Totally." My whole body buzzed with pride in Milo, warmth spreading outward from my chest.

"I can't wait." The mom followed Milo and the girl to a table with Kellan, who was already setting up for a game.

"Can you get this to Chase's family?" I asked my mom as I carefully put the drawing back in its folder.

"Yes, of course." She sounded distracted, and her gaze was locked on Milo who was deep in concentration, pencil flying over his sketchbook while the girl laughed at something Kellan said. "I had no idea he was that talented. His mother never mentioned it."

"She might not know." I said the words lightly,

without thinking, as per my usual, and it was no surprise when my mom's mouth pursed. She'd always been excellent at reading between the lines.

"Any other secrets he's hiding?" Her voice was as dry as August grass and about as much of a fire hazard.

"Uh..." I took far too long answering and could see the complicated calculations happening in her head.

"I see."

"The mom gossip network doesn't need more info for their alert." I tried to pass it off as a joke, but she didn't so much as smile.

"Jasper." The way she said my name all serious and slightly disappointed had me grabbing my cards in a hurry.

"I better find someone to play with."

"You do that. Someone *new*." She drummed her fingers against the folder. This wasn't going to be the last I heard about this topic for sure. She wanted to protect me from hurt, and hell, so did I. But I also wasn't turning down this reprieve from a lecture, and I quickly found a patient waiting for a game. I'd seen the boy here several weeks ago, and he was back for another round of treatments and tests. He gave me a good game, slapping down cards and doing an excellent job of keeping my mind off my mom.

"Look at all these happy faces." Ned from the hospital foundation came into the lounge right as I lost to the kid.

"How's it going?" I asked as Ned came over to my table.

"I've got tickets for you for Friday night." He took out a thick envelope and handed it to me. "Anyone need an extra ticket for a plus one?"

"Nah. I think we're good." That earned me a very pointed look from my mom, but whatever. There was only one person I wanted as a date, no matter how ill-advised that might be.

"We'll be there," Kellan added, looking up from his table as Milo and the girl also glanced our way.

"Good. We have some very big donors coming. It's going to be such fun! Can't wait to see all the funny costumes." Ned laughed, all jovial and friendly, but Milo's face turned stony at the remark. Discomfort radiated off him as he returned to his drawing.

Which turned out amazing, the little girl as a mighty superheroine, big cape and a sword and shield. But Milo still wasn't happy as he accepted the praise from the girl's mother and others nearby as we all got ready to go.

"He didn't mean funny like laugh-at-people funny," I said to Milo in a low voice as I packed up the decks.

"I know." Milo didn't sound too sure and didn't meet my eyes either. "Can I go ahead and get changed?"

"Sure. We still on for pizza?"

"You know it." He smiled but the rest of his expression stayed flat, no sparkle. "Think your mom will actually send the drawing to Chase?"

She and April were already gone because she needed to do a conference call before dinner.

"It'll probably be in the mail tomorrow. She always follows through."

"She doesn't like me." Milo stretched, rolling his

neck from side to side. I wanted to rub it, but the room was still half-full.

"She... It's complicated."

"I get it. I screwed up. I was terrible to you and a lot of other people in high school. Guess I can't outrun that." His shoulders slumped and he looked away.

"Yes, you can." I risked grabbing his shoulder anyway because I couldn't stand seeing him this down. "I believe a person can change. God knows I'm not the same person I was in high school either."

"I've noticed." He faked a heated look, but my ego knew the difference between false praise and the genuine desire he'd shown me this weekend.

"Good." I held on to his arm so that he couldn't ignore what I was saying. "But my point is, screw what other people think. Including my mom. Just keep proving them wrong. I believe in you."

"Thanks. You... That means everything."

"Everyone deserves a second chance." I hoped like hell that he didn't test that belief of mine. He met my gaze, expression deadly serious, almost as if he were starving for someone to believe in him, and there was nothing I wouldn't offer him in that moment, fresh chance to break my heart included.

CHAPTER TWENTY-FOUR
MILO

GOING OVER TO JASPER'S TO get ready for the ball was a mistake. Not because I wanted to back out of my commitment to go, but because a simple kiss hello turned into us tangled up on the bed, costumes entirely forgotten, clock ticking away as I reacquainted myself with his mouth. Grinding against my thigh, he stroked my face.

"You shaved."

I'd showered and shaved both, exactly like this was a hot date, which wasn't that far from the truth. "Neptune has to look his iconic best for his big night. I went to the barber too. My hair was getting shaggy."

"Ha." Stretching, Jasper dragged his own mop of curly hair against my neck. "Maybe I should cut mine too."

"Don't you dare." I chuckled wickedly, memories of what we'd done Wednesday hanging between us. "I like holding on to it."

"I noticed. Can we do that again now?" He plucked at my shirt buttons. "I can be fast. Bet I can make you fast too."

"You're rather confident." I shifted as my blood all rushed south.

Dropping a kiss on my collarbone, he skimmed a hand down my torso. "Hey, I know where my talents lie."

"Which would not include being on time." Reluctantly, I rolled away before his nimble fingers could reach my fly.

"Fine. Be the responsible adult," Jasper complained even as he too sat up.

"First time for everything." And speaking of first times, I had packed my bag as carefully as I'd showered. I couldn't wait for later.

My nerves were dancing even before Jasper winked at me. "We're coming back here afterward, right?"

"Better be." I pulled out my costume and finished the job Jasper had started on my buttons.

"Why do you have to torture me?" Jasper moaned as I put the shirt and my jeans on his chair. "It's like eating a double chocolate doughnut in front of me."

"Don't look at me like that," I warned. The appreciation in his eyes was a drug I couldn't get enough of.

"Or what? You'll drag me back to bed?" Even though he sounded hopeful, he went ahead and started getting his own costume ready.

"Dude. You did get a bow tie." I gestured at the fancy upgrades to his outfit.

"Kellan came through. New hose too." He preened as he adjusted his velvet breeches. Kellan had fashioned him a matching coat with long tails and a jaunty lavender bow tie.

"It's a mirror image of my drawing," I marveled, circling him.

"Kellan's good. But so are you. He loved your drawing. Expect him to ask you for one of him and Jasmine. Make him pay. No more freebies." He wagged a finger in my face. "Both of them have loaded parents."

"Feels weird drawing for other people, let alone taking their money." I scratched the back of my neck.

"Customers, Milo. They're called customers." He tugged his costume this way and that as he examined himself in the mirror on the back side of his closet door. "How many fifty-dollar drawings do you think it would take to cover your moving fees?"

"I shouldn't have told you that I called," I grumbled as he left the mirror to come and hug me from behind.

"Sure you should have."

I'd called on Thursday morning after a spectacular Wednesday evening of pizza and making out followed by returning to my cold and empty little room and having to listen to Luther and James argue over their game. I needed out of that place. So I'd called. And talked with a very nice graduate student in charge of finding a new roommate for a group house close to Professor Tuttle's place in the historic district. They weren't doing formal applications, but they did require an interview with the housemates and two references.

I didn't have the first idea of how to act at an interview with a bunch of über-geniuses. But at the same time, I kept seeing that rainbow on the flyer. I could have Jasper over and no one would likely care. I could put up my drawings, and maybe my bread and peanut butter would remain unstolen. I wanted that vision so much my muscles ached, but I wasn't sure how to get it.

"I have news on your housing quest too."

"Oh? Tell me you didn't meddle." I carefully added my coat over my toga. Didn't match the costume in the slightest, but it was too chilly outside to skip it.

"I didn't... Okay, okay. Not much. I saw Professor Herrera on campus today and asked him if he could say you're a cool guy who needs a chance and how you're learning how to cook for groups."

"That's definitely meddling." My heart thumped against my ribs. Jasper would take over this quest of mine if I wasn't careful, and I wasn't entirely sure how I felt about that. "What did he say?"

"Maybe. Said to bring you to another game night so he can talk to you more."

"Oh." That wasn't a no, but it did feel like I was on probation for a spot in Jasper's life and for earning a new start for myself. Interviewing for a room. Begging for a reference. Trying to prove to Jasper and others that I was truly changing. I wanted to earn it, though, no question.

"Come on, Neptune. We'd better not be late, especially since you made me skip more making out."

"I'm so cruel." I followed him to the door. "How about I drive, Speed Demon?"

"Not too nervous?" He raised an eyebrow even as he handed over his keys.

"Less nervous about my ability to go under the speed limit," I teased him, although my pulse still sped up at the thought of driving with passengers. "And besides, I wanted to offer because I heard Kellan say that this thing will have an open bar. If you want to drink something, I can drive back."

"Nah, if you're not drinking, I'll skip too. I'm more of a soda guy anyway."

"I know." I clicked his door shut behind us.

"Looking good, Jasper!" The second we stepped into the hall we encountered a group in the hallway playing some sort of board game and splitting a pizza. And maybe I was an idiot, but I hadn't been prepared for this, people seeing us leave his room together and seeing us in our costumes out of the context of the hospital or the ball.

"Thanks." As usual, Jasper didn't look disturbed at all. And he undoubtedly wasn't sharing my internal freak-out about what these people might have heard through thin walls. I shuffled my feet, fighting a churning stomach and the urge to flee.

"Need to get Prince Charming to the ball before midnight?" One of the girls laughed.

"Something like that." Jasper glanced at me and frowned. "Have fun, guys."

Heading to the stairs, Jasper walked quickly. "Sorry. Didn't know they were out there."

"It's okay." I knew better than to share my churning thoughts, but I had the feeling he'd picked up on my discomfort anyway because he was quiet on the way to the car and slumped in the passenger seat until I parked at the upscale hotel that was hosting the ball.

"My car makes the others look like they're slumming it tonight." Jasper laughed, but he was right—his beaten-up, dusty car was in between a BMW and a Lexus.

"Yeah," I said weakly. Maybe Jasper was slumming it too. I hadn't thought of it that way before, but it fit. Jasper went to a near-Ivy, had rich friends like Kellan and others, and had a stadium-lights bright future waiting for him. He wouldn't drive a crap car forever. He didn't belong with a guy with limited prospects like me. Now I was the quiet one as we made our way to the grand ballroom and checked our coats at the coat-check room.

"*Wow.*" Jasper inhaled sharply at the entrance to the ball. The place looked like a very upscale prom—lots of silver and gold decorations, multiple areas for taking pictures, tables for the silent auction items, a dance floor, sitting areas, and a fleet of waiters circulating with appetizers. Even the guests' costumes were classy—lots of flappers and 1930s-era suits and elaborate celebrity look-alikes. More women than men were in costume, with a lot of older men in classic suits and tuxes hanging out in clumps. They exuded a wealthy vibe, as if they were too important for costumes.

We'd been told by Ned's assistant that we'd be mainly working the photo areas, hanging out if people wanted pictures, encouraging people to check out the silent auction items. A couple of other charitable cosplay groups were also working the event. A number of Star Wars characters and popular superheroes were already hanging out near where people were snapping pictures. We met up with Kellan and the rest of the group, and I relaxed a little, feeling less like all eyeballs were on me.

The group was a little smaller than usual, a few people having had other obligations and April having not come because she'd had a low-grade fever Thursday and Jasper's mom was worried about potential germs at a gathering this size. I felt bad that she'd had to miss this as she probably would have appreciated all the fancy stuff more than I could.

"Oh, honey, come here. I want a picture with Toga Guy." A slightly tipsy woman a little younger than my mom in a silver dress dragged a guy in an elegant black tux over to where we stood. It took me a second to realize that I was Toga Guy. Jasper made a go-ahead motion, and I went to stand next to them by some columns and a gold backdrop.

"Of course you do," the guy groused. "Couldn't catch me dead wearing nothing but a sheet."

I opened my mouth, but no sound escaped my throat. I wanted to defend Kellan's handiwork because this costume was so much more than a *sheet* and I had not straightened all my various gold accessories for nothing. I wanted to make some quip like Jasper would about how I'd never owned sheets with a thread count this high or whatever. But I did what I always did when I felt uncomfortable or embarrassed: nothing.

I did, however, smile for Jasmine who took the picture with the woman's phone, an almost reflex on my part. *Smile. Don't let the discomfort show. Hope it would be over soon.* Which it was, and after they had wandered away, I returned to Jasper's side.

"You okay?" he asked.

I shrugged, knowing he'd see through a ready lie. "Guess not everyone likes costumes."

"Nope. But as long as they open their wallets for the cause, who cares?"

Me, apparently, but I wasn't admitting that. "But you like it. I still haven't exactly figured out what you like about dressing up so much."

My tone must have been a bit sharp because he frowned. "Haven't you ever wanted to be someone different?"

"Yeah." I bit my lip. Every damn day, honestly, although that burning, awful need to get out of my own skin was getting somewhat better the more time I spent with Jasper.

"Me too. And it's fun. An escape. A chance to be silly."

"I get it. I just wish others saw it that way and not as... embarrassing."

"Screw that." Jasper's frown deepened and his voice hardened. "Are you seriously going to live your life in fear that someone might laugh?"

"Uh..." I knew the right answer, but I also knew myself. It was hard. And I wasn't entirely sure we were still talking costumes.

"If you're continually afraid of being embarrassed, you're going to miss out on a lot of fun." Jasper shook his head as if he was already tired of me being such a drag. And before I could apologize, he added, "I'm thirsty. How about I get us some sodas?"

"Sure." I might be a disappointment to him, but at least I could be an agreeable disappointment. However, as he walked away, I couldn't help feeling like I'd screwed up. I wished there were a way to show Jasper that I might be slow but that I was trying to get better.

While Jasper waited in a long line at the bar, a few other people wanted pictures. However, in between photo taking, I took in the gathering, people-watching. At first I was looking for more people like the rude guy, people looking for a chance to laugh at us, but everyone seemed occupied with their own friend groups, too busy and happy to make fun of some college kids in wacky costumes. Shoulders unknotting, I started picking out costume ideas for my drawings. I liked the idea of doing more superhero drawings for kids at the hospital.

My gaze landed on the dance floor where a tall Superman was swaying along with a shorter Batman. They were only one of several couples dancing to a classic ballad, but they captivated me. Both men were probably in their late thirties or early forties, and the easy familiarity with which they danced spoke to a long relationship. And there they were, wearing tights and fake muscles and capes and laughing and moving together without a seeming care for what anyone else thought.

I want to be that brave. The thought slammed into me. And more than that, I wanted a love like that. Someone who knew how I danced and what I liked and what made me laugh. I glanced back at Jasper who was almost to the front of the drinks line. Maybe that wish wasn't as far out of reach as I thought. And maybe there was a way to show Jasper that I was working on the brave part. Maybe.

CHAPTER TWENTY-FIVE
JASPER

"DID YOU GET INTO TROUBLE without me?" I asked Milo as I handed him a soda in a clear plastic cup. I tried to keep my voice light, like we hadn't taken a left turn into Awkward Town ever since Milo had turned into a walking corpse when we'd run into the people at my dorm. Stiff. Pale. Monosyllabic. So much for progress.

"Nah. Stood for some more pictures. Thanks for the drink." Milo's tone was cautious, like he was trying to suss out if I was still irritated with him. Which I was, a little. But while in line, I'd resolved not to sulk all night.

"No problem." I gave him a smile, a real one because even uncomfortable, he was still who I wanted to spend my evening with. "I looked at some of the auction items on my way back, and the bids are high. They should raise a ton of money tonight."

"Good. I hope the foundation can help more families like yours." He sipped at the soda.

"Me too." Maybe small talk was the best we could do right then, but Milo seemed to be marginally loosening up. A pair of women in fairy costumes wanted pictures with us, and he even managed some jokes along with a grin for the camera.

As they left, he turned back to me. "I still might not entirely understand the cosplay thing, but even I can see the good your group does."

"Yeah? Not embarrassed to be seen with us?" Okay. Perhaps I wasn't entirely over my earlier funk.

"No. You guys are great." He gestured at Kellan and Jasmine and the others. "Good people. I like your friends."

"Thanks. I think they like you too." More like *I* liked him. Way more than I should. And with each picture he stood for, I liked him a little more, especially when he'd remind people to go bid high on the auction items. As the party progressed, the requests for pictures slowed, and we ended up standing near the back of the room, eating fancy food and watching people spin on the dance floor. A sappy song came on and more people headed to dance. There were several same-sex couples, including a Batman and Superman duo who were particularly good dancers.

Dynamic duo. That was what Milo had called us, but I knew in my gut that wouldn't be us. Milo? Making lovey-dovey eyes where other people could see? Not happening. Not to mention the chances of him wanting something permanent and public were next to nil. I exhaled hard, trying to keep my earlier resolution about not getting bent over things out of my control.

Right as I breathed out again, a hand brushed mine. Milo. But instead of flinching away, like I'd expected, he kept his hand there, against mine, fingers tracing my wrist and palm.

"What are you doing?" I whispered.

"I believe it's called holding hands." He laced our fingers together, squeezing my hand like we were alone in the car and not five feet from my friends who were not going to miss this development.

"It is." My heart clattered against my ribs, which were entirely insufficient to withstand this surge of emotion. "And I'm not complaining, but I feel honor bound to point out that we might be noticed."

"That's okay." The back of his neck was flushed as were his cheeks, but he didn't pull away even though I could feel the tension in his grip. "Maybe we should dance."

"Here? Now?"

"Well, maybe not this song. This song is pretty terrible. But your friends are dancing." He gestured at the dance floor where Kellan and Jasmine were swaying out of rhythm to a Disney love song. "We should too."

"That's going to be even more noticeable than holding hands. People are going to think we're together." I was starting to worry that I was having an out-of-body experience. Or maybe that Milo was.

"What was that you said earlier? Let them."

Yep. He'd definitely been kidnapped by aliens and this was his cry for help. And he might sound resolute, but he'd also turned pale and stiff again.

"You look like you just rode that roller coaster. You don't have to do this." I didn't drop his hand, but I did pitch my voice low and soothing as I loosened my fingers, so he'd know I wasn't tethering him to another uncomfortable situation. But to my surprise, he tightened his grip.

"I might be nervous. And not really know what I'm doing or how to do it right, but I want to." His tone was firm, as if he needed to sell us both on this turn of events. "I like holding your hand."

"I like holding your hand too." No way was I letting go now. He was trying. And in that moment, it was everything. He was scared and he was trying anyway—for me. It was almost too much. "And you're doing plenty right. Trust me."

"I just want you to know that I'm not always going to be embarrassed about us." He nodded sharply as the song crested, our own little movie-perfect moment as my heart did its best to leap over those protective barricades I kept erecting to present itself to Milo on a platter for the taking.

"There's an us?" I had to joke so that I didn't let myself get carried away by what his declaration meant. But he'd used an *us* and an *always* in the same sentence. And that was something.

"There's an us." He was emphatic, but then bit his lip. "Right?"

"Yeah. There is." I squeezed his hand and tugged him closer. The velvet of my jacket brushed his bare arm. "And even when I wear my costume? I don't want you embarrassed to be seen with me."

"I'm not."

I raised an eyebrow because I didn't believe him.

"Seriously. Any issues I have are with myself. And sure, I don't like eyeballs on me or being made fun of. But I'm working on not caring. Anyone would be lucky to have you."

"Thanks." Heart. Milo's. Done deal. Delivered with two-day express shipping, no returns accepted. And right on cue, the music shifted to another love song, this one from a movie popular the year we graduated from high school. And for once the thought of high school didn't make me nauseated and angry. The past was fading. Not gone. Not forgotten. But not as important, not as vital as this moment right here. "This song better?"

"Yeah." Milo nodded but didn't move.

"We don't have to—"

"I want to." Still holding hands, Milo took a few halting steps toward the dance floor.

"Okay." I took over, leading him to the edge, near a speaker, and while not hidden, it was a little more out of the way. It had my intended effect as Milo huffed out a breath and relaxed enough to move into a dancing position. We had a bit of a tussle as we sorted out how to stand. Of course, Mr. Ideal Platonic Formal Dance Date assumed he'd lead, but I'd sort of automatically taken that stance too. But we figured it out, and like with kissing, Milo went from instigator to happy follower, letting me direct us as we shuffled and swayed. *Dancing with the Stars* we were not, but there was music and we were dancing and it was possibly the best moment of my whole life, especially when Milo kept looking at me like he too couldn't believe we were here.

"This is…"

"Perfect." I finished the thought for him, because it really was. I could tell he was still a little nervous, and that made it all the sweeter because he was trying. Trying to be here with me. And that mattered.

"Exactly." He gave me a tentative smile that lit me up from the inside out. A new song started and we kept dancing. "Jasper?"

"Yeah?"

"Tell me we can get out of here soon." The heat in his gaze made it clear this request was motivated by something other than discomfort, and my body finally caught up to my brain, taking notice of how close we were standing, how delicious he smelled, how good his hand felt in mine.

"Are you in a hurry?" My laugh was strained from holding back the urge to kiss him.

"Yes." Milo glanced back at the door to the ballroom.

"Good." I didn't kiss him, but it was a close call. Instead, I dropped his hands and led the way back to my friends where we made the world's fastest goodbyes before heading out into the cold and clear night. "You'd better drive. I might be tempted to speed if you keep looking at me like that."

"Like this?" Milo gave me an exaggerated leer that had me preening.

"It's a wonder my costume hasn't spontaneously combusted."

"It's a risk." He gave me a fast kiss right next to my car. The parking structure was otherwise empty, but I still thrilled at the gesture.

"Okay, we really need to get out of here." Charged energy crackled between us the whole way back to the college. "Hurry."

Laughing, we raced toward my dorm, but I slowed when Milo pulled up short, grimacing. "Damn it. These sandals. Still not used to them."

"Sorry. I should have remembered about your leg. Can you do the stairs? I don't want to make it worse."

"Oh, I'm doing the stairs." His mouth was still tight, but the heat was back in his gaze. "Totally worth it."

"Yeah, it is. But we can go slow." We took the stairs at a more sedate pace, and when we emerged on the fourth floor, the board game among my fellow residents was still going on.

"Hey, Jasper!" A biology major who was a senior like me, with a love of loud K-pop, looked up from the game.

"How was the ball?" Another girl spoke up, shuffling some cards. "And Prince Charming?"

"Excellent." I inched toward my door.

"You guys want to play?" She held up the cards.

"Later." Milo's expression was less alarmed than earlier, more like he was vibrating with the same need to be alone as me.

"Sorry." I wasn't entirely sure what I was apologizing for as I closed my door behind us. We threw our coats on the chair where neither of us would be sleeping that night.

"Don't be sorry. Kiss me."

"That I can do." First, however, I quickly connected my phone to my speakers, which were cheap but effective.

"What are you doing?" Milo had followed me over to my desk, a most welcome stalker. Within moments, a playlist I used sometimes for unwinding my brain for sleep filled the room. Wasn't perfect, but I hardly had seductive music at the ready.

"Privacy. In case you wanted to make good on your earlier promise…"

"Oh, I do."

"Excellent." I pushed him until he was seated on the bed, sinking to my knees in front of him, but he shook his head and hauled me up next to him. "What?"

He stretched to grab his backpack from the floor next to the bed. "I…I brought stuff. If you want to…"

"Because you think I need that?" I tilted my head as I considered him. He was blushing again, but he didn't seem anywhere near as uneasy as he had earlier. And his eyes still glowed with sexy intent.

"Because I need to. Want to, I mean. With you." Abandoning the backpack, he gave me a slow, soft kiss.

"Okay." Like I could have refused right then. My pulse thrummed, anticipation and nerves in equal measure. "I have supplies too, you know. Could have saved the cash."

He offered me a crooked grin. "I figured you might, but I didn't want to presume. Really wanted to be able to do this tonight. Together."

"Nice." I kissed him back, but I couldn't let go of a rogue thought that kept making my neck prickle. "Does that bug you? That I've done it before?"

"Not really. I mean, like, I'm mad jealous, but also glad one of us knows what they are doing."

"Well, I wouldn't say that..." My laugh had a definite nervous edge to it. "Don't want to get your expectations too high here."

"It's you. And you haven't let me down yet."

If he hadn't already snagged my heart earlier, he'd have it now. All his. His belief in me, his absolute trust, meant the world to me. I only hoped I could find it in me to trust him, trust *us*, half as much as he trusted me. And I didn't want to let him down either. My hands shook as I pulled him close. I wanted to make all his dreams come true and just hoped I was up to the task.

CHAPTER TWENTY-SIX
MILO

"I DON'T WANT TO EVER let you down." Jasper was way too serious for a guy about to get lucky.

"You won't." I matched his somber tone. And I truly believed that. He wasn't the type to maliciously fail me or to stop trying. He cared, and the fact that he'd slowed down enough to talk about this was proof.

"You're awfully sure of that." Jasper bumped shoulders with me, still not back to the kissing and joking mood we'd been in before. The music was slow and nostalgic, which made me more relaxed and talkative than was maybe wise.

"I am. And I'm the one who let you down. You...you're the most reliable, generous person I've ever known." I wasn't sure whether I could ever apologize enough, and my stomach churned with worries that never totally went away.

"You can't keep beating yourself up for past mistakes." Jasper squeezed my hand. Yup, kind and generous to a fault. "You were really brave tonight. That matters. And I want us to move on. Forward. Together."

"Together," I echoed before kissing him, putting all my surging emotions into it, all the things I didn't even have words for. I meant what I'd said at the ball. I wanted an us, however scary and unlikely that concept might be.

We tumbled backward on the bed, kissing for long moments, before I finally pulled away to catch my breath.

"We're gonna ruin our costumes." I laughed as I grabbed for my backpack and retrieved the things I'd bought with flaming cheeks at the store earlier that day.

Jasper made fast work of removing his costume down to his boxer briefs, and my body took notice of all his creamy skin and adorable freckles. I was down with anything that got us horizontal again fast, but I still carefully stripped off my toga and set it on the chair with our coats, loving how Jasper watched my every move like a kid waiting for an ice cream cone.

"You really want to do this? I'm totally good with what we've been doing," Jasper said as I climbed back onto the bed.

"Me too. Love all that we've tried. But...I've spent a lot of years alone in my room fantasizing about this too." Admitting that made my face go from warm to supernova, and I had to study the comforter instead of Jasper. "And I want it to be you."

"Wow." Jasper rewarded my honesty with a gentle kiss, and figuring we were finally out of things to say, I tried to tug him backward. But he resisted. "But...um... can you be more specific?"

"Specific?" I wasn't sure I had much if any talent for dirty banter. And we'd agreed to do it, so I didn't know what else we were supposed to talk about.

Jasper wasn't giving up easily either, bumping my shoulder.

"Like, when you have this fantasy, what are you doing? And for the record, I'm good with any answer there."

"Oh." Now I got it. My skin prickled because I'd thought that part went without saying, but of course Jasper the king of careful consent was going to make me spell it out. "Uh…I'm not the one doing. You are. That's what I want."

"Yeah?" A grin slowly spread across his face as he stroked my cheek.

"Yeah." He was going to kill me slowly, all this talking, but I did love how much care he was showing.

"It can be a little uncomfortable the first time. Like, not everyone enjoys penetrative play—"

"Love your big words," I growled, tugging him until he was on top of me. This time he went easily. "And I didn't say I'd never fooled around on my own. I know what I like."

"Oh?" His eyes went wide. Shocking him was worth the mild embarrassment of admitting that. But if there was anyone on earth I trusted to do this with, it was Jasper. He made even my deepest desires safe and normal and possible.

"Yeah. So, you good with that?"

"More than. You've got no idea…" Jasper gave a shaky laugh then held up a trembling hand. "I want you. So much. You're not the only one with fantasies."

"Good." I kissed him until he wasn't the only one breathless and shuddering.

"We'll go slow—"

"Not too slow. Want it. Promise." I wriggled under him,

trying to make my point, but only succeeded in turning myself on further.

"Me too. I want everything. Especially this..." Jasper rained little kisses down my neck, across my shoulders, and meandering all around my chest, like some sort of very adult version of connect the dots. Whatever it was, it was torture, all the little sparks with each drag of his lips against my overheated skin.

I cursed low under my breath. "You want to kill me."

"Definitely not. Then I couldn't do this." He added licking and nibbling to his explorations but didn't add even a little speed, if anything slowing further.

"This is the opposite of hurry." Leaping out of my skin seemed like a real possibility. I touched every inch of him that I could reach, stroking his slim but strong shoulders and his gorgeous mop of hair.

"Don't rush me. I'm going to have this night on replay for years. Might as well make it feature-film length."

"I'm going to remember this too." There was so much else I wanted to say. Words. Declarations. Promises. But my throat already burned with the effort of admitting as much as I had. This was already the best night of my life, bar none. Dancing with him had felt like climbing a big, scary mountain only to find it wasn't as hard as I'd thought, and this part was the exhilarating rush of celebrating having conquered some of my fears.

"You'd better." He kissed my belly again, mouth everywhere except where I wanted it most, deft fingers on their own journey down my sides, over my thighs.

"Gonna remember that you were an evil tease." I spread my legs, trying to encourage him to do this sometime this century and preferably before I detonated from nothing more than the rasp of his breath against my skin.

"Better this way. Trust me. Last thing you want is to rush into this…" His eyes flickered. There was a story there, but now was not the moment to ask for it. Still, though, I stroked his wrist, trying to let him know that I got it and that I appreciated his care.

So I let him take his time, let him lead like I had while dancing, trusting him to take us someplace good. And he did, one stroke, one kiss at a time, until finally he reached for the lube and I nearly wept with relief.

His touches were featherlight at first, and I had to bite back a reminder that I wasn't made of crystal. But then he got more purposeful and suddenly it was moans, not snark, that I was holding back, trying not to be louder than the music. The speakers played a song from a cheesy movie, and somehow I knew those notes were going to be imprinted on my soul right along with this moment.

"Maybe…slow…not terrible," I panted. "More."

"If you roll over, it might be easiest on you." Ever considerate, Jasper stroked my side with his other hand.

"Don't want easy. Want you." I'd done enough on my own to know that what I truly craved was watching his face like this, seeing the way wonder and awe and arousal battled for space, sharing more than simply physical sensations.

"God, you're so beautiful, Milo. Can't believe how lucky I am."

I'd been a lot of things in my life. I wasn't sure beautiful was one of them, but in that moment I believed him. "Now. Now. Please. Want it."

"Well, since you asked nicely…" Jasper's hands were shaking again as he reached for the condom box. The evidence of how deeply he cared, how much he wanted to get this right for me, made my chest tight. I didn't deserve him, but I also wasn't going to push away the incredible gift of his affection.

"Do it. Please," I demanded, forcing a lighter tone so that I didn't drown in all the emotions that surged every time he looked at me like that, like I was precious. Like I was worth something. Special. His.

"Your wish is my command." Laughing, even as his eyes stayed serious, he positioned himself. More of that caution and restraint from him, a careful press forward. And maybe all that buildup had been necessary because this was a little different than fooling around on my own. Okay. A lot different. I had to suck in a breath, try to will my body to relax.

"Ah…" Inside. Jasper was inside me, and my body was still trying to decide what it thought about that even as my mind thrilled.

"Okay?" His furrowed forehead said he'd stop the instant I told him it was too much. Which it wasn't. Just…different. Overwhelming, but not in a bad way. And I'd wanted this far too long to turn back now.

"Yeah. We're good." I met his gaze, wanting to reassure him, but the depth of emotion in his eyes was almost my undoing. So much there. Jasper. Me. Everything. And then he shifted his body, moving so we could kiss, and the change in position sparked something deep inside me. Different and almost too much became incredible in a space of heartbeats. "You're good. It's good. So good."

"It is." There was so much wonder in his voice. "Clearly I need to work on my powers of imagination where you're concerned…"

I knew exactly what he meant. "Me too. Never thought…"

"Me either." He stroked my face and neck. I couldn't get enough of looking at him, watching his reactions, hearing his murmured praise and soft moans. "You're amazing."

"Ditto." I was rapidly losing the power of speech and rational thought. This was everything I'd ever wanted, every fantasy, every feverish late-night imagining, all right here, a thousand times better because it was Jasper. "Need…"

"I've got you." And he did, reaching for me right as I did the same thing. I let him win though because his was the touch I craved.

"Jasper." My head fell back and my whole body started to tense. "Hurry."

And this time he finally complied, and then there was no more talking, no more thinking, only pleasure that seemed to go on and on. No beginning, no end, exactly like my feelings for Jasper. I couldn't remember how I'd lived without him, without us, without this moment where we were more than our ordinary selves. Jasper would undoubtedly have some complicated math term to describe how this wasn't addition but something more. Something extraordinary, and I never, ever wanted it to end.

"Wow." At some point, Jasper had stiffened along with me, our moans mingling, and now he sounded as out of breath as I felt. His face was flushed and sweaty, and I wanted to look at him like this forever, memorize him in this moment.

"That was…" I was no better at speech than he was, voice all rough and rusty.

"Exactly." Jasper gave me a tender kiss, brushing my now-damp hair. "You okay?"

"You have to ask?" I sounded drunk still, but this beat any other substance I'd tried, the best high I'd ever experienced.

"Always." His eyes were serious again. And I knew he meant it, knew he always would ask, and that made my chest expand. Seeing that level of caring from him for me of all people was nothing short of breathtaking.

"You're the best." So many other things I could say, so many things I wanted to put words to, but I was still sex-drunk and drowning in the emotions I saw in his eyes.

And maybe he could sense that because he laughed and pretended to preen. "I try."

"Me too. Don't give up on me." There. That was what I wanted to say—or part of it at least.

"I won't." The laughter was gone now, and I wanted it back because the sudden tension in his muscles reminded me of all the ways we could still fail. All the ways that I could still let everyone down. And now, so much more seemed to be on the line. I'd never dared to imagine something this good, and now the thought of losing it made my skin all clammy. I held him closer, trying to keep him with me as long as I could.

CHAPTER TWENTY-SEVEN
JASPER

"HOLD STILL." MILO'S FACE WRINKLED. He was adorable when he concentrated.

"How am I supposed to hold still if I don't know what you're doing?" I ignored his request and twisted around to try to see. He was especially adorable like this—naked other than a pair of boxer briefs, sprawled in my desk chair, feet on the bed near where I lay, sketch pad in his hand.

"If you can't tell..." He waggled a pencil in my direction. It was late, probably past when we should have tried for sleep, but we were both weirdly awake and energized. We'd both made use of my limited hot water after sex, then had a late-night snack, and now it was apparently arts-and-crafts time. Milo had retrieved his sketchbook amid some mumbles about a brainstorm. Which apparently involved me needing to hold still and not touch my postshower hair.

"Funny. Come on, am I at least going to get to see?"

"Maybe." Milo reached for our half-eaten bag of popcorn and fed me a few kernels. "Here. Maybe this will keep you quiet."

"This would be a better incentive." Rising to my knees, I gave him a fast, salty kiss as my body tried its best to convince us both that going again would be a most excellent idea.

Laughing, Milo pulled away and made a show of going back to drawing. "That's going to end with no drawing and pencils and popcorn in weird places."

"You're lucky you're cute when you're all strict and serious." I flopped back on the bed and tried to hold the position at least. It was kind of cool that he wanted to draw me, even if staying still had never been my strong suit.

"Not sure anyone's ever accused me of being serious." Milo bit his lip as his pencil flew over the page.

"They don't know you." But I did. I'd seen the serious kid who could obsess over minute Lego details for hours, and I'd seen the man now who didn't smile nearly enough and who thought to fold his toga before losing his virginity because of course he did. He was Milo. And under the whole jock facade, there was a warehouse of seriousness.

"True." Milo's smile was faint before his gaze went more distant. "I wish…"

"What?" Anyone who didn't think Milo could be serious didn't know his talent for brooding. And being hard on himself.

"Nothing. Just that I wish I'd valued being understood more than being popular and anonymous."

As if one of the best-looking guys in our year could have ever been anonymous. But I got what Milo was saying—being with the jocks and popular crowd had let him stay hidden, maybe even from himself. "Perhaps you weren't ready to be seen."

"Yeah." Milo exhaled, pencil coming to a halt again, point snapping. "You're right. And even now, it's…"

"Scary?" I was still proud of him for dancing with me at the ball, pushing his comfort zone that far.

"Yeah." He didn't meet my gaze as he resharpened his pencil.

"But worth it?" I reached out and tilted his face up.

"Oh, yeah." He leaned in for another kiss. "Especially the fringe benefits."

"Orgasms make everything better," I said with authority as I resumed my pose.

"They do." He was quiet for a few moments as he worked on his drawing, humming along with the song playing on my speakers. "Jasper?"

I had started to drift off a little, but the sound of my name had me lifting my head. "Yeah?"

"Is sex always this good? Like, no matter who you do it with?"

"No. God, no. I wish. But no. This is…well, maybe not rare, but the exception, not the rule. And special. It's different with each person, but with you…yeah, special." I was babbling, trying not to reveal how much better this was than anything that had come before it for me and how much of that had to do with the almost terrifying intensity of my feelings for him.

"I'm glad." He gave me a warm smile before turning more thoughtful. "It…uh…hasn't always been good for you?"

I gave a harsh laugh. He was too perceptive as always. "Sex is weird. Like, when it's good, it's spectacular. And when it's bad…well, it sucks. And not in the fun way. I think almost everyone ends up having bad sex at some point in college. Probably a rite of passage."

I was aiming for a worldly tone, but judging by Milo's deep frown, I didn't quite hit the mark.

"Doesn't matter if it happens a lot. It still sucks. And I hate that it happened to you." Milo reached out and rubbed my leg.

"You're sweet. And it wasn't that bad." I made a vague gesture, like that alone could tell my memories to go take a hike.

Milo went back to the drawing, but the past lingered in the room, a weird unspoken tension, until finally he gently said, "Want to tell me about it?"

And surprisingly, I sort of did. I didn't like talking about unpleasant things—being the fun, upbeat guy everyone needed was way easier, but maybe Milo's seriousness was rubbing off on me.

"Well, before I figured out that I like having regular boyfriends more than hookups, I did have a few hookups freshman year that made me feel like crap. Good lesson."

Milo frowned. "I'd like to teach the other people a lesson, all right."

"You're cute jealous. But put your inner caveman away. I'm just saying it's way better with someone you…care about."

"I'm sure." Rubbing my leg again, Milo gave me a tender look that made me shiver with all the things we very carefully were not saying.

Milo's tenderness gave me the courage to keep going. "And

sober. You're not the only one who's got regrets in that respect. I was a little drunk the first time I bottomed, and so was the other guy. It was fast and rather uncomfortable and then I never saw him again."

"He hurt you." Growling, Milo totally looked ready to do battle on my behalf.

"Not that way, not really." Actually, the physical discomfort had been not insignificant, but I didn't need Milo any more indignant. Also, the lack of prep and advance conversations paled in comparison to my embarrassment later. "Oh well. Live and learn."

"Yeah, but sometimes learning a lesson sucks, and it's okay to be mad, especially at jerks."

I had a feeling we weren't still talking about my bad sexual experiences. And sure, I'd been mad at Milo back then. Furious, really. But I also didn't like what being angry turned me into. And I'd also found that more and more what I truly needed was Milo to forgive himself. "I don't really do mad. Moving on is more productive anyway."

"You're almost too mature for your own good." He shook his head and I laughed because *mature* and *me* were not often used in the same sentence. "Get mad at that dude. Heck, I'm mad on your behalf. Your first time should have been way better."

"Not everything can be fairy-tale perfect."

"Mine was." Milo leaned in for a soft kiss that melted all my muscles. "Everything about tonight. That's why I'm not sleepy. I don't want it to end."

"I'm glad. I wanted that for you." If anything, having a less-than-great first time had made me super determined to make it good for Milo, and knowing I'd succeeded made my whole body warm in a way that had little to do with arousal.

"I want that for you too. I want you to have...everything."

His tender look was almost too much for me, and I gave a shaky laugh. "I'd settle for a peek at your drawing."

"Okay." He nodded like he knew that I'd reached my breaking point for heavy, emotional talk before passing over his sketchbook. "It's not done..."

Mr. Humble as always had undersold his talent. It wasn't simply me on a bed like I'd expected. No, he'd given me some sort of Victorian fainting couch, something that the frog magician would approve of, and the pieces of my costume were strewn about me.

"Oh, Milo. This is...incredible. Sexy. Perfect." It was. He'd captured my likeness down to the freckles on my shoulders. My very bare likeness. My cheeks heated even as my heart tried to clamber its way out of my chest. "Like, I'm never letting anyone else see it, but I love it."

"I'm glad you like it." Ducking his head, Milo reclaimed the sketchbook, but I wasn't going to let him get away with being bashful. I crawled into his lap on the chair, which probably wasn't designed to hold both of us but oh well. If it broke, it would be more than worth this moment, his lips on mine, his hands skimming over my body. The kiss went on and on, and him holding me close like this was everything I'd ever wanted.

Buzz. My phone rudely vibrated right in the middle of a decent song and our spectacular kiss.

"That's my mom's tone. I need to check it, make sure nothing's wrong."

"I felt bad for April tonight. I know she wanted to come."

"Me too," I said as I grabbed for the phone and scrolled to my messages. "And yup, that's what this is about. Mom's up late because she's stressed. She wants me to come to dinner after work tomorrow so I can tell April all about the ball, maybe cheer her up with some company."

"That's a good plan." Milo absently stroked my sides like I was a lap cat, and I stretched into the attention.

"You should come."

"To dinner at your mom's house?" Hands stilling, he sounded like I'd proposed a public execution.

"You don't have to sound so horrified. You've eaten there before." I turned so I could see his face better.

"Yeah, but that was back when they liked me."

"They can like you again." *Just like me.* The unspoken words hung between us. But honestly, if I'd found my way to liking Milo again, so could anyone else. "Give them a chance. If they can see you've changed—"

"Feels like it might never be enough." Sighing heavily, Milo held me tighter. "And like, I get it. If I were a parent, I wouldn't like me either. I was a jerk. They're entitled to their grudge."

"Maybe, but they can get over it. Like I said, mad isn't productive. They—and you—need to move on." I needed Milo to believe in his own changes even more than I needed my parents to. They could get over their anger because I'd seen it before, but I wasn't as sure about Milo, who seemed determined to flog himself for all of eternity for past mistakes.

"I get that." His mouth twisted. "Dinner still feels…"

"Scary? I'm not saying we waltz in there holding hands. I meant it when I said I wouldn't out you. You can come as a friend. Which you are. And if you're a friend who's planning to stick around—"

"I am." On this point he was firm, and he punctuated the words with a kiss on my forehead.

"Good. And so, if you're going to be part of my life, they need to get used to that. April already likes you. Mom's making lasagna, which probably isn't going to be up to Italian grandma standards, but it is still awesome. Let me text her back that you're coming too? I'll just say that you and I already had plans to hang out, but that I'm bringing you to dinner first. Easy."

"Not sure I buy 'easy.' But, okay. This means something to you, so I'll come. But I don't think this is gonna be that simple."

"It might be." I squirmed on his lap, almost toppling us before I gave him what I hoped was a reassuring kiss. And he returned the kiss, but his tension remained.

"I hope you're right."

I hoped that too. I needed my family to see this Milo, the changed guy, the one who was funny and tender and an amazing artist. The one who had spent years hiding, but who might finally be ready to poke his head out into the larger world. I clung to the memory of dancing with him at the ball, the look in his eyes, the gentleness of his hands. He cared, and what I needed most of all

was him to get out of his own way. I wasn't sure whether
all my conviction would be enough to make it happen, but
I was sure as heck going to try.

CHAPTER TWENTY-EIGHT
MILO

"I'M STILL NOT SURE THIS is a good idea." I slowed my steps as we approached Jasper's house. Because Jasper had to work and the weekend bus schedule was so awful, I'd driven, and my heart rate was still elevated from Saturday night traffic. Driving was getting easier, but I doubted I'd ever completely lose my tension over being behind the wheel.

"I am." Jasper bumped shoulders with me as we walked up the little path that wound around the house. Handprints of various Quigley kids and pets decorated the stepping-stones, and if I looked hard enough, I could bet that I'd find one of my own. The sunny day when Jasper's mom had recruited every-one's help in making the path seemed a million miles away. "Listen. I promise no matter how awkward it gets, we can still go back to my room after and I'll make suffering through worth it."

"It's a plan." Some neighbors I didn't recognize had been in their yard when I'd found a parking spot down the street, and not kissing him hello had been torture. Funny how I could live years and years without kissing and touching, and now a few hours without him had me desperate. Rather than head to the front door, Jasper rounded the house so we'd enter through the mudroom. I knew this place almost as well as the one I'd actually grown up in, and I categorized all the little changes that showed the passage of time—windows with new curtains and not the handmade school art projects that had graced them in the past, newer paint job and storm door, and some unfamiliar garden fixtures.

"Now smile," Jasper commanded as he opened the mudroom door. "And be prepared to have to scrub up. Mom's in serious mother-hen mode after the scare over April earlier in the week."

"I get it. I'd be worried too."

After hanging up our coats on a crowded rack, Jasper bent to remove his shoes. "Mom? We're here."

"Jasper. You made it." His mom swept into the cluttered but clean mudroom, catching him up in a big hug before turning to me, smile dimming. "And Milo."

"Hey, Mrs. Q." I offered her a smile I didn't quite feel, nerves still making my stomach slosh around. But I did remember my manners. "Thanks for having me."

"No problem." Her guarded expression said otherwise. "Leave your shoes here and wash up."

Carefully lining up my shoes with his, I followed Jasper's lead in scrubbing my hands like a surgeon prepping for the operating room.

"Smells good," I observed as we made our way into the

kitchen where Jasper's mom was mincing garlic and supervising a number of pots on the stove.

Jasper's mom shrugged, not bothering to look my way. "Probably not up to your grandmother's standards."

"Nothing ever was." It was the truth. She'd been an iron-willed woman with strict, exacting rules, and I'd been rather terrified of her as a kid. It was no wonder my mom had stopped trying to live up to her in-laws' standards, culinary or otherwise. However, when Jasper's mom deepened her frown, I softened my tone. "I'm sure it's great."

"Thanks." She bashed the heck out of the garlic, making me hope I never pissed her off when she had a cleaver nearby.

"I..." I wanted to apologize, but I wasn't sure where to start. And would she even believe me? So instead, I squared my shoulders. "Can I help? Set the table?"

"Okay." She motioned at a nearby cabinet. "You probably know where everything is."

"I'll help." Jasper grabbed a stack of plates and handed me cups and flatware. We made fast work of setting the table for five and were finishing up as April came bounding down the stairs, looking chipper as ever.

"Neptune! You came!"

"Oof." I wasn't expecting either her hug or its strength, but she hugged us both before stepping back. She had Jasper's habit of bouncing on her feet when excited.

"Tell me everything about last night. Even the boring parts."

"There were a lot of boring parts." Jasper gave her an indulgent smile. I could see why they were so close, and not simply because they were the last two Quigley kids at home. They had the same mannerisms and even the same sense of humor. "A lot of the rich old guys didn't even wear costumes."

"Losers." April rolled her eyes.

"Huh. I hadn't thought of it that way." I'd been so caught up in what they had thought of *me* that it hadn't occurred to me to judge *them* in return. As soon as April said it, though, I had to agree that not wearing a costume to a costume ball was slightly rude.

"If I were rich, I'd have a whole wardrobe of different costumes. Like Kellan but even more so. Like, what's the point of money if you don't have fun occasionally?" Beaming, April took a seat at the table.

"True." I sat next to her, both to keep talking and because it seemed safer somehow than sitting with Jasper, all but waving a sign that we were a couple now. Which wasn't untrue, but it would be nice if Jasper's mom at least tolerated me somewhat before she figured that out.

"If you won the lottery, what would you do?" Leaning forward, April talked with her whole body, exactly how Jasper got when excited.

"Uh…" Guys like me didn't get lucky like that, but I didn't want to spoil her fun. I closed my eyes briefly, trying to visualize. "Get my mom a better place. Repay Bruno for…some stuff. Move to an apartment on my own, no more roommates. Maybe…look at taking some art classes."

"Those aren't bad wishes." Jasper's mom sounded slightly less irritated as she set a steaming platter of broccoli on the table. Jasper sprang up to help her with the rest of the food while April bellowed for their dad.

"Something smells delicious." Wearing an old T-shirt advertising a basketball team that no longer existed, Mr. Quigley ambled into the dining room. Like Jasper's mom, he had a cool nod for me. "Milo. Good you could join us."

"Thanks for having me." I tried to do better at turning on the charm, especially when we started passing the food around, but nothing seemed to clear away the awkward energy at the table. Jasper and I told April all about the ball, and all my people-watching paid off in the amount of detail I was able to recall. Meanwhile, Jasper shared the latest gossip from his friend group. But his parents stayed largely silent, and I could sense entire conversations happening with their eyes, almost certainly about me and my presence at the table.

His dad had a few polite questions about my job, but I tried to steer the topic back to the ball because I didn't want to get into my current living situation. Luther and James were likely even bigger villains than me in this house, which was yet another reason why I needed that group-house interview next week to go well. How could I prove to anyone that I'd changed if I didn't ditch the friend circle at the heart of so much of the past I regretted?

Finally, the eating part was done, and while the food truly had been delicious, I was already counting down to our departure. But then Jasper's mom brought out a platter of cookies. "Who wants dessert?"

"Oatmeal raisin? I remember how awesome these always were," I said as I passed the platter.

"I thought you might like them." Jasper's mom rubbed her eyes, like the dinner was every bit as exhausting for her as it was for me. But she'd remembered. And maybe that meant she wouldn't hate me forever.

April took two cookies even as she groaned. "What I really want is a game. Please, guys?"

Jasper glanced my direction. I nodded because even if I were uncomfortable, no way could I say no to that face. "Sure. But we should help your mom with the dishes first."

"You and I can handle that while April gets her cards."

"Let Jasper shuffle for you," their mom warned as April headed for the stairs. "Last thing you need is another paper cut from a card sleeve."

"Mom. I'm fine. Seriously." April put her hands on her slim hips. She was so delicate. I understood why the family was so protective of her, but I also could see how she chafed under all the concern. It reminded me of when I'd had to stay with my mom after the accident, how narrow the line was between caring and smothering.

"I just worry." Jasper's mom handed him her plate and fork as we cleared the table.

"You need that on a T-shirt." Jasper kissed her on the top of her head. "Thanks for the food. It was great."

"You and Milo can divide the leftovers. We've got enough stuff already in our freezer."

"Thank you." I offered her another smile, and this time she didn't frown. Baby steps. Like Jasper said. Maybe I only needed to be patient. Carrying dirty dishes, I followed Jasper to the kitchen.

"See? That wasn't so bad."

"It wasn't terrible," I allowed in a low whisper as we tackled the dish mountain. Same as in middle school, we fell into an easy rhythm where he washed and I dried and put away. "But the lasagna noodles were easier to slice into than that tension."

That got a deep laugh from Jasper. "Could have been worse. And I could sense Mom coming around. People want to give you a chance, Milo. You only have to keep giving them reasons."

"Wish I had your faith." I wanted to kiss him so badly, but Jasper's parents were still at the table and we weren't nearly hidden well enough for that. I was debating whether I could at least get away with touching his arm when my pocket buzzed.

Reflexively, I pulled out my phone. And immediately regretted it as I read the message, my back tightening. "It's my mom. She's talked to Bruno. He should be back stateside and able to visit in two weeks."

"That's great, right?" Jasper glanced up from loading the dishwasher, leaving the pots for the handwashing.

"It's not the worst." Anytime Bruno was out of danger or at least in *less* danger was good news. "But two weeks...it's not enough time. We've still got two cards to go."

"Have you thought about coming clean to him?" Jasper handed me a pot to dry.

"No." My tone was a bit harsh, and I wasn't surprised when Jasper's face drooped. Clearly, he'd wanted a different answer, but I wasn't sure I had one to offer him. "I mean, I want him to see all the things I'm trying to change—staying sober, looking into art classes, ditching my loser roommates, getting you back as a friend—and I want him to be proud of me for once. Not hate me."

"I don't think he'd hate you." Jasper met my gaze, eyes warming me through as much as if he'd been able to touch me. The way he cared for me and wasn't afraid to show it was perhaps the most inspiring thing I'd ever seen. And I wished I had even half his optimism. Instead, all I had was a roiling gut and a lot of old memories that said otherwise.

"Don't be so sure. He's a good guy, but he holds grudges. He wrote down for me exactly how much he had to spend on me so that I could repay him over time. And don't you remember that time I crashed his bike in fifth grade? He didn't speak to me for almost a month. And that was a bike!"

"And you were kids back then," Jasper said reasonably as he wiped down a counter.

"Exactly. And now I'm an adult and supposed to not be a dumbass anymore."

"I get that." Body tensing, Jasper paused for a long moment, mouth opening and shutting a few times. "It's just…"

"Yeah?"

"I get wanting to show him that you've changed. But I also think he's not your dad and you're not fourteen anymore."

Ah. I got it now. Jasper was afraid that I wasn't ever

going to tell Bruno about the two of us. And while I was worried about that—okay, terrified—I'd also promised Jasper that I wasn't going to hide forever. I hadn't gotten as far as coming up with a plan for telling Mom or Bruno, but to me, that was a separate deal. "This isn't about coming out."

"Okay." Jasper didn't sound like he believed me. "I'm only trying to say that if it was, you've got friends now. You've got me. I'm not going anywhere, even if Bruno gets mad at you."

"Thanks." A quick glance at the dining room revealed that Jasper's parents had finally left the table. Thank God, because no way could I not kiss Jasper after a declaration like that. He truly was the best of guys. I brushed a soft kiss across his very surprised lips, loving the way his mouth curved into a smile even as we kissed.

"I still want to find those cards though." For whatever reason, I just couldn't seem to let it drop. And maybe Jasper was right and coming out was somehow wrapped up in all of this in ways I didn't particularly want to consider, but regardless, I wanted to make this one thing right.

"Then that's what we'll do." Jasper nodded like the universe would simply have to bend to his mighty will.

"You're incredible."

"I try." Jasper's shrug was so much like his mom's that it was almost eerie. He seemed eons more mature than me in that moment as he patted my arm with a damp hand. "And so do you. I wish you'd give yourself more credit."

"I'm trying. But I want to earn it too." My ribs ached with all that I wanted to get right in my life.

Jasper didn't let go of my arm, gazing deep into my eyes like he could see all that yearning churning inside of me. "And that's admirable. Truly. And I want to help."

"Thanks." I didn't deserve this guy or his faith in me. He seemed so certain that I could deal with whatever was coming my—our—way, and I wished I shared that attitude, wished my stomach wasn't churning, wished we had more time. Jasper might believe, but I wasn't so sure that doom wasn't lurking right around the corner, waiting for us.

CHAPTER TWENTY-NINE
JASPER

"WHAT ARE YOU DOING HERE?" My Wednesday was already going haywire when George walked into the game store. I'd had an early morning class and now was helping Arthur because another employee had called in sick and there was a bunch of new merchandise to inventory before the weekend rush. I'd have to hurry to make it to the cosplay group on schedule, and I did not have time to deal with freaking George of all people.

"Now, is that any way to greet a paying customer?" He looked slick as always—expensive sneakers, pristine clothes despite slushy weather, perfectly arranged hair, and weaselly expression already in place.

I narrowed my eyes at him. "I thought Arthur banned you from the store."

"Correction. He banned me from playing here. Not shopping. My money's as good as anyone else's, and I need some booster packs for a draft party I'm having tonight. Thought I had enough but it looks like I'm more popular than I anticipated."

With anyone other than George, draft parties were super fun as everyone got a set number of card packs and raced to build decks with the cards they scored and then played each other for prizes and bragging rights.

"Planning to cheat more so-called friends out of premium cards?" I wasn't going to bring up Milo by name, but I couldn't resist a dig.

He made a scoffing noise. "You're jealous that I'm a superior player."

"Superior at cheating, sure." I shrugged, no closer to retrieving the packs for him.

"I could go pro and you know it, Quigley." His sneer transformed him from slick to slimy and no way could I let that stand.

"Prove it." Slapping my hands on the counter, I stared him down.

"How?"

"Rumor has it you recently acquired Frog Court cards. Play me for them." I could already hear Milo's protest in my head, but I was too pissed to reconsider my brash proposition. Milo might hate the idea, yet I'd also bet he wouldn't turn down the missing cards. I'd almost qualified to the finals at the Philly tournament. I could do this for him as well. Even simply thinking it had my shoulders lifting. I wanted to be the one to do this for him.

"In your dreams." George made a dismissive gesture. "Even if I had said cards, why would I wager them against you? What's going to be your bet? Even that beat-up roller skate you call a car isn't worth as much as a single one of those cards."

He had a point, but I also knew exactly what would tempt him. "I have a ticket to the launch party in NYC."

"Keep talking." He was playing it cool, but the light in his eyes gave him away.

"Play me in the new tournament style they just announced. Best two out of three." I liked this format because it was newer and therefore less likely that George would have already found a hack. "Bet me those cards."

"I might think about it." His smug smile had my fists clenching.

"You do that." I finally gave in and slapped the booster packs down on the counter for him. "Now how many did you need?"

"Fifteen from the latest set." He pulled out a gleaming credit card. "Why are you suddenly so interested in rares? They hardly fit your...style."

"None of your business." It was, however, Milo's business, and he was undoubtedly going to have lots to say about me trying to goad George into a game. In fact, it might be better simply not to tell him yet. Wait to see if George actually took the bait.

At least that was how I attempted to rationalize things on the way to the hospital. I was a couple of minutes late, and Milo was already in costume, sitting in the waiting area with Kellan, laughing at a story Jasmine was telling while April sat on his other side. Watching him with my friends gave me a strange pang. I loved seeing him integrated into our little group, loved him getting better taste in friends, but I also knew how much more it was going to suck if things didn't work out between us. It wouldn't be only myself who was let down.

"Hey." Milo noticed me hovering. "I was getting worried about you. You better change fast."

His concern felt almost as good as a hug and I smiled at him. "Will do."

When I emerged in my costume a few minutes later, Milo and Kellan were deep in conversation with April.

"Jasper! You know how Mom doesn't want me doing any crowded big events? She was going to make me skip the revue at the college despite us having tickets. But Kellan has a work-around."

"Tech rehearsal tomorrow night. Full run-through. Limited audience. I can get you guys in, get you seats away from anyone else."

"I might have already said yes." Milo gave me a crooked smile that melted me even more than his earlier concern. "Your sister is pretty persuasive."

"Better extend that persuasion to Mom," I warned. "But sure. I can pick you up if Mom says it's okay. Where is she, anyway?"

"Dropped me off so she could do a conference call in the car." April made a face. "And had a million warnings about keeping my mask on."

"She's not wrong."

"But you'd like to do your own remembering. I get it," Milo added, an unexpected bit of compassion from him. While I figured he was referring to his own mom, I also hoped he didn't think that I was a nag, trying to get him to change more than he wanted to. I wanted him to find his own way. But not pushing was hard.

"How'd that group-house interview go?" I asked him in a whisper as we all made our way to the lounge.

Milo groaned. "Postponed. One of the housemates is sick."

"That sucks."

"Yeah." His posture deflated, and I wanted again to hug him, but I refrained.

"Looking splendid today, everyone!" Natalie greeted us. "And Prince Neptune, your fame precedes you. The family that you did the drawing for last week showed it around, and I've had a number of inquiries as to if you'd be with the group today."

"I'm here." Milo blushed deeply even as he hurried to get a sketchbook out. "If I skip playing, I can probably do more than one sketch."

"We'll give you a reprieve," I joked as I waved him over to a table. Even once I was set up for a game with a kid who was new this week, my attention kept wandering to Milo, watching him draw a thin boy with a heavy cast as a mighty Viking warrior complete with shield and horned helmet. Pride made my shoulders lift and my chest expand. He was incredible. And, at least in that moment, he was mine.

"Tell me it's pizza night," Milo joked as we packed up. We were the last two of our group left because Milo had kept drawing past our usual ending time. His final tally of sketches was four— the little Viking, a flying superhero, a hulking strongman, and a special request for a mermaid.

"You have definitely earned your pizza," I replied as we headed for the hall, letting my tone turn low and flirty. "And I owe you—"

"Dude. Lionetti. What the hell are you wearing?" Two of my worst nightmares greeted us before we could reach the elevators. Luther and James, in gray janitorial outfits with matching scowls, were pushing big utility carts that stood between us and an easy escape. High school had taught me to always be aware of the exits where the two of them were concerned, and even Milo's presence wasn't enough to stop the chill racing up my spine.

"Forget what he's wearing. What are you doing with this Willy Wonka reject?" Luther gawked at me.

"Aren't you a little old for playing dress-up?" James sneered at me. "What are you supposed to be, anyway?"

I opened my mouth to defend the Frog Wizard costume to them, but then closed it because I knew these guys. They'd just twist my words, make it worse, and I wasn't about to give them fresh ammunition. No, the best thing to do with bullies like them had always been to walk away fast.

But they were blocking an easy escape, and Milo appeared to have put down roots next to me. His eyes were wide and stricken, and his skin had turned a pasty, pale green.

"You look f-ing ridiculous. Both of you. Who put you up to this? Is it some sort of prank?"

"Blink once if you need a rescue." Luther laughed as Milo continued to stay silent. "Better make sure no one takes a picture of you two. You wouldn't want it to go viral."

I was dangerously close to decking him because this wasn't high school. I wasn't risking my scholarship prospects with an expulsion. I didn't have to take this heckling, and even if Milo had turned into stone, I didn't have to stay there and wait to see what if anything he was going to say to his friends.

"Come on. Let's get out of here," I said firmly to Milo because I didn't want to abandon him, but I also wasn't going to stand there and let Luther and James pick us apart. However, when I stepped forward, Luther playfully swung his cart into my path.

"Okay, now I'm mad." I glowered at him, and right when I was about to shove his stupid cart, Milo suddenly came to life and stepped in front of me.

"Stop," he said, and time came to a screeching halt while we all waited to see what he was about to do.

CHAPTER THIRTY
MILO

"STOP." FINALLY, I'D RECOVERED MY ability to speak. It had taken me a few moments to get past the shock of seeing Luther and James at the hospital, exactly like I'd been dreading. And it was high school all over again, Luther and James hassling Jasper, and me doing nothing to stop it. It was like they started their shit and my voice fled along with my convictions and my courage.

But unlike high school, Jasper now looked more furious than scared, and I had a sinking feeling some of that anger was probably directed my way. And also in contrast to the past, I now had way more on the line. I'd promised Jasper and myself that I was going to be a better person, and that better person was definitely not a scared-rabbit statue who let my roommates get away with harassing anyone, let alone someone who meant as much to me as Jasper.

"Knock it off," I said to Luther. My stomach issued a Category 5 hurricane warning. It might have been a little dramatic, but I swore I could feel my entire future hinging on the next few minutes. My stomach could deal. "Let him pass."

"I'm so sorry, Zeus. Or is it Apollo? Sorry. I didn't pay attention to ancient history." Luther laughed harshly.

"It's Prince Neptune." I pulled myself up to my full height, which was taller than Luther and wider than James. "And you both need to cut it out."

"Or what?" James shook his head. "Since when do you hang out with Quigley, anyway?"

"You don't know everything about me."

"Clearly." Luther swept his gaze over my costume again, openly mocking. "Like I said, you'd better be careful. People might get the wrong idea."

"Right here, guys," Jasper said from behind me, tone still dripping with irritation.

"Or maybe they'll get the right one." My stomach was in full-out revolt now, bile burning my throat, but I forced my hand backward, fumbling for Jasper's. Holding his hand at the ball had been scary, but this right now was like the difference between a high dive and skydiving. With an iffy parachute. And the landing zone was on fire. But whatever. I was doing it.

Jasper inhaled sharply but he didn't flinch away, grabbing my hand back, not letting go.

"Okay. Very funny." Luther rolled his eyes as if there was no way I was serious.

"I don't have time for this shit." James yanked his cart past Luther's.

"No. No way." Tilting his head, Luther quirked his mouth like he might be seeing me for the first time ever. My clammy skin broke out in goose bumps under the scrutiny, yet I held firm to Jasper.

"There's no room in my life for you...*experimenting*, Lionetti."

"It's not your life. It's mine." Even as my muscles started to quiver, I still stared James down.

"No, I meant that literally. No room. You can pack up your crap and get the fuck out." James's expression was as hard as his tone.

"Yeah." Luther sounded more resigned than mad. "Way to choose that—"

I cut him off with a growl. "Watch it."

"Everything okay here?" An older portly security officer stepped off the elevator and strode toward us. Heck. All we needed was someone to have complained about our argument.

"Yup, Officer." James spared me a last glare before steering his cart toward the elevators. "Moving on. Moving the F on."

"You do that." I scowled back until they were both out of sight.

"You need me to call the cleaning company supervisor?" the guard asked. "I know how much the kids love the costumed visitors like you two. That cleaning company's workers are supposed to stick to the remodel on the next level up."

"No. It's fine," I said, even though it most definitely was not. Jasper muttered something under his breath about a complaint not being a bad idea, but I pretended not to hear, instead trying to look casual while waiting for the guard to head down the corridor.

"Wow. That was…" Jasper exhaled about a decade's worth of tension.

"I know." Swaying slightly, I squished my eyes shut.

"Hey. You okay?" Jasper steered me toward one of the couches in the waiting area by the elevators.

"No." Collapsing onto the couch, I put my head in my hands. Jasper made soothing sounds and rubbed my back, but I was concentrating too much on not hurling to appreciate the contact. "What did I do?"

"You stood up for me. For yourself. You were amazing. But I get that it was probably intense for you." Jasper sounded amazed but all jazzed up, like we'd just conquered some ride together. And as always, now I was the one about to puke.

"That's one way to put it."

Jasper gentled his tone some and slowed his hands, like he was calming a nervous puppy. "You did good."

"Should have done it a long time ago, but still…" I held out my shaking hands.

"I'm not trying to say it wasn't hard for you." Giving me a kind smile, Jasper squeezed my biceps. "But I was impressed."

"I'm now impressively homeless." After removing my crown, I scrubbed at my hair.

"Hey." He stilled my hand while I still had hair left. "Do you want to call your mom?"

I lurched away from him, gut roiling again. "God, no. I'll figure something out, but I am not needing another rescue."

"Fair enough, but I meant more that maybe you need the support."

"I'll be fine." I pushed myself to standing even if my knees were still decidedly wobbly.

"You don't look—"

"I just need a minute." I dragged in a rattling breath before striding toward the restroom. "I'm going to get changed."

"Good idea. I'll do the same."

Toting all his usual bags, he followed close behind me, almost as if he expected me to make a run for it. Which I definitely was not about to do in this toga. And Jasper might be my only friend. I was feeling like crap but I wasn't stupid enough to flee. So no fleeing, but my self-loathing had reached new depths, and I wasn't surprised when I ended up puking while changing. I hated how much I now needed Jasper. And I hated that it had taken me this long to stand up. Oh, and that I'd been this unprepared for the inevitable reaction.

"Where to?" Jasper asked as I emerged from the stall, doing a pretty good job of pretending like he hadn't heard me getting sick even as he passed me a pack of mints. "You want to collect your stuff while they're still at work, right?"

I quickly rinsed my mouth and popped a mint that did nothing to quiet my still-anxious gut. "What I'd like is to not think for a while."

It came out too loud, too sharp, and Jasper took a step back, feet hitting his bags. "Okay."

"Sorry. That came out harsh. You're trying to help. I get it. I hate being such a mess—"

"This isn't your fault or your mess. It's theirs." He

rubbed my arm before picking up his bags and following me out of the restroom. "And like you said, maybe this was way overdue."

"Yeah." I paused for a drink at the fountain by the elevator. His tone had been pragmatic, not accusatory, but he was right. I'd waited way too long to stand up to Luther and James. He'd be justified in being pissed about that. Yet if he was, he was doing a good job of hiding it as he waited with patient expression. "Let me help. Please?"

"I guess I could use a ride back to the apartment. Everything I own should pretty much fit in my car."

"And then?"

"You can be in charge of pizza." I forced out a laugh as we got on the elevator.

"I'm serious. You can stay with me tonight while you figure out what to do."

"Thanks. I don't like imposing—"

"You're not an imposition." Jasper was quick to interrupt me with one of his mom's favorite sayings. But the soft way he gazed at me wasn't familial at all and was way more caring than I deserved. "You're my guy."

It was a nice thought, but I still felt like the world's biggest burden as we stepped into the chilly evening. For weeks I'd felt one move away from my life collapsing like a faulty block structure, a build with a fatal flaw—me. Now it was happening and I had no one else to blame. Even with Jasper by my side, I wasn't sure I'd ever been so alone.

CHAPTER THIRTY-ONE
JASPER

MILO WAS IN A FUNK. And I couldn't blame him. He'd come out to his friends, who weren't really ever true friends, but they'd been a part of his life for almost a decade, and he'd lost his place to live all in one grand gesture. Which had been unbearably sweet. And scary. The moment when he'd reached for my hand was something I'd remember forever. My inner fourteen-year-old had waited years for him to stand in front of me like that, to stand up, not only for me but also himself. I'd wanted to cheer him on, even if my adult self understood that the real-world consequences sucked. So I got why he was brooding. I simply wished I had a way to make it better.

"Is that everything?" I asked as I closed a box of clothes.

"Yeah. Thanks." He'd grudgingly let me handle packing up the closet with the boxes we'd picked up at my mom's. She did so much online shopping that it had been easy to raid the stack awaiting recycling in the garage. And it hadn't taken many boxes at all to pack up Milo's tiny, bleak room at Luther and James's apartment. Nothing on the walls, not even any of his amazing drawings.

A bed and dresser he didn't own. No signs of the Milo I'd come to know so well over the past few weeks. Even his art supplies and sketchbooks were a meager stack that he'd kept stored under his bed. We'd mainly packed in silence, and the quiet continued as we carried the last boxes down the single flight of stairs.

Milo didn't spare a last glance for the place as he tossed a key on the kitchen counter, not that I blamed him. There was nothing homelike about this place. I wanted so much better for him.

"Are you sure your mom is cool with me parking there?" he asked when we reached our cars. A loaded-down classic car in the huge parking lot at school would be a major theft magnet, so when we'd grabbed the boxes, I'd asked Mom if Milo could park behind the garage, out of view from the street and curious passersby.

"Yes. I didn't even have to tell her the whole story—"

"Might as well." Sighing, Milo unlocked his car. "Everyone is going to know soon enough. Luther can't keep his mouth shut."

"As well I know." I spared a glance around the deserted parking lot before patting his shoulder. "It should still be your choice who and how much you tell."

"Ideally." He pursed his mouth, looking off into the distance. Sad Milo always tugged at my heartstrings, but this version was something different and way harder to read.

"Hey. Are you mad at me? I didn't make—"

"No." Milo rubbed my arm as he steered me toward my car. "I know you didn't. You didn't make me come out to them. It was the right thing to do. But sometimes doing the right thing sucks donkey balls."

"That bad?" I tried to get him to laugh by making a silly face, but all he had was the ghost of a smile.

"Yeah. Let's get out of here."

Later, after his car and belongings were safely stored at my house with a minimum of Mom interactions, we split a cheap pizza on the floor of my dorm room. Even with a lax RA and all, Milo wasn't going to be able to stay with me indefinitely and that knowledge hung between us, a ticking clock warning that we needed a new plan for him. And not surprisingly, he barely picked at his food. I'd ordered plain cheese and plain breadsticks, trying to go easy on his stomach, but he only played with his crust and shredded a breadstick.

"Not hungry? Stomach still upset?" I asked. I'd thought about grabbing some soup for him at Mom's, but he'd asked for pizza and I didn't want him accusing me of coddling him. Even if I kind of wanted to. I liked taking care of him.

"A little. Sorry."

"Quit saying 'sorry.'" I put the food away in my mini-fridge and retrieved a clear soda for him. "Do you want a movie or other distraction? I was going to do more card searching after cosplay, but—"

"That. Let's do that. I need some good news." Milo leaned forward as I brought out my laptop and set it between us on the bed. I called up all my bookmarked card-searching sites. A spare five grand might nab us something, but now more than ever, Milo needed a bargain. He deflated further with each lead that didn't pan out.

"The universe hates me," he groaned. "I want this one thing to go my way, put the whole mess behind me."

"I know." I stroked his back. We were alone in my room so I could touch him as much as I wanted, but he was still stiff and tense under my hand. "We'll find something. Do you want me to call Professor Tuttle? He might have a lead."

"Nah. No sense in bothering him. We'll see them Saturday, right?" Earlier in the week, Professor Tuttle had messaged about a game after I worked on Saturday and specifically told me to bring Milo along. Milo had readily agreed, but now seemed less than certain. "If I'm still invited..."

"Of course you are. In fact, if you tell them what happened—"

Frowning, Milo pulled away from me. "Didn't you say it was up to me who I tell? I don't want anyone's pity. I can sort this out on my own."

"People like helping—"

"Not everyone. And not all help is free." His tone was ominous, like he was echoing his father and his strict grandmother along with some painful past lessons. I understood, but I also didn't reach for him again. I didn't want to make things worse, so I only nodded.

"Sorry." He gave me a fast pat on the knee. "I'm being a pain."

"You're allowed a bad mood."

"Yeah, but I shouldn't be taking it out on you." He rested his head on my shoulder, and I hugged him close, wishing there were more I could do. "How about that movie? You can study and I'll try to tell my brain to shut up."

"It's a nice brain." I kissed his forehead.

"Not as nice as yours." His crooked smile was his first real one in hours and the kiss he gave me was that much sweeter for the wait.

In theory, what happened next was him watching a movie on my tablet while I got out my notes for my senior seminar. But in reality, I set my notes aside and played with his hair and stroked his shoulders while he used me as a backrest. Every so often he'd remind me to study, and I'd try, but I kept getting distracted by how much I wanted to help him. As the final credits rolled on the movie neither of us had paid that much attention to, Milo yawned big and leaned further into me.

"Tired?"

"Yeah. Head is still buzzing though." He groaned and rubbed at his thoroughly messed-up hair.

"Tired but wired sucks." I dropped a kiss on the back of his neck while I snaked a hand down his torso. "I know one thing that might help…"

"Sorry." He stilled my hand and reversed our positions so that he was cuddled behind me, face buried in my hair. "Not right now."

"Okay. It's all good." It was a challenge to sound as accepting and accommodating as I wanted to while Milo was squeezing me so tightly that I had to keep from squawking.

"Oops. I'm squashing you." He arranged us in a marginally more comfortable position, but the bed certainly seemed a lot smaller when we weren't all tangled up in each other on it. "Do you want me to take the floor bed?"

"Not unless that what's you want." I snuggled into him, trying to give off platonic vibes, which was difficult with him right there, smelling so good, but I truly was fine exactly like this. I loved being near him however I could get him.

"No. I just want to lie here like this." He held me close, gentler now, breathing like he was doing a meditation class.

"Does that help?" Now I was the one yawning, but I wanted to stay awake if he needed to talk. And maybe also to memorize this moment that felt both achingly sweet and infinitely fragile.

"Holding you always helps." He kissed my temple. I'd meant the breathing, but I wasn't going to turn down the compliment. However, somehow I also didn't believe I was doing enough to assist him through this crisis. I was good for more than being a human body pillow. And for all my ability to scheme and plan my way out of tight situations, I couldn't help Milo if he wouldn't let me.

CHAPTER THIRTY-TWO
MILO

"IS EVERY SONG IN THIS thing about being lonely?" I looked up from the program we'd snagged from a stack in the lobby. The tech rehearsal audience was bigger than Kellan had advertised, but Jasper, April, and I had found seats off to the side away from a rowdy mix of undergraduates in the middle of the theater. Mrs. Q had been full of reminders to use hand sanitizer and have April home on time, and Jasper was all about taking his big brother duties seriously.

"I think there's a deeper meaning than that." Leaning over Jasper, April pointed at a paragraph that explained how they'd picked the various musical numbers for the revue. It was a mix of well-known hits and newer songs. "It's iconic songs of personal power."

"Way to quote the program." Jasper laughed from in between us. "Speaking of alone... Any luck with your...new project?"

He gave me a pointed look. We hadn't had much time to talk that day. I'd had to leave while he was still asleep to make the bus to work for the early shift I was scheduled for. I couldn't afford to miss work, not right then. Then after work, Jasper had been in class, so I'd hung out in the Gracehaven library, scrolling through housing ads and trying not to get too discouraged by dead ends.

"Maybe," I answered cagily, not wanting to involve April in my drama.

"Good." Jasper had brought me soup from the dining hall after his class. He was so good at the caretaking thing, but nonetheless I hated how much I needed him. I wanted to solve my own problems, and he made it too easy to sink into his cozy nest of favors and nice gestures. Unsurprisingly, I hadn't told him how fruitless my searching had been when we'd fetched April together. And now he was all questions. "What about—"

"It's starting." April shushed us, and I was grateful for the distraction.

The revue was a lot of fun with high-energy musical numbers that lifted even my bleak mood. Watching groups of people run around and sing and dance while navigating quick costume and scenery changes was more enjoyable than I'd anticipated. The revue took a number of songs out of the context of their respective plays and did fun twists on the staging of the numbers. Later, the frantic energy of the early numbers gave way to a somber performance of a medley of songs from *Wicked* recast as a lesbian coffee-shop romance.

"Oh, wow." I didn't realize I'd gasped aloud until Jasper squeezed my hand. Reflexively, I started to pull away, but then the music crested, and it hit me that I didn't have to. I didn't have to hide. Not ever again. Not if I didn't want to. The worst had happened, and in a way, it was freeing. I gripped his hand back. Let people see. I was damn lucky to have someone like Jasper on my side. The soloist hit a high note and my soul soared along with the music. Seeing the two lead singers so fearless and defiant made me newly resolved to figure out my current situation.

"That was incredible," I enthused after the performance as everyone took their final bows.

"I know." Jasper had a tender look for me as he released my hand.

"Should we find Kellan?" April asked as we made our way to the lobby.

Jasper made a face at that. "Nah. I mean, I'm sure he's all about the kudos but it's going to be packed backstage, and Mom wouldn't be happy with the germ potential."

"Okay. Party pooper." April pushed at his shoulder, but good-natured as ever, Jasper simply laughed and took it.

"Yup. Let's get you home."

"Can we at least take the long way home?" April asked as she pulled on her coat. "We could get drive-thru milkshakes at—"

"Quigley." The sound of Jasper's last name drowned out the end of April's request, and it was the last voice I wanted to hear right then.

"George." Jasper gave him a cool nod while I merely did my best to set his smug face on fire with my eyes, super-hero style.

"Oh, and pretty boy." George gave me a once-over

that had my skin crawling. "Fancy seeing you at an institution of learning."

A growl escaped my chest. "I have a name."

"So you do." His tone was dismissive and made my hands ball up. "What are you doing here? Wouldn't have taken you for a patron of the arts."

"I could say the same for you," Jasper interjected with a laugh.

"I'm seeing the soloist of the third song. He's got an audition next week for an off-Broadway show. He's going places."

"Not with you," Jasper said firmly. My chest swelled with pride at how easily he put George in his place, and I resolved to ask Kellan to give the singer a warning that George was a piece of work.

"Cold, Quigley. Cold." George sounded almost as impressed as I was. "Guess I can see why you're suddenly interested in the Frog Court cards."

Wait. What? My eyes narrowed, but Jasper spoke before I could.

"Like I said. None of your business."

But it was mine, and I gave them both a hard stare. I was not going to contradict Jasper in front of George, but he was going to need to talk fast as soon as we were alone.

"I might be interested in that offer of yours." George gave Jasper a considering look. "Might."

I couldn't stay silent any longer. "What offer?"

George's arch look soured my stomach even before he spoke. "That's between Quigley and me."

No, it wasn't, but before I could protest, a crowd of people came through.

"Message me, Quigley." George gave us a little wave as he backed away. "I find I'm...intrigued."

He wasn't the only one, but we still had April with us, and no way was I interrogating Jasper around her. So I settled for beaming questions at the back of his head as we left the theater.

"Are either of you going to tell me why Milo's car is at our place?" April asked as we made our way to the parking lot. "Or is that need-to-know information?"

"Yup." I tried to keep my tone light.

Jasper must have picked up on my efforts, because he added, "If you don't bug him about it or make a big deal to Mom, I'll get you that milkshake."

"Jasper. I'm not nine." April did an impressive eye roll while waiting for Jasper to unlock the car. "But okay. Lucky for you I'm hungry."

I wasn't. But I wasn't going to stop the two of them from picking up shakes from the fast-food place next to Lee's Bakery that April liked.

"Stomach again?" Jasper whispered while April dictated her order.

"Yeah." If I blamed my wallet, he'd offer to treat me, so I went with the easier excuse. Seeing George had killed whatever limited appetite I had, but I did need to save every dollar.

Finally, we delivered April and her drink safely back to the Quigleys' where Jasper's mom must have been waiting by the door, lights going on as soon as we pulled into the driveway. Jasper glanced at me as if he was debating going in, then shook his head before I could speak.

"Tell Mom I'll call her soon. And that Milo says thank you for the parking space."

"Yeah. I appreciate it," I added.

"Okay. Don't get into trouble with the rest of your night." She winked at us as she exited the car. "Or rather, get into lots of trouble, but tell me all about it."

Jasper and I groaned in unison. "April..."

"I'm going, I'm going."

I waited until her door shut and Jasper was back on the road before I unleashed the question that had been burning a hole in my brain ever since George's appearance.

"What did he mean?" I asked as Jasper turned toward campus. "Offer? When did you talk to him, anyway?"

He sighed like he'd been expecting this question. "Yesterday."

"And you didn't think to tell me?" Heck. I sounded like my mom, and it was not a comfortable comparison. Shifting in my seat, I looked out the window.

"You were a little busy yesterday." That flimsy excuse got me whirling back around, and Jasper quickly added, "And I didn't think it was that big of a deal."

"Well, it is. I don't trust him."

"Oh, neither do I." Once we arrived back at his dorm, Jasper did a parking maneuver that had me sending up a quick prayer.

"Then what were you doing making him offers?"

"Chill." Turning the car off, Jasper twisted toward me. His command had the opposite effect, making all my muscles tense, but I waited for him to continue. "All I did was suggest a friendly game. My ticket to the launch party wagered against at least one of the cards. I'm going to argue for him including all of them—"

I held up a hand before he could go further down this absurd path. "No, you're not."

"I'm not?"

"I don't want you playing him!"

"Because you don't think I can win?" Jasper took on a pinched expression.

"Because he'll cheat and you'll lose that ticket, and your whole future is riding on your contacts at the game."

"Well, maybe not my whole future..." Shrugging, he looked right at me, holding my gaze until I swore years passed between us.

My face heated. God. I wanted him. But he couldn't pin a whole future on me. On us. "You know what I mean. You can't lose your shot at that job."

"I don't know. Maybe staying local wouldn't be the worst thing." He still had that stubborn tilt to his chin to match his speculative tone, like I was anything other than an iffy bet at best.

"Don't be ridiculous. You are not risking your future for me."

"Who else would I do that for?"

My heart trembled even as my soul thrilled. But I couldn't let myself wallow in his sweetness. "Be serious."

"I am. You're insistent that you need those cards. I

want you to have the cards. Ergo, playing to get you the cards makes sense."

"No, it doesn't." I didn't need fancy Latin words to know I was right. Jasper was always so quick to want to solve things for me, and right then, the math simply wasn't adding up for me.

"Are you jealous of George?" Jasper studied me more intently, parking-lot lights glinting off his eyes. "Because I can tell you that he's a piece of slime with zero appeal to me."

"Not helping. I don't want you having to associate—"

Buzz. Jasper's phone clattered around in the console. "I better check."

"Fine." I didn't blame him for grabbing the excuse, but I didn't have to like it.

"Good news!" He shook the phone like it might shower us with glitter confetti.

"It better not involve George." I glowered.

"It doesn't." Jasper patted my knee. "Professor Tuttle put Arthur in contact with this retiree looking to offload their whole collection. There might even be some Frog Court cards in the lot."

"Sounds good, but what's the catch?" There was always a catch.

"The entire collection is unsorted. Just boxes of cards all mixed up. Arthur says if I stay late tomorrow and help sort, I can have dibs on an ultra rare if we find one."

"I could help too." Anything was better than Jasper playing George, even cataloging cards.

"I was hoping you'd say that." He hadn't lost any radiance from his smile even with our earlier argument. "See? Things are looking up!"

"Maybe." I wasn't going to count on anything right then.

"Still mad at me?" Jasper let his head fall onto my shoulder before giving me a puppy-dog smile that had me laughing despite myself.

"I can't seem to stay mad at you," I admitted, putting an arm around him. "I still think you should have told me."

"And that's a fair point. I'll try to do better at keeping you in the loop." His earnest tone went a long way to making more of my upset vanish, but the deeper unease at the idea of letting him play George lingered.

"Good." I kissed the top of his head.

"Things will work out, Milo. You'll see."

I wished I believed him, wished I could channel even half of his endless optimism. But I couldn't shake the feeling of doom that had plagued me the last few days. What I could do, however, was kiss him, my mouth finding his right there in the front seat of his car. He tasted sweet, like the chocolate shake, and his mouth was soft and giving as he melted into me. Moaning quietly, I tried to bottle up this moment when he believed so surely in me, in us, in our chances.

"Race you to your room?" I asked when we reluctantly pulled apart.

"You're on." He beamed at me, lips still shiny from the kiss. This was all probably still going to collapse, but I wasn't going to waste time arguing with him now. There'd be time enough for that later.

CHAPTER THIRTY-THREE
JASPER

IN THE END, NO ONE raced up to my room. We walked. I wasn't going to let Milo strain his leg again. But we did turn the speed on by the open door of my RA. Last thing I needed was him noticing that Milo had stayed over consecutive nights. I wasn't sure what the max was for visitors, but I probably needed to look that up soon.

Later.

Because right then, my door was shutting behind us and Milo's lips were on my neck and all I could think about was the precise number of steps to my bed. Our coats and shoes made an inelegant heap on the floor as even Milo forgot to be a clean freak for once.

But as he tugged me the four-and-a-half steps to the bed, my inner good-guy nudged my shoulder.

"Are you sure?" I asked.

"Uh-huh." Milo seemed to have a thing about my neck right then, and I'd need a shirt with a collar tomorrow. Which I didn't care one bit about, but Mr. Good Guy wasn't done lecturing me yet, and I ducked another kiss.

"Last night—"

"Was last night. And I'm sorry." Milo landed his next kiss right in the center of my throat, making me give a happy sigh.

"You don't have to be sorry. You had an awful day yesterday. And you don't have to—"

"I want to." Milo cut me off by tumbling me onto the bed. "Can't you tell how much?"

"Maybe a little." I wiggled so that our torsos were aligned, and yeah, there was no mistaking that he was into this. That inner Good Guy of mine breathed a sigh of relief as I told him to go take a hike. I had this. And for right then, I had Milo, and I was going to enjoy every ridiculous moment.

"Who are you calling little?" Laughing, he kissed the tip of my nose.

"Definitely not you."

"Good." He sat up enough so he could pull off his shirt. And I probably should have removed my own clothes, but all I could do was marvel at the wonder that was Milo naked.

"It's too bad we weren't together when I accidentally took that poetry class sophomore year. I could have written my final portfolio all about your muscles. One of each type of sonnet."

"Ha. More like a limerick. There once was a jock from around the block…"

"Dork. But I'd read that." I laughed and went ahead and removed my shirt.

"Maybe we're both dorks." Milo dropped a kiss on my bare shoulder in between us scrambling out of the rest of our clothes.

"Totally." I gave a happy sigh as we settled back onto the bed together, skin to skin.

"Jasper?" Milo sounded serious, even for him, and I hoped we weren't about to renew the George debate.

"Yeah?" I said warily.

"I'm sorry I wasn't around your sophomore year."

Regret was way easier to navigate than irritation, and I'd been doing a fair bit of thinking on this myself.

"I'm not." My voice was firm.

"No?" Frowning, his face creased with way more hurt than I'd intended.

"I wasn't ready. Not for you. Not for this. You weren't the only one who needed to grow up." I wouldn't go as far as to say that I needed every breakup and hookup that went nowhere, but that time post–high school to discover who I was truly meant to be had been key, had led me here to this place where it was possible to forgive, to move on, and to build something real and solid and distinctly more lasting than a teenage fling.

"Yeah. I get that." Milo held me close, his chest hairs tickling my back. "But I can still wish I'd been there for you."

"You're sweet." I sagged against him. "I could stay exactly like this the rest of the night."

"And you're stealing all my best lines."

"That's the best you've got?" I pretended to scoff.

He turned me slightly in his embrace so he could peer into my eyes. "I think I'm falling in love with you."

My next breath strangled in my throat, and I made a choking noise. "Okay. That's…"

"Too much?" His cheeks took on a bright-pink stain and he sounded like he'd been running.

"No." I stretched to give him a gentle kiss, trying to put my awe and appreciation into it because God knew I lacked the words. And courage. "Never too much."

"Good." Milo soundly kissed me back, putting what felt like his whole heart into it. Mine was so full I wasn't sure I could stand it. I'd wanted to hear this. *Needed* it. And still this fluttery voice kept saying it wouldn't last. He'd change his mind or take a different Jasper-less path out of his current situation. *He's just grateful,* the voice added, a chill racing up my spine. He was undoubtedly waiting for me to say it back, but my worries kept coming instead.

"But this is what I meant earlier. About the future—"

"Which we are not thinking about right now." Voice commanding, Milo pulled back to hold me by the shoulders.

"But—"

He silenced me with a kiss that was less sweet and more ravenous. It was like a campfire threatening to leap out of the fire circle, heat licking at the base of my spine, warmth spreading through all my limbs. We kissed until I was a fire hazard waiting to happen, no more thinking about the future or about Milo's declaration or anything other than how much I needed him right that minute.

"Okay. Brain officially off-line." I groaned as he kissed his way down my neck, more purposeful now.

"Excellent." He leaned over the edge of my bed, fumbling for his backpack and coming up with the supplies we'd used the other night. He handed them to me before falling back against the pillows, grinning up at me.

"Wait."

"Brain." He danced a finger down the side of my face. "Go away."

"No, I meant we don't have to do it that way. If you want to change it up..." My neck heated. Felt polite, offering to switch since he still hadn't experienced both sides, and I didn't have my usual trepidation where bottoming was concerned. I wanted to share that with Milo, give him that first too.

"I don't need different. I know what I like." Grinning wickedly, he tugged me on top of him. "And what I want."

The last of my reservations rolled away. I knew what I liked, and him wanting that too was beyond sweet and perfect. He kissed me like he was trying to inhale a piece of my soul, and the hunger in his kiss and roving hands made my whole body thrill. I met him need for need, both of us moaning and moving together until I almost forgot the plan.

But Milo hadn't. He pulled back, breathing hard and eyes glassy. "And what I want is you. Now."

"Bossy," I chided even as I reached for the stuff.

"You love it."

"Maybe." Maybe my brain and all those insidious voices weren't going to let me say the words, but I tried to put all my racing emotions into our next kiss. And it must have worked because his head fell back, eyes closing as he groaned.

"Hurry."

"Slow, remember?" I wanted every time with him to be as good as the first time, never wanted to rush him even if his head was more impatient than the rest of his body.

"As long as you keep kissing me like that, you can go whatever speed you want."

"Good answer." Taking him at his word, I made a five-course holiday meal of kissing my way down his torso.

"Maybe not that slow—" His voice trailed off on a groan as I lightly raked my fingers against his ribs. "Hey. That tickles."

"Serves you right for complaining."

"Not complaining. Requesting." He made big, pleading eyes, and I was torn between laughing and giving him everything he ever wanted.

Indulging him won out as I added slick fingers into the mix of exploring his magnificent body. I loved how responsive he was, how his movements and low moans showed me exactly what he liked.

Milo groaned as I pushed a single digit inside, still going slow. "Oh. Wow. I'm not sure how it gets better, but it does."

"I can do even better."

"Brag—" Milo's whole body arched as I crooked my finger in a particularly deliberate way. "Okay. Yeah. That. Now."

"This?" I withdrew my finger and took care of the condom in record time.

"Yes."

I was going to suggest again that Milo flip, but he looked particularly debauched like this, sprawled on his back, eyes hot and needy, mouth slack. I wanted him exactly like this, forever. Slowly, I pushed in, watching his expression to gauge how fast to go. He felt incredible, but even more than that was the way he made me feel. Like I was the one who was the sea god or maybe a rock star. *A hero.* Someone powerful and adored, and someone who was worthy of sharing this with someone as amazing as Milo.

"Say it again," I demanded and he nodded, a little smile tugging at his lips even as his body surged with mine.

"I might love you."

Even the *might* was endearing, the way Milo qualified it as his eyes still bared his soul. The words spurred me on, and we moved faster and faster together. Our bodies were in perfect sync, like a complex equation with a singular solution, running on an infinite loop. Urgency built and I reached between us, knowing what he needed and loving how his body tensed further, back bowing.

"Jasper." He said my name like both a question and a prayer.

"Yes." I would have promised him anything in that instant, and while the power of speech rapidly slipped away, my soul crowed with the words I couldn't say aloud yet. My body moved like this was a song I'd heard a thousand times, like I knew exactly what to do and when. The physical pleasure wasn't entirely new, but it was different somehow, tinged with everything I felt for him.

Watching him feel it, too, was a new level of pleasure for me, and I reveled in Milo's reactions as the silent melody guiding us swelled and peaked. We both went over the edge at almost the same instant, and I was left drained, emotionally as well as physically spent.

"Wow." He sounded all dreamy and I loved knowing I was the reason why.

But I was also still me, and I needed to hear him say it. "Okay?"

"You need me to write you a sonnet?" He cracked one eye open.

"No. Just be you. And be okay."

"Always." He pulled me close enough for a tender kiss, soft and sleepy and *everything*.

"Always," I agreed.

I was a smart guy. I knew that *always* could be a rather finite amount of time. Short. But in that moment, I didn't want to think about that or any of my worries from earlier. I wanted to pretend that *always* meant forever and that meant having everything I'd ever wanted, even if it wasn't going to be easy. And as I rested my head on his chest a few minutes later after we'd cleaned up, snuggling in to drift off, I tried to ignore the way his heartbeat sounded suspiciously like a ticking clock.

CHAPTER THIRTY-FOUR
MILO

THERE WAS A CERTAIN WEIRD energy that the world took on after midnight. And I'd seen midnight enough to know, especially lately. Being in the game store this far after closing time was weird, especially as all the other downtown lights flickered off one by one, even the bars hitting closing time. Arthur's bulk card haul had ended up being boxes and boxes of assorted cards in apparently random order, and we'd spent hours trying to make sense of them, taking over the private game room at the back of the store with our sorting.

"If I see another scroll card, I might scream." Jasper, who usually was such a fountain of cheerfulness, sounded exhausted, and I rounded the table so I could rub his neck.

"You? Getting frustrated? Never."

"Hey, you don't have the market cornered on brooding and bad moods, you know." He stretched into my touch like a cat demanding more. His funk was far faster to fade than the one I'd been fighting for days now.

"Sorry. I don't mean to be so down." I kept rubbing his neck because it felt like the least I could do since he was putting up with me and this seemingly endless quest for the lost cards.

"You're going through a lot. I get it." Of course he did because he was like the most understanding person ever, which simply made me feel guiltier.

"I don't think I could be as nice as you," I admitted. He was in all respects the better person, and I remained in awe that he'd decided to turn all his wonderfulness in my direction again.

"Many have tried. Few have succeeded." He gave a regal nod, adopting his Frog Wizard persona for a beat, which earned a laugh from me.

"Goof."

"You love it." Moving away from my massage, he preened on his way back to his pile of cards.

"Maybe," I said cagily. He'd never said it back the night before, so I wasn't about to make another grand declaration right then while surrounded by piles of cards and Jasper's boss being in and out of the room. This thing between us was still relatively new. Fragile. I understood why he probably wasn't ready to say the words, but that didn't make having been the one to blurt it out easier.

Jasper, though, was not deterred. "You do."

Neither wanting to start an argument nor to put myself out there again, I tried to dodge my way out of that line of conversation, busying myself with my own sorting. "What I'd really love is to find one of the cards."

"Or anything of value," Jasper agreed as he separated out still more scroll cards. Unless they were a few select rare types, scrolls in *Odyssey* were penny cards, something experienced players bought in stacks to flesh out their deck. They might make the game go, but they were too common to offer much value to collectors. In the past few hours, I'd received quite the education on the types of rares and what cards actually fetched a decent price. And we'd uncovered precious few of those in this lot.

"I lost to this card in Philly." Jasper held up a card. "But it's a cheap common. Worthless unless it's in the right deck. I'll leave Arthur a buck for it, but it's sad that that's the best card I've seen in hours."

"See? Even you're discouraged."

"Jasper? Giving up?" Jasper's boss, an ex-military guy named Arthur who reminded me of some of Bruno's buddies, came into the room. He had that same sort of intimidating attitude as the special forces types I'd met, but he did seem to have a soft spot for Jasper. "He never quits."

"Thanks." Jasper offered him a weary smile.

"I'm heading out soon." Absently shuffling a stack of cards, Arthur rolled his neck. "I'm not up to all-nighters anymore."

"You're not that old," Jasper teased because Arthur wasn't Professor Tuttle's age by any means. "I'm pretty sure there are some mountain ranges with a few years on you."

"Ha. Can you and your boyfriend lock up when you're done? Triple-check the alarm."

"Okay, boss. Will do." Jasper glanced at me, clearly expecting some objection from me at the label. But it wasn't inaccurate. At least I hoped it wasn't. And ever since coming out to James and Luther, I'd felt strangely at peace. I wanted to be brave, like the singers in the revue the night before. To that end, I simply nodded and told the fluttering in my stomach to behave.

"Sure thing." I tried to project an air of trustworthiness to Arthur. "I'll make sure he sets the alarm. Thanks for the sandwiches and coffee."

Some hours earlier, after he'd seen the last customer out, Arthur had ordered Jasper to take a break and produced mugs of coffee and homemade sandwiches for us. I was starting to see why Jasper liked this little store so much. Arthur might be gruff, but he was kind, and the store was full of interesting displays and little treasures. It had a warmth that drew people in, and I appreciated that sort of hominess now more than ever.

Arthur pointed at my empty cup. "Glad someone appreciates my coffee."

"Install a soda machine and I might be more impressed," Jasper tossed back.

"Score me a stack of rares other than that Frog Court card you've got dibs on and I might consider it."

The two of them were fun to watch, and I had to laugh. But I was also genuinely grateful to Arthur for letting us have this shot at one of the cards we needed. "Thanks, man."

"No problem." He gave Jasper a few more reminders before heading out.

As the back door shut, Jasper stretched and waggled his eyebrows at me. "Alone at last."

"Us and a giant mess." I gestured at the sloppy piles covering the table.

"Why don't you put your urge to clean to good use?" Jasper suggested as he handed me some empty card boxes. "I'll sort and you stack and put away."

I did that, falling into a nice rhythm of straightening stacks and carefully labeling the boxes as Jasper directed. "This reminds me of sorting Legos together."

He reached out across the table and ruffled my hair. "We make a good team."

"We do." Our eyes met, and I was debating whether we could get away with a break for making out when my phone buzzed with a message.

"It's my mom," I said as I scrolled down my list of alerts.

Concern flashing across his face, Jasper pursed his mouth. "Bruno news?"

"Yeah. Not bad. But he'll be here next weekend. *Next weekend.* And Mom wants to make a big dinner."

"And you're worried about her cooking?" He did an exaggerated nervous expression, trying to earn a laugh, but this time it didn't work.

"Everything else. It's not enough time."

"It'll work out." He came around the table to hug me, but even his warm presence at my back wasn't enough to make my muscles relax.

"Says you." My retort made him step back, and I regretted it immediately, turning so I could pull him to me again. "But thanks. I'm lucky to have you, no matter how this goes."

"Maybe your luck is about to turn." He pointed at a box on the floor. "Last case."

"Okay. Maybe this is the good stuff." I hefted it up and peered over his shoulder as he opened it up.

"Maybe. I'm crossing—"

"Fuck." I didn't let him finish the thought because I knew what I was seeing and it wasn't good.

"More scrolls." Even Jasper sounded beyond dejected. "Okay. Let's actually dig. There might be something hiding."

But there wasn't. This wasn't a treasure hunt, and there wasn't some secret panel on the bottom of the box hiding a cache of rare cards. Jasper checked, even going so far as to turn each of the boxes upside down. Nothing.

"All right. This isn't an utter disaster." The way Jasper was wringing his hands said otherwise, right along with my stomach, which was making me regret those sandwiches. I popped two mints, but the sour feeling stayed.

"How so? Bruno's home next weekend. I'm out of time."

"We are not out of time." He drew his shoulders back, the commanding leader who wrangled his cosplay group into shape making an appearance. "I'll play George and—"

"I told you. I hate that idea." I might really enjoy bossy Jasper, but not right then, and not about my life. I pushed away from the table and stalked to the other side of the small room. "And it's not your call."

"Actually, it kind of is." Jasper followed after me. "It's

my ticket to the launch party. And it's my need to help you. Let me help you."

"Not like that." A faded poster on the wall welcomed newcomers to *Odyssey*, mocking me.

"Okay. I think you're being stubborn, but whatever." Jasper slumped into one of the folding chairs. I hated how defeated he sounded and was about to rub his shoulder when he added, "Maybe the best thing is to own up to what happened to Bruno."

"No. I can't do that." I took three steps backward, running into the wall. "I mean, here I am, life a mess again. Lost his cards. Lost my place to live—"

"But think about what you've gained." Jasper turned in his chair, eyes boring into mine. And I wasn't stupid. I knew what he meant. Self-respect. Ambition. Pride. Friends. *Him*. Definitely him and everything that included, every wonderful moment of the past few weeks. But none of that was going to matter. This wasn't one of Jasper's equations where one side balanced the other.

"He won't see that."

"You don't know that."

"Sure I do. He's been a success at everything. School. Special forces. Every sport and game he's tried. And me? I keep messing up. And now I'm a failure. Again."

"Gee. Tell us how you really feel." Jasper leaped out of his chair, took a step toward me, then apparently changed his mind and stomped to the other side of the table.

I held up both hands. "I didn't mean that being with you is a failure."

"No? Because it sure seems like you're trying to punish

yourself for being gay, chalking that up as one more black mark Bruno is going to hold against you."

"He stood up for me. All the time with Dad." I'd lost Dad, if I'd ever really had him. I'd lost James and Luther and a bunch of other pointless acquaintances. But I couldn't lose Bruno too. I just couldn't, and I needed Jasper to understand that. "He'd tell Dad to lay off me or he'd help me do my chores faster. And then when I had the accident—"

"I get it. He's been there for you. And you *did* make a big mistake with the cards. Which is why I want to play George for you. If it's that important to you that Bruno not know, let me do this for you. For us."

The thought of him playing George filled me with such rage and shame. Stepping back and letting him do that for me was more than I could bear. My back tensed, every muscle rigid. Jasper was always so quick with the solutions, the genius right answers, and I loved that about him, but I also simply couldn't stomach the thought of turning over my problems to him for the quick fix.

"This is my mess. I'll sort it out. Somehow."

"On your own," Jasper said flatly.

"I need to." I didn't know how I could expect him to understand when I didn't fully get it either, but fresh resolve drove me, like a pebble of an idea had started rolling and now it was a boulder and I couldn't stop it. And what was worse, I didn't know whether I should stop, whether my pride was about to trash what was left of my life or whether this was me making a long overdue stand.

"You came to me, you know. You asked me to help—"

"I know. And you've done so, so much. I can never repay you." I crossed the distance between us, but his expression was guarded, eyes narrow, fists clenched.

"I don't want repayment. I like helping you. It's what friends do. And we're friends, right?"

"More than. You know that." I reached a hand toward him, but he didn't take it.

"Do I? Because you're not acting the most like it right now."

"Sorry. It's because we're friends—boyfriends—that I don't want you playing George. I don't want you to have to rescue me." I wasn't the same guy who had walked into this game store all those weeks ago, and I needed to prove that to both of us. "I want to be the one protecting you sometimes too. And that includes from creeps."

"Milo." Jasper surprised me by touching my arm. "I don't need protecting. I don't. And you don't have to handle this yourself."

The air crackled, a charge sweeping through the room, reaching my stubborn brain. *Handle. Yourself.* And in that instant, I knew what I had to do, and maybe I'd known it all along because certainty settled over me like a heavy cloak.

"I think I know what I have to do." But it wasn't going to be easy, and as with most things, I didn't want an audience. "I need to go."

"Right now? Alone?" Jasper dropped his hand as his mouth went slack.

"I've got some stuff to work out in my head." What I really needed was a long, cold walk to grant me clarity. I wasn't like

Jasper, human search engine for a brain, quick-firing neurons. I needed to think. Also I knew he'd try to talk me out of this plan before I even got it settled. "Trust me?"

"I'm trying."

"Fair enough." I grabbed my coat.

"Milo. I hope you're not making a mistake," he warned.

My heart galloped because I hoped that too. But if it was a mistake, it was going to be my own mistake. And it was Jasper who made me brave. I was finally, finally going to solve everything, and this was a chance I had to take.

CHAPTER THIRTY-FIVE

JASPER

THE DOOR SHUT SOFTLY BEHIND Milo. No slamming. No screaming. It wasn't even a storming off as much as a bid for space, which even if I wasn't as introverted as him, I did sort of understand. I'd grown up in a big family with space at a premium. Finding a spot to be alone to think had been a challenge at times. But with Milo, I wanted to be together. A team, like we'd been earlier. The dynamic duo, solving all Milo's problems. Him shutting me out hurt. If he didn't want the same kind of partnership I did, I wasn't sure where that left us.

But mainly, I was super worried about Milo. As I cleaned up the last of the card mess, I kept debating exactly how worried I should be. He was a big guy, sober, on a clear night that for once was showing signs of spring. If he needed a walk in the dead of night, so be it.

However, his parting words had been rather...ominous. I took my phone out. No messages. Should I text someone? My mom? His? A friend? I didn't want to call for backup this late at night without a good reason. I didn't think Milo would do anything too rash. For all that he could brood, he'd never shown a tendency to self-harm, but I was still worried.

I stacked boxes and wiped the table with quick, jerky movements. And maybe some of my concern was because I had a strong feeling where he was headed and why he hadn't told me. He knew I'd stop him. Which I probably still would. I knew exactly how long it would take Milo to walk there at a slow pace, so I'd let him get a head start, finish up here, then go talk some sense into him.

Thump. I was almost done cleaning when I tripped over Milo's backpack. Heck. He had to be really worked up to have forgotten it. His sketchbook was under it because he'd been noodling with a drawing earlier while I'd been busy doing stuff for Arthur to close up the store. When I lifted up the backpack, the motion pulled the sketchbook open. And what I saw took my breath away.

Me. Over and over again, me. Me as the Frog Wizard, me as a regular guy in my hoodie, happy, joking, quiet, sexy, a myriad of different moods. I crouched low to get a better look, transfixed. I should have shut it fast, but I couldn't. Because there on those pages was *love*, bold and fearless. He'd said the word the night before, but I'd been half-convinced that was sex talking. But here on these pages, his pencil didn't lie.

He saw me like no one else had ever seen me. Saw beyond the joker and funny guy to the parts of me that were softer, more serious. Vulnerable. More like him.

My legs cramped from holding the position, but I didn't

care. If he could see me so well, didn't I owe it to him to try to see him too? Not simply my stack of assumptions about him and what he needed, but him as he actually was, all of him. I'd spent days trying to come up with plans for him, but had I seen him amid all my scheming?

Because there he was on the pages too. Self-portraits and cartoon Milo both. Cartoon Milo was more like me, joking and open. In so many ways, we'd always been mirror images of each other. Seeing him like this underscored both our differences and the ways we complemented each other. He was always saying how I was nicer and a better person, but he made me that way, both as part of my past and now as what I wanted for my future.

Seeing his more serious self-portraits, it was easy to grasp his complexity—the artsy, almost poetic parts dancing alongside the sporty, brash parts. He had visions for his future, too, little sketches for how he might arrange a small room and one of cartoon Milo holding up a drawing. I'd wanted so badly to rescue that Milo, the one that had been afraid to let those different parts of himself see the light. But what if he'd never truly needed my rescue? What then?

Speaking of rescues, there was one of Bruno too, looking heroic in his uniform. The love was apparent there, too, and I understood better than most how family ties could run deep. Jeff's distance still hurt, and even Katie and Brenda getting their own lives was bittersweet. April would grow up someday too, need me less, but I wasn't suddenly going to stop being her big brother. Maybe it wasn't fair of me to ask Milo to stop caring so much about what Bruno thought of him. It mattered to Milo.

And Milo mattered to me.

Buzz. My phone vibrated on the table above me, and I unfolded my stiff body to reach for it.

Triple-check the locks. Not a word about why he'd left or where he'd gone, but he'd promised Arthur he'd remind me, so he had. My chest pinched, a deep, hard pang.

Are you okay? That was what I truly needed to know.

Yeah.

Good. There was so much I wanted to say, but none of it would fit in a text. My words would have to wait.

And I was going after him—as soon as I triple-checked the locks—but I was no longer racing to stop him from doing something stupid. Rather, I was ready to listen, really listen with my whole heart, and open my eyes and *see* him. Only then could I hope to actually *help*.

CHAPTER THIRTY-SIX
MILO

"I KNEW YOU'D COME." I didn't look up as Jasper plopped himself down on the paver closest to where I was sitting. And I had, had known even as I shut the shop door that he'd follow. Honestly, I was surprised it had taken him this long. Perhaps more surprising was that I'd wanted him to come and had been actively missing him since about three minutes into my cold trek here. I hadn't been lying. I had needed the walk to clear my head, sort through the muddle of emotions that had arisen during our argument. But now he was here, and I wasn't upset to see him.

"I'm always going to come." Like me, Jasper kept his voice down. "Even though you don't want me—"

"I want you. I can want space and still want you to chase after me. I'm a fickle guy."

"Not fickle. Complicated." Even now he was loyal to me.

"How'd you guess I'd be here?" I gestured at his parents' yard. I'd been taking a chance that they hadn't installed motion-sensitive flood lights or something, but I'd been sitting here awhile now and no alarms had sounded and the house had stayed dark and quiet.

"Maybe I know you." Jasper raised an eyebrow at me. Dawn was still a way off, but there was a dim alley light close by, casting long shadows over us and glinting off his hair and eyes.

"You do." I sighed, because I was still working out how I felt about that. It was entirely possible that he knew me better than anyone else. "Did you come here to stop me?"

Jasper was silent for a long second, joining me in staring at my car. He knew. I knew. There was no point in either of us playing stupid. It was my one thing of value, the end-of-game card I'd been holding all along, and maybe we'd both known how this would play out.

"I was. I was going to come and try to talk you out of whatever plan you've got. But not now."

"No?" I turned more toward him. He looked older, somehow, in the night air. Taller, back straight, gaze locked on the car, not on me. "What changed?"

"I found your sketchbook."

"Oh." It said something that I only realized in that instant that I had left my backpack behind.

"I brought it and your bag. And yes, I know it was a huge invasion of privacy to look, and this is probably where I should start by begging forgiveness—"

"You don't have to beg. I made mistakes tonight too," I admitted. It didn't bug me that he'd seen my sketches as much as make me wary of his reaction. "And I was working up the nerve to show you the whole thing for a while now. I was worried it might scare you away."

"Never." He scooted closer, touched my arm. "You're not getting rid of me that easily. Or scaring me away with your gorgeous drawings. They're amazing. You're amazing."

"Thanks." My skin heated even in the chilly air. "But how did my drawings change your mind about stopping me?"

"I saw myself. I saw you. And I realized that I wasn't doing the best job of listening. I've been doing a lot of telling. Telling you to get a new place to live. Telling you that I'd play George. Telling you to come clean with Bruno."

"You meant well." I returned the favor and patted his shoulder. Touching him felt good. Necessary even. I settled an arm around him. "And a lot of it was good advice."

"But I wasn't *asking* you what you want and why, and actually paying attention to your answers. Really listening. Like you always do."

"I do?"

"You hear even the stuff I don't say. I joked about how I know you, but you know me. I could see it in each sketch. And it made me want to do a better job of seeing you. Hearing you."

"Wow." I'd done my own thinking during our time apart that evening, but he might have outdone me in the profound realization department. My neck relaxed, a tension I hadn't even known I'd been holding ebbing away. "Thank you."

"So this is me, asking. Not telling. Not trying to solve the problem. What are you going to do?"

"I think you already know." I pointed at the car.

"You're going to sell it?" Jasper put deliberate emphasis on the word *sell*, a question, not a statement.

"It's the right thing to do. And you made me see that." I pulled him closer, both because of the cold and because his nearness made it easier to make these big confessions.

"I did?"

"When you said that I didn't have to handle things myself, I realized the opposite. I *need* to handle this. I spent weeks running from the real solution. And not simply the owning up to Bruno part—you're not wrong there either— but I have the way to make this right."

"But it's your dad's legacy. You said that yourself. It's the one thing you can't part with." Jasper bit his lip like he was trying hard not to be too argumentative.

"And maybe it's the one thing I should," I countered. I'd been round and round on this point in my own head, but saying it aloud actually helped me to feel more definite about the idea. Mom liked to go on about how people like Dad and Nona were guardian angels now. And I'd never bought that, especially in the case of Dad who could have done a lot more protecting when he was alive. I was done elevating him to a pedestal he didn't deserve. However, if he were watching over me, was it so terrible to use the car to ensure my future?

"If I sell, I might get enough to replace the cards and to help make finding a new place to live easier. Maybe even have something left over to take a few art classes. I can make my dreams come true, at least some of them."

"You can make your dreams come true even without the car, but I get what you're saying." Jasper exhaled, his breath warm against my neck. "I hate to think of you parting with it though. Your dad wanted you to have it."

"And I did. I kept it even when I probably should have sold it to repay Bruno after the accident. I kept it even when I was scared to drive it. But like you said the other day, I'm not fourteen anymore. I can't live my life by what he would have wanted for me. He wouldn't have wanted any of this." I did a broad, sweeping gesture encompassing myself.

"He didn't know what he was missing." Jasper gave me a soft kiss on the cheek, but I turned in to him so that our mouths met, more comfort than sizzle, but so very necessary right then.

"Thank you." I hugged him against me. "I mean that. Thank you. And you do see me. You see all the parts he didn't. And I'm done trying to hide the real me. The truth is that he wasn't a very good dad—"

Jasper was quick to cut me off. "He wasn't terr—"

"Yeah, he kinda was." I appreciated him trying to be tactful, but I was done with dancing around the facts. "It's okay. We can say it now. He was narrow-minded and mean. And yeah we built that car together and not all my memories are bad, but that's okay. I'll keep the good times. Now I'm going to use what he left me to have the life I want—need, even if it's not one he would have agreed with."

"Okay." Jasper nodded like he'd finished a page of equations and was happy with the solution, even if it wasn't the one he'd wanted. "So you'll sell it then?"

"Yup." As I said it aloud, a weight rolled off me, like leaving all my winter gear behind to enjoy spring and summer. I was free.

"You were so sure that I'd object that you couldn't tell me the plan back at the store?" There was no mistaking the hurt in Jasper's voice, and I didn't blame him. Walking away had been a dick move on my part.

"That and I thought I wanted to be alone to do this. Solve everything on my own, and then come to you with it all fixed. Be more worthy of you. But then my leg started to ache on the walk here—"

"Oh crap." Jasper flipped from justifiably annoyed at me to worried. "Do you need—"

"It's fine." I waved off his concern. "And then this car passed me, full of rowdy teenagers. A soda can landed right near my feet."

"I should have—"

"I'm not trying to make you feel bad. I'm the one who left. My point is that I was cold and my leg hurt and these kids were laughing at me out the window. And then I thought, 'What the hell am I doing here?' Because if I was trying to make a point about how I could do it all on my own, I was doing a shit job at it."

"Wanting to be self-sufficient isn't a bad goal. I get that desire. I do." Jasper was so earnest, I very nearly had to kiss him again, but I wasn't done yet.

"Thanks. But what I realized in that moment was that I was acting exactly like my dad would have. Angry. Storming off alone. Insisting on no help."

"Oh, Milo."

"But maybe there's a better way. Maybe I don't have to

do it entirely on my own." I exhaled hard, because this was tricky, the balance between being needy and being resourceful, between being a loner and being independent, and between being stubborn and being smart. Even now I wasn't sure I had it right.

"You don't have to do it all. But I don't think you're in the wrong for wanting to. And I was trying to take over a bit. I get why you needed me to back off." Jasper's expression was as earnest as I had seen it as he held my gaze. "You're not your dad. You're never going to be your dad. You're a way better person and always have been."

"Maybe not always." Unable to keep looking at him, I studied my scuffed shoe.

"No, I mean it." Jasper tilted my chin up with his fingers. "Unlike him, you've owned up to your mistakes."

"I'm trying." I met his determined gaze, wanting to convey how much it meant that he believed in me.

"You're doing a good job."

"Thanks." That did it. I had to give him another kiss, this one more lingering. "And maybe it's okay to admit when I need help."

"And when you don't. It needs to be *your* plan."

"Yeah." I nodded.

"So tell me what the plan is and how I can help. I want to help." Jasper squeezed my arm.

"I figured I'd wait until morning, then take the car to my dad's friend, the one storing Bruno's car, find out what a fair price would be, hope I don't get screwed—"

"Is this the part where I can offer help?" Jasper was

practically bouncing next to me, a sure sign that he'd had a big idea.

"You can offer to help."

"I might not be a car guy, but I am an expert at pricing rare items and at research. I can make sure you're getting a good deal. If you want, I mean."

"I want." I kissed his temple. "I do want your help, and I want *you*."

That little speech earned me another kiss from him. The paver was cold under my butt and the air still nippy, but things were heating up right where they counted. In Jasper's parents' yard. In the middle of the night. *Oops.* I pulled away, breathing hard, and he laughed.

"And we can cross-check my research with Professor Tuttle tonight. He knows classic cars. If that's okay."

"It's okay. What I realized is I don't have to do it all on my own and neither do you."

"Assemble the team!" Jasper pumped a fist upward like his invisible cape might carry him skyward.

"Shh." I was laughing too hard to do a good job quieting him. "Dork."

"You—"

"Love you. Yeah. I just might." I went ahead and said it because maybe he needed to hear it. And maybe I needed to say it. "And yes, assemble the team. The dynamic duo rides at dawn."

"Maybe not dawn." He yawned wide. "How about first some sleep, then we save the world?"

"Deal." I still didn't have all the answers and neither did he. I had no idea how things were going to turn out—the car, the cards, Bruno, my living situation—all of it. But I knew I had Jasper, and that was what truly mattered.

CHAPTER THIRTY-SEVEN
JASPER

"OH, GOOD. YOU'RE HERE." PROFESSOR Tuttle was laughing, expression sly as he opened his door. "What we need is a heist."

As the professor moved aside so we could enter, Milo leaned in close, whispering, "When I said assemble the team, I didn't mean criminal masterminds. We can't let the old guys get arrested on my behalf."

"They won't." Of that I was pretty sure, and I sneaked a quick pat on his back as we shed our coats. He was still a little jumpy after our late-night soul-baring conversation. Professor Tuttle being apparently ready for grand larceny was not helping matters.

"A heist?" I asked louder.

"A cookie heist." Professor Herrera came into the hall, drying his hands on a dish towel. "They're cooling. And none until after your game and after the snack I'm making."

"Darn." Professor Tuttle gave him such a fond look that my stomach cramped from the sweetness. *Maybe someday.* Despite the lack of sleep, Milo and I had lain awake, talking more until the sun was teasing the sky, and then we'd finally drifted off for a couple of hours. Waking up with him was fast becoming my favorite thing on earth.

"And Milo! Exactly the nongamer I was hoping to see!" Professor Herrera clapped Milo on the back. "Want to learn some new knife skills? I'm making a new sheet-pan nachos recipe with my homemade salsa."

"Uh. Okay. Thanks." Milo blinked, clearly not expecting this welcome.

"I want to hear all about this group-house situation Jasper mentioned to me too," the professor added as he led a befuddled Milo toward the kitchen.

"They'll be all right," Professor Tuttle assured me as we headed to the dining room table. Apparently not needed for the revue that night, Kellan was already there, fiddling with the cameras.

"No Jasmine?" I asked as I set my stuff down.

Kellan made a sad face. "She had a paper to write. Not everyone has the cupcake of a last semester schedule like you."

"By design." I pulled out a deck and started shuffling while waiting for Professor Tuttle to get situated. "I front-loaded my year because I knew I'd be ready to be done."

"Done?" Kellan shot me a skeptical look. "Thought you were the one who wasn't ready to graduate and move on."

"That was before…" My voice trailed off because so much had happened in only a few weeks. Milo. The cards. New certainty about what I wanted. "Yeah. I am ready. Bring on whatever's next."

"Absolutely agree. I've got two interviews for summer-stock costuming positions."

"Seriously? That's awesome." I was going to miss my friends, no question. And I'd miss my family if I moved away, even a short distance, but I finally felt ready. Ready for graduation. Ready to see Kellan crushing it with Broadway and Hollywood costumes. Ready to let people move on even as I kept others close. Like Milo. As I set up my play mat, I could see us squashed into a chair together, scrolling social media, seeing where everyone else ended up. The future might still be big and scary, but it was way more hopeful now.

"Now, Jasper." Across from me, Professor Tuttle slapped a deck down on the table. "I have a new gambit play I want to explain and then have you demonstrate defending against."

The professor's move was truly devious, and I couldn't decide which I liked better: the play itself, which involved discarding an entire hand, or defending against it, which took a certain deftness.

"Aha!" I crowed as I finally mastered the timing for getting my block ready. "I see your plan and not today! Countered!"

"Excellent, Jasper," Professor Tuttle cheered.

"Oh, this would be perfect against cheaters like George," Kellan observed as he gave the signal that we were off-camera again.

Right then, Milo came to the doorway, his speculative expression revealing that he'd probably heard George's name. I tried not to feel a pang of regret that I wouldn't get to play hero for him, swoop in and restore Milo's cards, and crush George in the process.

"Food's ready."

"Cookies!" Professor Tuttle skipped the nachos to take two cookies while Professor Herrera clucked at him. They were almost too cute. The rest of us made plates of food while Milo proudly explained what was in each component.

"Did you know dicing and mincing are not the same?" Smiling shyly, he handed me a soda.

I blinked at him, adjusting my future vision from earlier to include lots of trips to the grocery store. "I do now."

"Okay, you two. Tell me about this car of Milo's and what you've found on the internet already." After putting his reading glasses on, Professor Tuttle pulled out a fancy pen and a little notepad, exactly like this was one of his seminar classes.

Milo explained the whole history of the car, its year and make, and the prerestoration condition. He then launched into everything that had been done to it as well as how he maintained it. It was a lot, and I was staggered by how much Milo had put into the car himself, not simply assisting his dad. I wanted to tug on his sleeve, to ask him if he was absolutely certain he wanted to part with this car, but I'd promised not to talk him out of this. If Milo thought selling was the right call, then I was going to support that, even as I marveled at this side to Milo I hadn't really seen before.

"So anyway, the heater's really the only drawback, but it's functional and a top-of-the-line part. Oh, and it's clean. I'd detail it again before selling—"

"You could perform surgery in the back seat," I joked.

"We don't need to know how you've seen the back seat," Kellan tossed back.

"Gentlemen," Professor Tuttle gently reminded us that he was still there, taking notes. "I think what you've found is accurate as far as asking price. But go up a few thousand. Let the buyer talk you back down. And I agree about asking the collector who's storing your brother's car. However, I also know a few collectors myself who won't haggle with you too much. Can I make some calls?"

I liked how Professor Tuttle asked instead of telling. I was trying to get better at that myself. Milo seemed to like that, too, nodding thoughtfully. "Yeah, I'd appreciate it. I need a fast sale. And not just because Bruno's coming back. I can't keep crashing with Jasper in the dorms."

"Yes, you can." I'd go to bat with the RA myself before I let Milo sleep in his car or something else drastic.

"I don't want to get you in trouble." Milo's eyes were serious.

"That's a good point." Professor Herrera stroked his chin. "I think I might have a temporary solution."

He and Professor Tuttle did some sort of longtime-couple-communication magic with their eyes before Professor Tuttle pronounced, "Brilliant idea. I concur."

"We have a spare room—"

Milo held up a hand. "I can't impose like that on you guys. You've been so nice already."

"Oh, this isn't me being nice." Professor Herrera's eyes sparkled like he was holding a winning card and knew it.

"The room is full of boxes. Boxes that I need removed if we're going to have more guests. And since we moved our room downstairs after Gus's fall, I've had a list of furniture I want rearranged, but I can't do it on my own. Trust me, I'll make you earn your keep while you're visiting."

"I could do that," Milo allowed, licking at his lips. The hope in his expression made my chest hurt. I wanted him to have so much more than a safe place for a couple of nights.

"I can help. I'm good at moving stuff." I patted his biceps. "Maybe not as good as these muscles, but I can help, spare Professor Herrera's back."

"But only until I find something more permanent." Milo remained somber, regarding all of us like this were a treat that might be yanked away. "I don't want to take advantage."

"Are you going to assist in eating all the odd recipe experiments Julio dreams up?" Professor Tuttle turned toward Milo, merriment sweeping across his craggy face. "You're not taking advantage. You're exactly what we need."

"Me too," I added. And he was. He was exactly what I both needed and wanted.

"Dude, I'm not sure whether to ask for a group hug or text Jasmine and tell her about the new epic levels of adorableness reached tonight. Maybe both." Kellan chuckled as he grabbed another cookie. "And I'll come help tomorrow with box-o-palooza. We can do an assembly line."

"Wow. You guys don't have to help me." Milo darted his gaze between us, still looking wary, like the offer might evaporate any second.

"We want to," Kellan and I said in unison.

"Thanks." Under the table, Milo tapped my foot with his.

"Did you want to stay tonight or did you have...plans?" Professor Herrera raised an eyebrow in my direction as he spoke to Milo.

Milo glanced at me. We weren't as skilled at the whole wordless conversation yet, so I spoke up. "He has plans."

"But tomorrow." Milo had turned a delightful shade of pink at the mere implication of sleeping together. "We can't expect your RA to ignore us forever."

"Sounds good." Professor Herrera led us in cleaning up before Professor Tuttle got too worn out. Milo proved what an awesome house guest he was going to be as he washed the big pots while Kellan and I put stuff away. Meanwhile, the professors worked putting their dining room to rights again.

"I saw George last night backstage at the revue," Kellan said as we worked. "He was talking smack. Are you gonna put him in his place? I wanna see that."

"No. Probably not." I couldn't keep the regret from my tone, and I very carefully avoided looking at Milo.

"You really want to, don't you?" Milo asked me softly.

"Yeah. I do. But you asked me not to do that, so I won't, but man, stomping him would feel so good."

"And if you lost?" Milo's mouth was a thin, narrow line.

I shrugged. "At least I would have tried. Even heroes have off days."

With damp hands, Milo turned me by my shoulders, so we were eye to eye. "You're already my hero."

I'd waited maybe my whole life to hear those words, and my jaw dropped open, mouth filling with so many words I wanted to say and—

"Aw, you guys..."

I'd totally forgotten Kellan was still three feet away from us. "Kellan—"

"I'm going. Heading out now. Catch you both tomorrow." Laughing, Kellan grabbed his coat and ducked out the back door.

"You mean that?" I asked the second the door clicked. "I'm your hero?"

"You are. No matter how this turns out. You saved me from myself, and that makes you a superhero in my book."

"Wow. I always wanted to be the hero." I could admit that aloud to him because he knew. He knew the kid I'd been who had wanted the cape and fancy costume and the big, daring rescues. It was part of why I loved being an older brother so much—I got to be April's hero now and then. And Milo also knew the guy I was now, the one who let that urge to be the hero get the better of him sometimes. Like last night. Milo didn't *need* rescuing, and I knew that he needed to do his own saving sometimes. However, all those big realizations didn't stop me from wanting to swing in with the win anyway.

"You don't have to win me the cards, but it means a lot that you want to try, even if I hate the idea of you anywhere near that scuzzbucket."

"I know." The air went out of my superhero fantasy, cape

deflating. I wasn't going to go behind Milo's back or risk making him upset, not when we were finally in such a good place together.

"Too bad you can't do a fake-out." Milo looked away, studying the refrigerator art which as usual was a collection of tickets to upcoming events, magnets from their travels, and random drawings.

"What do you mean?"

"You're big on me asking for help. Why not ask Conrad to hook you up with another ticket? Call in a favor. George doesn't have to know you've got the hookup, and then it wouldn't feel so much like you're gambling your whole future on me."

"It would be worth it though. I'd bet everything on you. On us." I met his gaze, trying to convey how serious I was. I'd risk everything to be with him, and in the grand scheme of things, the ticket to the event was nothing compared to how I felt about him. My future employment could work itself out.

"I know." Milo nodded slowly. "And I'm still selling the car. Whether you win or not."

"Of c—*Wait*. You're going to let me play him?"

"You don't need my permission." Milo made a sour expression. "I don't want to be that kind of controlling boyfriend—"

"Hey, I'll take you being a boyfriend, period."

"Be serious for a sec. You deserve a non-dickhead boyfriend and to make your own choices, same as me. If you want to play George, play him. Like Kellan said, a lot of people would love to see you win."

"Thanks." Another thought occurred to me. "Two tickets would mean I could bring you along. If I won."

Another magical night with Prince Neptune? I was totally in favor of that, but also the scheming side of my brain was already thinking of ways to show off Milo's art to the right people.

"You'll win." He sounded absolutely convinced and I hoped he was right. I didn't want to let him down, but more important, I didn't want to let myself down.

CHAPTER THIRTY-EIGHT
MILO

"OKAY, VERY FUNNY, GUYS." GEORGE sneered as he entered the room, a supermodel-attractive girl and a guy who looked familiar from the revue following him. "This isn't a duel at dawn. Did we really need fifty texts laying out the terms of engagement? Seconds? Neutral location? Judge? Isn't this overkill?"

"Nah." Game face on, Jasper slapped his deck bag down onto the table in one of the student union's private study rooms. He had Kellan and me flanking him, exactly like this *was* a duel as we stared down the competition.

"I could have hosted." George took out a leather-and-wood deck box that probably cost more than the heater for my car, never mind the pricey cards inside.

"I don't trust you." Jasper echoed my sentiments, voice cool and conversational. I'd come with him to reserve the room earlier in the day, and I'd been the one to push for a neutral location. I didn't trust George either, and while it was rather caveman of me, I didn't particularly want us entering his space. Luckily, Jasper had agreed. "You probably have one of those eight-grand custom gaming tables with secret panels. Or hidden cameras."

"You're giving me ideas." George's wicked smile reminded me of how I'd fallen prey to his charms to start with and made my stomach lurch. *Ugh.* How could I have been so stupid?

"Ideas? More like your MO." I rolled my eyes at him. "Arthur wouldn't even agree to you being at the game store after hours."

"Your reputation does precede you," Jasper added.

"Rumors." George made a dismissive gesture.

"We'll see." Jasper matched his indifferent tone, like it hadn't taken a ton of tense negotiating to get to this point where he was about to play George for one of the two cards I still needed. We'd agreed to here, two witnesses each, and a judge to enforce tournament-style rules.

"I'm here. Sorry, my seminar ran over." Professor Tuttle bustled into the room, leaning on his cane, backpack with a math book sticking out over one shoulder.

"That I got an A in last term's seminar is the only reason why I agreed to the ridiculous idea of having a rules judge." George moved aside for Professor Tuttle to take a seat. "And I still say we should film this as an episode of the show."

"No." Professor Tuttle had firmly put an end to that idea already. "I can't have gambling on the vlog. And this is where I should point out that a gentlemanly exchange might be more civilized than a bet—"

"But what's the fun in that?" George all but cackled at the notion of being a gentleman.

"Let the history books record that for the first time ever, I'm agreeing with you." Shuffling his deck, Jasper didn't bother looking up. I was enjoying this badass side to him, the way he was projecting a confident, devil-may-care attitude. The way he'd chattered the whole walk over here revealed that he was actually amped up and nervous, but he'd settled down the minute we'd spotted George, almost like how he sank into his role in the cosplay group.

"Shall we get started?" Sounding like a bored host, George fanned out his deck, showing off his custom sleeves. "I assume the judge needs to see our decks."

"Tournament rules," Professor Tuttle reminded both of them as he inspected the decks. Jasper had been up late last night tweaking his deck for the new rules and trying to predict what George was likely to bring.

"Big and flashy," I'd guessed, and I was right, as his opening play was a mirror card—an ultra-rare card type Jasper had introduced me to that was prized by players because it bestowed extra powers. He ramped up quickly after that, but Jasper attacked him with a single-minded focus that was weirdly sexy, the way he went at George, knocking down threat after threat.

"You're more aggressive than usual, Quigley. I might be impressed." George raised his eyebrows before smiling at his entourage. "Might."

"Your turn." Jasper tapped the table.

"Look at you. No trash talk even."

"Nah. Just winning." Unlike George, who kept playing to his audience, Jasper hadn't glanced once at Kellan or me.

He was deep in his own head, and it was almost scary the way he dismantled George's deck. For all he'd always counseled me about not attacking too early in a game, he was aggro in the best way, attacking methodically over and over.

Kellan whistled low under his breath. "Geez. Don't ever get mad at me."

"Tell me about it," I whispered back. "I might be afraid to ever play him again."

"Oh, he'd be gentle with you. Especially if you asked nice," Kellan teased. And for once, the double meaning didn't make me squirm. It was getting easier and easier being a public couple, holding hands in his dorm and exchanging long looks as we walked across campus. But then, random strangers weren't truly the issue. It was easy not to care about them and their opinions, but telling myself to do the same with Bruno or my mom was another thing entirely. Fresh dread gathered in my stomach at the thought of the coming weekend and the conversations that had to happen.

However, those thoughts took a back seat to the game as both players traded blows. Momentum stayed with Jasper, though, and he took the first match handily.

"Bad deal." George shrugged like he couldn't care less about being on the ropes.

And indeed, he didn't play like someone on the verge of losing. If anything, he became more relaxed and fluid while Jasper tightened up further and further. Even his grip on his cards was tense.

"Not so smug now, are you?" Rolling his neck, George pushed back in his chair like he was about to order a drink. As I well knew, his charm tended to increase as he sensed a win. The snake.

"Take your turn." Jasper's mouth was a thin line. From my vantage point behind him, I could see his cards, and I'd been working to keep my face neutral with each draw. Also, I'd watched and played enough to know that he'd gotten screwed by his opening hand. His nerves probably weren't helping, but like always, he played better as he slipped further behind. However, despite scrappy play, he wasn't able to recover from the bad start, which meant everything would come down to the third match.

"See?" Flashing a victory smile for his friends, George stretched. "I just had an unlucky deal that first round."

"You sure about that?" Even with the loss, Jasper seemed to have recovered some of his swagger.

"Of course." George gave a lazy shrug.

"Put your money where your mouth is." Jasper leaned forward as if he were about to pounce. "Put up a second card for the final round. Winner takes all."

Kellan and I gasped in unison from the sidelines, and I watched George carefully. He loved escalating bets, as I well knew. Would he take the bait?

"Tempting. You putting up a second ticket?"

Oh. That I hadn't been expecting. At all. George wasn't supposed to guess our fake-out. And Jasper had scored a second from Conrad, but it had come with the warning that the event was now completely sold out. No other help was incoming.

Jasper made an indignant noise. "I don't—"

"You're crap at bluffing. Of course you've got the

hookup. Come on. You want me to go double or nothing, you do it too."

Jasper subtly darted his gaze my direction. *Crap.* Way to put me on the spot. I'd told him not to gamble his future. But I also believed in him, believed him when he told me the job situation would work itself out. It wasn't so much that I thought this was Jasper's only chance, but rather my own mixed-up emotions as to how much I wanted him to stake on me. He was a sure thing. Me? I was the bad bet. I didn't want to be the reason he lost even a single opportunity. But I was also supposed to be working on trusting him more. Letting us each make our own choices. He was trusting me about selling the car. Maybe I was supposed to do the same here.

I shrugged, then gave the barest of nods, trying to convey that it was up to him.

"You're on." Jasper smacked the table for emphasis, eyes glinting. Yeah, he'd wanted this moment, wanted to have it all on the line.

And now he did, but he was playing like it too, slow, cautious moves that kept getting blocked. Where was aggressive Jasper? Was his confidence shot because of the loss? Was he too nervous now? I bit my finger, trying not to reveal my worry but probably failing.

"You're on the rocks, Quigley. Better have a good comeback."

I held my breath, unsure whether Jasper could pull this off. I wanted to believe in him, wanted this for him more than for me, but things were looking decidedly bleak. Everything came down to his next move.

CHAPTER THIRTY-NINE
JASPER

"WELL? I'M WAITING. I'VE GOT plans after I win." George's cockiness was infuriating as always. I rearranged my hand of cards, like it might give me different answers if I sorted them in a different order.

"You and your *plans* can chill." I shot a look at his two companions who'd seemed super bored the whole match. The guy had his phone out and the girl had filed her nails, written in a leather day planner, and read over some printed handouts all in the time we'd been playing. At least she was getting shit done. Unlike me. "I'm thinking."

Really, I was less *thinking* and more counting. Calculating. I wanted to try Professor Tuttle's gambit from Saturday night. I had an idea for a twist that was all my own, and it might be my only hope. The episode hadn't aired yet. I might manage to catch George unprepared for this sort of move, but for it to succeed, I had to precisely weigh my odds of getting the cards I needed. Milo was always marveling about my big brain, but I needed every spare neuron as I built a mathematical model in my head. I also needed to not glance at Milo because his faith in me was more than a little intimidating.

I kept tensing up, wanting to make him proud. This would be so much easier if it were just him and me at the pizza place, me showing off about the game or stochastic processes.

Wait.

I was making this far too complex. I remembered how I'd explained things to Milo, making predicting seemingly random events like which cards were likely to show up in a given card draw easy to understand. I had it. Now to show off.

"Quick change," I announced as I played the card. I'd added it at 2:00 a.m. I hadn't been able to sleep after Milo left for another night at the professors' house, and I had kept fiddling with my deck rather than confront how lonely my bed seemed without him in it. And how nervous I was about this match. But I couldn't show my nerves. I'd let them get the better of me in round two. I wasn't going to lose twice.

"What fresh hell is this?" George snatched the card up, as I'd known he would. It wasn't an expensive card, but it also wasn't common. Few players wanted to discard their entire hand and take the risk of all new cards. But I'd done the math. This was my best chance.

"Response?" I tried to sound bored, like I didn't care if he countered the card. But everything hinged on him letting the card through. I also didn't dare look at anyone. If Kellan or Professor Tuttle caught on to my move, their expression could give me away.

"Whatever." George waved his hand dismissively. "Do your Hail Mary."

"Don't mind if I do." I discarded the five cards I'd been holding, then drew a fresh five. I didn't waste time reviewing them. In that moment, I was the Frog Wizard and my ability to deceive and mislead was more important than what I'd actually drawn. "Your turn."

"This is getting pointless." George took his turn and shaved another few points off my life total. Another turn and he'd have me.

Showtime. My turn. I slapped down a hasty warrior princess, schooling my expression.

"Tell me you're not attacking." George shook his head like he was already deciding what to wear for the launch party.

I considered everything I'd counseled Milo about patience and not attacking too recklessly. And threw that advice out the window. Bring on the balls-to-the-wall heedless attack.

"Attack." I threw everything I had at George. Well, almost everything.

"All in?"

"Yup." The part of me who was Milo's boyfriend was trembling. I needed a certain response from George or else this was going to fall apart. However, my inner Frog Wizard winked. *You've got this.* George wouldn't shake. He'd revel in the moment. Which was what I did, leaning back in my chair.

"You've miscalculated," he scoffed, exactly as I wanted. "Let me see how I want to block."

Taking a breath, I waited until he lined up his cards. "Kill them all."

Snap. I put down Grave Mistake. It had been in the lot of bulk cards Milo and I had sorted. I'd said it needed the right deck, but really it needed the right move and the right player. Me.

"Vicious." George whistled but didn't move to remove his cards. "And illegal."

"Rules?" I'd been anticipating this.

"According to the official guidebook…" Professor Tuttle held up his phone to reveal the Odyssey website, the rules committee page, and quoted the specific provisions that related to what I'd done. "Allowed."

"Do you have a counter?" I asked George, who still hadn't moved and also hadn't offered his hand.

"No. The rules website has it wrong, though. You can't be that sneaky."

"Says the king of sneak attacks," Milo huffed from behind me. *Almost. Almost.* I still couldn't look at him.

All I needed was George's concession, but the moment dragged out, George's eyes narrowing, his hand glued to his side. His mouth pursed like he was doing internal math. I didn't care what he calculated as long as he came to the same answer as me, saw his inevitable loss.

"Fine. You win." George huffed as he stuck out his hand. "But don't go blaming me when you get a rep."

"For winning?" Finally, I let myself smile. All the air returned to my lungs in a whoosh, and leftover adrenaline made my hands shaky. A single glance in Milo's direction was enough to have my eyes burning, the way he looked at me like I'd captured the sun.

"Don't go getting cocky, Quigley. It doesn't become you."

"Sure it does. Cards, please." I tapped the table.

"Whatever. Here." He removed two triple-sleeved cards from his deck bag, stopping just short of bending them as he slapped them down. "Don't think you'll get me to play you again."

"Don't imagine I'll want to." I shrugged, remaining sitting even as George packed up his stuff and beat a hasty retreat.

"Oh, my God, that was spectacular." Kellan launched himself out of his chair as soon as the door shut behind George and his friends.

"You were such a badass." Milo rubbed my head as he came around the table. "I can't believe you did that."

"Bold, Jasper, bold." Professor Tuttle smiled. "That was a professional player move. Championship spirit."

"Hey, I learned from the best." I moved so that he could pass with his cane. I went ahead and unfolded myself from my chair. My shirt stuck to my back. I'd started sweating at some point and hadn't even noticed.

"So, how are we celebrating?" I asked Milo as I handed over the cards. Kellan and the professor were still nearby, so I figured anything racy was off the table, but I couldn't resist shooting him a sexy look.

"Wanna come for a drive with me?" His look was too

shy to mean back-seat action was imminent, but still, this was a guy I'd follow anywhere. Especially in this mood where I felt like…a hero at last. His hero. I'd saved the day.

"Sure." I beamed at him as we waved goodbye to the professor and Kellan. As we made our way out of the student union, I turned back to Milo. "You know, now that we've got the cards, you don't have to sell."

"Yeah, I do." Milo gave a solemn nod, which was pretty much what I'd been expecting.

"I get it." Maybe I hadn't saved the day as much as given him options. Which was okay. I didn't have to do the huge save to still help Milo and to still be a good boyfriend.

"I agreed to terms right before the match. I'm taking it tomorrow morning."

"So soon." I couldn't help the wistful sigh. I understood that he needed to do what he thought was best, but I still felt bad.

"It feels right. Feels like time. This way I can pay Bruno back for some of what he spent after the accident. Clean start. And having a little nest egg for the future… That's huge. For the first time in forever, I feel like I have choices."

"You do. Did…did the win help with that?" Maybe I was a praise junkie but I kind of wanted to hear it.

"Absolutely. And that you were willing to risk so much…"

"I'd do it again."

"I know. So, come with me?" Milo stopped by his car, which was gleaming under a parking lot light. All his boxes were currently stored in my parents' garage, and he'd washed and cleaned it so carefully I was almost scared to get in. "One last drive."

"Okay." I cautiously settled into the front seat. Milo didn't head for the highway, and I wasn't at all surprised when his drive took us a few streets over from my parents' house.

"New family seems settled in." I gestured at his old house where two kids were riding scooters in the driveway. It was early evening still and the night air had lost almost all of its winter bite. Spring wasn't far off now.

"Yeah, they do." He stared for a long moment before driving on. He turned toward our old school. "I'm going to tell Bruno everything. *Everything.* He deserves the truth and he deserves to hear it from me."

"He does," I agreed as he passed the school, heading for a narrow park where we'd learned to ride bikes together. I waited until he'd pulled into the nearly empty parking lot before adding, "I'm proud of you."

"I'm proud of me too." His bashful smile made me melt.

"Did you bring me here to seduce me? Because I'm good with that plan."

"I spent three hours detailing this car. You're tempting, though." He gave me a fast kiss that was all too light.

"No butt prints, got it." I grinned at him.

"Goof."

I didn't tell him that he loved that about me because the emotion was already there in his eyes, waiting for me to say it back. And even now the words felt too big for my mouth. Bigger than maybe my brain and my heart could hold. I felt them, but speaking them was scary, an admission of how very much I was trusting Milo, how much I stood to lose, and how much I wanted that forever with him. Instead, I kissed him again, this time getting the lingering kiss I craved, and hoped he knew what I couldn't yet say.

"I never taught you to drive a stick," he said mournfully as we broke apart. "And now I can't risk the clutch—"

"It's okay." I silenced him with another kiss. "There will be other cars."

"Yeah. There will." He met my gaze, eyes glowing in the evening light. We'd get more chances. More adventures. "I'm ready now. Ready for whatever happens with Bruno."

"You are. You're inspiring." I stroked his prickly jaw. I was super into his scruff, and the fact that he'd been too busy cleaning the car to shave was a nice bonus.

"Me? An inspiration? Nah." Grinning sheepishly, he shook his head.

"You are. I didn't think I was ready to move on after college. Didn't think I wanted what came next. But now I do. And a lot of it is because of you. Especially this last week or so, watching you be brave."

"If I'm brave, it's because you've shown me the way. And you believed in me, even when I didn't entirely believe in me."

"I'm never going to stop believing in you." The words rose in my throat again, the scary ones that wanted to come out, but then he claimed my mouth in another soft, sweet kiss and the words fled. I'd get there. Eventually.

And I was starting to believe that we'd get a future filled with chances. But first, Milo had one more mountain to conquer and

I was going to be right there, cheering him on. Whatever happened with Bruno, he'd have me, but I really hoped his big brother didn't break his heart.

CHAPTER FORTY
MILO

THIS WAS GOING TO BE hard. Jasper might believe in me, but right there on the front step of my mom's little apartment, I wasn't sure whether I agreed. Brave. Jasper had said that about me more than once, but he was the truly fearless one as far as I was concerned. And my courage was in short supply as I raised my hand to knock.

"Milo!" The door swung open before I finished the knock. Bruno stood there, a weird mix of military haircut and posture and civilian sweats and bare feet. His hair was damp and he had a huge smile for me. He looked both exactly like I remembered and completely different.

"You made it." I gave him a back-slapping hug.

"Yup. A little while ago. Caught a transport flight up from Virginia then had to battle traffic. I'm still catching up to the luxury of having easy hot water." Chuckling, he finished drying off his hair with one of Mom's good towels with the angel print. "How are you, man?"

"I'm good." It surprised me how much I meant it. I was. I still had some uncertainty about my living situation, but I'd had a promising interview that morning. Yesterday, I'd taken care of business with the car and handled the money aspect with the professors' help. I felt lighter. Free. Ready, like I'd told Jasper.

When we'd been parked at the playground, he'd offered to come with me tonight, but as much as I'd come to rely on him being my emotional support human, I'd wanted to do this part on my own. I'd told Mom that I was bringing a friend tomorrow when more friends and family would be stopping by for a homecoming party for Bruno. But I wasn't the type to do a big public announcement at the party, and it didn't seem fair to ambush Bruno or put Jasper on the spot. No, this way we could talk first. The mature choice, Jasper had called it, even though his eyes had said he wanted to come. But then he'd kissed me, warmed me in places I hadn't even known were chilly, and my plan had seemed smart.

But now I was actually here, missing that warmth, stomach doing its usual rumba routine, and I wouldn't have minded having Jasper's hand to hold as we made our way to the kitchen where Mom was pulling ingredients out of the fridge. Setting her armload on the counter first, she had a huge hug for me.

"What's the plan for dinner?" I tried to sound upbeat, not wary.

"Tacos. Easy and you guys always loved those growing up." She gave a sheepish smile that looked an awful lot like the one I saw in the mirror each day. "I got all your favorite toppings too."

"I can help." Draping my jacket over the back of a kitchen chair, I rolled up my sleeves. Opening the fridge, I added an onion and a head of garlic to the collection on the counter. "Do you have canned tomatoes? Fresh is better, but it's the wrong season."

She blinked at me before handing over a can. "Who are you, and what did you do with Milo?"

"I'm both impressed and scared." Bruno laughed as he took a seat at the table. "But I might trust you with a knife more than Mom."

"None of that. I can cook. I kept you both fed." She waved a package of cheese in our direction. "I spent all day picking up stuff for the party tomorrow. Rolls from that new bakery. The cold cuts from the deli with that ham Bruno said he can't get in Virginia. Cake from the place that did your graduation cakes. Oh, and brownies for dessert tonight from the pizza place Milo told me about. The house is stocked for my boys."

"Thanks, Mom."

Working together, she and I made the dinner. My onion dice wasn't as perfect as Professor Herrera's, but I was getting there. Her eyes got wide when I deftly drained the beef. Her new kitchen was tiny—barely enough room for all the appliances and a small dining nook—but we made a good team. It was fun surprising the two of them with my new skills, and Bruno kept up a steady conversation about being stationed abroad.

"And then our SEALs came in—"

"I love how you claim ownership of the SEALs," I teased as I warmed tortillas.

"Hey, I save their bacon all the time. Highly classified stuff, but you'd be amazed at how much the support personnel does. And I'm up for an advancement in rank later this year. Might get even more responsibility then."

"That's awesome." I gave him a high five. Mom had lots of questions about what the new rank would be and what he'd be doing, and his answers took us most of the way through eating. Afterward, Bruno and I cleaned up like old times while she made herself a cup of tea.

"Mom got a case of Sam Adams for tomorrow's party thing. You want a cold one?" Bruno took two bottles out of the fridge.

"Nah. I...uh...I don't drink anymore."

"Like, at all?" Bruno put a bottle back. "Good for you, though. Will it bother you if I have one?"

"No. I can be around it. It's more that I don't have to have it now. I like who I am better sober, that's all. I make dumbass mistakes drunk, and I'm done with that."

"I like you better sober too." Mom kissed the side of my head before heading to the living room with her tea. "I'm going to find a movie for later. You two catch up."

Bruno put the second beer back and returned with two sodas. My stomach didn't really need carbonation right then, but I appreciated the gesture a lot.

"To no more dumbass mistakes." He clinked cans with me. "Proud of you for making that change. Now if you could just convince those idiot friends of yours to give up drinking too, then you might actually get somewhere."

"Well..." I wasn't going to get a better opening than

that. "I'm done with them too. But first I did make another dumbass mistake. That's why I stopped the drinking. I can't keep making the same mistakes over and over."

"What'd you do?" Bruno sounded much more guarded now, which I hated.

"It's a long story, so let me finish before the inevitable lecture?" I asked as I took a deep breath. *Now or never. Time to be brave.*

"I'm listening."

Slowly, I told my story of what happened with the cards and the quest to get them back. Retrieving my backpack, I spread the four out as I explained. I kept thinking about the way Jasper had played the final round yesterday, the way that he'd left it all on the table. Fearless. This story wasn't the same without him in it, and I wasn't the same without him in my life.

"I seriously had no idea the cards were worth that much." Bruno chewed the edge of his lip as he considered the cards in front of him.

"What?" I hadn't considered that possibility, although maybe I should have.

He made a dismissive gesture. "Would I have kept a ten-grand item with my other cards? I'm not stupid. I won them off a guy. I knew they were ultra rares, but not that much money. You could have told me what happened, saved yourself some hassle."

"I know that now." I fiddled with the cracked edge on the little dining table. He might not be stupid, but I was. "I messed up, though. Again. And I didn't want to admit it to you. At the time, that seemed like the worst thing in the world."

"Well, I'm not *happy*," Bruno admitted. "And it was an idiot mistake. But I could have added it to your tab."

"And that's exactly what I didn't want. I owe you too much as it is." Fumbling with my pocket, I withdrew the check I'd stashed there earlier and handed it to him. "Here. I told you, I'm done making mistakes like that and I'm trying my best to make up for past ones."

"What the hell?" Bruno held the check like it might burst into flames at any second. "Did you sell a kidney? You're not making this kind of money at your job."

"No. I'm not." I had to pause, let my pulse slow and tell my roiling stomach to deal. I couldn't hurl. Not now. "I sold my car."

"No." Bruno tried to hand the check back to me. "You're not doing that. Dad wanted you to have it."

"He wanted a lot of things." I let that hang between us.

Bruno's expression hardened further. "He wasn't that bad."

"For you, maybe. You were the perfect son." An edge crept into my voice that wasn't there before. I'd tried not to think about that too much, but Bruno being so freaking perfect hadn't made it any easier to be myself.

"Maybe he was a little...rough on you. I'll grant you that." Retrieving a beer from the fridge, Bruno cracked it open. Apparently we were done with the solidarity part of the evening. "But was he bad enough for you to spit on his legacy like this? You can repay me eventually. It's just money."

"It's just a car," I countered. And it was. I'd been sad, saying goodbye to it the day before. I'd gotten choked up and had to look away as the new owner drove it away. He was a friend of Professor Tuttle who'd only tried to shave a little off the asking price and who'd looked at the car like Jasper did double chocolate doughnuts. Nice guy. And a weight had rolled off me as he left, even through my tears. I'd been free. It wasn't simply the money, but rather everything that car represented. And in the end, it was a car. Only a car. Like how Dad had been a man. Not a giant. Not a guardian angel. Just a flawed, human man, and it had been time to say goodbye to him and the car both.

"Why couldn't you tell me? About the cards and now this. You say you want to stop messing up, but you're not stopping to think, and that's a problem."

"I'm gay." The words had been there the whole conversation and now they flew out, another level of freedom reached. Not holding them in any longer had me weirdly giddy.

"What?" He sputtered around a mouthful of beer. "No, you're not."

"I am. I've got a boyfriend now, and like I said earlier, I'm good. Better than I've ever been."

"And this is why you couldn't talk to me?" The hurt and pain in his voice were palpable. I wanted to reach for him, but I couldn't bear it if he yanked his arm away.

"Part of it," I admitted, drumming my fingers on the table. "I'm sorry."

"Fuck. This... It's a lot." He scrubbed at his short hair. "You sure you're not shitting me?"

"No. It's Jasper. My boyfriend. You remember him from when we were kids?"

"Of course. You guys lived in each other's pockets... *oh*." His eyes went wide, and I swore twenty-two years of history passed between us. He kept staring at me as if he'd never seen me before. And maybe he hadn't.

"He helped me get the cards back. He's pretty incredible. And I want you to meet him."

"I..." Bruno pushed away from the table, taking his beer with him. "I need to think. This is..."

"A lot." I echoed his words from earlier. We weren't that different, he and I. Running from hard conversations. Thinking we needed to be alone to make sense of things. I understood him, but his dismissing me still stung, made me feel raw and exposed.

"It is. The cards. The car. The boyfriend. The *boyfriend*. Hell. I'm gonna go lie down."

"Okay." My voice was small. "Do you want me not to come tomorrow?"

"Just let me *think*." With that, he left the kitchen, heading for the spare room. I put my head in my hands as I heard the door shut. I had no idea how long I sat there before a gentle hand landed on my shoulder.

"You'll come tomorrow." Ruffling my hair, Mom plopped into Bruno's empty chair, regarding me with sad eyes.

"He doesn't want me here. I don't want to make it worse. I already ruined his homecoming." I dropped my head onto the cool wood of the table.

"You didn't. At least you didn't hit him with all this

while he was deployed. Thank you for that." Voice as weary as it had been in the days after my accident, she rubbed my back.

I turned my head so I could look at her. "More like I was too chicken to do it sooner, but yeah, I didn't want to distract him in the field."

"He'll come around. You heard him. He needs to think. Process."

"He might get madder." I slumped down farther at that thought. Him surprised and confused was one thing. Him actively angry... I wasn't sure I was strong enough for that.

"He might. But you're still coming tomorrow. With your friend." Her voice didn't leave room for argument so I nodded.

"But what about you? You upset too?"

Might as well get it all out there if so. See where my cards lay and all that.

"I had my time to process. Thanks for that." Her smile was distinctly strained.

"Sorry." I sat up enough to give her an awkward pat. "There were maybe lots better ways for you to find out."

"Oh, Milo. I've probably always known." She touched the back of my hand. "And I did a crap job protecting you from your dad. I can't make excuses for the past, for not standing up to him more."

"You loved him."

"I did. But I didn't see how...problematic he was until it was much too late. It wasn't fair to you."

"We all made mistakes."

"Yeah." Her eyes were on something far away. I joined her in staring at the clock above the sink. Pretty, with a little poem and twin angels decorating the face, it had been in our old house too. Still had a crack from the time Dad slammed a door too hard and it fell. Finally, Mom looked away and straightened her shoulders. "But I'm not making new ones. You'll come tomorrow. We'll get through this. As a family."

"Thanks." My hand hit the edge of one of the cards. Crap. Bruno had left both the cards and the check behind. "Can you keep this safe? I'm not taking it back. No matter what Bruno thinks of me selling the car, I still want to pay him back."

"You already have." Standing, she kissed my head. "Now, just be patient. Give him time."

But it felt like time was the one thing we didn't have. The party was tomorrow. Bruno only had a short visit. And then he'd be off, sent on a mission to some far-off place. I had a narrow window to make things right with him, and it was rapidly closing.

CHAPTER FORTY-ONE
JASPER

"I'M NOT READY." MILO MADE no move to open the car door. I'd had to park down the street from his mom's apartment complex, and that was probably a good thing as no one could look out the window and see us sitting here. Milo's back was broom-handle straight.

"We can stay right here." I patted his thigh. He looked nice, hair all tamed with product, and khakis and a button-down shirt that had both seen an iron recently. Anywhere else and I'd be enjoying dressed-up Milo, but we'd talked late into the night last night about how things with Bruno did not go as he'd hoped. And now dread rolled off him in thick waves, like choppy surf, and it sucked that I couldn't figure out what would help. "As long as you need."

"Just a minute maybe." Eyes closed, he breathed in and out slowly, and I pulled out my phone, scrolling messages to give him some space. But then I saw one from Kellan that had me legit gasping.

"Hey. Uh. This is either really cool news or not what you want to hear—"

"What now?" He cracked an eye open.

"You went viral." I clicked the link Kellan had sent so I could see for myself.

"I went what?"

"Chase's parents got your picture. And they put it up on their social media as part of their updates on Chase's health." I held up my phone so he could see one of the posts. "And now...you've got a zillion shares and dozens of people in the comments wanting a drawing like that and wanting to know if you have a website."

"I don't have a website." Milo's voice was halfway between horror and regret.

"Yet." Grinning, I winked at him. I wasn't letting this opportunity pass him by.

"Yet," he echoed, studying me intently before he smiled too. "I'm totally getting one by bedtime, am I right?"

"You're not wrong." I rubbed his arm before gesturing at the nice day outside. "Feeling any more ready?"

"Yeah. No point in staying here until it's dark."

"Oh, there's always a point to being alone in an enclosed space..." I waggled my eyebrows at him.

"Hold that thought for later." He groaned before opening the car door. "Have a feeling I'm going to need the distraction."

"Think the professors can spare you for the night?" I bumped shoulders with him as we headed down the sidewalk.

"Definitely. I'll text them that I've got plans to work on

a website with you." His laugh was most welcome after some of the more serious conversations we'd been having lately.

"Among other plans." I looked him up and down. "I might like this look even more than the toga."

He chuckled self-consciously at the praise. "Stop making me think about sex."

"But you're less nervous now, right?"

"Yeah, I am. Thank you," he said as we reached the apartment. He took one more big breath before knocking.

"Milo. Jasper." Milo's mom opened the door and surprised me with hugs for both of us. "It's so good to see you again."

I nodded, but I didn't return the sentiment. I might have forgiven Milo for being fourteen and confused and scared when he ended our friendship, but I wasn't entirely over the role his parents had played in our story. Sure, by all accounts she was supporting Milo *now*, but where had she been back then when Milo desperately needed more people unconditionally on his side? My fists clenched. I'd told him that I didn't regret our time apart because we'd both had a lot of growing up to do. Which was true. But it was also true that his road could have been a lot easier.

Could *still* be a lot easier. I wasn't impressed by Bruno needing to think. And seeing him now, sitting on the couch, flanked by aunts, not looking up to greet Milo, I was similarly not predisposed to like the man. But I was there to support Milo, not make a scene, and I'd follow his lead.

He looked at the cramped living room full of people spilling out onto a little patio, but then shook his head as he sighed and headed down the hall to the kitchen.

"Milo, who's your friend?" one of the many aunts asked as soon as we entered the kitchen, which was narrow with a little eating nook on one end.

"This is my boyfriend, Jasper." Milo turned bright red, and his hand shook as he grabbed mine, but I'd never been so proud of him as I was right then.

"Nice." She hugged Milo and shook my hand. "Make sure you feed him some of my ziti. He looks too skinny."

And that was that. She pushed Milo in the direction of the loaded-down food table before grabbing a glass of wine and heading back to the living room.

"Wow. Your mom expecting even more people?" I hadn't seen this much food in one place since the holidays at my parents' house.

"Nah. It's how Mom rolls. She wanted to have all Bruno's favorites here, and then the aunts can't come empty-handed and they try to outdo one another."

"My family's the same way." I laughed as I remembered another text that had been on my phone. "By the way, Mom says she's making chili for Wednesday after cosplay."

"I'm invited?" Milo was cute when he was surprised, and I couldn't resist jostling him with my shoulder.

"I think she's figured out that we're a package deal now."

"We are." He smiled at me, a special, private one that had my toes curling in my sneakers. I was trying to figure out whether I could get away with a kiss when he pointed at the table. "There's cake. Do you remember Bruno's high school graduation? When we made ourselves sick on the chocolate cake? This one is from that bakery."

I groaned. "As if I could forget. I think I'll stick to a cookie."

"And a soda. She got your brand." Milo handed me one from a cooler on the floor.

"I'll thank—"

"Hey." All of a sudden, we weren't alone in the dining nook and Bruno was right there, regarding us both intently. He was in jeans and a NAVY sweatshirt, but he didn't need to be in camo to exude badass warrior vibes.

"Hey." Milo nodded stiffly at him.

"Just got an interesting text. This your stuff?" Bruno held up a shiny phone opened to a social media app with Milo's drawing on it. "Figured there's not too many other Milo Lionettis out there…"

"Uh…" Milo turned bright pink.

"He's brilliant." I dared Bruno to disagree with me. "Parents were lined up on our last hospital visit to get him to draw their kids too."

"That's pretty cool." Bruno's tone was careful, like he was on a tightrope over some alligators. "It's good of you to do that for the sick kids."

"They do as much for us." Milo sounded exactly like I always did. He finally understood why I kept going back, week after week.

"I bet." Bruno nodded again, then flicked his gaze my direction. "So…this is the boyfriend?"

"Yup." Milo managed to sound both defiant and proud. I loved him. I might not be able to *say* it yet, but I loved him so much in that moment.

"Jasper, man." Bruno extended a hand to me. "You went and grew up."

"So did Milo." I regarded him coolly as I returned the handshake. I wasn't letting either him or their mom off the hook that easily. And Milo had been doing a ton of work the last few weeks, and he deserved credit for that.

"So he did." Bruno and Milo exchanged a long glance. "So, Bro, this...art thing. You gonna do something with that?"

"Maybe. I've been looking at classes." Milo sounded way more tentative than the guy who'd lain awake with me two nights ago, dreaming out loud and spinning a future for both of us.

"He's too talented not to pursue it." I stared hard at Bruno. If he dared to crush Milo's burgeoning dreams, he'd answer to me, badass warrior or not.

But all he did was roll his neck like he'd been thinking hard. "Good. You should. I want you to use the money for that. Go back to school. Make me proud."

"I'll try." Milo's voice was thick.

"You'll do it. You're a Lionetti. We don't quit." He cuffed Milo on the upper arm.

"Yeah." Giving him a tentative smile, Milo asked quietly, "You sure I still am?"

I hated that he had to ask and I glared at Bruno.

"Still my brother? Yeah. I'm sure. You're not getting rid of me that easily. I'm sorry if I was a dick last night."

"I put a lot out there all at once—"

"You did. You really did." Bruno's self-effacing laugh was identical to the one Milo did when nervous. "But that took guts. I can respect you for telling me even if it made my head spin with everything all at once."

"Sorry." Milo looked down at the tile floor.

"Don't be sorry. We're family." Bruno pulled him into a tight hug that made me fear for Milo's ribs before he thumped Milo's back. "How about next time, though, you try talking to me? About everything?"

"I will." Milo hugged him back before releasing him.

Bruno grabbed a soda and a piece of the cake before turning to me. "Take care of this guy, okay?"

"You don't have to ask." I regarded him solemnly, trying to tell him with my eyes that Milo was the most important thing in my life. And maybe he got the message because he nodded sharply before heading back to the living room full of relatives.

"Wow." Milo gripped the edge of the table hard enough that his knuckles turned white. "That...that was intense."

I knew him. I'd seen him this shade of pale before. "You okay?"

"Yeah." He took a shaky breath. I didn't entirely believe him, and I rubbed his back until he returned to more of a normal color. "Thanks. For being here with me. It...you mean everything to me."

"Ditto." I licked my lips. I wasn't about to kiss him in his mom's kitchen, but damn, I wanted to. To distract myself, I pulled out two pages I'd printed earlier. "And speaking of going places together..."

His eyes went wide as I handed them over. "The tickets to the launch party?"

"Yeah. You coming, Mr. Viral Celebrity? Still got time for us little people? Alden and Conrad said we can crash at their place after."

"I wouldn't miss it." Putting an arm around me, he pulled me close. "It doesn't matter how many reshares I get on social media. I'm always going to need you. Always."

"Good." And then I really did need to kiss him, but he was already on it, a quick brush of his lips across mine. We were going places. Together. The two of us. Bruno not being a complete ass helped, but it was Milo I was truly proud of in that moment. He was the star I wanted to set my internal compass by, the one constant I needed as we ventured forth into the still uncertain future.

CHAPTER FORTY-TWO
MILO

"I'M GETTING AWFULLY FOND OF this toga." I admired myself in one of the highly polished windows. The expansive event space hosting the launch party was a beyond-swanky loft, and even the back corner where we were hanging out was modern and glitzy.

"You do look...okay." Conrad had clearly been about to compliment me on my Neptune outfit, but then thought better of it as his über-serious boyfriend narrowed his eyes. "You look fine. Both of you."

"Why, thank you." Jasper adjusted his velvet jacket. No mask, but he looked dapper as ever as the Frog Wizard. The invite had specified that cosplay was encouraged, so we'd opted to go in costume. Conrad's whole department at Odyssey had decided to go as soldier tokens, so he was in a uniform that called to mind World War I. Alden was in a nice shirt and pants, but no cosplay for him.

"You're not chilly?" Alden asked me.

"Nah. It's finally spring. And the costume's grown on me." I did a silly twirl just to make Jasper laugh. It felt so good to be here with him and his friends. Forget the exclusiveness of the event. Just making it to this point, that meant something.

"Oh my God, I think I spot another Neptune." Jasper peered around Conrad.

"What? I'm not unique?" I pretended to pout. "At least I'm the best."

"Yes, you are." Jasper patted my face.

"I'd tell you two to get a room, but seeing as you're crashing on our floor, please *don't* get a room." Conrad laughed and shook his head.

"Don't worry." Jasper made a dismissive gesture. "We brought sleeping bags."

"Somehow I'm not reassured," Alden replied dryly.

"Zippers are sexy," I teased. Their tiny apartment was way too small for Jasper and me to do more than hold hands and whisper, but I was still looking forward to those quiet moments alone late at night. The whole launch-party experience was another adventure for us, taking the train into the city together that morning, our first little overnight trip.

"That's all you." Jasper gave me an indulgent look, and I almost reconsidered the whole no-fooling-around thing.

"I'm surprised no one's asked for a pic with you yet." Conrad stretched.

"The Neptune thing? You said there are others here. Maybe they wear the toga better…"

"Never." Jasper pretended horror at the notion.

"You're so loyal." Conrad chuckled. "No, I meant the

whole minor celebrity thing. I wanted to ask you for a drawing of us, but I bet your going rate is increasing by the day."

"Have you seen the website? You fill out the form, and then the calculator I programmed tells you your approximate wait time." Jasper was only too pleased to remind us that he'd put all sorts of bells and whistles on the website I hadn't known I wanted until a few weeks ago.

"Okay, okay. I'll fill out the form."

"Nah. Don't do that. I'll draw you tomorrow morning. You can trade me those bagels you were talking about and we'll call it even."

"Sounds like a plan." Conrad snagged an appetizer from a passing server. I grabbed one too, some sort of little toast thing that was prettier than it was tasty. Knowing the food was likely to be sparse, Conrad had promised us pizza after the event, he and Alden only too happy to show off their neighborhood spots.

"I've got another drawing to do on the train back too," I said to Jasper. "Bruno emailed a little while ago."

"Bruno wants a drawing?"

Things had been...interesting with Bruno since the homecoming party. Not strained exactly, but not entirely back to normal either. However, it seemed to have more to do with my decision to sell the car than with coming out, as in each message he made a point of asking about Jasper and he'd said he wanted to play a round of cards with us next visit.

"A buddy who has everything has a birthday apparently. Bruno thought he'd get a cartoon-style drawing done as a T-shirt—"

"Merchandise." Jasper's eyes went wide. "That's it. That's the next step to your empire."

"He's certainly your best hype man." Conrad took a sip of something bubbly. There was an open bar, but I wasn't tempted to join the line. I'd meant what I'd told Bruno. I liked myself more sober, and besides, this was the sort of night where I wanted to remember each moment.

"He is." I tugged Jasper closer. The whole public boyfriends thing was easier now, and there were a ton of other same-sex couples at this thing, holding hands and dancing and hanging out in clumps with friends, exactly like us.

"Conrad. Your whole department is looking spiffy." An elegant older woman flanked by several younger people strode toward us.

"Thanks." Conrad tweaked his collar. The entourage made the woman look important, but the way Conrad, Alden, and Jasper straightened told me this was the Odyssey boss, the one who made gaming dreams come true. I let go of him so he could pay attention if destiny was calling.

"Excellent work on this set. I hear great things from your department head," she enthused, making Conrad turn even more pink as he made introductions for the rest of us. She had a broad smile that seemed especially wide for Jasper. "So nice to meet you in person. Excellent costume choice."

"It's my favorite character." Light danced in his eyes. He might be good at playing it cool during a game, but he was clearly starstruck with the Odyssey creator, and it was cute. This was the moment he'd been waiting for, and I was so happy for him that I had to resist the impulse to cheer.

"I saw the *Gamer Grandpa* episode with the diabolical gambit using quick change. It might be my favorite one yet, although I liked last week's on defending against Reaper decks a great deal." She spoke authoritatively, and it was entirely possible that she'd seen more episodes than I had. Which was funny because I got good boyfriend points every time I attended a taping or watched the finished product.

"Thanks. That gambit...it's useful." Jasper rubbed his neck as if he were remembering his match with George.

"Graduation must be approaching for you, right?" She had a thoughtful expression, and my pulse sped up for Jasper, who didn't look nearly as eager as I felt.

"Yeah."

"Excellent. Shall I have Marsha put you on my schedule for a call Monday morning? I want to discuss your future and how Odyssey might fit in it."

Jasper shot me a quick look, face more tense than I expected considering that this was what he'd been both wanting and debating all year. He'd be a fool not to hear her out, and my guy was definitely not a fool. I nodded at him, and maybe that was he was waiting for because he exhaled. "That would be good. Thank you."

"Fabulous. I see some more people I need to say hello to, so you all take care."

Goodbyes were said all around, and then Conrad decided he wanted a drink refill.

"Come keep me company in line," he said to Alden, casting a glance at Jasper and me. He was a perceptive guy, and undoubtedly he'd picked up on my burning need to get Jasper alone.

As soon as they were out of earshot, I turned toward him. "What was that hesitation? That was the connection you wanted to make, right? The whole point of this party?"

"Yeah. I guess it was. But I don't want to leave—"

"Your family. I know. But trust me, they want this for you too. I bet April and your mom will visit, and you can take the train on weekends and—"

"You. I was going to say *you*. I don't want to leave you."

"*Oh*." I took a step back, hitting a low bench facing the window. I sank down, and he followed, sitting close enough that our knees touched.

"My family will deal. And chances are good that Kellan will end up with a Broadway job. We can do cosplay at a kids' hospital here in the city maybe. I'm less worried about leaving my life behind anymore. Except you. I don't want to leave you."

"You're not getting rid of me that easily," I said, echoing Bruno's words. Even though my stomach was wobbling, I tried to smile at him. This might be the most serious moment in my life, and all around us the party swirled, glasses clinking, costumes swishing, but all I could see was him.

"I'm not sure that visits are going to be enough." He took my hand.

"Me either." I squeezed him back. "But this is the opportunity you have to take."

"Maybe. But I was tempted to tell her that we're a package deal. Dynamic duo. Two-for-one special."

I flashed back to the *Odyssey* artist at the tournament in Philly, and I wanted that. Wanted the lines and the iconic cards with my art. Wanted to work with Jasper, make something enduring. A legacy.

"Someday. I want to get better first. Wasn't that you saying I need to build my empire?"

"Better? You mean the art school idea?"

I nodded. "Bruno was serious about me using the car money to help with that. And you're not the only one who can use Google. Professor Herrera has been helping me research schools. He says I need to dream bigger than an online course or some community college classes."

Somehow, I still hadn't moved out of the professors' guest room. The group house hadn't worked out, which was fine because the box sorting was an epic project. Then there was the furniture moving. And the dining room needed painting. That made the living room clash, so it got a fresh look too. Now, it was spring and there was planting to do. Stolen moments in Jasper's dorm room aside, I'd never been as happy living somewhere. I'd spent the last few years feeling like I didn't belong anywhere. And now I did. I belonged with Jasper and everything that went along with that.

"You should listen to the professor." Jasper's expression was speculative. "What are you thinking?"

I fished my phone out of the little pocket Kellan had thoughtfully included in the toga. "This."

Jasper whistled as he considered the screenshot I'd saved of a school here in the city. "I don't know art, but I'm pretty sure that's—"

"A top ten program. Number five for illustration."
The hand holding my phone wavered right along with my
stomach. "It takes a portfolio to get in, not test scores.
There's a whole section about help for learning differences too. And there are scholarships, but it's still a major
reach—"

"No, it's not. You're ridiculously talented. I believe in
you." He pulled me close like we were alone and sharing
these dreams under the covers in his room. A few months
ago, being snuggled up with another guy at a big, fancy
event like this would have seemed impossible, but now here
we were and anything, absolutely anything, seemed possible.

"And I believe in *you*. Take the Odyssey job. Dream
big. And I will too."

"You're going to apply?" A slow smile crept across
Jasper's face.

"Pretty sure the professors will be disappointed if
I don't." We'd made lists. And then the lists had sublists
because I didn't do great with broad concepts. Little goals
and concrete tasks were easier, so Professor Herrera broke
it down for me, exactly what had to go in the portfolio.
Professor Tuttle took careful notes that I could later review
at my own pace. "Deadline's coming up."

"When were you going to tell me?" Jasper tilted his
head, considering me with cautious eyes. Behind us,
someone laughed as there was an announcement over the
loudspeaker, but no card reveal or prize package could steal
my attention away from those eyes.

"Now. When you decided to go for the Odyssey thing. I don't want to be the only reason you take it, though. If you truly want to stay close to home, I'll look at local programs. Keep my job. But my supervisor says they might have hours for me if I put in for a transfer to one of the city locations. Like I said, you're not getting rid of me so easily."

"Dynamic duo?" He offered me a fist bump. What I really wanted was a kiss, but I'd take it.

"Always." I bumped him back, then captured his hand again in mine.

"Think you might need a roommate if—when—they accept you?" Jasper asked, brain going to the same place mine had as soon as I'd seen the pictures of the school. "It's not too far from Conrad and Alden."

"I'm not unaware of that fact. And yeah. You asking me if we can live together?" I pretended to need to think about this concept, deliberately wrinkling my forehead.

"Yeah." Jasper sounded a little wary now.

"I dunno." I shrugged, enjoying this far more than I should have. "That's a pretty big commitment—"

"I love you." Jasper blurted it out, eyes going wide, like he was both pleased and surprised by himself. And a little worried. Which he didn't need to be, because my entire body thrilled to those words.

"Well. There is that." Somehow I managed to play it cool, get another smile out of him.

"I know I haven't said it. But I've meant it."

"I know." And I did. I'd said it a few times, both joking and serious, and he still hadn't. But I'd known. Every kiss. Every late-night chat. Every long look and every adventure. But I still had to tease. "And not just because you want student-priced housing?"

"Oh, I'm totally hitching my star to yours," he teased right back, eyes sparkling and not only from the lights.

"You're a goof." My throat was tight.

"And you—"

"Love you back. Yeah. Completely. I love you too." This time felt more real than the other times I'd said it, because he'd said it back and it meant something. And we had the start of a plan for the future. All those big dreams meant nothing if there wasn't love to back them up, and I'd known there was, but hearing him say it was a rush, a sudden kick of adrenaline making me even more certain that this was the right path for me. For us.

He leaned in, giving me plenty of time to turn away, but no way was I going to. Party? Who cared? Jasper loved me and he wanted to kiss me right here and so we would. There was a low whoop. Might have been Conrad. I still didn't care until Jasper deepened the kiss and I had to break away, laughing.

"Hey, now, I'm wearing a toga. None of that."

"You're my favorite prince." He trailed his fingers down my smooth face. I'd done the shave-and-haircut thing for the event, wanting everything perfect for tonight. For him.

"Better be your only prince," I growled.

"Only one I'm ever going to want," he shot back before smiling tenderly.

"Promise?"

"Always."

I caught sight of us in the big window, Prince Neptune and the Frog Wizard, having a moment. We were as cute as our characters. But we were also Jasper and Milo, two guys in love. Two guys meant to be together, meant to be here in this place, at this time, no matter what had gone before us. I wasn't ever going to stop regretting high school, but when I saw us side by side like this, what I saw was my future, not my past. Jasper wanted us to dream big. And I did too, but I also knew that no matter how far we went, nothing was ever going to rival that feeling in my chest when he said he loved me.

"Say it again," I whispered.

"I love you." His eyes met mine in the reflection. Yup. Always and forever, this was right where I was supposed to be.

CHAPTER FORTY-THREE
JASPER

August

"YOUR PRINCE IS HERE," KELLAN announced loudly as he joined us on the patio, plunking down a six-pack of good beer and a tray of cookies. He was looking tan and shaggy after his stint at a summer stock production, and Jasmine was hanging on his arm in a way that showed off the engagement rock she'd gotten graduation weekend.

"Ha. Very funny. My prince and I came together." I gestured at Milo who was across the table from me in the professors' backyard, which was rapidly filling up with all our friends.

"We do that now." Leaning back in his lawn chair, Milo nodded archly.

"Dude. We were on the same train." Conrad rolled his eyes at both of us, an impressive feat. "If you say the words 'our place' or 'together' one more time, I'm going to die of sugar overload."

"Was that not you last fall doing the exact same thing?" I

asked pointedly because I still remembered how much it had sucked when he'd been all in love with Alden on their visits and I'd been oh-so-very single.

"It was," Conrad agreed, exchanging some sort of private message with Alden.

"It maybe still is." Alden gave a rare smile. He seemed a little more relaxed than usual, enjoying the last weekend before school started for him—his first year teaching at a junior high near where he and Conrad lived.

"I'm just saying that the unbearable cuteness that is you two hipster wannabes—"

"He called me a hipster." Milo faked indignation.

"You're an art student in Brooklyn who does cosplay on weekends. Were you thinking you still passed as a jock?" Kellan laughed and everyone joined in, including Milo, but then he got quiet.

"No. I guess not," he said softly. And it was true that he didn't look nearly as sporty these days. His hair was bushier and he'd forgotten to shave again. We'd been late getting ready to leave our tiny student housing near the art college campus for *reasons*, so he was in an *Odyssey* shirt someone had thrust at him last time he visited me at work and old shorts. His leg scars were more faded now, and he could comfortably wear chunky leather sandals for more than short cosplay stints.

"You'll always be my jock," I said fondly to him. And that was also true—he still smelled deliciously of sporty aftershave and I still got to hear way too much about what European soccer players got paid and which teams had the best chance at a World

Cup. And sometimes he'd lift weights and get all sweaty and... Yeah. Still my jock. *Swoon.*

"If you want to kick the soccer ball around later, we can do that," Conrad offered. Between his asthma and Milo's leg, it would likely be a low-key thing, but they'd done that a couple of times in the park when we'd met halfway between our neighborhoods. "Let Alden play Jasper for the game episode."

Milo stretched, flexing his leg out in front of him. "I've got a couple of kicks in me."

"I might join you guys, work off this beer." Kellan rubbed his stomach. Milo hadn't had a drink since winter. We didn't really talk about it that often, but I added it to the list of things I was super proud about for him.

"I can feel it. Today I'm going to win against Alden." I pumped both fists like a boxer promising victory.

"Not likely." Alden spoke factually, not the sort of trash talk that Conrad and I excelled at. And probably also literally because he usually did win, whether we were playing casually at their apartment or with Professor Tuttle for the show.

"I believe in you." Milo saluted me with his water glass.

"Thanks."

"Who needs more food?" Professor Herrera brought over a big platter of sausages and grilled vegetables, and Milo was first to leap up to help him arrange the food, as always. Thanks to Milo, I already knew the location of every specialty grocery store near us as well as exactly what size chicken our tiny oven would hold.

"I'm stuffed. But I'll help with dishes," Milo said, moving so Professor Herrera could pull up a chair. "And what's the deal with the flyer on the fridge? You looking to replace me so soon?"

"You? You're irreplaceable." Professor Herrera gave him a fond smile.

"I agree." My loyalty got a round of groans from everyone else at the table who was tired of us being so adorable. They could just deal with us being so in love. I'd waited *forever* for something like this, and I wasn't wasting it.

"Actually, we enjoyed having Milo so much that we've decided to add a renter or two this fall." Professor Tuttle tapped his cane against the patio.

"The *Gamer Grandpa* expansion pack. I dig it." Kellan sat back in his chair with one of the sausages in a roll we'd brought with us from the city.

"They don't *have* to game." Professor Herrera laughed. His continual bid to get Professor Tuttle interested in different hobbies had been the source of great stories when Milo had been living with them in the spring.

"They don't?" Conrad faked horror.

"They will learn," I said all ominously to big laughs.

"Goof." Coming around the table with his empty cup, Milo dropped a kiss on my head.

"You love me." Tipping back in my chair, I gazed up at him.

"I do." His eyes were as serious as ever about that. He could joke a lot more easily now, but never about that. And I never got tired of hearing it, either. "Now go win your game for me."

"Yes, dear." I pretended an obedience we all knew I'd never reach.

"Are you staying here or at Jasper's parents' place?" Jasmine asked as she grabbed one of the cookies.

"Jasper's mom may not let him out of her clutches the rest of the weekend," Milo groaned as he rested against a planter near me. He could pretend irritation all he wanted, but personally, I couldn't wait to be alone in my old room together. I'd waited almost a decade to kiss Milo Lionetti in there, and I was going to enjoy the opportunity. Quietly. Very, very quietly because April still delighted in teasing us. Mom, however, had adapted to us being together quite well, making it her life's mission to keep Milo supplied with recipes and food storage ideas.

"And Milo's mom?" Jasmine's ring caught the sunlight again. I wanted one. Not the cookie. The ring. Maybe with less glitz. *Someday.* Timing wasn't there yet. But someday.

"Brunch on Sunday," Milo answered. Between our two moms, we were going to be so stuffed when we rolled back into Brooklyn Monday. But happy. We'd be happy. "We'll see her again in two weeks when Bruno's in town as well."

"And I'm going to win against him too," I announced. Bruno was a damn good player. Ruthless. But I'd snuck in a few wins against him on his visits. He said that when we went to Virginia to see his base that he might let me play against some actual SEALs. I couldn't wait.

"You could start by winning against me," Alden reminded me.

"Oh. My. God. Make Bruno play Alden." Kellan gestured like his head just exploded at the idea.

"Or Conrad. I can play, too, you know. Just a bit." Conrad gave him a look, then laughed.

"Just a bit." Alden arched an eyebrow.

"Do you guys play all day at work?" Kellan asked as he took more food. "Like, what does a hard day at the office look like for you guys? 'Oh, I lost to Conrad all day again, someone feel sorry for me and rub my feet'. Because I might need a career change."

"Says the guy with three interviews next week for Broadway shows." I flicked a piece of ice at him. Actually, I'd never in my life worked harder than I had that summer for Odyssey. I loved it. But it was still work. Meetings. Forms. Reports. Boring stuff. But I also got to see one of my best friends most days, so it was still winning.

"True. Okay. I'm not quitting my daydream yet. I'm just saying you guys have the coolest jobs ever."

"Hey, it's hard work!" Conrad protested.

"I'm gonna find out. Someday." Milo gave a little smile. We'd been to a few more regional tournaments together. Official Odyssey business. And I always found Milo in the artist alley section, looking at the lines. Someday. He was going to get there. I knew it.

"Noooo," Conrad moaned. "Then I'm gonna have to be that boss who has to lecture Jasper about not kissing next summer's interns in the conference room."

"The boss?" I stared him up and down. "Never."

"You never know. Maybe I'm gonna run the place someday." Conrad grinned at me. I grinned back.

"Play you for it." I leaned forward.

"You're on."

"You'll win," Milo said sometime later when we were alone in the professors' kitchen, washing dishes together. "Against Alden in a few minutes. But also against Conrad. You're going to be the one to beat at Odyssey."

"How do you know?" Heedless of the running water, I wrapped myself around him from the back, resting my head against his neck. I inhaled deeply. Yup. Still my jock.

"Because you're my hero." He turned so he could give me a soft kiss. "And I believe in you."

When he said stuff like that, I believed him. Believed in myself a little more. I was a hero, exactly like I'd always wanted to be. And not only was I a hero, but I also got the guy in the end. "Love you."

"Always." He gave me another kiss. And I believed that, too, believed in the love I saw in his eyes. It got easier and easier to trust that this was indeed my actual life. I really did get to wake up and kiss Milo Lionetti every morning. I'd gotten my prince, exactly the one I'd needed, and now I wasn't ever going to let him go.

Go back to where it all began:

CONVENTIONALLY yours

Available now!

CHAPTER ONE
CONRAD

"YOU CAN'T KILL ME," I said. "You don't have the strength."

In reality, I was already dead. My fate had been sealed by my own stupidity, but I wasn't going down with a whimper. No, the last of my life might be spinning away, leaving me with only a dwindling collection of scrolls and my wits, but I'd rather go out fighting—or at least laughing.

I leaned back, feigning confident disinterest. "Come at me."

"You're rather confident for someone with no defenses." Alden, my least favorite opponent, sounded almost bored, which only made me even more determined to hold on.

"And *you're* so predictable," I shot back. Maybe I could egg him on, push him into making a mistake. It seemed like the only option I had left.

"Dude. You are so screwed. At least your carcass is going to be pretty." My sometimes-friend Jasper wasn't helping any, taking great glee in my predicament.

"Beg for mercy." Payton, as always, was more pragmatic.

I neither needed nor wanted an audience for this latest humiliation, so I tuned everything out, focusing every resource on staying alive.

"I move to attack," Alden said. The swing came, just as I'd anticipated, with Alden going all in, trying for a fatal blow.

"Yeah, well, attack *this*." I slapped down a card to create four tiny frog soldiers. Not much when facing off against everything Alden had at his fingertips, but it was the best I could manage.

One more turn. It had become something of a mantra over the last hard, seemingly endless year. And yes, this was only a card game, and no, another loss to Alden wouldn't really be the worst thing to happen to me. But regardless, I still wasn't going to let him see me falter.

"Really? That's your response?" Alden shook his head, his weary expression making him look far older than twenty-three. He didn't seem cowed in the slightest. He did superior better than anyone I knew, full mouth curving, lock of dark hair falling over his forehead as his hazel eyes gleamed. Fresh dread gathered in my stomach. My cheap-yet-effective mercenaries should have been just enough to hold him off and to get me to my next turn. But then Alden shook his head again and activated five scrolls, turning them sideways with long, clever fingers. "Unblockable Quest."

It was a hundred-dollar card, the sort of comeback that pro players trotted out like jelly beans, and so far above my current gaming budget it might as well have been gold-plated. But I had one final answer, my last card and my last scroll to activate it. "Peace Offering."

It would mean the sacrifice of my soldiers, but at least it would get me that *one more turn*.

"Conrad." The irritated way Alden sighed my name always made my teeth grind. "Peace Offering is one of the cards that got outlawed with the new rules. It's no longer tournament legal. Didn't you freshen up your deck last week like everyone else?"

No, no I hadn't updated a damn thing because I'd needed my last forty dollars for food, not cards. But I wasn't telling Alden that, wouldn't give him the satisfaction of pitying me. Instead, I stuck my hand out. "Guess I forgot. Good game, man."

"Yeah, good one." Alden barely glanced at me as he gave a perfunctory shake.

"That's right. You missed the release event last week when they unveiled the new cards and revised rules. Hot date?" Payton asked, leaning forward, long hair swishing over their shoulders, the soft hint of southern in their lilt making *date* sound old-fashioned and dirty at the same time.

"You know it." I leaned back in my chair. I wasn't about to admit I'd been working extra hours at the pizza place, trying to replace that money I'd spent on food. I'd spent hours dodging irritable parents and hyped-up kids instead of being here at my favorite game store for the unveiling of a set I'd been looking forward to for months.

Alden made a disgruntled noise. "Can we film his death reaction now?"

"Sure thing." Professor Tuttle swung his handheld camera in my direction. "Die, Conrad. Make it good."

On cue, I sank low in my seat, almost sliding under the table as I made noises like I was melting, like a cartoon character getting hit with acid. Elimination reactions were something that Professor Tuttle's audience always loved, almost as much as his "Gamer Grandpa" game analysis. *Gamer Grandpa* was one of the most popular *Odyssey* vlogs, with Professor Tuttle analyzing our in-person card play as well as matches on the wildly successful online version of the game. He made game theory accessible to the masses, and we were all regulars on his channel. Jasper did a lot of the editing for him, Payton did some special effects, and Alden...

Well, Alden did all the winning. He had a combination of the best decks and exactly enough infuriating skill to make him darn near unbeatable.

Oh and me? I liked to think I was the eye candy of the group. Or maybe the comedic relief. I brought the sort of trash-talking our viewers loved. That it never failed to rile Alden was only a bonus. And I'd take being seen as cocky over the truth, which was that I was the professor's latest charity case—a scrappy player with cheap cards, a fucked-up life, and a missing future.

"Great. That'll do it for this game." Setting the handheld camera aside, Professor Tuttle bustled around, disconnecting the overhead cameras that pointed at our play mats.

"They're going to want the room back soon." Jasper moved to help, collecting dice and counters and rolling mats. He worked part-time at the game store where we filmed the shows and was the reason why we got the private play room so often.

"Arthur can wait." Payton was one of the few people not

rattled in the slightest by the store owner's gruff exterior, and they gathered their stuff slowly.

"Give me a minute and I'll grab you some of the latest card packs, Conrad. I bought two set boxes, so I've got some to spare." Ignoring Payton, Jasper continued to aim for employee of the year, wiping down the table.

"Thanks, man." There was a time when I'd been one of the store's best customers, but those days were long gone, and now, even borrowing Jasper's employee discount, I could barely afford to keep playing. I should have been too proud to accept the packs, but it was probably my only shot at updating my decks. I couldn't afford to buy individual cards on the secondary market like Alden or Payton. No, I'd be limited to whatever came in the packs. And I supposed I could get lucky, score some rares, but luck and I were hardly on speaking terms lately.

"I've got some commons you can sift through too." Alden reached for his deck bag—one of those custom deals that held a bunch of decks in their boxes securely, nothing jumbling around like my duffel, which was often where good cards went to die.

"Nah. I'm sure I'll be okay with whatever Jasper can spare." I might able to live with myself in accepting handouts from the professor and Jasper, but not Alden. I'd sooner stop playing than take his castoffs.

"Suit yourself." Alden gave a shrug of his elegant shoulders. Not broad. Not bulky. Not even a swimmer's lean build or the more technically accurate *slight*. No, the only word that worked for describing Alden's body type was elegant. Or perhaps regal if one was feeling even more fanciful, which I decidedly was not.

But it was undeniable that Alden had a presence to his posture, a way of holding himself that took up far more than his share of space, and that frequently made me forget that I was technically the taller, bigger one.

"Wait. Before you guys head out, I've got something to share." Professor Tuttle sported a gray T-shirt that proudly proclaimed "Gamer Grandpa" with his Einsteinesque wild-hair logo beneath it. Like Alden, he had a professional-grade deck bag, along with assorted camera and laptop cases. Checking three different bags, he finally came up with a thick manila envelope. "Do you know what this is?" He waved the envelope in front of us before reaching inside. Practically vibrating with excitement, he didn't wait for any of us to take a guess. "This, my friends, is the trip of a lifetime."

He laid five white tickets out on the table. They looked expensive—large rectangles of thick, creamy card stock with gold lettering that proudly proclaimed, "Massive Odyssey Con West" on them.

The room went silent, the kind of eerie stillness that often preceded a summer storm back home, but in this case, it was anticipation, not a tornado, building, energy crackling as I waited to see who would speak first.

"But MOC West has been sold out for *months*. I know. I tried." Payton's green eyes were wide. Among all of us, they were probably the only one of us who could easily afford the high price of admission for the fan convention taking place in Vegas next month. Giant in scope, it rivaled the largest of the Comic Cons in popularity. Better yet, not only was it a showcase for the game, but also a huge tournament for players, with prize money and even seats on the pro tour up for grabs.

A spot on the pro tour could be *life-changing*.

"I know. But my contact at Odyssey Games said they're really impressed with what our channel is doing. They want us to come— me to sit on some panels and make fan appearances, and you guys to play in the tournament. Then we'll do a recap video about our experiences afterward."

"Wow." I whistled low, visions of an invitation to the pro tour and the end of my money worries dancing in my head.

"All we have to do is get there." Professor Tuttle nodded so enthusiastically that his unruly white-gray hair bounced.

And hell. Just like that, my vision went poof, lost in a cloud of reality. "You mean we have to cover airfare?"

"Well, yes, travel expenses are ours, as are meals and—"

"Not a problem." Payton already had their phone out and was clicking away, probably telling their trust-fund manager that they needed a boost of cash.

"For you, maybe," I grumbled, already digging my duffel out from under the table. Time for me to get going. That ticket might be my one last decent hope of digging my way out of the hole my life had become, but the cost of airfare wasn't even remotely within my pitiful budget, and I needed to escape the excitement of the others before my disappointment ruined their fun.

"Slow down now, Conrad." Professor Tuttle could do stern when he wanted to. I slumped back into my seat, bag in my lap. "I've got a travel plan for those of us with more...challenges to face."

More like those of us with nonexistent bank balances, but I didn't say anything. I'd worked hard to make sure that as few people knew the extent of my situation as possible. The professor knew more than most, but no way did I want the rest to realize just how screwed I really was.

"I don't fly." Alden stared at the tickets as if they might hop up and bite him. I had to blink at that. In the couple of years that I'd hung around Alden and the rest of our play group, I'd never known him to be anything other than rigidly in control. Our perennial winner had a weak spot?

"Since when?" I asked before I could think better of it. I'd learned long ago that Alden, conversation, and I seldom mixed well.

"Since ever." Alden gave me the scathing look I'd been expecting. "I just...don't."

"Which is fine." Professor Tuttle had moved from stern teacher back to peacemaker. "You don't fly. C—*Some* of us have limited funds. And I have a plan."

Pulse pounding, I eyed those tickets again. Forget Alden and his blinged-out decks. I could hold my own in that tournament, and I knew it. I could solve so many of my problems. But rather than being giddy with hope, I felt like I'd swallowed Alden's huge deck bag, a heavy weight pressing on my vital organs.

Whatever this plan was, I wasn't at all sure I was going to like it.

CHAPTER TWO
ALDEN

I STRAIGHTENED MY SHOULDERS, NOT letting my body lean forward like it wanted to. I wasn't going to let myself be overeager. Not yet. Real-world plans had a way of seldom working out in my favor, which was why I loved *Odyssey* so much. In the game, all my careful strategies could come to fruition, as they had when I'd won out over Conrad a few minutes earlier. Across from me now, he had gone pale, his usual Disney-hero face gaunt and more than a little green.

"A plan?" he croaked. I had to admit, it was nice to see the Prince of Swagger off his game, even a little. He deserved to be off his game, in no small part thanks to his endless needling and mockery. He called it trash-talking, but I'd never seen the difference. It was hard not to take his comments personally when they always felt so targeted.

My fingers itched to reach for the tickets, to make sure they were real, but I wasn't going to be the first to grab. I also wasn't about to let Conrad—or anyone else—see how badly I wanted to go. Payton and Conrad undoubtedly wanted a ticket so they could party with other gamers, and Jasper was likely already envisioning the cosplay possibilities, but all I could think about was that tournament. A seat on the pro tour. Yeah, that would be worth something after the tire fire that was my last year.

A win like that would validate all the time I'd spent honing my game, but more importantly, it would give me the one thing my life was sorely lacking: control. I'd spent the past year racking up disappointment after disappointment, and here was my chance to seize a fresh new direction for my future that had nothing to do with the increasingly claustrophobic path my family had set me on.

I swore I could already hear the cheers, feel the weight of the trophy, the intense wave of pride washing over me. But behind the daydream was the bitter splash of reality. I didn't like to fly. It was what had kept me limited to cons and tournaments within driving distance here on the East Coast and what had held me back from registering for MOC West when it first opened.

"And it doesn't involve flying?" I asked, trying to not sound as skeptical as Conrad.

"Nope." Professor Tuttle offered a wide smile. "I've had a bunch of midwestern local game stores ask for signed books. And they've been clamoring for something of a tour. So my idea is to drive with whomever wishes to join me. We can share time behind the wheel, stop at my favorite local game stores along the way, play a few hands of *Odyssey* with their regulars, see the sights... It'll be fun."

That was easy for him to say. He had friends all across the country thanks to his storied career as a mathematics professor as well as the reputation he'd built with his vlog. He loved travel, but I knew full well that he was only proposing driving because he thought that was the best way to get us there. He'd been friends with my family long enough to know about my issues with flying. Also, Jasper was perennially short of funds, and I was never quite sure what was up with Conrad lately. He'd had to drop out of school for reasons he was cagey about, and I could never tell whether he was as broke as Jasper, or just didn't care, or possibly a mixture of both. For all his bravado, he was tough to read—something that irritated me even more than his swagger and constant needling.

"Can it be the sort of fun that I hear all about when I see you guys at the con? Road trips are so not my style, and I've got plane tickets already up on my phone." Payton waved their phone, managing to sound dismissive without outright knocking the professor's plan. I desperately wanted to learn their trick for always managing to seem above the fray without being rude about it. They were never emotionally invested in anything, whether it was grades or relationships or even the game itself. Me? My adrenaline was still thrumming from the win, my stomach yet to settle from that sick feeling when I'd thought Conrad might be about to best me. Holding back his soldier tokens had been a stroke of genius.

Not that I'd ever tell him that. *He* didn't need the ego boost.

"The convention is right after the term ends for summer break." Professor Tuttle still taught part-time, despite devoting most of his retirement to his vlog. "I say we take two weeks—five or six days there, three days for the convention, five or six days coming home. It'll be a grand adventure. Who's in?"

I expected Conrad to agree first, because no way would he turn down a chance to go party with Payton and be a minor celebrity with *Gamer Grandpa*'s following. I'd been forced to overhear too many stories of their wild antics over the years to think otherwise.

In the end, though, it was Jasper who nodded first. "I'm up for it. I'll have to talk to my folks and Arthur, though, make sure I can be spared."

"Excellent. Conrad?" Professor Tuttle prompted. Relief rushed through me that he hadn't asked me next. I still hadn't sorted out my reaction to this turn of events. Unlike the others, I wasn't the best at reading situations and never coped well with sudden change. I *wanted* to go. That wasn't the issue, but there was a ton of other mental clatter going around in my head that was making it hard to focus.

"Uh…" Conrad still sat across from me, still holding his duffel like a shield. "Work, you know? Might need to rearrange some things…"

That was typically vague. I wasn't entirely sure what job Conrad currently had. He seemed to have an endless supply of side hustles and part-time gigs that never lasted long. Rumor was, he got fired almost as often as he went out and partied. I'd once tried to help him see that the two probably were related, but he'd almost bitten my head off, so I tried not to get involved anymore. It wasn't my business anyway.

"That's fine. How about you guys think about it? The tickets are yours, but you can tell me your decision about the road trip when we play Sunday afternoon."

"Time to think is good." That gave us a little under forty-eight hours, but it was better than being put on the spot. I nodded along with Conrad.

"The tickets are ours?" Conrad licked his lower lip as he took one from the stack. I couldn't shake the feeling he was mentally working out what his ticket might fetch on a reseller site. And see, this was why I needed to go. I was the only one of us who truly cared about the game and the tournament.

I grabbed mine before anyone else could think about taking it.

"So, you think you're going?" Conrad nodded at the ticket in my hand. His midwestern flat affect took a turn for the country with *you* sounding more like *ya* when he was agitated. I'd never figured out exactly where he was from—some corn-fed rural state where they grew their guys naturally athletic and tall as water towers. Conrad always looked like he'd escaped some minor league baseball team to come slum with us nerds at the game store.

"Maybe. I said I'd think about it." I didn't owe him a peek at my inner turmoil, didn't want him to know how rattled I was, and my tone came out way too snappish. Something about Conrad always made me feel even more out of my depth socially, and that uncertainty tended to come out as combative—little verbal swipes that accomplished nothing other than to ensure that we were always at odds.

"Chill, Alden." Jasper was more Conrad's friend than mine, and the long-suffering look they exchanged grated on my last nerve.

Whatever. I wasn't in this to make friends. I was here for one reason, and one reason only—the high I got from winning. Sure, the satisfaction of deck building was nice, and the aesthetics of the game weren't entirely lost on me, but nothing compared to the rush of victory. And right now, at this point in my life, I needed that rush in the worst way.

Payton would accuse me of being overly dramatic, so I'd never admit it aloud, but there were days when the game kept me going. Just knowing we'd had the filming today had been good. Getting to do this professionally? Being able to call this a career choice and not an expensive hobby? That might be worth whatever it would take to get that seat on the pro tour. I still wasn't sold on Professor Tuttle's plan, but that ticket was mine, and I wasn't letting go.

Book Club Treasure Hunt

Jasper and Milo spend much of *Out of Character* on a treasure hunt for rare cards...but did you notice the secret clues scattered throughout the book? They'll help you find the answers to these questions.

1. Jasper and Milo used to be friends but had a falling out as kids. As they're thrown together again, what instructions does Jasper give in his first text to Milo?

2. What does Milo get Jasper to drink at the bakery, and what do you think it means that he knows Jasper so well?

3. Where does Jasper find Milo after their big fight?

4. Milo uses his art to express himself even when the words won't come. What does he draw after he returns from Philadelphia? (And what do you think it means?)

5. What unexpected couple does Milo see dancing that gives him courage?

6. Milo has a lot of complicated feelings about his car—but what's the one thing he really doesn't like about it?

7. What flavor of pizza does Jasper order for Milo, and why is that important?

8. What code name does Milo suggest they use?

9. What does Milo's heartbeat sound like to Jasper, and why?

10. Jasper's frog wizard costume is as vibrant as it is grand. What colors are most prominently displayed?

11. Each Odyssey player has their own unique style. What type of card does George play first?

12. *Out of Character* begins with Milo in a tough place, uncertain of his future. Where is he when the book ends?

Acknowledgments

No book can take place without an amazing team behind it. I want to thank Mary Altman of Sourcebooks and Deidre Knight of the Knight Agency for making my dreams of a *Conventionally Yours* sequel come true. Mary and Christa Désir's careful edits helped push me deeper into making my vision for the book ring true. Stefani Sloma is a publicity wizard and part of a larger unsung Sourcebooks team that does amazing things. I appreciate every opportunity you have found for me and for your enthusiasm for these books. The audio team from Dreamscape have also been so fabulous. I can't say enough good things about the cover art by Colleen Reinhart and also the promotional art from artist Lauren Dombrowski. Lauren has been particularly wonderful to work with and their drawings give life to my imagination.

Jasper had an amazing cheering section on the home front too. Melinda Reuter went above and beyond with her thoughtful beta, especially on the gaming details. Karen Stivali was my sounding board for all things East Coast and mothers, and I appreciate her friendship most of all. My personal assistant, Abbie Nicole, is also a dear friend and probably heard more about Jasper's tribulations than anyone else. This was my first beta from my unicorn-loving bestie, Gwen Martin. I'm so, so glad you came into my life at the perfect moment, and your comments and enthusiasm helped so much. So many other friends provided key support, and I must thank all the readers of my Facebook reader group, Annabeth's Angels. The group is often the brightest spot in my day, and everyone's desire for more from the True Colors universe kept me going.

This book also comes from years of playing tabletop games, and I'm so grateful to all the podcasts, vlogs, and websites that helped round out my knowledge. I especially appreciate those that patiently explained the secondary market for rare collectibles in terms even this newbie collector could understand. Jasper and Milo also required a deep dive into the world of geocaching, which was fun and informative. Thank you to my family and friends for all the hours spent gaming over the years and for dealing with my many questions with grace. My family also put up with a lot of late dinners and distracted conversations during the final push for which I am so grateful.

The book was written during the quarantine and social distancing of the great pause, and it was so lovely to get to escape into a world without Covid-19, where conventions and fundraisers and hospital visits could still take place. The decision to leave Covid-19 out of the book was very deliberate, and I hope readers enjoy this little bit of escapism as much as I did. I loved the group scenes so much, and I can't wait to live in a world where such gatherings are commonplace again.

And finally, thank you to my readers. I have the best readers anywhere. Every share, picture, post, tag, like, and message are so appreciated. Your word of mouth is everything, and your enthusiasm is why I keep writing. I love hearing from you! If you love Jasper as much as I do, please consider telling a friend or leaving a review.

About the Author

When she's not adding to her keeper shelf, **Annabeth Albert** is a multi-published Pacific Northwest romance writer. Her popular LGBTQ+ romances include several fan-favorite and critically acclaimed series. She lives with her spouse and two children in Oregon. To find out what she's working on next—as well as other fun extras—check out her website or connect with Annabeth on Twitter, Facebook, Instagram, and Spotify.

Website: annabethalbert.com

Goodreads: goodreads.com/author/show/6477494.
Annabeth_Albert

Twitter: twitter.com/annabethalbert

Facebook: facebook.com/annabethalbertauthor

Instagram: instagram.com/annabeth_albert

Newsletter: eepurl.com/Nb9yv

Fan group: facebook.com/groups/annabethsangels

ROMANTIC COMEDY AT SOURCEBOOKS CASABLANCA

Boyfriend Material
Wanted: One (fake) boyfriend
Practically perfect in every way

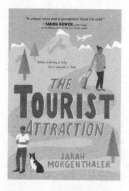

The Tourist Attraction
Welcome to Moose Springs,
Alaska: a small town with a
big heart, and the only world-
class resort where black bears
hang out to look at you!

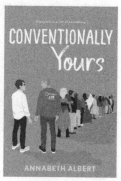

Conventionally Yours
Two infamous rivals.
One epic road trip.
Uncomfortably tight quarters
(why is there only one bed??!!).
And a journey neither
will ever forget.

Bad Bachelor
Everybody's talking about the hot
new app reviewing New York's
most eligible bachelors. But why
focus on Prince Charming when
you can read the latest dirt on
NYC's most notorious bad boys?